Flight of the Valkyrie

K. S. Daniels

K. S. DANIELS

ACKNOWLEDGMENTS

I'd like to extend much gratitude to the many people who contributed to the novel. Many thanks to my amazing beta readers, Jeremy Hicks, Allen Vu, Heather Wilkins, and Mike Zambrano, for lending me your eyes and allowing me to see the project as a whole through them. Just as many warm thanks go to Susan Basham for being the best damned editor out there. Thank you to my family, Hank and Rebecca Daniels, for putting up with me as I locked myself away for hours and days on end to complete this project. Thanks must also go to my horde of animals, Yuki, Saeliia, Freya, and Kiba, for being good listeners and even better snugglers. And to all the rest of you who've had my back from day one and beyond. I firmly believe my friends are the best friends in the universe. Much love to you all.

Edited by Susan Basham

Cover Art by Ana Cruz

ISBN-10: 069224610X
ISBN-13: 978-0692246108

Other Books and Stories

by K. S. Daniels

<u>The Valkyrie Series:</u>

"Children of Ymir" (#0.5)

The Valkyrie Profiles (#1)

<u>Other Stories:</u>

"Chimera", *Luna's Children: Stranger Worlds*

CONTENTS

K. S. DANIELS

Always and forever,
for Granddaddy.

K. S. DANIELS

Flight
of the
Valkyrie

K. S. DANIELS

1

DEIMOS

Vladia Robespierre stared out of *Freya*'s cockpit into the never-ending sea of blackness. It was the same view as yesterday, and the day before that, and the twenty-something days before that. She was on the brink of slumber when the gentle squeak of the hatch below her feet roused her to full attention. Had another six hours already slipped by?

Swinging her legs away from the ingress, Vladia made room for Rehel to poke his head out. The Valkyrie was cramped for one, let alone two. The only ship built for melee style combat in space, it was designed to accommodate syncing up with a single pilot. Its legs and arms and everything else became the pilot's. The sensation was incredible; you felt as big as the colossus itself, as if nothing stood between you and the vastness that was the rest of the universe. Yet neither she nor Rehel, though for entirely different reasons, had synced up with *Freya* on the long journey to the Red Planet and as a passenger vehicle, a Valkyrie left much to be desired. As a robot, Rehel couldn't connect with Freya; in her case, it was fear.

The robot would shut down for hours at a time and remain in the belly of the ship to give her as much room as possible. He'd offered to remain in hibernation for the duration of the trip to Mars, but Vladia wouldn't have it. She'd go raving mad if left to her own thoughts for the three and a half weeks it would take to reach their destination. So, with not too much trouble she convinced the robot to boot up every six hours and spend some time with her.

"We're getting close," she said. "Another half-hour, tops."

Rehel nodded. "We should disengage the autopilot soon. If I may, I'd like to come up and check a few things."

"Of course," Vladia complied, moving from the pilot's chair and squeezing into the sliver of space behind it.

Rehel seated himself and checked their gauges and coordinates. Once satisfied, he turned to Vladia. "Would you pilot *Freya* in once we've received clearance? I can do it on manual, but this is your ship. Syncing up will make for a much smoother approach."

"No."

The firmness of her response startled even her.

She'd been prepared never to pilot *Freya* again. The first assault on Luna had cost Vladia her right arm. To thank her, Earth dropped her classification to cyborg; second-class citizens didn't get to be pilots. Didn't matter she'd been flying for years or that she'd been top of the class. It mattered even less that she lost her arm saving her captain and half-brother Tolen Malthus and that he was the one who opted her out of the regrowth option in favor of a robotic arm to get her back on battlefield faster. He'd had her declassified, then framed and arrested for his own war crimes.

But they weren't on Earth anymore. They might never see it again, and those laws shouldn't hold any meaning to her. Yet her hesitancy persisted. The truth was she didn't know if she could sync up with *Freya*, and now was not the time to test that theory.

"As you wish," Rehel answered without question.

"I'll handle the comm. News travels fast, a hell of a lot faster than this ship, so we don't know what we'll be up against."

Rehel slowed the ship and disengaged the autopilot. He appeared to be getting quite used to his new role.

Thinking of Malthus, even in the remotest fashion, made Vladia clench her jaw. She'd never forgive him for his betrayal, and she'd never forgive herself for letting it all happen. She was the only one with the power to stop him, but because of her own weakness, her silly notion that they should stick together, that their blood bond was the end all be all, many lives had been sacrificed. And for what? So Earth could have Luna securely pressed under her thumb once again?

Vladia questioned Malthus' interest in the whole Earth-Luna affair. Why did he care if Luna was independent or not? He had said he wanted a peaceful, unified solar system, but something was missing. There was more to it than that. She'd given it serious thought during her hours of isolation, but Vladia still couldn't quite find the true end to his means. Not yet, anyway. What she did know was what her half-brother needed, which was a stable, ruling government, a high-ranking position, and nanobot technology.

Inching closer to the robot's side, she could see the Red Planet in the distance, growing larger by the minute. Would this strange world now be home?

It was almost funny that she'd ended up here after all the times Maria's former co-workers had begged her mother to immigrate. Yet never did she relent, and in the end that cost her everything. Vladia couldn't help but wonder if Malthus had been right when he'd called her mother stupid in her refusal to leave. Maybe Maria would still be alive if she'd have left Earth. Some ideals are worth one's life; Vladia wasn't sure this had been one of them.

"Vladia," Rehel interrupted her thoughts, "We're being hailed. No visual."

"Good. Open the channel." She'd learned long ago that making the first move could be detrimental, especially in an unknown situation. This would give her what she needed to approach the Martian government appropriately.

"Valkyrie Class ship, identification number 57R061, this is Lieutenant Marxx. You do not have permission to land. I repeat: Valkyrie Class ship, identification number 57R061, you do not have permission to land."

"Lieutenant Marxx, this is Colonel Robespierre. I seek

medical assistance, which under the guidelines of the Expedition Treaty you are obligated to provide," Vladia demanded.

She knew full well they could, and probably would, refuse her on the grounds that she was a fugitive. She also knew Mars held no particular love for Earth and whatever they officially said might not be what they officially did.

"Colonel Robespierre, you know as well as I do that not a treaty in all the worlds means anything if you're a fugitive. I'm sorry, but I cannot allow you to land. If you try we will shoot you down."

It was the expected response. Though judging by his tone, Marxx didn't sound too inclined to shoot anybody. Mars wasn't exactly known for their military prowess; it was brimming with technology, but their military had little use for it. Mars was peaceful, full of scientists and civilians more than anything else.

"You can't mean for me to starve out here in the depths of space, Lieutenant," Vladia began. "If I could just land for supplies, I would then gladly be on my way."

There was a long pause, hopefully one of consideration and sympathy.

"Robespierre, I cannot allow you to land on Mars. You are a Terran fugitive. We cannot risk any involvement with you. You may, however, briefly land on Deimos to refuel and be on your way."

Well, it was better than nothing. There was just one more thing to take care of now.

"Lieutenant, has another Valkyrie made contact with Mars in the last day or so?"

"Negative. Other than scheduled transports, you're our first visitor hailing from Earth in over four months."

"Thank you, Lieutenant," Vladia signed off. She couldn't hide the disappointment in her voice. If Abel hadn't made it here…

"Vladia," Rehel began. "I know you are worried about Abel. I, too, am concerned at this point, but we should proceed to Deimos with haste. There are many other options to deliberate other than the most dire. We will be better prepared to weigh those options once we land."

"You're right. To Deimos it is."

Vladia retired to the floor once again. It would only take a few minutes to get to Deimos, and she told herself she wouldn't think about Abel until she'd stretched her legs. But that didn't happen. Her mind was racing with the possibilities of his whereabouts. She refused to consider the most obvious conclusion, for now at least. Maybe he had not approached Mars as they had. Maybe he went straight for the fueling station. Maybe this Dr. Weston had met him before he was in sensor range of Mars. Maybe Lieutenant Marxx had lied to her. Or, maybe *Gunnr* had been damaged in battle and he was behind schedule. No, that last one was getting too close to things she wasn't ready to consider yet.

"Incoming message from Deimos," Rehel announced.

"Great. They might be turning us away as well," Vladia huffed.

"I don't think so. The message is just landing coordinates."

"Coordinates for Deimos?" Vladia couldn't help but chuckle. "Why would we need them? That moon's no more than, what, a couple hundred kilometers?"

"Four hundred and seventy-nine."

"And a good deal of that is cratered. Can't be too hard to find a fueling station on that rock."

"I would normally agree. However, it appears Mars has made a few special modifications to Deimos."

Rehel zoomed in the viewscreen.

What she saw could hardly be called a moon anymore, in the sense that a moon is a natural satellite of a planet. This rock was all man-made, completely spherical, and looked to be more than ten times the size it should be.

"That's no moon. It's—"

"A space station," Rehel confirmed. "Surrounding a moon."

Deimos' surface, once craterous, was now covered in port

entrances, giving it a sleek appearance disturbed only by the comings and goings of other ships, of which there were many.

"There's a lot of traffic. It will make for good cover," Rehel said.

"Or a quick discovery. Some of those are bound to be Terran trader ships."

"These coordinates will take us to the lowermost port."

"I'm starting to think the Martians might be embarrassed by us," she grumbled.

Her sarcasm wasted on the robot, Rehel continued, "There's less activity at the poles, and these ships are just your standard supply transports; there's no reason for them to be looking for us."

The robot eased *Freya* along, flying as casually as one could. Vladia held her breath as they neared their destination. A Valkyrie class ship would stand out against this lot. If anyone bothered to look away from their tasks and take stock of their surroundings, they'd be spotted.

As Rehel closed in on the coordinates, a small circle on the surface opened up for them.

Vladia exhaled, releasing her tension as the ship breached the outer crust of the sphere.

"Into the belly of the beast, then."

"An apt analogy," Rehel commended her as *Freya* slipped wholly into the surface of Mars's smallest moon. "The word 'Deimos' translates to 'dread'."

∞

The inside of Deimos was uniformly gray and dull, a sea of metal walls, floors, and ceilings, interrupted only by the thin fueling cores jutting up from the floor like natural stalagmites. It created a feeling of both claustrophobia and endlessness all at once. Not a place you planned to stay for long, which was obviously Mars' intention. The last thing they'd want was any Terrans feeling the least bit welcome. Immigration had officially ceased a few years ago; it was the only thing the two planets had managed to agree on in decades. Mars wanted no more Terrans polluting their gene pool, and Earth's population had sunk so low due to their contactphobia that they needed Terrans to stay firmly put.

From what Vladia could deduce, there must have been over a hundred pods that served as fueling stations or repair pits. Each pod appeared to accommodate no more than five small crafts and a single large one. And this was just the surface level; there was no telling what was going on in the core.

Rehel landed *Freya* with only the slightest of difficulty. "Atmospheric readings are stable. We can disembark."

The hatch opened with a weak hiss. The air was fresh and new in comparison to the recycled air she'd been living on for the last few weeks. Vladia sucked in a deep breath, filling her lungs to the brim; then, almost reluctantly, she exhaled.

This small taste of comfort was all it took for her to push aside brooding thoughts of their dismal situation and replace them with a powerful longing for two simple things: a cold glass of fresh water and a long, steamy shower. *Freya's* water recycling system was not meant for long trips. Its only intended use was for emergency situations, like getting stranded for a few days, a week tops. She'd used it well beyond the safety guidelines, and in the last two weeks it'd become obvious the filter needed to be replaced. Needless to say, even if she'd had the resources to waste on a bath, she'd wouldn't have had the space to take one.

She'd been religious about preventing muscle decay by spot contracting her entire body in cycles at least once every waking hour. Still, standing erect for the first time since leaving Earth pained her more than she thought it would. She'd felt confident about her endeavors until now.

Reaching to her toes, her legs throbbed as she stretched them out. She ached down to her bones, except for her right arm and shoulder. It no longer had bones, or muscles, or proper nerve endings. This kind of pain, the ache of absence, stung much more than the rest of her. No amount of stretching would end this hurt.

Putting her self-pity aside, Vladia stretched through the stiffness until she was sure she'd be able to descend the ship safely.

Rehel had no such muscular limitations and was already out and investigating the area by the time Vladia's feet hit the floor.

"There's no one here," the robot said.

"Guess we should help ourselves. You take care of the fuel while I poke around," she said, still fantasizing about that shower.

Rehel nodded, then went straight to work.

The pod was large and empty except for the six fueling pumps, all of which were covered with plastic sheeting, and one large ship occupying the far end of the pod. The ship was old and looked to be in disrepair. Vladia didn't recognize the make or model, but it was clearly massive enough to fit her own ship within it four times over.

Scanning the walls, she attempted to locate an exit, but it appeared the only way in or out was the direction from which they came.

There was no need for panic; as long as they had *Freya*, escape was not impossible. In all likelihood, the absence of both people and exits marked the Martians' desire to keep their distance from the fugitives of Earth. Vladia couldn't blame them for that.

Still, she was being watched; she'd felt a pair of eyes on her ever since she had disembarked. And then there was this other ship. The closer she grew, the more she began to think it was, in fact, operational.

"Something's not right," she whispered, clenching her jaw.

"Very perceptive! I expected nothing less," a disembodied voice boomed.

Vladia reached for her weapon, only to remember that she hadn't been armed since her encounter with Malthus on the *Dragoon*.

In her peripheral, a nearby viewscreen flickered on. There, a man with stark white hair, dark skin and a wide, toothy smile spoke: "Nice to finally meet you, daughter of Robespierre."

Rehel stopped fueling and made to advance towards the monitor, but Vladia motioned for him to wait. "Don't concern yourself with this, Rehel."

"Of course," he complied and returned to his duty.

Vladia turned her attention back to the screen. "Who are you?"

The man frowned. "You don't… remember me?"

"No."

"That's so harsh! To think after all those sweets I sent to you and your mother and you don't even remember poor Dr. Weston! Come to think of it, I never did get any thank you notes…" The man seemed genuinely hurt. He was certainly from Mars, the way he threw around words like 'daughter' and 'mother' as if they were nothing.

"Could it be that you never received my care-packages?" he went on in serious contemplation. "Though, to be honest, they were more bribes than anything. Maria always had a soft spot for candies; I just knew that was the trick to getting her to immigrate. It was so sad when–"

"Dr. Weston," Vladia stopped him sharply.

"Sorry, sorry, sorry," he said, waving his hands back and forth.

"What do you intend to do with us?"

"Eh?"

"There's only one way in or out of this pod. Are we to assume you are trying to capture us?"

"You? A captive?" Weston laughed. "After what you two pulled on Earth, I seriously doubt I would be able to contain you for very long."

"Then what is it you want from us?"

"Just a little chat before you're on your way. Nothing more, nothing less."

"Right, then. Come out and talk. Just make it quick."

"Oh, I'm afraid we'll have to have our chat like this. Mars is quite serious about having no involvement with you at this time. In fact, what I'm doing now would be frowned upon."

Vladia huffed. She didn't like having her back to everything and her attention so divided. Glancing back towards the large, aged ship, she sized it up once more. A whole mess of armed forces could be hidden within its hull. There were far easier ways to capture, or kill her, she decided. For now, she'd trust Rehel to be the eyes on the back of her head and let her suspicions go. For now.

"Start talking," Vladia consented, after a quick glimpse back at Rehel.

"I've been keeping tabs on you for a long time," Weston began in nostalgic reflection. "At first it was just out of curiosity to see how the child of a dear friend fared the harsh reality that is Earth. Forgive me for saying this, but you'd lived in a kind of fairytale reality until Maria was executed. A loving mother, a house of your own with all the toys and robots a person so inclined could dream of. I wanted to see that you made out all right. And you did, so I gradually began to lose interest in you. No offense."

"None taken."

"A while back, I received an encrypted message from Earth. It was impressively secure. Too secure, I think, for a Terran working alone." Weston paused and looked in the direction of *Freya* and the fueling core. "Might I assume you encrypted the message? Rehel, was it?"

"I did," the robot answered.

Vladia hid her surprise, but inside she fumed. What else had Abel and Rehel yet to tell her?

She folded her arms across her chest and merely waited for Weston to proceed.

"Yes, yes. It was much too clever for a human to have put together. Anyway, it was from one Lt. Commander Abel Duren. I won't bore you with all the details, as I am sure much of it would be repetitive. He expressed his concern about Earth's current situation, specifically mentioning his Captain, Tolen Malthus."

Vladia grimaced at the name. She wanted to banish the words from her universe so she'd never have to hear them spoken aloud again.

Weston continued: "This Duren fellow also seemed to believe you were key in stopping whatever it was Malthus was planning, mostly because of your, by Earth's standards at least, unconventional relationship with him. Needless to say, my interest in you returned. His main reason for contacting me, however, was to secure an escape route for himself and several others, if it came to that."

Vladia suppressed the urge to ask after Abel, even though there was a fair chance Weston knew her comrade's whereabouts. She couldn't trust Weston yet, and if he learned of Abel's importance, she risked turning her friend into a weapon against her. So, as far as Weston was concerned, Abel would remain a disposable means to her end. Nothing more.

"You're right. All of this was repetitive," Vladia bluffed.

Weston smiled. "Well then, I'll begin my questions. What is Malthus' plan?"

"To unify the solar system by force. Mars will obviously be his next target, followed, eventually, by the outer moons. Before he can continue he'll need to gain more power within Earth's government, so we have some time." There was no harm in telling him that which he had clearly already figured out on his own.

"And what will Vladia Robespierre do with this time?"

Vladia shook her head. "Oh, no, you don't. My turn now."

Weston shrugged and gave her leave to proceed.

"If you know Earth is planning to attack, even if it isn't for another few years, why does Mars turn me away when I am the only one who has the means stop him?"

"So you do believe you can stop him, then?"

"I'm possibly the only one who understands how his mind works. It gives me an advantage Mars will absolutely need."

"That doesn't answer the question," he pointed out.

"And you have yet to answer mine, Doctor," Vladia persisted.

"Fair enough. Because Mars has no choice."

"There is always a choice."

"Suppose we take you in? Then what? You have nothing to

offer us. You alone cannot protect us from Earth's wrath. As it stands we cannot protect ourselves, either. Helping you will all but ensure Earth will attack, and attack sooner at that."

"I take it some don't believe Earth is a threat?"

"Correct. I've shared my findings with the highest officials I have access to, but I have no hard evidence. And this, as you are well aware, is a world built on science. We don't put too much stock into theories that are based solely on speculation. Mars wants evidence."

"What happened to Luna is not proof enough?"

"Luna is a moon," he said with a dismissive wave of his hand. "It is Earth's moon at that. Possession is implied and has been for thousands of years. The situation is far too different to serve as evidence."

Vladia hated to concede, but the man had a point. It wasn't so long ago that she was the one waging war on Luna with no qualms whatsoever.

"And, believe it or not, many people here are still very sentimental about the mother planet. Most of the inhabitants here immigrated before the war, you see, and Earth has never made a move against us. So, our view of Earth is not as tainted as you might imagine," he went on. "However, we can worry with the politics of it later. For now, you need to make yourself an asset to Mars. Your connection to Malthus, your sureness of beating him based on your shared blood, isn't enough. One does not win wars that way."

Vladia knew what he was getting at. "You need an army."

"Precisely. We've got technology enough. And though Mars is naturally resistant to the idea of war, it can easily be converted into weaponry for that purpose. What Mars lacks most is manpower."

"What of your robots?"

"There's not enough. Even if there were, each one would have to be stripped of the three laws. Even Mars is afraid to do that on the scale you're thinking. We may not fear robots as Earth does, but the disastrous results of the Anglo-Eastern War made us just as cautious."

"Fine. I'll get you your army," Vladia said. She didn't have much choice in the matter. Mars was closed to her until she could provide them with something of value.

There was only one place to go from here: the Outer Moons.

Dr. Weston seemed pleased by her sureness. "You do that, and Mars will gladly open her doors to you."

Rehel had finished fueling and was now making his way towards Vladia. The doctor watched his approach eagerly. It was a rare specimen, an Earth robot. She wondered just how different Martian robots were these days.

"Dr. Weston, I had hoped you'd be willing to assist us in locating Abel Duren."

"I was wondering when you'd ask about him. I suppose an apology is in order now."

On cue, the loading ramp of the large ship behind them screeched open and clunked to the floor.

Vladia again reached to her empty holster.

Abel sauntered down, still clad in his green and black Valkyrie flight suit and his trademark grin. Bandages swaddled his right hand almost up to his elbow; otherwise, he looked unscathed, just tired and a bit more worn around the edges.

As he approached, Rehel stepped forward with an extended hand to greet his friend first. "You are injured, Abel."

"Had to do a little rewiring mid-trip and singed myself a bit. It's nothing." Abel took the robot's hand with his wounded one and shook it firmly to prove it.

"How long have you been here?" Vladia asked, her arms still neatly folded over her chest.

"Ah, just a few hours. Maybe ten, tops."

She could sense he was taken aback by her coldness, but it was for the best. They'd gotten too close, and Vladia decided she must put an end to it. Nothing was simple now; any and every relationship she forged could be used against her. Malthus had proved his resolve and would not hesitate to exploit Abel to get to her. During the flight to Mars, she'd worked over a dozen scenarios in which Abel could be used to prevent her from stopping Malthus. She couldn't let that happen, but Vladia feared the death of her friend even more than failure. She would shut him out to save his life. Abel would understand her decision in time.

"The large ship," Vladia turned her attention back to Weston, "Is it ours?"

"Yes. She's not much to look at, but she's armed, and your Valkyrie will stow inside nicely."

"*Gunnr* is already tucked away inside," Abel added. "There's lifts on the far side of the hanger we can use to load *Freya*."

"What's her name?"

"She came here as *Devil's Run*, but that can be wiped," Weston offered. "I assume a new captain would in turn call for a new name?"

"No. *Devil's Run* is just fine."

"As you like," the doctor continued, "I've loaded several different identification codes; they'll come in handy for docking on the sly. I've also stocked you up with a bit of Martian gadgetry. Some tracking devices and a few other little goodies. Nothing showy enough to link you to us, of course, but I think you'll find the Outer Moons rather barren as far as useful technology. This'll give you a leg up, as they say."

"Thank you. Your aid is much appreciated."

"I've told Abel he's more than welcome to stay. He is not a wanted man like you and your robot. I could arrange some immigration papers for him, but he insists on going with you," Weston explained.

Vladia had half a mind to demand Abel remain on Mars. It would be the safest option and the surest way to distance him from her, but the truth was she needed his help. The Outer Moons came with a rough reputation, and now she was tasked with raising an entire army. She didn't know if she could get the job done without him.

"He's indispensable, Doctor," Vladia praised her comrade, then gave Abel a firm nod. "It'd be too much to ask him to stay behind."

Abel smiled at her; she caught just a glimpse of it as she

turned back towards Weston. Her coldness towards him was more difficult that she thought it'd be. She truly was so very happy to see him.

"We should get going then. The longer we stay, the more we are imposing on your goodwill," Vladia said.

"Wait," Abel cut in. "We're waiting on two more. Cornelia and Takashi. They're coming too."

Vladia frowned and stole a glance at Rehel, who, to her surprise, was looking away from them both. She had already put Cornelia out of her mind. Her own insensitivity sickened her.

"There's no one else coming, Abel."

He immediately caught her meaning. "Both of them?"

"Cornelia went down with her ship. Takashi's status is unknown, but considering the circumstances of their relationship, I wouldn't expect him to be coming any time soon," Vladia explained. She didn't have it in her to tell him the whole story, how Malthus had sabotaged Cornelia Arnim's Dreadnaught and sent it crashing into Luna to deal the final blow of the war. She owed him the truth, but not now, not in front of a strange man on a strange moon. Somehow, Vladia felt as if that would cheapen Cornelia's sacrifice, and that was something she could not do.

"All right then. Let's move out. Thanks, Weston," Abel said, his voice only the slightest bit shaken.

"Glad to be of assistance. Of course, I am not doing this for you so much as I am doing this for Mars."

"We're grateful, whatever your reasons. And next time you see me, it will be in front of your army," Vladia promised Weston. Turning to Abel she said, "Let's get *Freya* loaded so we can get out of here."

"I'm on it," Abel said, walking towards the lifts.

Vladia moved to follow, but Abel continued, "Rehel and I can handle this. Go have a look at your new ship. Maybe grab a shower."

"You calling me smelly?"

Abel laughed. "I guess I am."

Vladia smiled. So much for keeping him at arm's length. She really couldn't make this a habit, though.

As she moved towards her new ship, she heard Weston call out to Rehel to come closer. They spoke for only a few seconds, and in low enough tones Vladia couldn't make anything out.

Once they concluded their whispers, Rehel lightly jogged to catch up with Abel.

"What was that about?" she asked herself, imagining Abel was asking the same.

She watched the two for a few more seconds before heading inside the ship. She wondered if they were just catching up, or could it something more. Either way, that shower was calling her name. The long haul to the Outer Moons would provide ample time for further questioning about Weston and his interest in her robot.

∞

The ship was certainly a hunk of junk on the outside, but the inside wasn't so bad. Weston had splurged on quite a few upgrades. In fact, Vladia wondered if he'd purposefully left the outside a dilapidated mess as camouflage.

It was brilliant, really. The ship looked as if it could, and would, simply fall apart at any given moment. It was old, clunky, a bit rusty even, but on the inside it was a fine war machine. The blasters had state of the art energy coils, as did the engine and shields. No one could imagine this ship as a threat. It was truly perfect.

The amenities, on the other hand, were lacking, but not beyond reason. The crew's cabin didn't have private baths. There were beds, if you could really call them that. They were more like cubbies in the wall with a thin layer of padding. Stacked three high and only about a meter deep, there was nothing to keep you from falling out if you were a restless sleeper. The Captain's cabin had its own computer terminal, but other than that it was just as sparse as the crew quarters.

The bridge lay at the heart of the ship, creating easy access to it from any other area. A corridor surrounding the bridge in an oval and connected it to everything else: engine room, cabins, showers, med center, and the mess. Since this had been a cargo ship, it was half storage, all of which could be found on the lower deck with the loading bay. It was an efficient design that Vladia admired.

She ended her self-guided tour of the ship in the showers. There were three shower heads lined up a meter or so apart on the back wall. Waist-high metal rods with dingy curtains protruded from the wall separating them into stalls. It wasn't the most female-friendly set-up, but she hadn't expected even that amount of privacy.

Vladia peeled off her uniform and tossed it on the ground. She felt cleaner already. After a brief moment of letting her skin breathe, she reluctantly scooped her garments up and toted them over to the laundry unit. She'd be better off torching her clothes rather than washing them, but it was all she had at the moment. She set the cycle and proceeded to the nearest shower head.

Despite the archaic interface, she managed to turn the water on and set the temperature with relative ease. Pressing her hands against the rough wall, she let her head sink below her shoulders and her blonde hair cover her face. Steam enveloped her, and for the first time in months she could almost relax. She dialed the heat up until it hurt, pricking her skin like a barrage of searing needles against her back and arms.

It took every ounce of her being to not curl up on the floor and let the water overtake her until she felt emptied of the last several months. But every drop she used must be recycled. Since she didn't know the specs on this ship yet, it'd be best to play it safe with a short shower.

She touched the interface to start the shampoo cycle, but after a few minutes it became clear the shower wasn't cycling properly. All it could do was spray water. It felt fantastic, but this wouldn't get her clean.

Stepping over to the next shower head, she immediately discovered it didn't work at all. The final head worked, but it was stuck on the shampoo cycle. She could work with this at least.

Once she was lathered, she moved back to the first stall and rinsed clean. Just one hurdle left: the drying cycle. To her great relief, it worked just fine and she was ready to re-dress in no less than five minutes. After a few cold minutes of waiting for the laundry unit, Vladia was soon dressed and ready for a more thorough examination of the ship, starting with the bridge.

The bridge was much smaller than the one on her Dreadnought, the *Spartan*. This ship could be manned by as little as three: the captain, the pilot, and the weapons master. The captain's chair was the central point of the bridge, with the pilot and weapons station a few meters forward at the bow along with the viewscreen. The nav center and all other scanners and read-outs were against the back and side walls, interrupted only by the various exits.

She entered to spy Abel lounged in the captain's seat, his legs swung over one of the armrests and his head propped up on the other.

"It's a good ship. Though you could have warned me about the showers."

Abel leaned his head back and tossed her an upside-down smile. "Well that wouldn't have been much fun, would it? You see the engine specs? Weston went all out, didn't he?"

"Top of the line. We'll make the trip out in record time," Vladia said, leaning into the archway of the entrance. "We'll need to hire a crew first thing. It's bad enough there's only three of us, but at least Rehel can pick up the slack for now. An engineer is a must, preferably one with experience."

Abel swung his body around and sat upright in the chair. "We should get a dedicated medical attendant, too."

"Agreed. I think I'll have Rehel attend to the duties of weapons master and you should stay on as pilot."

"Why's that?"

"Because you're good. And I don't want some stranger in

control of the ship."

"But you'll let a stranger treat you in the med bay? You sure have some odd priorities."

Vladia shrugged. Honestly, she wouldn't be the one in the med bay in all likelihood. Her nanos would stitch her up, both flesh and machine. Maybe Abel had forgotten she wasn't really human anymore.

"You know, your chair's pretty damn comfy," he said, standing up and motioning for her to take it.

"It's not my chair. I may be next in command, but you're the puppet master of our little play," she smirked.

"We're not in the military anymore. There is no next in command," he explained. "I knew a long time ago that if it came to this, you'd be the one to lead the way."

Vladia made her way to the Captain's seat but didn't sit. Instead, she stood beside it, letting the chair hold the space between them. "Abel, why did you contact Weston? What I mean is, why him of all people?"

He hesitated, as if weighing the truth versus an alternative. "It seemed logical to find someone who'd be sympathetic to the situation. Someone already familiar with you, I mean."

Vladia shook her head. "You dug up Maria's records too, not just mine."

"We wanted to be thorough."

"We? You mean you and Rehel? Which translates to you ordering him to help you."

"Hey, he broke a number of protocols to get to those files. He wouldn't have helped if he didn't think it could be important."

"That's my point, Abel. Those records were protected. They weren't any of your business."

It had shocked her when she'd discovered he'd rifled through her personal files a few months ago. Vladia had been angry then too, but with Abel telling her from a hospital bed after his brush with death made her more reserved about showing her disapproval. It had apparently made her more forgiving as well, since she really hadn't given it another thought. Somehow, this was worse. It felt like Maria had been summoned from the grave only to be put on display, then dissected, labeled, and sorted.

"Look," Abel continued. "Once I realized who you were, I needed to find something, anything really, to prove you could be better than Malthus. That you could be the one to stop him if it came to that. That your connection to him wasn't a threat, but an asset."

"That's a pretty weak justification, and you know it."

"It's not, Vladia. I had to know who raised you before you met Malthus. And what I found was just what I'd been hoping for. When all her colleagues immigrated, including Weston, she stayed behind. Maria would not be bullied into leaving her life's work. It was selfless of her to try and save her robots. That's the kind of bravery and self-sacrifice that will be Malthus's undoing."

"It's not your privilege to judge what kind of person Maria was to me or to anyone," she said, still managing to remain calm despite her instincts.

"If you'd been raised in the system with the rest of us I wouldn't have had to do any digging or grasping at straws. All my files? Open access. But not yours. No, yours were classified. One of the perks of the aristocracy, I suppose. And you can't tell me you haven't looked into my records."

She didn't deny it. She had looked after all that business with Ceres Forté and the explosion at the research facility came up.

"All I did was level the playing field," he added.

"Who is your mother, then?" she shouted. Her fury had finally exceeded her control.

His jaw dropped ever so slightly and his body went distinctly rigid at her vulgarity.

"No? Who's your father then? Your brothers? Your sisters? No one knows, do they? Not you, not your comrades or your superiors, not even the rearing facilities that taught you how to make words and dress yourself. Safely anonymous. How nice that must be."

Vladia paused, taking a moment to regain her composure and dull the sharpness of her tongue.

Abel started to speak, but she put her hand up to silence him. "It's not a privilege of the aristocracy. It's protection from the rest of you. It's the only way we can live anything close to a normal life on Earth. You didn't level the playing field; you destroyed it."

Steps rebounded from the corridor walls, silencing them both temporarily. Rehel rounded the corner. Wrapped gently in his arms was a pile of grey fur.

"I found a cat," the robot announced.

"What d'you mean you found a cat? Why is there a cat?" Abel said, taking a few steps back. "Why is there a cat?" he repeated, this time looking to Vladia, the rift between them momentarily pushed aside.

"It's a ship's cat, I suppose. Though I don't see why a space ship would need one," she mused aloud.

"This particular breed was developed by early Martian terraformers to detect changes and anomalies in the still-developing atmosphere of the planet," Rehel explained. "The cat's coat would change colors to indicate a possible spike in nitrogen or carbon dioxide levels, for example."

"Wouldn't they just use machines? Seems a bit backwards to use animals." Vladia said.

"Early settlers had limited resources. Repairs were costly. Much was still imported from Earth, and taxes were high due to the cost of travel. It only made sense to find a sustainable resource for as much as possible. Only a small colony of cats needed to be genetically altered to have an endless supply of essentially free equipment. The Outer Moons still utilize cats to detect leaks or increases in radiation, mainly due to the primitive, and often faulty, equipment aboard their ships."

"So it just came with the ship then?"

Rehel nodded.

Abel edged a bit further away. "With Weston's upgrades we don't need it. Go take it outside and leave it in the hangar. Someone'll be 'round to pick it up, I'm sure."

Rehel turned to do as requested.

"Wait a minute," she called to the robot, who paused mid-step.

"If it's customary to have a ship's cat in the Outer Moons, don't you think it'd look odd if we didn't have one?"

"You do have a valid concern," Rehel admitted. "If we hope to obtain more crewmembers on arrival it could create an issue. Many potential crewmembers would hesitate to board a ship they view as unsafe."

"But it's not unsafe," Abel objected. "We've probably got better systems than those hillbillies have ever seen."

"That's not the point, and you know it. If we break custom we may get a crew, but it'll create an atmosphere of unease, which is not ideal. The cat stays."

It'd never really occurred to her before, but facility children had probably never been around animals of any sort for fear of the diseases they carried. That, and they were few and far between these days. Earth had killed off most species in the course of her history. Even she'd only been around a few animals.

"This is insane! Wild animals don't belong on a spaceship," Abel continued his protest.

"Actually, this cat was bred specifically for life aboard a ship. To remove it from its natural habitat could be greatly distressing for the beast," Rehel said.

"We wouldn't want that would we, Abel?" She smiled at him playfully. "The cat's part of the crew, and that's the end of it."

"I realize you have never been around animals, Abel, but there is minimal danger associated with having the cat stay," Rehel explained. "I've already scanned it for both disease and deadly bacteria, and as I suspected it is perfectly healthy. Also, the medical bay is fully equipped to handle cat bites and scratches in case of incidents."

"Great. That makes me feel so much better."

Rehel put the cat on the ground, and it scurried from the room.

"See? It doesn't like you either," Vladia pointed out.

"Good!"

"On a more important note," the robot proceeded, "I need both of you to come to the medical bay for injections. Being Terran born, neither of you are equipped with a strong enough immune system to even handle the gentlest of viruses. Dr. Weston has provided us with vaccines for the most common diseases present in the Outer Moons."

"What about the uncommon ones?" Abel questioned.

"I would recommend hand-washing and limited contact with the locals."

"This day just keeps getting better and better," he grumbled as he walked towards the exit. "I'll go first so you can finish looking around."

"Thank you."

Abel brushed by Rehel, who remained in the doorway. "One more thing that may be of interest to you."

"What's that?" Vladia asked.

"Dr. Weston also provided more recent data on the Outer Moons that should help you decide which group of moons we should plot a course to. I've sent the information to your cabin."

"I'll look it over at once. The sooner we plot a course and get moving the better. Once you've finished with Abel, tell him to take us out past Mars and wait for further instructions."

"Yes, Captain."

It'd take an hour or so to pour over the information from Weston, but for now they still had to get away from Mars. Terran ships still swarmed about Deimos, and they wouldn't be welcome here again empty-handed.

2

WATCHDOG

General Tolen Malthus took his seat to the right and three chairs down from Grand Admiral Clovis. Seating arrangements in the War Council Chambers were everything. They told a story: your rank, your reputation, your merits in battle, your trustworthiness; but most importantly it unofficially mapped out the order of ascension. After his promotion to General from his previous post as Captain of the Valkyrie Squad, he'd only moved up one position. Thanks to both his efforts at the Battle of Emden and his rooting out of the war criminals Vladia Robespierre and the robot Rehel, only four people now stood between him and the Grand Admiral. It wouldn't be much longer now; he'd be in Clovis' inner most circle by year's end.

It wasn't that he was in a rush. He had much to do before he took over as Grand Admiral. Even though the war with Luna was finished, the treaty still had to be finalized. That was the main reason for today's discussion, which was boring and predictable and he already knew the outcome. But every puppet wants his chance to sing and dance before the king. So, twenty men and women sat around taking their turn to banter ideas back and forth. Malthus remained quiet and distant. His turn would come soon enough.

The current dispute was about the Lunites' right to research. The argument steadily increased in intensity, and as that happened logic and reason declined. He watched Clovis closely. As much as the man wanted to believe it, he was not cut out for war. Unlike Malthus' blood-born father, Admiral Urada Malthus, the Grand Admiral took a rather passive approach to leadership. His decisions, almost exclusively dictated by those closest to him, only resembled those of a well-bred leader. His transition out of office would be all the smoother for it. Really, he couldn't have asked for a more perfect commander.

Despite his father's superior qualities, in his sixty-odd years of service Urada Malthus never did any better than Admiral. At thirty-two, Tolen was on the cusp of that rank himself and his two biggest obstacles to his next move were already surmounted: Vladia had been removed from Earth, and he'd freed himself from his father's shadow.

It hadn't been easy. Though his records were sealed– as the records of all children raised outside the rearing facilities were– he had the unfortunate responsibility of bearing the man's surname. And even though no one knew he'd been raised by his father, all suspected that Urada Malthus must undeniably be his father. That was disgusting enough for most. Vladia had been raised by their father only after her mother's execution. But since she carried her mother's name, no one knew of their relationship or shared past.

Maria Robespierre's execution had been quiet and quick. In fact, the only people who even remembered the woman existed were few and far between. The remaining roboticists knew of her work, but since it had been banned they'd not dare admit it. He'd bet every scientist on Mars knew of her though. But Mars was different. There, people still raised their offspring. There were families, brothers and sisters, mothers and fathers. No one would shun you for being blood-born because they were all blood-born. It was archaic, but rather beautiful in a way. Even if Mars reached the kind of population and disease crisis that Earth had in the past, they would never end up like this place. Mars still had the drive to explore the stars, encouraging discovery and coveting knowledge, while Earth merely wanted to control all within her reach.

"You're awful quiet there, Malthus. Care to weigh in, or had you plans of day dreaming through today's session?" Admiral Vorros bellowed.

That was his cue. Vorros was close to Clovis. Not close enough to be a real threat, but just enough that Clovis would listen to him with caution. Vorros hated Malthus only because he allowed it. Hate, second only to love, was the easiest emotion to manipulate. He wondered if Vladia had learned that lesson yet.

"If everyone has finished their pointless chatter then, yes, I am quite ready to participate."

"By all means then, General. Grace us with your opinion on the matter of the Lunites' right to actively continue scientific research."

"The answer is simple. No."

"No to what part exactly?" the Grand Admiral asked with genuine interest.

"All of it. You argue about regulations, policies, special permissions, and so forth, but this is pointless. Luna attacked us with research that we gave them permission to conduct. How stupid do you think it will look if we give them even the slightest bit of allowance on this point? Mars will be laughing so hard that the vagabonds of the Outer Moons will hear them loud and clear."

"Why the hell should we care what Mars thinks? They're no threat to us."

"Of course they aren't. We may know this, but they may not."

"What are you getting at, Malthus?" Clovis asked, leaning forward on the table with his elbows.

"Perception is everything. Luna was no match for us, but she thought otherwise. Hence, we had a war."

"Which we won," Vorros boasted.

"Yes. But at what cost? The death toll on our end alone exceeded three thousand in just two short months. These are resources that are becoming harder and harder to replace. And what of our ships? How many were lost? How many destroyed? How many damaged beyond repair?"

He paused to let his words take full effect.

"If we show any compassion in dealing with Luna, we are perceived as weak. We are not weak, but if Mars thinks she has a chance at us she will take it. And though Earth shall again prevail, you must ask yourself: at what cost this time? War is expensive, comrades; this treaty costs nothing but our time."

What followed was muffled whispers of agreement and some head nodding from all, except for Vorros, whose face had turned a bit red.

"A valid point, as always, Malthus," Clovis commended. "I like your assessment. No leniency and a firm grip on Luna is what the situation calls for. I think we can safely say this treaty will be finalized and delivered to our defeated insurgents by week's end now. Well done, comrades."

Clovis pushed back his seat to stand and conclude the meeting, when Vorros spoke, "Grand Admiral, might I make one more suggestion before we dismiss?"

"So long as it's brief," Clovis said, still standing.

"General Malthus seems to be very perceptive when it comes to this Luna situation. I'd dare to say he's one of the best men we have in that regard."

"Thank you, Admiral Vorros. But I seek no praise."

"Of course not, General. But my point is this: I think it would be a great asset to have a man of your skill in a position where we could make the best use of that talent. A position that would give you real, direct contact with the Lunites in order to study them and give us a clearer understanding of their motives. Perhaps this will help deter any further aggression from them, or at least help Earth act in a way to diffuse any potential issues before things get out of hand."

"You're suggesting I give up my post here and become Earth's Ambassador to Luna?" Malthus allowed himself to reveal the slightest look of displeasure.

Vorros smirked, "I can't think of a finer man for the job."

"I will, of course, serve Earth in any way the Grand Admiral thinks best, but I feel my place is here, on the War

Council, not on Luna as a watchdog."

"The position of ambassador is not to be taken so lightly, Malthus. It is a great honor," Clovis insisted.

Malthus knew better. For most, being sent to Luna in any fashion was like forced retirement. Only a rare solider came back from such a far-removed post.

"Besides, there's no reason you can't still be on the War Council just because you are physically on Luna," the Admiral continued. "The first few months after the treaty is signed will be shaky at best, and we need someone with tact who can handle this delicate situation. Vorros is right. There is no better man for the job. General Malthus, I hereby appoint you as Ambassador to Luna on behalf of Earth. We'll work out the transfer orders later. For now, you're all dismissed."

Everyone waited for Clovis and his Special Forces Guards to exit before making a move to leave. Several shot Malthus sympathetic glances, while others refused to make eye contact at all. After all, as far as they were concerned, he was no longer a useful connection to maintain.

Vorros made his way over to Malthus' chair and put a gloved hand on his shoulder. "You had a good run of it. And I must admit I'll miss our backstabbing banters. Surely you must have known I wouldn't just stand by and let you take what's mine."

"I would never take anything that was rightfully yours, Vorros. Unfortunately, your inflated sense of self-worth has you grossly delusional about what exactly it is you're entitled to."

The man's grip tightened on his shoulder as he leaned closer. "Listen here, you little shit: you're done. You understand that? Clovis won't let you come back from Luna; I'll make sure of it. So you enjoy your new gig, watchdog," Vorros hissed as he released his hold with a shove before marching out.

Now Malthus was alone. The room would be vacant for another hour.

"That went just as you said." His comm buzzed to life with

the sound of a woman's voice.

"Obviously. How are the preparations going on Luna?"

"I've secured a facility, and the cargo has been delivered. We have a final count of twenty-two humans and one robot in need of serious repair."

"Any more problems?"

"No."

In no time at all, Lunite marauders had taken to killing Terran survivors found in the carnage of the crash site. It had been quite the feat for Isobel to do her job because of this. She had the advantage, though; she knew which parts of the ship would be the most likely to have remained intact enough to have survivors. She'd been able to get her hired hands in and out before the Terran rescue team arrived. The marauders hadn't been so lucky.

"I adjusted the records for the facility to label it as radioactively condemned," she continued. "Also, the workers hired for the recovery and delivery of your cargo have been dispatched."

"Elaborate, please."

"A malfunction with one of the airlocks on the mining expedition they began as their next legitimate job. It was clean. All bodies were accounted for."

"Good. Looks like I'll be formally assigned to Luna in the next few days. Make sure you've finished up on your end."

"Aren't you taking a risk leaving Earth? Vorros is right. Getting assigned to Luna is a dead end. I could have gotten everything to Earth. It would have taken longer, but—"

"It's fine. There are too many suspicious eyes and ears on Earth now. On Luna, I am, as Vorros stated, the watchdog, and everything that is to be reported to Earth goes through me first. Luna is perfect."

"If you say so," she said. He half expected more of an argument from her. It was a relief she was becoming more compliant.

"What's the status on the other end of the spectrum? Have you encountered any difficulties yet?"

"They're orbiting Deimos. No trouble yet."

"I suspected Mars would turn them towards the Outer Moons. As soon as they set a course, let me know. Replicating has been successful as well?"

"Yes. I've multiplied enough to infest their new vessel. The Valkyries and the robot are still unattainable for some reason. I suspect the robot created a program to block me after the L4 incident."

"Just make sure you're only observing. No interfering without my consent."

"Of course."

Again, he expected more of a protest. For the first few weeks of Isobel's transformation, her request for a robotic body had been incessant. He'd told her he was steadily working to obtain one for her, that her life as a swarm of nanbots was temporary. But that'd been a lie.

There was no chance of getting his hands on a robotic shell without going unnoticed. And though Isobel imagined otherwise, the damaged one they'd retrieved from the *Iron Maiden* wreckage would serve another purpose, assuming it could be repaired. More importantly, she was of no use to him in any other form.

He'd been buying time with his promises, and it had paid off. Her requests had tapered off and now had stopped entirely. Not because she had accepted her fate, but because she'd all but forgotten why she wanted a body. Replicating, as he had suspected, watered down her soul, or personality, or whatever it was that made her human. It also explained why she'd stopped being difficult about following instructions.

Isobel's love for him would soon fade, and then he would have exactly what he needed: sentient, obedient nanobots with a hive-like mentality and completely void of humanity's greatest flaws. Of course he anticipated some complications, but he'd deal with those all in good time. It was swarm robotics at its fullest potential. He couldn't help but think Maria Robespierre would have been more than a little impressed. Even if she would have disapproved of his methods, he got results. Whether Vladia wanted to believe it or not, her mother had been more like him that she could ever imagine.

"Do you want me to send you the list of names?"

"No. No more transmissions. It can wait."

Malthus smiled. If anything, Isobel should thank him. If he hadn't transferred her consciousness from her body to the swarm, she'd have died after the first full-fledged battle with Luna. And for once he couldn't take credit for the fortuitous circumstances. Call it fate, or a happy accident, but Isobel's death was solely Vladia's doing. The death of her body, anyway.

In her foolhardy attempt to save his life, she had put both Abel, Isobel, and herself in harm's way. It was no surprise Abel had come out relatively unscathed; he had been his best pilot. Isobel had never been all that great, having barely passed the Valkyrie training exams, and if Malthus hadn't discovered her other uses so soon he'd have dismissed her. Perhaps Vladia paid the highest toll for her endeavors: declassification from human to cyborg. Even now, though she had escaped far from the reaches of Earth, he imagined the mental weight of the experience was quite trying. He wished he could watch her struggle, but reports from Isobel would simply have to do.

"As you wish," Isobel agreed. "But there is one name that I think will be of interest to you."

"Really? Let's have it, then," Malthus prompted.

"Cornelia Arnim."

3

SPACE COWBOYS

Li Fey lounged back in his office chair and took a deep puff off his cigar. It was a Titan Tobacco, and it was his last. He wasn't quitting; he'd just run out. And the way business was looking, it'd be a good long while before he'd be able to afford another box.

He savored the bold taste of oak and almond, and as he slowly exhaled he could pick up hints of the caramel undertones. It was good stuff. Made him wish he'd set up shop on Titan instead of Ganymede. He'd grown up on Titan with his mom and two younger brothers, but he'd made trouble there when he was young and stupid and decided it'd be best for his family if he left.

Now he was rapidly approaching sixty. He still got to see his brothers when he was in the neighborhood, but his mom had passed not five years after he'd left home. He'd been in deep space making a run to Mars when he'd gotten word. All he could do was send money for the funeral. Even though he'd been on Titan many times since she'd died, he'd never been to her grave. Didn't feel like he deserved to go.

Li ran his hand over his slick head and took another pull off his cigar. His hair'd let loose a decade ago and all that lingered of his black mane were a pair of thick salt and pepper sideburns. He may not have been in his prime anymore, but he was still in good shape. His muscular, dark frame remained attractive despite the wear of time. Sure, his back got achy now and again, but he could still shoot straight and go a few rounds if he needed. And win, too; long as the fight didn't last too long, that is.

Seemed crazy to have to start over at his age, but what could he do? Competition had gotten fierce the last few years and that, combined with a few of his own poor decisions, made business slow. Slow enough that he couldn't always pay rent on this office or the dock, and his ship was in sore need of a number of parts. But today had been the big blow. The finishing move. Irei Kodokun, new successor to the Ganymede Crime Syndicate, had purchased the port where Li docked his ship. The previous owners had been more than lenient with his late payments. The Syndicate was not. The docking fee had doubled and payment was expected now. If he couldn't pay, they'd take his ship. No ship, no business.

Call it luck, but as fate would have it his ship was currently on a series of short-range runs. Right now, half his crew was on their way to Io for a mining equipment drop-off. Short-range work didn't pay well, so the money they made off this lot wouldn't cover the new docking fee plus last month's late fee. It did at least buy him some time to plan his next move.

The lift doors squeaked open, and down the hall swift footsteps approached. Li frowned, reluctantly capping his cigar and stowing the last half of it away to enjoy later.

"What's this garbage I hear about us going under?!" a woman's voice shouted as door the banged open, bouncing so forcefully off the wall that it almost swung shut again.

Nova caught the door with her hand and shoved it away. Standing in the threshold, hands on her hips, she continued, "I'm sitting at the docks chatting up this cargo master, when Armstrong comes sauntering over with his big, stupid grin and hands me a package. He says it's a going away present, seeing as how Li Fey can't pay his docking fees and the goddamned Syndicate owns our ship."

"What was in the package?" Li asked, the taste of his cigar still lingered in his mouth.

"What?"

"The package. What was in it?" he calmly asked.

"Who bloody cares what was in the package, Li!"

"Well, if it'd been money, it might've helped."

The woman sunk down into one of the chairs on the other side of Li's desk. "So it's true, then?"

"No. Well, not yet anyway. The ship's still ours as long as Ten and Erro are out on runs. Once they dock, that's another story."

"When were you planning on telling us about this?"

Li shrugged. He'd been hoping for a few more days to come up with a plan before he broke the news to the crew. But she was right; he should've told her.

"I'm sorry you found out that way."

"Me, too."

Nova stretched out her long legs and then kicked them up on his desk. Her Rokurokubi tattoo on her left shin glared at him; its neck, elongated and slender, twisted around her leg so slow you almost couldn't be sure if it was indeed moving.

"Get that thing off my desk."

Shrugging, she re-crossed her legs, covering the ghoul's face. Flecks of dirt fell from her ankle-high black boots onto his workspace as she moved, and Li brushed them off with the back of his hand.

"What were you doing at the dock, anyway? You're not exactly dressed for work," he said, referring to her lack of weaponry more than her clothing, which was made up of a pair of slick green shorts and a black lace top that hung slightly off of one shoulder. Her hair was a deep teal today, long but braided on both sides and pulled into a faux-hawk.

"I've got my short knives tonight," she said gently patting her thighs. "I told you I was chatting up this cargo master. He works on Galmen's ship, *The Jazz Queen*. Anyway, they just got back from Mars with a shipment of assorted parts, many of which we need, so I thought I'd see if I could nab us a little discount."

"I don't like thievery."

Nova shot him a glace, calling his bullshit.

"Well, thievery amongst one's peers anyway," he clarified.

"They're not peers, Li. They're competition. Besides, I wasn't going to steal them. I was gonna take them as compensation…for services rendered."

"The pleasure of your company is not worth what you seem to think it is."

"You don't have to be an ass about it. I was just trying to do my part for the business."

"Well, that won't be necessary anymore."

"Sorry."

"Noted. So, if that's all you need," he said, motioning towards the door.

Nova sniffed at the air. "You've been in here smoking."

Li sighed. She had no intention of leaving.

"It's my last one and, no, I'm not in a sharing mood. Thought I'd enjoy it while I figured us a way out of this mess."

"How'd that work out for you?"

"It didn't," he grumbled.

"Well, we've got at least another week before Ten and Erro get back. I could do a few runs between domes on my skiff. Those jobs are crap, but if I do enough of 'em it might make the ends meet."

"Even if we manage to pay this month. What about the next? We've been losing the big jobs for a while now. And with the docking fee doubled, we need those big jobs more than ever."

"If we had the upgrades, we could get back into some serious bounty hunting. Could we get a loan?"

"Doubtful. The Syndicate doesn't loan money to people who already owe it to them."

The two sat quietly, each thinking in vain for a way to escape an impossible situation. Li still longed for the last half of his cigar. It was a simple pleasure. Made life feel simple too, even if it was just for a moment.

"I don't know. Maybe it's time for a career change," Li broke the silence.

"Don't say that."

"You guys'll be fine. You're young and fresh still. You could get on with any ship you wanted. And you, you've got your side business and quite the reputation with a weapon. I honestly have been wondering why you've stuck with me so long. Certainly isn't for the money."

"Guess I'm just a creature of habit."

"Why don't you spend a little more time making the rounds. See if you can find a large ship that's hiring. With any luck, we can all get on the same bucket."

"I just told you–"

"Even if we can't, it's just for a while. We can save up, pool our money, and buy a new ship."

Nova frowned.

"Look, with no overhead, we can save up fast between the four of us. In less than a year we'll be able to buy the fastest ship the Outer Moons can offer. And that's what we need to get the big jobs."

"I don't like it."

"I know. But this is the best we can do now, kid."

Nova stood up and stretched. "I'll think about it," she said. "I'm not in the mood to fight with you tonight. Don't get me wrong, I'm mad as hell. But, I'm going for a drink instead. You want in?"

"Pass."

"Suit yourself. You know, you can pick up some good info over a drink. Information sells just as much as cargo these days."

"Heard anything I might be interested in?"

"Maybe. But you can't afford it," she laughed.

Nova had some good connections in the information trade circuit. They'd used them well in the past when they still dabbled in illegal trade and bounty hunting. Li had been trying to keep his business clean the last few years, though he knew Nova still picked up one-man jobs that were less than savory.

She didn't do too bad, and she certainly had enough set back to pay a few months' worth of docking fees. But she knew better than to offer him money. He'd go out of business before he became a charity case.

"I'll keep an eye out for recruiters, but they'll have to take us all. Package deal."

"You know where to find me."

With a curt wave, Nova closed the door soundlessly, a marked improvement over her entrance.

Li reached in his top desk drawer and pulled out his cigar box. He opened the lid and stared at the contents for a few moments before tucking it all back out of sight. Talking to Nova, saying what he'd been thinking for days out loud for the first time, was tough. He didn't want to waste his last Titan Tobacco on a foul mood.

He'd save the last half for a happy occasion. He hoped it wouldn't spoil before that happened.

∞

Nova kicked up the stand to her skiff and sped off towards The Gryphon's Nest Tavern. It took all she had to remain calm back there with Li. Not because the Syndicate was breathin' down their neck, but because the whole reason they were in such a heap of financial trouble was Li's fault.

A few years back, he suddenly got very selective of the types of jobs he'd take. He never said why, and he was the boss so they all kept their traps shut about it.

Then there was the Garbel incident. The whole crew had been tracking this guy once before when he'd just vanished. Almost a year later she got a hit on his location: the Callisto water mines. The bounty was still high, so she took it to Li. He'd declined the job, and as usual he wouldn't say why. That time she refused to just stand by and watch someone else take her bounty. She went behind his back, got Erro and Ten to help too, rented a ship and nabbed him with only a minor fire fight. Ten had taken a hit, but he'd shook it off as usual like it was nothing. The three of them split the reward and never told Li.

Months went by, and money became tighter and tighter. Li

wouldn't take any high-risk jobs, which meant he wasn't taking any high-paying jobs either. Nova had to rely on her side business more and more. The ship needed repairs and the money just wasn't there; that further limited the jobs they could take to nothing out past Jupiter's moons.

Out of frustration, she began tailing him at night. After about a week she found what she was looking for. Li had a kid. A little sprout no more than three. She watched him go in to this woman's house, hand her a chunk of his earnings, then visit with the kid for over two hours. Li and the kid played; the woman didn't show back up until he was getting ready to leave. And that was it.

Li didn't want his kid to know he was a smuggler, a bounty hunter, and an illegal trader, so he'd quit those gigs. She supposed he also wanted to make sure he stayed alive long enough to watch the sprout grow up.

Nova slowed as she got into the thick of the city.

"Remember, rain is scheduled for today at three a.m. and will continue until six-twenty a.m. Thank you and drive safely," the Artificial Weather System chirped its friendly reminder across the city.

It was all very noble and sentimental, but it was sinking their business. She'd figured out his schedule and followed him every time he went to that house, which was once a month. She didn't know why she did it. Maybe it was out of spite. Or maybe because it hurt that he was hiding all this stuff, this whole life from her, Ten and Erro. She'd thought they were his family, but apparently he had fulfilled that need elsewhere.

Then there was the night of the big fight. Li hadn't brought the woman any money. Work had been sparse that month, and everyone had had to chip in to replace a burned out fuel cell so they could get that lump of crap they called a ship off the ground. They screamed for twenty minutes straight before he stormed out. She'd caught bits and pieces, but Nova visited on different nights just to confirm what she suspected.

Sure enough, the woman had a string of men coming by, passing her money to see a kid they thought was theirs. Hell, she'd probably just found the kid on the streets and decided to use him as a means of income. Whatever the truth of it was, it didn't change the end result: Li ran out of funds, and apparently so had their business. And even though he'd freed himself from his illusion of a family, the money'd been spent. Nova knew it'd be hell to crawl out of the hole he'd put them in.

Still, she hadn't realized just how bad off they were. Of course, if the Syndicate hadn't doubled the docking fees they might have had a shot at getting back on track. Wishful thinking certainly wasn't going to help anybody, so her plan was to just keep on working.

She parked two blocks away from the Nest and had to hoof it the rest of the way through the crowded streets of the Mid District where most of the bars could be found. Ganymede was made up of twelve dome cities, each connected by tunnels. December, her city, was one of the bigger domes and further divided into districts: Upper, Mid, Lower, and Under. The names really spoke for themselves.

"How's the crowd tonight, Tomy?" she called out as she approached the bouncer seated outside the Nest.

"Nova! Is your lucky night! New band inside. Very good music," he answered in his thick Titan accent.

He extended a muscular hand that Nova clasped firmly to exchange both friendship and a twenty credit piece.

Popping a colour cap in her mouth, she swallowed and then asked, "What's the cover?"

"Beautiful women get in free tonight."

"You flatter me."

"No," he said, pointing to a sign in the window that read exactly that.

"Well then, shall we proceed?" Nova asked, holding her arms out from her sides and slightly spreading her legs.

Tomy pulled his weapons detector from his holster and flicked it off before scanning her. It was twenty credits well spent. Catching her reflection in the window, she watched her hair fade from teal to mahogany red. It wasn't her favorite color; but she had a surplus of red caps, and the dark colors helped her blend in against the ultraviolets.

"Looks good. Where are your twins tonight?" He referred to Erro and Ten.

"They're out on a run. Hope to have 'em back in a week or two."

"You shouldn't send the boys out alone. They lack your intuition, I think, and I'm sure it is well missed."

"Yeah, but they can handle themselves on the little stuff."

"As you say. Have a good night!"

"Will do. I'll send you a shot out later. Wouldn't want you to get too thirsty," she tossed back as she entered the bar.

The band blasted, and the crowd in front of the stage moved like a choppy ocean as neon lights of blue, green, and pink glinted rhythmically across the surface. Tomy was right, the band was good, but drinks came first.

She skirted the edge of the crowd, making her way to the back area. People swarmed around the bar, and Nova had to fight for a spot close enough to place an order. She flashed the bartender a few coins to get her attention. Moments later she had a cold drink in each hand.

She threw the first drink back quick and chucked the cup into the crowd. She lost sight of it in the light show and never saw it land. Taking a few sips of her second drink, she waded into the sea of people.

Closing her eyes, she listened to the music, danced, and blended in. Everyone around her was doped, she imagined. A popular pastime among bar-hoppers that Nova did not partake in. She needed to be on her game at all times, not slushed out of her mind and body. She envied them a bit. It must be nice to just switch off for a few hours.

She wished Tomy hadn't mentioned Erro and Ten, or 'the twins' as he called them. They were twins, identical even, except for the hair, which they wore differently to help ease the confusion. Ten's black hair stayed long, often in a fashionably high ponytail, while Erro kept his short and parted on his left.

Tomy thought himself clever for calling them that, but it

aggravated her a bit. Drawing attention to their oddness always bothered them. They'd never say so, but she could tell. Guess that was her intuition as well. She loved both of 'em as brothers and didn't like them being picked on, even if it wasn't malicious in intent. And maybe she missed them a little bit, too.

Three more songs flew by. Nova took the last swig of her second drink. She pitched her second cup into the air as she had her first and watched it evaporate in the lights.

The crowd thickened, and the dancing continued. She felt a pair of hands encircle her waist. It wasn't uncommon. Dopers often got touchy, but a gentle push was all it took to move them on to the next person. They wouldn't remember any of this tomorrow, anyway.

Nova lightly tried to extract herself, but these hands held firm. It wasn't a doper.

One hand slid up her back and then to the side of her face, placing a micro-receiver in her ear.

"It's me," a male voice spoke. It was her contact.

She had no way of verbally responding. All she needed to do was listen.

"I've got intel on a pair of fugitives from Earth."

Nova shook her head. She had no interest in Terran bounties. Too much work to deliver them, and she had no desire to help them catch anyone. As far as she was concerned, anybody that wronged Earth was no enemy of hers.

"This case is special," her contact continued. "There's a bounty of ten million, but someone has gone to a lot of trouble to erase all evidence of it. We found out via a transmission we picked up by accident on Mars. As far as we can tell, no one beyond Mars knows about these two except us."

Nova continued shaking her head. She still had no interest.

"We know someone on Ganymede who will pay triple that price to have these two delivered to them alive. Now are you interested?"

Nova nodded. That came out to thirty million. Jesus, of course she was interested now.

"All the data we have is on the chip," he said as he placed his hand inside her back pocket to relieve her of the coins she'd put there and replaced it with the sliver of data.

"Until next time," he signed off. Removing the receiver from her ear, the man vanished into the crowd. She didn't try to look for him; it was no use.

She stayed through the band's first set, then made her way out.

"They send you out a shot like I asked?" she shouted at Tomy as she briskly strode in the direction of her skiff.

"Indeed they did! Goodnight, Nova!"

Once at her skiff, she popped the chip into her onboard reader.

The text read: Ten million dead or alive. Vladia Robespierre: Wanted for war crimes against Earth and for the deaths of over one thousand Terran officers and Lunite civilians. Escaped during prisoner transfer. Last witnessed fleeing Earth in Valkyrie Class ship, 57R061, with a robot accomplice, identification number HCV-1178. Very dangerous.

There was also a picture of the woman, clearly taken from her military id, and a video loop.

Nova played the footage. It was her escape, or the last part at least. Cover fire blasted from above, and then an explosion that made the rest of the video hazy at best. She could barely make out a hand pulling Robespierre into the cockpit of a ship she assumed was the Valkyrie mentioned in the text.

That was it. A picture, ten seconds of footage, and some meager bits of text was all she had on this one. This woman could be anywhere in the solar system.

"What a freakin' rip-off!" she yelled into the still crowded streets.

With a disgruntled huff, Nova revved up her skiff and sped off.

The AWS chimed once again, "Remember, rain is scheduled for today at three a.m. and will continue until six twenty a.m. Thank you and drive safely."

4

THROUGH A GLASS, DARKLY

Rehel injected the last of the vaccinations into Abel's left shoulder, causing him to flinch not from pain but the coldness of the fluid itself.

"Some of these may cause nausea, dizziness, and/or drowsiness. I don't recommend any strenuous activity for a few days at least," Rehel explained as he prepared the next batch of inoculations for Vladia.

"Not a problem," he said, hopping off the only table in the otherwise bare medical bay. "Guess we should stock this place up once we reach the Outer Moons. You should make a list of the things we need."

"I have already made two lists. One with my recommended stock and another with only the absolute essentials."

"I don't know how far the currency Weston gave us will actually stretch. You might need to make a third list. Call it 'things we'll die without'."

"It does help that I won't need anything, and Vladia would require medical treatment in only the most dire circumstances."

"Right."

He'd forgotten about Vladia's nanobots. Now he felt like an even bigger piece of shit for the things he'd said earlier.

For a long time, back when he and Rehel first began looking into her, Vladia was less a person and more an ideal or a symbol. She was to be their last resort if Malthus turned out to be the devil Abel suspected him to be. She was hope and that made it easier to justify the liberties they were taking with their investigation of her history.

"I estimate we'll need to hire at least three more people to run this ship at optimal efficiency."

"What about those scans Weston wants you to run?" he asked, changing the subject. "You really think it's just curiosity?"

"I can only assume. It appears harmless enough, and he himself professed interest in Maria Robespierre's work. I would be his only chance at studying one of the models she completed after his immigration to Mars."

"I guess. I just don't see why he needed to be so secretive about it," Abel said. He wanted to trust Weston, especially after all he was doing for them. But he just couldn't quite shake the feeling there was more to this than just plain curiosity.

"I sympathize with your suspicions, but I cannot see anything to be gained from scanning my systems other than what he has stated."

"You think he knows about Vladia?"

"I would assume so. All the newsfeeds refer to her as the cyborg fugitive, not a human. Though you forget, Martians do not share the same prejudice as Terrans. They do not have classifications of citizenship. In fact, many humans on Mars would be considered cyborgs by Earth standards."

"Speaking of Terran sentiments, what other materials did Weston provide to prep us for the Outer Moons?"

This worried him a great deal. Going from Earth to the Outer Moons was about as extreme as it got. He didn't know how Vladia expected them to blend in. Maybe it'd be easier for her since she'd been raised outside the system. He truly had no clue just how different her upbringing was from his.

"We have cultural assimilation units available for several of the moons, as well as language units. The Outer Moons speak a very primitive form of Standard. Structurally, the language is still similar, so it shouldn't be too hard to pick it up."

Abel nodded. "As soon as we set a course, send me some units."

"I must warn you, Abel. These units only explain the customs. They will do little to prepare you for the experience."

Rehel seemed genuinely concerned on this point. For good reason, too. The barbarism of the Outer Moons was drilled into Terran children at an early age. It was a breeding ground to some of the most vile natural diseases. Casual sex was rampant, leading to overpopulation and even starvation and homelessness in some of the poorer areas. Drugs, violence, and other illegal activities were staples in these communities. Of course there were drugs and violence on Earth as well, but the rearing facilities preached so carefully against them that few strayed from the righteous path set out for them. And at any rate, serious slums on Earth became labeled a blight and were swiftly sectioned off from the rest of the population.

There was no real government, only the gangs and mafia. Since the moons couldn't be terraformed as Mars had been, whole cities, called ports, lived under biodomes that were all connected by a series of tubes. And even though Abel was well aware that his views on the Outer Moons were just a part of his conditioning, all those people breathing the same disgusting air over and over again made him queasy.

"I'll go get Vladia," he said, taking a few unsteady steps before his knees gave out from under him. Rehel caught him by the arm and moved him back to the table.

"You have a slight fever, which may become worse if you push yourself too soon. You should rest here. I will get Vladia."

"Fine," Abel groaned as the dizziness grew more intense.

"Shall I give you something to help you sleep?"

Abel shook his head.

Rehel nodded and then pointed towards the comm station to the right of the table. "If you need me, the comm is operational and connects to every area of the ship. Also, there is a bucket under the table in case—"

"I got it," he said, laying back on the cool metal table. Just thinking about vomiting made it worse.

"Rehel, is she…is she much changed?"

"Vladia?"

"I haven't been around her much since…" he couldn't quite form the words, only in part because of the sudden nausea.

"Since her declassification, or since Cornelia's death, or since General Malthus tried to have her imprisoned, or—"

"All of it. Since everything."

Rehel considered the question for a few moments, then said, "I think any human would be changed after her recent ordeals. Vladia and I did not speak about any of these events during our journey to Mars, but I have noticed a hardness about her, if that makes sense. I cannot say for certain, since this is out of my area of expertise, but if I had to describe her current emotional state, I would say she is afraid and sad."

"Afraid and sad?" He hadn't expected that by a long shot. Angry, sure, but afraid and sad?

"Yes. I think she is afraid of what she might have to do in order to stop Malthus and sad that she must do it at all."

"Earlier, I may have been a bit careless in my attitude towards her. I haven't seen her since before the battle, and I'd not thought about how all this might have affected her. Honestly, I made an ass of myself," he admitted reluctantly.

"Should I pass on an apology?"

"Yes. Please."

His body began to gently shiver. He'd not felt like this since, well, he couldn't recall. Maybe never.

"This is not an uncommon reaction to vaccinations, especially since your body has been stressed from your trip to Mars," Rehel assured him. "I will return soon."

"Good."

Rehel disappeared from his view, and moments later he heard the gentle swish of the door close behind him.

Abel didn't want to sleep, but fighting off the wooziness that filled his brain was out of the question. Before he realized it, he'd drifted off into a strange world of nannies that looked like beggars softly singing broken childhood hymns.

"Sterilize the body, sterilize the mind.

The only germ we cannot fight's
The germ that we call Time."

∞

A twelve–year–old Vladia lounged peacefully under one of the many elder sycamore trees that populated her father's estate. She'd only just closed her eyes for a quick afternoon nap when the rustling of rapid footfall made her push up on both elbows. Shielding her eyes from the sun, she could just make out the figure of Tolen sprinting her way.

"Aren't you supposed to be with Mr. Hendri for Calculus right now?" she asked once he was in earshot.

The boy slowed his approach. Tossing his brown satchel to the ground, he sat down beside her. "I'm sick today. Had a slight fever around lunch so of course they quarantined me. I slipped out the window after an hour or so. They really should do something about those vines if they expect me to stay put."

"You shouldn't do that. You'll fall."

"Says you. You do it too, and I know it."

Vladia shrugged and laid back down. She wasn't in the mood to talk to him. He'd given her a good beating at fencing yesterday, and she was still pretty sore about it.

Tolen pinched at her knee and snapped her bio-blocks against her skin. "Why are you still wearing those?"

"Too much trouble to take them off. Besides, I'll just have to put them right back on before I go in for Physics."

"You're messing my experiment up, Vladia."

"One time won't make any difference. Besides, don't you need a control?"

"The rest of the planet is the control. You're just being lazy."

He was right. She'd wanted to be lazy and take a nap during her break, but now he'd ruined it. She didn't see why she had to participate in his experiment anyway. Tolen had this theory on germs and natural resistance. He said if they stopped wearing the bio-blocks, they'd build up a natural resistance to some sicknesses. All it'd got both of them so far were runny noses and fevers.

Tolen stood up and began ascending the tree until he found a solid perch on a branch directly above her. Summer was fast approaching, and soon it'd be too hot to spend her afternoon break outside. She didn't mind the heat, but if she came in sweating and smelling of dirt and grass, the maids would have a fit.

"You and me getting sick all the time, it just re-enforces their belief we're disease-ridden abominations," she said.

"I don't care what they think. Do you, Vladia?"

"No. Well, sometimes I do I guess."

"You need to let that go."

"Let what go?"

"Your need for affection and approval. No one here's ever going to give you either."

She stared up at him, this cold, stoic boy of fifteen. His words always cut so deep. He was right about the maids and their father. They'd never care for them. But what really hurt was that she knew he included himself in that statement as well. Maria would be the only person in all the worlds to have ever truly shown her genuine affection. And she was dead.

"I think you want to be sick. I think you want to be so sick it kills you," she fired back.

"Could you blame me if that were true? I think there's something in all of us that longs to test our limits. Well, there used to be. Before Earth became a nothing more than a prison."

"What are you talking about?"

"Never mind," he sighed. "Anyway, I brought you something."

He pointed to his satchel. As Vladia reached over and tugged the bag lightly across the grass towards her, he continued. "I know you're taking ancient history with Griggs. If I remember right you should be in Rome by now."

"We started it two days ago."

Vladia took out a thick set of books. "*The Decline and Fall of the Roman Empire*, Volume One. Gibson," she read the title of the top tome aloud. "I take it I'm supposed to read these in addition to what Griggs has assigned me?"

"What Griggs has you read is crap. And a lot of it just plain wrong. These are what you need to read."

"I'm surprised you're not making me wait to fill in the holes of my education until after I've earned my entry code to the library."

"I thought about that, but didn't think it would serve anyone's best interest. And honestly, Vladia, it could be another year yet."

"Thanks," she said, under-enthused.

"After the course I can get you the books you'll need to fill in the rest of the gaps. Just wait till you take History III. Last week, we covered the entire nineteenth century in ten minutes."

"Did you speak up?"

"There's no point. All I'd succeed in doing is getting an unfavorable report to the Admiral, a lecture on knowing my place at the next interview, and suspension from the library for a few months."

"Sounds like you've tried it before, then."

Tolen frowned.

"Wow. You made a mistake? I didn't think it possible!"

"It wasn't a mistake," he spoke not with anger, but with impatience. "I acted without sufficient knowledge of the situation and learned a valuable lesson. It would only be a mistake if I let it happen again."

Vladia giggled. "Still sounds like a mistake to me."

"As usual, you miss the point entirely and instead focus on what you wrongly consider a small victory over me."

She stopped her quiet laughter and waited for him to proceed.

"The point here, at this estate, is to learn. Not to try and change anything or point out shortcomings and injustices. Just learn as much as you possibly can. Taking a stand will achieve nothing other than keeping me from one of the few real sources of knowledge left on this planet."

Tolen gripped the tree branch with the backs of his knees and let go so his body hung upside down from his perch. If Vladia stood up and leapt into the air, he'd still be well out of her reach.

"You take our situation here too lightly. It will be hard for us once we leave. Children raised at the rearing facilities are bred differently. They're like a species of their own. Even with our records sealed, we'll stick out. But none of this can be helped, so the best we can do is take our only advantage and make the most of it."

"And that is?"

"The library, obviously. Those kids come out of the system knowing only what the government allows them to know. The lessons we get here are roughly the same, but with the library we have access to so much more. Knowledge is the only real power in this world, and we have enough to swim in it here."

"Do you think any of Maria's books are in there?"

"No," he answered sharply. "When one is executed in disgrace one's stamp on this world is eradicated completely. Her books were confiscated and burned, as is Terran custom."

Vladia wasn't quite sure she believed him but said nothing. Once she gained access to the library, she'd do her own search for her mother's books.

The sun had lowered below the cover of her tree, just enough to pierce her eyes with its dying light. Vladia stood up and brushed her clothes off. Looking up into the tree, she couldn't see Tolen anymore. Had he climbed even higher?

Someone called her name in the distance, and she had the sinking feeling she might be in trouble again.

∞

Vladia jerked her head up from her desk. Rehel was standing beside her, and for a brief moment she couldn't remember where she was.

"I'm sorry to wake you, but I wanted to talk to you about

the vaccinations."

She rubbed her eyes with the heels of her hands, and as she did her fingertips grazed a slight indention in her forehead. Looking down, she realized she'd fallen asleep on the datapad she'd been reading.

"Are you all right?" the robot asked.

"No. I mean, yeah, I'm fine. Just had a dream, or a dream of a memory, I guess."

It was in her mind still, but all jumbled up. She'd been the one who'd had the fever that day, not Malthus. And it was she who had climbed out the window and gone to find him in the garden. There'd been something else a bit off too, but it was fading fast back into the fog.

"What'd you say you needed?" she asked, letting the dream go completely.

"It's about the vaccinations. Abel's experiencing some side effects. I cannot determine yet how severe they will be, but it is safe to say he's in no condition to work for a few days at least."

"That's fine. Nothing much to work on, anyway."

"I'd also like to hold off on your vaccinations until he has recovered."

"Is he really that bad off?"

"His reaction was both faster and more serious than I had anticipated, though not entirely atypical. I will be monitoring him closely."

"Well, there's no reason mine can't wait, though I feel confident my nanos would prevent me from any major complications."

"You are most likely right. However, Abel's reaction requires that I should, as he would say, play it safe, if you have no objection."

"Of course not. We've got plenty of time."

"I take it you've selected our destination?"

"I have. The information Weston provided helped a great deal. I'll have to remember to thank him."

This was one area she thought the Admiral's library would've given her no advantage. On Earth, propaganda was the only info on the Outer Moons. But as it turned out, many of the moons very much resembled more primitive civilizations of Earth, something she had studied a great deal in her youth. That knowledge, combined with Weston's up-to-date data, made the decision all too easy.

"I narrowed it down to Titan or Ganymede pretty fast, since they're the central hubs for their respective areas," she began. "Through sheer luck, distance proved to be far less of an influence than I initially thought. It really came down to how each moon is governed. Both are for all intents and purposes run by criminal organizations, but the way these organizations treat the population seems to vary quite a bit.

"On Titan, you have more of an old North American-style mafia organization. They usually look out for their own, but the rest of the community they see more as resources to be used, not a people to be taken care of. On Ganymede, it's much more similar to an Asian Yakuza organization. They take care of their communities because they consider themselves protectors, not consumers. Both are, of course, wary of outsiders, violent, and dangerous, but based on Ganymede's interest in protecting the moon as a whole, I think I at least have a chance at persuading them that Earth will become a threat to them if left unchecked."

"I agree with your conclusion. Their desire to protect, and hopefully their willingness to listen, should give us the best chance at our goal. If you'd like, I can go make the necessary calculations and plot our course immediately," Rehel offered.

"Thanks. Then you should get back to Abel."

Rehel nodded.

The ship would be on autopilot for the next several weeks as they traveled to Jupiter. Technically speaking a Valkyrie was one of the fastest class ships in the system and could cut their travel time almost in half. But the thought of crawling back into the cramped cockpit of Freya for yet another long journey made her nauseous. Besides that, they'd likely suffocate before the trip ended in such a small craft built only for battle.

Devil's Run was built for deep space. Even with both

Valkyries stowed in its belly, she still had room in the cargo hold to spare. What was another month of travel compared to not having a ship to get them there at all? Besides, she had much to do in that time. She needed a plan of attack, she needed to become fluent in the language, customs, and culture of Ganymede, and she needed to re-strengthen her body after the muscle decay caused by the trip from Earth to Mars. She would not be bored.

"Before you go," Vladia continued, "what was that last bit of business with Weston?"

"He asked if I would be willing to record some data on my systems during our trip out. He seemed eager to study me since he has not had access to any of Dr. Robespierre's robots since his immigration," Rehel explained. "If this presents a problem I will decline ,of course, but I had intended to comply with his request. After consulting with you, that is."

It seemed a harmless request on the surface. But Vladia imagined there must be more to it than just curiosity. "Have you already checked out the diagnostic equipment?"

"Yes. I found nothing out of the ordinary. Should we be suspicious of Dr. Weston?"

"Maybe. Your model number was constructed before his immigration, so he had access then," she pondered. "Obviously he's interested in you particularly. Did he say why?"

"He did. Though I fear he will not receive the results he is hoping for."

"Well?"

"He wanted to gain access to a robot that had, as he put it, lived through the Robespierre ordeal. I assume he is referring to the execution of Maria and the brief chaos that ensued at the facility during that time. He seemed to think it might have changed me, or rather damaged me, somehow."

"Why would he think you're damaged?"

"I do not know."

"And does he plan on sharing his findings with you?"

"I was led to believe so, yes."

Vladia leaned in, elbows propped up on the desk. "Go ahead and send the data then, but do it sooner rather than later. If someone is actually able to decode your encryption they could trace us to Ganymede. In fact, for the moment set a course for Titan. Once you've sent the data and received your report from Weston, we'll re-route to Ganymede."

"This will add at least a week to our journey."

"I'm aware of that, but what's one more week at this point? It's a small thing to avoid potential, if improbable, detection."

What she wouldn't tell him was that if Weston really was concerned about him, then so was she. She needed him for the task ahead, more than she needed anyone else.

"Understood. I'll set course now and will run the diagnostic from the med bay so I can continue monitoring Abel's condition."

"Let me know when he improves and send me a copy of Weston's report as soon as you get it. I'm eager to study his findings as well."

"Of course, Captain," Rehel said with a quick, stiff bow but made no move to leave.

"Is there something else?"

"Actually, yes. Abel wanted to apologize for his behavior earlier. Though he did not say exactly what transpired, he explained that he had 'been an ass', his words."

Vladia laughed, and Rehel looked as shocked as a robot could manage. Hearing him call Abel an ass, even if he was simply repeating Abel's own words, made the whole confrontation worth it.

"Tell him I accept his apology, but only because it came through you."

"As you wish."

Vladia exhaled raggedly and put her head on the desk. She felt tired. Her energy levels were all out of sorts. Sleep would have to wait, though.

"Are you sure you're all right?"

"I will be, and that's all that matters," she said, lifting her head grudgingly. "You've no idea how much I envy you sometimes, Rehel."

"I don't understand."

"No, I don't suppose you would," she said thoughtfully. "Never mind me. Abel needs you now."

The robot bowed once more and left.

Vladia waited until she could no longer hear his footsteps before reluctantly standing up. She stretched a bit then headed out the door. The circular corridor that wrapped around the bridge was perfect for a run. She needed to be combat ready, and a run would clear her head. The remnants of the dream still clung to her. And like a heavy shadow latched to her feet, she dragged it behind her as she began her sprint around her ship.

5

LUNA

Ambassador General Tolen Malthus strode down the ramp of the shuttle *Tiberion*, flanked by two escorts from the Grand Admiral's Special Forces Guard. If he hadn't known better he'd have thought himself a prisoner. In a way he was really, though it was of his own choosing. He'd not be able to leave Luna for quite some time, and those on the War Council who felt threatened by his rapid and glorious ascension towards the throne would breathe a sigh of relief, misplaced as it was.

The shuttle bay's routine procedures had clearly been interrupted during the chaos that ensued after the Battle of Emden. The right half of the platform had been converted to a makeshift aid area, which consisted of a mixture of bunks, desks, and first aid stations. He found the disorganization of the entire area offensive. If he didn't have other duties, he might have taken a small pleasure in restructuring the entire facility.

He'd not expected any sort of welcoming party, after all Earth had just decimated their central and most powerful colony in a single blow, but protocol dictated that there should be at least someone to greet them and show them to their quarters. Too consumed with their own tasks, no one lifted an eye towards them.

"Ambassador?" the guard to his left asked, probably in hopes that he knew where they should go. Both guards were to remain stationed here during his stay as protection, though he knew they had also been told to watch him. Not by Grand Admiral Clovis, of course, but by Vorros and perhaps a few others.

"Do not call me that. The Lunites will call me Ambassador. You should address me as General," he corrected, giving every outward indication that his station here was a grievance against him.

"Apologies, General Malthus."

Once he had realized he'd have company during his stay on Luna, Malthus had proceeded to research each man with care to determine how much of a threat they posed. The man who'd spoken just then was Commander Jet Gailmen. He'd been part of the Grand Admiral's guard for two years and demonstrated all the typical qualities of those in his position. He was loyal, sharp, and skilled in combat. In fact, Malthus imagined the man embodied everything his father had hoped he would have become: the perfect soldier. Judging by his record, Gailmen wasn't the kind of man who looked for trouble, so he posed a minimal threat.

The second man, Victor Whitlock, was another story. He'd been with the guard eleven years, by choice. Twice he had declined a promotion and raise that would have moved him to a more powerful position. This was a man who cared little for himself and all for Earth. A man with such unshakable ideals should always to be treated as beyond dangerous.

One more fact made him a threat: he'd been the officer who'd piloted the prison shuttle that had transported Vladia back to Earth after the Battle of Emden. He'd witnessed her attempt at escape and had had several minutes of contact with her. Granted, nothing of his behavior afterwards indicated she'd said anything of importance to him. But one could never be too careful. Whitlock seemed the kind of man who, once he'd got the scent of a rat, he'd not stop until he ran it down.

"I'll see myself settled in," Malthus said. "I suggest you two do the same. Dismissed."

"Sir, our orders are to accompany you to Viceroy Connell," Whitlock explained resolutely.

His response was as expected.

Malthus smiled and said, "That could be some time, judging by the look of this place. But, if you wish to follow me about in the interim, by all means proceed. I have no objection to your presence."

Malthus strolled towards the exit, hands clasped firmly behind his back, followed closely by the two guards.

Just as the three approached the egress, the doors glided open to reveal a tall, thin man of about seventy. It was obvious by his build he'd never been a soldier, and his formal garb of stately blue and gray robes signaled to Malthus that he must be a politician.

"Viceroy Connell, I presume?"

The man grunted. "You're early."

"No, I don't think so," Malthus insisted politely.

Another grunt. "As you like. Follow me. I'll brief you on the way to your quarters."

The group walked down the hallway, Malthus abreast of Connell with Whitlock and Gailmen in line behind them.

"How are you adjusting to your new duties, Viceroy?" Malthus said with feigned interest. One of the quickest judges of character was to study how a person responded to different stimuli, in this case friendly banter with the enemy.

"Never mind that. You're here to spy on me. I'll tell you right now I resent this in every way imaginable. Despite my feelings, however, you're here to stay."

"I assure you, Viceroy, I have no desire to be here, spying on you, as you put it. I intend to do my job then go home."

"Ha! Good luck with that, Ambassador!"

Malthus glowered slightly, making sure the Lunite saw it. Even the Viceroy thought he'd come to a dead end, and he had no interest in changing that perception.

"Your only job," the Viceroy continued, "is to express Earth's wishes to me and force me into seeing things your way, or Earth's way, I should say. In turn you are to take any concerns we have back to Earth. I trust you will at least pretend to do us justice. I'll give you fifteen minutes of my time every third day to discuss any issues that come up, and unless there is something pressing, I'd like to make that the maximum amount of time I must deal with you. What you do with the rest of your time is entirely up to you, but I assume it will be observing and reporting every move we make back to Earth."

"As you wish."

Connell stopped at the lift. "Your quarters are on level F. Your room is number twenty-seven and your guards' are thirty-four and thirty-six. That level's mostly for maintenance workers, but we've had so many officers displaced I've no other area to put you," he smirked.

The man wanted them scared. Luna's policies on the workforce differed little from Earth's. Children, though raised in family units, were still tested at fourteen and assigned to a job ladder based on IQ, physical and mental health, and personality. Those assigned to repetitive maintenance-type work had the lowest level IQ's and were less emotionally developed. Some even speculated that Lunites dumbed down random embryos to make sure they had enough worker bees to replace the loss of the robots who had once done that sort of labor for them.

Either way, worker bees had little in the way of reasoning skills; that combined with their emotional instability made them more likely to end up in a physical confrontation. If that wasn't enough, Lunites' phobias of germs and disease were not nearly as extreme as Earth's. Many of them wouldn't even be wearing bio-blockers. It mattered little to Malthus, but he would enjoy watching Gailmen and Whitlock squirm.

"Thank you for your assistance, Viceroy."

Connell frowned. He clearly expected more of a reaction from them.

"This counts as our first session. I don't want to see you again until next week. Good day!" he said indignantly, marching away.

Once he was well out of ear shot, Malthus said, "I'm sure I don't need to tell either of you this, but it would be a good idea to check your room for bugs. It would not surprise me if Luna aimed to spy on us as well."

"Will you be fine staying on level F, Sir?" Gailmen asked. "We could see about getting moved."

"He'll be fine," Whitlock answered for him.

His rudeness did not go unnoticed, by Malthus or Gailmen, but Malthus had no intention to discipline either of them on Luna. Whitlock did not like him, and now that he'd exposed his hand so early in the game, dealing with him would be all too easy.

"We'll all be fine as long as we keep to ourselves," Whitlock continued. "Connell put us here to cause trouble, so he'll not reassign us so easily."

"Commander Whitlock is right. He would refuse any attempt to move on the grounds that they haven't the space," Malthus said, stepping into the lift. The other men fell in behind him.

The lift doors closed, and as the platform under them seamlessly sank to the levels below, Malthus added, "Besides, requesting a reassignment shows weakness; that is a luxury no Terran can afford."

∞

Whitlock observed his room with the trained eyes of a seasoned soldier. The accommodations were modest, which suited him perfectly. The more cluttered and ornate a room was, the easier it became to conceal dangers, such as radiation bombs or enemy transmitters. There to his right lay a bed with both sheets and covers folded neatly at the foot and topped with a flat brown pillow. To his left was a meager table and chair with a screen on the wall above. A small, rectangular panel below the screen opened to reveal a computer. He would, of course, not be using it. He slid it out from the wall, setting it on the table for immediate disassembly.

Pulling the case open, he set about clipping wires and removing circuits, and in less than ten minutes he'd covered the tabletop with its innards. The screen was his next victim. Prying it from the wall proved harder than expected, but he managed, and soon it joined the mess of its counterpart.

At the back of the room sat a short grey chest of drawers that his baggage rested beside. He took out each drawer for examination before moving to the underside and back of the chest. Next he moved on to the table, the chair, the bed, and ended with skimming the walls, floor, and ceiling for hidden panels. The next item was the wash area, which tucked away nicely into the back wall, making it an ideal hiding place. Still, he found nothing.

The last thing to do would be to search his own belongings, which had passed through unknown hands a few days earlier on their trip here. As he unpacked his two bags, he searched each item with both his eyes and hands before loading it into the drawers.

Sitting down on the unmade bed, unlaced his boots. His relief at finding no tricks or traps would be short-lived; he would have to do this every day at least once. No matter how harmless and defeated the Lunites appeared, letting his guard down was not in his skill set.

The door chimed and, instinctively, he reached for his sidearm before calling out, "Enter."

Commander Gailmen strolled into the room.

Once the door had slid closed behind the man, Whitlock asked, "Find anything?"

"Nothing," sighed Gailmen, taking the only chair. "Hurts my feelings. Should we see about doing a sweep of Malthus' quarters?"

"No. He's got sense enough to do that himself. Remember, unlike most ambassadors, he's more a solider than a politician."

Whitlock pushed his boots under his bed. He watched Gailmen poke through the wreckage on the desk. His dark blonde hair, handsome face, and hard, yet bright eyes made him look a poster boy for the Terran military. It was a harsh contrast to his own dark features. Younger in years and experience, Whitlock knew the boy would grow restless at his station. They wouldn't stay here as long as Malthus, but it would be long enough that a less tested guard might find himself making trouble with the locals out of sheer boredom.

"What do you make of Vorros' request?" Gailmen asked.

Whitlock shrugged. "I don't take orders from Vorros. You can do as you like. There isn't much going on here, so if spying on Malthus keeps you out of trouble, so be it."

"You expect no strife from the Lunites?"

"I'm prepared for it, but after what I saw of the hangar bay, I don't look for it."

He'd carefully examined the faces of those who surrounded them in the hangar. They appeared utterly broken. The death toll and damages suffered had been high. They were but a moon, as Earth had so mercilessly reminded them. He did not revel in their misfortune, but was made glad by the return of peace.

"He called him a snake," Gailmen said, referring once again to Malthus.

"Most of them are, including Vorros."

Gailmen stood up and strode to the door, then said, "It's a shame the Grand Admiral sent him out here to rot. He handled the Viceroy well, don't you think?"

"He did."

Whitlock couldn't deny the man's virtues, but somehow they only made him more wary of the Ambassador General.

"I'm going to the mess. I hope the food here isn't as bad as they say. You coming? Might scout around a bit after."

"I'm not hungry."

"Suit yourself," he said as he passed through the doorway and into the corridor.

Whitlock rubbed his chin thoughtfully, then laid down on his bed. Staring up at the ceiling, he let his mind drift back to the Robespierre incident.

Those few minutes with the woman during her transport back to Earth had all felt a bit off. Staged, even. It hadn't been much, but it'd been enough to leave a gnawing pit in his stomach for days after. She could have killed the two men guarding her, but she merely disabled them. After all, what was two more lives on top of the hundreds that had died on the *Iron Maiden* and on the Luna base?

Once word had gotten out that she was no longer human, Whitlock realized she might have killed him too, but didn't. In fact, to escape she would have been forced to kill him, and that seemed to be the real reason behind her inaction. It wasn't that she was unwilling to die in the attempt, but that she was unwilling to kill him. No, not unwilling. It was something else he couldn't quiet put his finger on. Something almost akin to fear.

After he had recovered from the injuries he sustained during her escape, he'd looked through her and her accomplice's training records. There was nothing that indicated any of them had the skill to create the program used to send the *Iron Maiden* hurling into Luna. Even the robot was devoid of the knowledge needed to program at that level. No attempt had been made to hide the evidence, either. It revealed itself easily, as if it longed to be found and put out on display.

But what stood out the most, what still kept him up at night, were the woman's eyes. They were not those of a cool, calculating murderer, nor were they the eyes of a crazed madman, as one might expect of a person who in the blink of an eye had killed hundreds.

What he'd seen in Robespierre's eyes was pain. The kind of pain one might see in a soldier's eyes after a long battle lost and upon realizing all one's comrades had fallen. She wasn't a murderer; she was a survivor.

In truth, the Robespierre incident had fostered within him a growing distrust of Tolen Malthus, the man she supposedly tried to kill just before getting caught. There appeared no reason for her to go after him in particular. He'd been her Captain, and there had been no reports of any difficulties between them. Other than that, they had no real ties that he could deduce.

If indeed Robespierre committed the crimes charged

against her, perhaps Malthus was involved, too. Perhaps he had a hand in all of it. It could be a sign of his betrayal that she should want him dead. If that was the case, then he was a threat that needed to be removed. Or perhaps he'd used Robespierre as his pawn, maybe without her even knowing until it was too late. In that instance, Malthus was all the more dangerous to Earth.

Either way, Whitlock planned to use his time in Malthus' company to uncover what he could. It was his proud obligation to see Earth and her citizens protected from both outside enemies and those from within. If that meant going up against Malthus, so be it.

∞

Malthus waited in his quarters with limited patience for Isobel to check back in. His first actual meeting with the Viceroy was fast approaching, and though he should have met with him several times already, the Lunite always seemed to have a reason to cancel their session.

He moved in front of the mirror near his bed and straightened his uniform. His Ambassador's garb lacked the stiffness he'd grown accustomed do with his former ensemble. Designed with a politician in mind, the crisp whiteness of his long outer coat and the ornate gold and blue embellishments were bold and off-putting. He much preferred the coarse material of his military uniform, or even the snugness of his old black and blue Valkyrie flight suit, to this.

His stay on Luna was well into its second week, and already it had become evident that Whitlock would indeed be a problem. The solider watched his movements closely, so much so Malthus hadn't dared to venture anywhere near the facility Isobel had set up for him. It wasn't impossible to give Whitlock the slip; the issue was more that giving him the slip was proof in itself that he had something to hide. Despite his altogether typical and rather boring routine, Whitlock had not let up in the slightest. The time for a new strategy to deal with this man had arrived.

Gailmen, on the other hand, he could make use of. His youth and impressionability made him easily manipulated, despite his military training. He didn't need the boy just yet, but the time would come soon enough.

His comm buzzed, gently flailing about on his desk. He scooped it up and inserted the piece into his right ear.

"Well?" he asked.

"I've secured the adjacent facility," Isobel explained, her voice all but lacking in its former humanity.

"Good."

He couldn't risk Isobel tampering with more facility records, so this one he had purchased under an assumed name. She did go in and alter the ownership records afterwards, but that involved little danger. Times like these made being raised outside the system quite the blessing. He'd inherited his father's estate, which left him with a seemingly endless supply of money. And one thing that remained a constant with humanity was its inherent vice of greed. There would always be those willing to sell their souls if the price was right.

"And how is our stock?"

"Alive."

"I want all of them moved to the second location tonight while they're still in stasis. Can you manage that?"

"Of course. And I will dispose of the help once complete."

"I'll be stopping in tomorrow evening."

"Should I ready the equipment for the first experiment, then?"

"No. This will merely be a social call. I think it's time I visited our old friend. Wake her up."

"And what if Whitlock files a report?"

"He won't. Not until he has evidence. He'll need something tangible, and he won't be getting that. Not just yet."

∞

Somewhere, a dim light hummed to life; it was in that

moment Cornelia Arnim dared to think she might not be dead. The cold and the dark and the shrieking echoes had convinced her she must be. Or, rather, she wished to die so it would end. Her numbed body refused her efforts to push up from the ground, and her eyes could see nothing but a grey blur. She gave up, hugged her stark legs to her chest, and buried her face from the light and the grey. But the echoes remained. They seemed farther away, but they lingered still. She feared they would follow her forever.

A sharp clack made her jerk involuntarily. What followed sounded like metal being dragged across the floor. She thought she felt the vibrations of it, but the numbness made her distrust her senses.

Someone else was here.

"Do you want to know where you are?" a familiar voice asked. She couldn't quite place it as the voice mingled with the echoes that distorted all she heard.

Slowly, she raised her head just enough to see the outline of a figure against the grey.

"You're on Luna."

"Am I a prisoner?" she asked in a voice that sounded unlike her own.

"Yes."

She lowered her head and resigned herself to her fate. If only she'd died with her crew. She'd be one with the echoes, not tormented by them.

"What you're experiencing is normal. Numbness, confusion, distortions in your vision and hearing. They will pass."

"Who are you?" she asked, refusing to look up a second time.

"You mean you really don't recognize my voice? Perhaps your symptoms are more severe than most. Stasis affects people to varying degrees."

She hesitated, then asked, "Captain?"

"I'm not your Captain anymore, but yes."

She couldn't speak. Should she be relieved? Or afraid?

"I've brought you some food. I apologize for its meagerness, but it's all I could manage for the moment," he said.

She hadn't realized, but the only thing covering her was a thin blanket. She pulled it tight around her body.

His footsteps approached her.

"Can you stand?"

"I can't," she heard the whimpering words escape her lips.

Malthus lifted her off the floor with surprising gentleness. The raggedy covering stayed firmly in place, as he carried her to the chair he'd brought in.

Her eyes finally started to adjust, and she could just make out his face.

Kneeling beside her, he placed a bowl of broth in her hands. On seeing she couldn't keep it steady on her own, he held the bottom of the bowl in place so she could take a sip.

The liquid tasted of salt and not much else. But it warmed her, and for that she was grateful.

After taking a few more sips, Cornelia looked him in the eyes for the first time since he'd come to her and said, "Tell me... what's happened."

"I'm not sure that is a good idea just now. You've only just awakened and–"

"Tell me," she interrupted, something she'd not ever dared to do in the past.

"Finish this first," he insisted, referring to the broth.

Cornelia choked down the last of the salty concoction and then waited for him to proceed.

"Your ship was infested with malevolent nanobots, much like we witnessed at L4. They took over your navigational systems and drove you into the moon's surface, destroying Luna's main base of operations. The incident, however unfortunate, did end the war," he said, taking the emptied bowl from her.

"How many survivors?"

"A little under a hundred on either side combined. Due to its location and the site of impact, the bridge of the *Iron Maiden* had several survivors."

"Where am I now? And, how is it that you're here?"

"After the crash, and upon realizing the war was lost, several Lunites decided to take matters into their own hands. Before Terran rescue troops could get to the scene, they went about the wreckage looking to kill any survivors. This place is where those not killed were taken. As far as I know, even the Luna government doesn't know about this place."

"Taken by whom?"

Malthus smiled and said, " By me."

Now Cornelia was sure. She should be afraid.

"The rescue troops would have arrived far too late to have accomplished any actual rescuing. I dispatched certain individuals to the wreckage almost immediately, which is how I discovered that the Lunites were killing survivors. I saved who I could using the only remaining connections I had on Luna."

"What will you do with me?"

"I'm going to offer you the chance to be useful."

Cornelia waited for him to elaborate, but it seemed he had no intention of going into details.

"What of Abel, Vladia, and… Takashi," she asked, fearing the answer so much she'd almost not dared to pose the question.

"Both Abel Duren and Takashi Gammarow are listed as missing in action. I can neither confirm or deny anything further for you."

"You're lying."

"Why would I lie about that?"

Now that, she couldn't really answer. Maybe to break her spirits? Though she worried that had already been accomplished even before such solemn tidings.

"Whatever you may think of me," he continued, "I don't much care for lying. I avoid it when possible, and I can assure you everything I've said thus far is the truth."

"Who sabotaged my ship? Can you answer me that, oh Speaker of Truths?" she mocked. "Or how about what happened to Vladia?"

"You want to force my hand? I'm afraid you might not like what I have to say."

"Who did it?" she spoke the words slowly between gritted teeth.

Malthus stood up and straightened his fine, clean uniform. "I did. I used your ship to end the war. Evidence was planted to frame Vladia, forcing her to flee from Earth to the Outer moons."

"And L4? That was you as well."

"In a roundabout way, yes."

"How could you kill all those people…"

"You sound just like Vladia. You do realize that you would all have likely died anyway? If the war continued to rage on, thousands more would be doomed to perish. And had your attack succeeded, how many Lunites would have died by your hand? How many have you killed in battles past? Where is the remorse for your own actions?"

"That's not the same."

"It's exactly the same!" he shouted, his voice resonated off the walls of her hollow cell. "You kill and you maim and only when it is your own that suffer do you then show the slightest bit of repentance. I am indiscriminate and therefore above your petty reproach."

Malthus paused to regain his composure.

He continued, "It was a necessary unpleasantry. They didn't die out of spite or greed or any other such base human desire. Their death had purpose."

"Well, then, go ahead and kill me too!"

"I can't do that, Cornelia."

"Can't? Or won't? I'll not help you. Whatever it is you want from me, you'll not have it."

Malthus smiled. "You remind me of her so much. How strange," he said, mostly to himself. "You'll help me; just like she did. You won't have any choice, you see."

He walked towards the door, his heels clacking loudly against the slick, chilled floor.

Cornelia grabbed the bowl he'd left at her feet and flung it wildly at the back of his head.

Too weak to put any force behind her throw, the projectile clattered to the floor at his feet.

"There's a bundle of clothes here," he offered, ignoring her attempt to injure him. "I suggest you make use of them; it does get rather cold in the night."

The door creaked shut behind him. His footsteps trailed off, leaving Cornelia to her solitude and her grief.

∞

"Why did you have me wake her?" Isobel's voice demanded through the comm.

Malthus ignored her as he made his way back to his quarters, all the while keeping a close eye on anyone who might be around to spy on him. Whitlock had easily been misdirected earlier, but that didn't mean the man couldn't accidentally stumble upon him now.

"She won't be of any use as a test subject now. We should dispose of her immediately."

Emerging onto his floor, she at least had the good sense to keep quiet in such a populated area. It was late, and most people would be asleep, but one could never be too careful of curious eyes and ears.

"Isobel," he addressed her firmly once his quarter doors closed behind him. "Does it not occur to you that there may be other uses besides experimentation?"

"No."

"Cornelia Arnim has not once, but twice, survived situations of almost certain death at my hands, as if the universe keeps placing her in my path. I'm beginning to think she will serve a greater purpose."

"What greater purpose could she possibly fulfill for you that I could not?"

Malthus refused to answer. No matter what she believed, she'd no right to any information regarding his plans for Cornelia.

"How odd, the way she got under your skin back there. I thought you above such pettiness," she continued. A hint of sarcasm tinged her voice.

If Isobel were half as intelligent as she believed, the reason would be obvious. Vladia's departure had clearly affected him in an unforeseen way, and Cornelia's similarity to her had thrown him off balance. This was the first time since he'd left for the academy at eighteen that she'd been so far out of his grasp. Of course back then, it didn't matter as it did now. Her removal from Earth had been crucial, but if Vladia strayed off the course he'd set her on, she could jeopardize all of his plans. In truth, he needed someone in the Outer Moons other than Isobel to make sure Vladia did as he needed her to. Only then could he feel entirely in control once again.

To Isobel, he said, "My behavior does not concern you."

"Everything concerns me." Her tone grew shades darker. He'd not heard such distinct emotion in her voice for weeks, and it caught him by surprise.

"I am everywhere and everything," she continued. "I am beyond you and your petty behavior! I am beyond humanity! I am eternal! I–"

The silence was sudden, a stark contrast to her growing fanaticism.

"Isobel?"

More silence.

"Isobel?" He said her name as if whispering a curse. If he lost her now...

"I am here," she said, her voice once again devoid of any feeling.

"What happened?"

"I'm not sure."

"Run a diagnostic. I need to know what just happened. It could impact everything we're working towards."

"As you wish."

The chance of instability had always been there, but she should have been far past the point for such an anomaly to occur. Depending on the diagnostic results, he might not have enough test subjects after all. Collecting more would be a great risk, but if needed Malthus would arrange his own trip into the Underbelly.

6

TO ERR IS HUMAN

Rehel sat at the helm of the *Devil's Run* alone. He'd just finished calculating the re-route to Ganymede and had laid in the course. Autopilot would take care of the remainder of the voyage.

Dr. Weston's report, still fresh in his mind, now occupied his thoughts once again. Rehel hadn't been permitted to closely examine his own diagnostics on Earth, and it was indeed strange seeing his insides in such a new way. The deviations General Malthus had been searching for, and consequently kept secret once discovered, were still present. But with Dr. Weston's insights on the raw data, everything finally made sense. His strange desire to keep certain pieces of irrelevant data and his slower processing time were caused by a mutation in his nanobots. A mutation, Weston had said, that could not have occurred naturally, but had been put there by someone else.

The mutated nanos had created new pathways to allow free will to weigh in on his actions. This free will led him to gather something like an emotional context for his decisions. Consequently, his systems slowed because more variables had to be accounted for. Currently, Rehel was running at ninety-two point seven one seven percent capacity. Not enough difference to be noticeable to the human eye, but he noticed it. He could feel it now, the passing of time. Sometimes it seemed like forever.

And this mutation would continue to change him, according to Weston. His capacity for emotion would grow. It would lead to irrational behavior, and it would slow his systems even further, possibly to the point of non-function.

Weston had not presented this report in a matter-of-fact way. He'd not even appeared remotely excited about this discovery, as most scientists might have. His concern overpowered all possible enthusiasm, and the report had read like a death sentence.

The report went on to explain that there was no known way of reversing the damage. Simply replacing the mutated nanos would only stop further damage. The pathways that had already formed were not so easily erased. But in deep space there was no hope for replacements anytime soon. It was equally doubtful there'd be the resources to replace them on Ganymede either, since nanobots were unneeded and virtually unheard of on the Outer Moons.

He couldn't even gradually replace his nanobots with some supplied by Vladia, since the mutated nanos would view the new ones as inferior and immediately upgrade them. Only a full transplant would do the job, and he could only get that on Mars. Furthermore, the likelihood of his survival until the next time they landed on Mars was also unknown, as neither the rate of mutation nor the possible damage could be determined based on available data.

Rehel didn't know what fear was, but he had an inkling he would soon find out.

Odder still, Weston was sure the nanos in his system were modeled after those designed by Dr. Maria Robespierre. He even cited *Essays and Research on the Robot Psyche: Progress and Implications*, her book with similar designs. Yet that book had been banned on Earth the moment Dr. Robespierre had been taken into custody. The books were confiscated by the Terran government and disintegrated. Even the copy stored in his memory had been wiped. It had been a thorough eradication. The chances of someone retaining a copy, having the ingenuity to expound upon Dr. Robespierre's work, and be granted access to his systems was statistically improbable.

Abel would of course immediately suspect General Malthus, and all known evidence did point to him, but that did not explain how he would have obtained a copy of Dr. Robespierre's book. And the likelihood of him independently coming to her same theories and conclusions was as close to zero as one could get. Malthus was not a roboticist; he didn't have the training.

It was then he recalled what Vladia had said about Titan and Ganymede over a week ago. She'd compared their organization to North American and Asian mafias. Only now did he realize how odd it was for her to possess such knowledge. It was non-standard information for a Terran child's curriculum, yet Vladia had grown up predominantly on her father's estates, many of which kept old world libraries. Surely her father, being contracted to Dr. Robespierre, would have a copy of the book. Still, it should have been confiscated along with the rest. No one would have risked hiding a copy for fear of the death penalty themselves; even Admiral Urada Malthus would not have been exempt.

The only way a book would have been missed was if it had been privately printed and at great cost to keep it off record. If that was indeed the case, its existence could not be confirmed, making it possible for a copy to escape collection.

Even if all this was true, that Malthus had managed to tinker with his systems, Rehel couldn't quite visualize General Malthus as the heinous monster Abel made him out to be. That is, not entirely. After all, he owed the General a great debt. It had been Malthus that had plucked him from destruction on not one, but two occasions. Most recently, there'd been the incident with his nanobots back on Earth that almost saw him decommissioned. Then there'd been the first time, many years ago before Malthus had even made captain of the Valkyrie squad.

He'd been scheduled for decommission, and Malthus had made the observation that the Valkyries needed a dedicated robot and somehow managed to handpick the robot of his choosing. It had been no coincidence that he'd pulled him from the decommission list. In fact, Malthus had as much as told him so when he'd spoke with him privately before he reported for duty.

"HCV-1178," Malthus had addressed him. "That's you're designation number, correct?"

"Yes, Sir."

"I've been perusing your records. Quite an interesting find you are."

"How is that, Sir?" Rehel had stood stiffly on the other side of Malthus' desk.

"Are you aware that you are one of only seven remaining robots personally constructed by Dr. Maria Robespierre?"

Malthus had motioned for him to take a seat, and so he had.

"No, Sir," he'd said. "I was not made aware of this fact."

"Of course almost all robots on Earth, however few they are in number these days, are constructed based on her original designs. You, though– you were actually built by the woman herself. Does that not make you special, HCV-1178?"

"I would have to answer, no, Sir."

"Well your answer is wrong. Very wrong indeed." Malthus had smiled at this. "Our paths were destined to cross."

At that he'd stood up and walked behind him.

Gripping Rehel's shoulders, Malthus had continued. "I think you need a proper name. I'll not be burdened with rattling off an identification number like you're a piece of equipment."

At the time that remark had seemed odd, as he had been the second person to comment on his lack of a name. It was only years later that he'd realized how truly strange it was that both Malthus and Vladia had made similar observations about him, with subtle differences.

"From now on your name is Rehel. You still must respond to others as HCV-1178, but to the Valkyrie squad you are Rehel. Understood?"

"Yes, Sir. May I ask, what does Rehel mean?"

"It means whatever you choose it to, Rehel. Do with it what you will."

And that had been it until just before Vladia Robespierre had joined the squad and before Abel had asked him to look into her sealed records.

Malthus had casually remarked one day, "You'll be happy to know Vladia Robespierre will be joining the squad soon. I expect you'll be glad to see her after all these years, no? Though I'd probably hold on to that locket she gave you. Seeing it after all this time would surely upset her. It might affect her initial performance grades, even."

Rehel had been unable to answer him, and Malthus had not waited for a response.

Once he'd learned of their connection to each other, it was clear to him that his former Captain had pulled him for this reason. Even though she wouldn't know it was him, Malthus had lifted him from the jaws of destruction and allowed him to see her again. And though his motivations remained unclear, the end result remained in Rehel's favor.

Rehel exited the bridge and took a left towards the med bay. For now, he must put all that aside. He had to get back to Abel, who was showing no signs of recovery yet.

He returned to the medical bay to find Vladia watching over his friend. Abel had been heavily sedated for several days now and had been put in quarantine. Vladia stood on the outside of the clear visoplastic encasing Abel.

"This is the second time I've had to stand over him like this. He's really making a habit of it," she sighed without turning around.

Rehel moved to her side. "I am sorry. I feel responsible, as it was I who gave him the vaccinations that caused this."

"You had to do it. Don't blame yourself."

Abel's fever kept spiking, then dropping and spiking again. It seemed reminiscent of a virus known on Earth as Mist. A man-made virus, it caused swelling of the internal organs, internal bleeding, and eighty point two three percent of the time it ended in death.

They'd used it in the Anglo-Eastern War. Dispensed by robots on the battle field, Mist targeted specific genetic racial markers on the side of the opposition. It wasn't designed to be fatal and was supposedly going to infect only those precisely targeted. Of course nothing ever goes exactly as planned, and soon it became clear that thirteen point nine seven percent of those not targeted also contracted the virus. In many cases the results were fatal. And it had spread like wildfire, both fast and fierce. Earth had managed to eradicate the virus, but only after several races of people had been wiped out, along with millions of others who thought themselves safe. In the end, robots became the scapegoat and Earth never fully recovered.

Those who'd immigrated to the Outer Moons had taken a horde of nasty diseases with them, mostly because so many who had left Earth had resided in the segregated slums and thus had limited access to medication. Many of the deserters who'd fled to the Outer Moons had been exposed to Mist and carried the contagion with them. It was rumored only half the people who left Earth even made it to the Outer Moons alive. Those who did make it had adapted to survive the illnesses but could remain carriers for generations.

The pair stood quietly listening to the chirp of the vitals display. Weston had bought the vaccines from Titan Traders, and in all likelihood Abel's reaction was due to a bad batch of vaccinations. Yet Rehel couldn't help but wonder if he'd delayed the vaccinations for a few weeks if Abel would have reacted this way to them. He had not been at peak physical condition due to the strain of the trip to Mars. The probability of that making the difference was slim, but still the doubt remained with him. Rehel fully believed the mutated nanobots were both creating and feeding this self-doubt. Humans dealt with this all the time, and he had always imagined the emotional burden placed on them to be unpleasant. Sadly, he was now learning just how right he was.

"I noticed you changed course earlier," Vladia said, interrupting his thoughts. "I take it Weston's report has arrived?"

"It has. I've forwarded a copy to you and to Abel as well."

Both Abel and Vladia had requested to see Weston's report. And to both he had sent a false report.

"What's the short-hand?"

"Everything looks in order. I fear Weston was disappointed in his findings," he lied.

The ease of his dishonesty surprised him. He didn't like that.

It'd been the first time he had lied to Vladia. It pained him to do so, yet he could not let her worry about something she could not do anything about, especially with Abel in poor condition. He told himself the information would hurt Vladia, and harming a human would be breaking his first rule of programming.

"Damn his disappointment. I'm just glad you're all right."

"As am I," he replied.

After a few moments of silence, Vladia redirected the conversation back to Abel.

"I know enough about Mist to understand what we're dealing with here," she said. "But there must be something we can do other than sitting on our hands and just waiting."

"There is one possibility," he began, relieved that the focus was no longer on him. "But there is no guarantee it will do any good."

"Let's hear it, then."

"We could give him a dose of your nanobots. Although they have never encountered these conditions, in theory they should still be able to eliminate the issue."

"But?"

"We could not remove the nanobots from Abel's system even after they have completed their task," he explained. "Since it would be the nanobots fighting off the infections, instead of Abel's own body, he will not develop an immunity to the infections as intended. If we remove the nanos, Abel will most die once exposed to the full force of the infections on Ganymede. If we do this, he will rely on these nanobots to be his immune system."

Vladia was silent. Rehel could see she now fully realized the implications of doing this. By Terran standards, these nanobots would effectively make Abel an altered human. And although they were no longer bound by Terran classifications, it did not change the fact that all humans of Earth had been raised to regard cyborgs as second class citizens. They despised them possibly more than robots, as evident by the number of Terrans who chose deformation or death rather than become what they regarded as a degenerate. Of course regrowth therapy made such a choice arise only in the most dire of situations. Vladia understood this more than most. She also understood that for someone like Abel, a child raised at the Rearing Facilities, it would be an even harder fate to accept.

"Do it," she decided.

"As you wish."

"But don't tell him," she added quickly, reaching out to gently clutch his arm.

Her touch startled him, and for a moment he worried she'd noticed.

Instead, her eyes looked back toward Abel. "There's no reason for him to know. Nothing would be gained from it."

"He will surely find out eventually."

"If he does, I'll deal with it then. For now, we just need to make sure he lives through this."

Letting go, Vladia took a seat and rolled up her sleeve.

"I think you have made a wise decision, Vladia," he tried to reassure her as he removed a syringe from one of the medical cabinets and prepared to take a vial of her nano-enriched blood. "If it helps, know that I can remove them once we've departed from the Outer Moons. He will not need them if we are to return to Mars, or even Earth, for that matter."

"Then I'll cling to that," she said half-heartedly.

He knew it was the right choice, but it was plain to see it had been a difficult call to make. It was not so long ago General Malthus had made a similar decision in regards to her. She firmly believed he'd only made the choice to later use her status as cyborg against her, though Rehel wasn't entirely certain of that. Knowing that she did this to save his life appeared to be of little consolation to her at the moment.

He could only hope that once Abel was awake and she could see him well again, it would ease her troubled conscience.

∞

Vladia crept down the ladder into the cargo hold where *Freya* and *Gunnr* gathered dust. The two Valkyries laid on their backs beneath thick, brown tarps, strapped to the floor with heavy gauged cording. She'd toyed with the idea of coming down here many times over the last week, but always was there a ready excuse in hand. Only now, when faced with the severity of Abel's deteriorating condition, could she see her own fears clear enough to tackle them.

Easing between the two ships, she caught the end of the tarp and dragged it beside her until *Freya* was exposed. Letting the sheeting slip to the floor, she unfastened the cord that ran over the cockpit hatch. She climbed onto the Valkyrie's shoulder and pressed the release button.

Freya's crown opened. The air within still smelled stale and used. Vladia grabbed hold of the cockpit's edge and pulled herself up and over, landing soundly in the pilot's seat.

Her key still hung from the ignition. With only a moment's hesitation, she took hold of it and twisted it to the left, starting only the computer, comm, and syncing systems.

"Good morning, Lt. Robespierre," *Freya's* greeting sounded automatically.

The ship hadn't been reassigned, or updated, since she'd last flown her, so naturally *Freya* thought her still a Lieutenant. Vladia wondered if it was really morning on Earth or if the Valkyrie's clock had simply picked up from its last shut-off.

Reaching behind her, she pulled out the cerebral connecters and reluctantly attached each one to the back of her neck. Settling down in her chair, she waited to sync with her ship.

Yet the expected queasiness never came, nor the slight

twisting of her mind as it unfolded and expanded itself into a larger presence. What did come over her was the dread she'd hoped to spare herself from all the weeks since she'd been removed from the Valkyrie squad. It had formed a small pit in her stomach weeks earlier, but only now did it threaten to burst from her body and overtake her wholly.

"*Freya*," she began in an unsteady voice, "can you run a diagnostic on the cerebral connectors?"

"Of course."

Not a minute later, *Freya* said, "Diagnostic complete. Cerebral connectors are fully functional."

Her mind always half suspicious of Malthus tampering with her life, it was possible he'd updated her ship to not recognize her in an effort to further foil any effort she might make against him.

She asked, "Have you experienced any updates within the last three months?"

"My repair log indicates no updates were received during the last three months."

"Run a full diagnostic just to be safe."

That would take a few minutes, but she had to be sure. Closing her eyes, she tried again to slip in sync with *Freya*. Still nothing.

Only a small percentage of the Terran population could sync with a Valkyrie to begin with. Perhaps this was a case of her own unsettled mind holding her back. The possibility was certainly real. In fact, she hoped for it. Only one other option remained, and she'd not think on that just yet.

"Full diagnostic complete: All systems operational. Would you like a list of suggested upgrades?"

"No. So you're detecting no connection right now?"

"There are no viable connections at this time."

"Okay. Is there an unviable connection?"

"Affirmative."

"And it is?"

"Unknown."

Vladia had never realized how difficult working with a

Valkyrie un-synced could be. When they were as one, their thoughts were fluid, as if the lines between commands and responses existed only in theory. She'd assumed Freya would be much like Rehel in an unconnected state, but the two remained worlds different in every aspect.

"Are you authorized to connect with Vladia Robespierre? With me?"

"Affirmative."

"Then why can't you connect with me now?"

"Vladia Robespierre is not connected."

"I know that. I'm asking why."

"An unknown organism is not a viable connection. Vladia Robespierre is not connected."

"But you're talking to me right now. You know I'm Vladia Robespierre."

"Of course. You are Lt. Vladia Robespierre; you are currently speaking. However, you are not connected."

Vladia flipped the ignition key off and, jerking it out of its receptacle, flung it out of the ship. A few seconds later she heard it clatter against the floor somewhere on the other side of the cargo hold.

Pressing her hands hard to her face, she wanted to scream. She fought the urge, curling her fingers under until her nails bit into her skin at her forehead. The pain mattered little, and her nanos would stitch up any damage done.

She laughed out loud. Laughed until tears lined her lids and spilled down her face.

She'd no control at all. Not even her own body could she bend to her will.

Wiping her face with her the backs of her hands, she pulled the cerebral disks off her neck and climbed out of the cockpit.

No one needed to know just yet. Not even Rehel.

Truly, she was no longer human.

∞

Whitlock's uneventful tailing of Ambassador General

Malthus had come to a sudden and unexpected halt, in that it turned from uneventful to pathetically impossible. After almost two weeks of following a man who did nothing but his job, his streak of boredom ended when Malthus suddenly vanished. Three occasions, three days in a row, the man disappeared for over two hours. When Whitlock finally managed to locate him afterwards, Malthus was always back in his quarters as if he'd been there the entire time.

This told him two things: Malthus was aware he was being watched, and likely had been the entire time, and that he had something to hide, something Whitlock felt must be linked to the Robespierre incident. It now fell upon him to uncover that something and determine if it could be a threat in any way to Earth.

The problem lay in that when Malthus wanted to disappear, Whitlock seemed to have no way of stopping him. His failure in this matter ate at him incessantly. He didn't like to admit it, but he might not to be able to deal with Malthus on his own.

At present, Whitlock sat in the mess several tables back from the man, waiting patiently for him to make a move. It had been days since his last slip, and Malthus had made no further attempts to evade him.

"Hey, man," a voice from behind greeted him, followed by a rough jab in the back.

Gailmen took the seat beside him, setting his tray of food down with a jarring clank on the tabletop.

"You eat early these days," the younger man continued as he popped the tab on his drink.

"Better for the digestion," Whitlock muttered dismissively.

He'd considered letting Gailmen in on his suspicions, but ultimately he'd decided against it. For one, he'd no real evidence to offer the kid; and two, it was a gross abuse of power to ask him to tail a man without just cause. On top of that, Gailmen didn't seem the type suitable for covert ops; he was a fighter, sure, but the last thing he needed was brute force. He imagined the boy would probably do more harm than good at this stage. If it came down to taking Malthus into custody, then he'd make a useful ally. Until such time, it was best to keep him in the dark.

Malthus stood up, carried his tray to the disposal, and then made for the exit.

Whitlock instinctively stood up.

"Hey, where're you going? I just got here, man," Gailmen said.

Ignoring him, Whitlock moved to leave, but his target stopped just short of the door, turned about-face, and headed straight towards them.

Whitlock returned his tray to the table and saluted the Ambassador General as he approached. Gailmen stood to salute as well, but Malthus waved their formality away, and the pair sat back down.

"Gentlemen," he greeted them, but remained standing.

"Can I help you, Sir?" Whitlock asked more sharply than he'd intended.

"The Viceroy made some unsettling accusation at our meeting earlier today, and I promised him I would look into the matter," he began.

"Accusations against us?" Gailmen laughed. "Well, I'm not surprised, but he's barking up the wrong tree."

"Not specifically against us, but it was implied. He claims there was a security breach involving trade communications between Luna and Mars."

"Trade communications? Why would that be of any value to Earth, or anyone, for that matter?"

"My words exactly. Personally, I think he's fabricated the entire affair to cause unrest. Nevertheless, I assured him we were not to blame and offered our services in settling the matter. After all, Luna is under Earth's protection once again, so it is our job to investigate."

"Why would he want us to investigate if he thinks we are the responsible party? There's no logic in it," Whitlock insisted. If anyone was inventing unrest, he'd put his money on Malthus, not the Viceroy.

"As I said, I believe it to be a fabrication, possibly to

distract us from something far more devious. I'd like you to head up to the LICB and check it out," he said to Whitlock. "Report your findings to me directly, and I'll forward them to the Viceroy. In the meantime, stay sharp and don't let this little incident distract you."

"Yes, Sir," the two said one after the other, followed by another quick salute.

"Man, maybe it won't be so boring here after all. I'll tag along to the LICB," Gailman suggested as he dug into his meal.

Malthus made his way towards the exit. Just as he rounded the corner, Whitlock stood up in pursuit.

"Hey! I'm talking to you, Whitlock," Gailmen said, grabbing for his forearm.

"I've got to go," he said, moving just out of the other man's reach. "The LICB is all yours."

"Seriously? You can't just tell me to–"

"Not now!" he snapped, not looking back as he paced towards the exit, abandoning his tray along with his comrade.

He'd not let Malthus get by him because that guy needed someone to sit with him while he ate as if they were kids back at rearing school. This LICB crap was just another way to throw him off. He was sure of it.

Once in the corridor, Malthus had vanished again.

He'd wanted to avoid using a tracking device since he'd have to obtain one on the sly from the Luna black market. And, of course, there was always the chance Malthus would discover it. If he managed to trace it back to him, he could easily levy charges of his own.

Yet he didn't appear to have a choice. He'd have to track him by less orthodox means. Even if it cost him his position and reputation, he would find out what Malthus was hiding.

∞

"Where is he now?" Malthus asked as he ducked into his supposedly condemned research facility.

The large, single-level building's sparse equipment was draped in brown sheeting to both hide and protect it in his absence. Malthus could only risk the bare essentials so as to not attract attention. If anyone were to wander upon the place, they wouldn't think much of his meager set-up.

"Whitlock has made his way into the central business district of Moretus City," Isobel reported.

Moretus City had another name: The Underbelly. It was one of the only pods near Luna's south pole, and it was ripe with criminal activity.

"He'll be getting a tracking device, I suppose."

"Shall I stop him? I can reveal his Terran identity easily enough and to the right people. You'll not have to deal with him further."

Isobel had infested the Luna surveillance cameras on arrival. Not only could she effectively track people of interest, she could also make sure he was essentially invisible to Luna's web of public surveillance. If she had enough footage of particular people, she could even manufacture recordings of them. She wasn't all-powerful though. She could only make the smallest of changes to prevent detection. It wouldn't do for her to be found out.

"No. Let him be. He's of more use to me alive for the moment. Besides, as he grows more and more desperate to track my movements, he increases the suspicion surrounding his own actions."

It was obvious Whitlock had no desire to involve Gailmen in his plans, probably because he thought the young man too inexperienced and would likely let his enthusiasm put them both in harm's way. His assumptions were most definitely correct; however, this would ultimately work against Whitlock no matter what. Gailmen would soon grow tired, and angry, of Whitlock's elusiveness. And that anger would turn to distrust soon enough.

He had presented the communications breach in such a way that he knew Whitlock would disregard it as a legitimate threat. His location confirmed both this and that he had likely delegated the task to Gailmen. Unfortunately for Whitlock, there had been a breach, albeit one of his own doing. Now Gailmen, not Whitlock, would find just what he needed to push his suspicions towards both his comrade and Mars.

"You seem to prefer many people alive and well these days," Isobel commented with just a touch of sarcasm.

Malthus took her meaning. She referred again to Cornelia Arnim's presence in the facility as a live prisoner instead of a dead test subject.

"Everything and everyone has their purpose."

"Perhaps if you would share those purposes with me, we could move along even faster."

"Perhaps. But as I have warned you before, faster does not mean better."

Isobel had been on the borders of perfection until her unusual outburst the day he had awakened Cornelia. Her emotional index had suddenly spiked and had yet to return to its previous levels. As a safety precaution, he'd been forced to lock her out of several systems in case she went haywire again. In a show of good faith, he had remained upfront about this, and she'd agreed it was a good idea. He hoped the fact that even Isobel showed some concern over her recent outpouring of emotion was indicative of a coming recovery.

"Now," he proceeded. "How did the first batch go?"

"Three of the four test subjects transferred successfully. Replication began at zero six hundred and as of now they are all in stable condition."

"At what rate?"

"Fifty percent. They will exceed known levels at any minute."

Known levels referred to Isobel's current level of replication. It shouldn't be much past that point that their humanity would theoretically be replicated into oblivion. Then he could begin field testing for stability.

He removed the sheets covering the swarm containment units and their readouts.

Scanning quickly over the data, he said, "Halt replication at two percent over and do an emotional index test. If it looks good, we'll begin field testing. If not, test every additional percentage over until the desired results are met."

"Understood."

"Now, let's have a look at our robot," Malthus said, walking to the far side of the facility away from the swarms.

Pulling the thin sheeting off a bar-height table, he revealed a crumpled heap that was the remains of a Generation C robot.

Under normal circumstances the unpredictability of humans proved to be more difficult than the stable and compliant robot. Yet despite his above average knowledge of robotics, he'd never actually repaired one. Modifying a working system he could handle, but essentially rebuilding some of the major components from the ground up would actually be a challenge for him. He couldn't even count on all the parts being here, let alone them being undamaged enough for use.

Still, this robot would be his creation. A smile glinted across his face at the thought. It would be his first attempt at perfection.

"We'll have to have a new skin," he said to Isobel. "Use whatever specifications you want. I don't want it to look like one of Robespierre's models. It needs to be able to blend in."

"I'll need to start on that now. Without access to hyper-growth hormones, the process will take some time."

"That's fine. This will be the only time we have to do it the old-fashioned way," Malthus promised. Next time, he'd be back on Earth and out of the shadows.

"I've got the index results ready."

"Let's hear it."

"They're at zero point two."

"Let's hold there for now and do a test run. Wake number 775. I'll be over shortly to begin."

Malthus abandoned the robot for the time being and moved to the replication station. Each swarm was held in an airtight container that was easily removable. At present only three of the dozen containers held any nanos, though to the naked eye they all appeared empty. The only way to tell them apart was by looking at the screen above each container. The empty ones had inactive screens, while the three containing nanos displayed their replication level, emotional index, and any other relevant data.

Malthus plucked a full container at random and pulled the corresponding display pad.

He had to move to the second facility to get to the test subject. The whole purpose of the additional facility was that if something went wrong, he could lock down the entire building and destroy it, without harming the most important components of his research. This, too, was one of the systems he'd been forced to lock Isobel out of.

"775 is awake," Isobel said just as he reached the other facility.

Malthus proceeded straight to cell 775, which was just beside Cornelia's. From the outside, he shut off the air flow. He'd have to do that to make sure the nanos didn't decide to go anywhere other than into the test subject.

Opening the door, he set the closed container inside.

The man on the floor mumbled something but was cut off as Malthus wasted no time in re-sealing the door.

From the data pad, he programmed the nanos with basic instructions to infest the test subject and perform a series of simple motions. Then, he remotely opened the container and engaged the viewscreen on the outside of the cell door.

There wasn't much to see at first; the swarm took a few minutes to infest the man. Only when they began taking control of the man's movements did anything seem out of the ordinary.

The test subject expressed the expected amount of confusion and fear at the loss of control over his own body.

His arms moved up and then down. He walked in a circle five times and then began a series of push-ups, all the while crying out in pain as his muscles had not fully awakened from stasis.

Malthus monitored the swarm's levels all the while. He was pleased to see they remained at optimal performance specifications.

After the last push-up, he had the man sit and take a rest. He was visibly shaken by the experience.

His blood pressure and pulse were elevated, but within acceptable levels.

To Isobel he said, "Let's leave it like this until tomorrow. We need to make sure there's no loss of control before we do any more strenuous tests."

As a safeguard, he left the air vents sealed and engaged the auxiliary air supply in the cell. The subject could survive seventy-two hours on back-up, assuming nothing else went wrong.

He made to leave the facility and return to work on his robot, when the man let out a sharp cry. Stepping back in front of the viewscreen, he witnessed the subject doubled over in pain.

According to his readings, his blood pressure had skyrocketed. With only the slightest bit of visible irritation, he watched the subject go into cardiac arrest.

"Never mind, Isobel."

He swiped his fingertips briskly across the datapad, ordering the nanos back into their receptacle.

"All clear," Isobel confirmed before he opened the door to the dead man's cell to retrieve the container.

"Let's do two more rounds of replication and try again in a few days."

"Shall I hire someone to dispose of the body?"

"Leave it," he said, marching out of the facility. His thoughts had already moved on. There was no point wasting his energy on the dead.

7

EN PASSANT

Whitlock tugged at the hood concealing his face as he treaded lightly into the borders of the Underbelly's black market. The streets reeked with an inexplicable dankness, and it was all he could do to keep down the remains of his freshly consumed meal. Luna, for the most part, adhered to Earth's stringent sense of cleanliness. But there were always the slums. Earth had done a fine job of segregating such areas off from the rest of the population; it seems her moon had not taken to that idea and let such blights rest within arm's reach of civilization. He couldn't complain too much, though; it did make for easy access and served his purposes well.

He would, however, take exception to hordes of people that now crowded the streets, many of them without shoes. He could only assume they lacked even the most basic forms of bio-blocks that were issued free by the government. Clamping his gloved hand tightly over his mouth, he proceeded into a shop whose window was decorated with all manner of electronic devices.

Despite the crowd in the streets, the store was empty except for the man attending the counter. Wiring and blinking circuitry hung from the ceiling like vulgar holiday decorations. Broken circuit boards clung to the walls and every surface was littered with Pre-Anglo-Eastern War junk. He couldn't imagine any of it actually working properly. Even if it did, who knew what any of the tangled mess could be used for these days.

The bell on the door clanked as it closed, drawing the attention of the attendant, who looked to have been busying himself with close examination of a large, swollen lump on his forearm.

"Greetings, Sir!" the man exclaimed.

Whitlock reluctantly removed his hand from his mouth and readied himself. He'd had training in blending into a crowd and adapting to new situations, but there was something to be said about the real thing versus a simulation. He needed to make this quick or he'd be found out.

"What can I help you find today? A transmission scanner to keep an eye on your girl, or guy, perhaps?" the attendant asked, leaping over the counter and motioning towards a wall of goods to his right.

"No. Nothing like that."

The doorbell chimed behind him as he spoke, and a dark-haired man came up behind him. His hand instinctively fell to his holster under his cloak.

"There you are, Rohan!" the stranger said, placing a heavy hand on his shoulder.

To the shop attendant he said, "Sorry, friend. He was just browsing to pass the time."

The attendant's amiable demeanor vanished as quickly as it'd come on, and with a grunt he went back to his station. The stranger pulled him towards the exit.

"Sorry to keep you waiting," he said loudly.

Whitlock kept quiet. It'd not do to start a commotion in front of others. If he could steer the intruder to an alley, he could end this with little trouble.

Once they entered the street, the man whispered, "You'll not find what you need in there, Terran."

Whitlock jerked away but did not run. Something in the man's voice...

"Relax. I can help you. But you'll need to trust me a little," he offered.

"Trust is earned, not given, friend."

The man smiled and nodded.

"True enough," he said. "But neither of us have the time for that, I think."

He pulled a key from his pocket and quickly flashed it before drawing it back out of sight.

"If you know what this is, then you know you can trust me," he said.

Whitlock knew what the key stood for, but he wasn't entirely convinced this stranger was its owner. Even if he was, that could make him Malthus' man. This could be a trap. But the risk would be worth the return if he could use him as proof of Malthus' treachery. And if he turned out to be a friend, well, he could do with a contact out here. Besides, he was the larger of the two. As long as he kept sharp and didn't let himself become outnumbered by more than a few, he could neutralize the situation easily enough.

"I'll hear you out, but I'll reserve my trust for a later date," he said.

"Follow me then," the stranger said. "The streets are no place for conversation."

Whitlock followed the man down alleyways and around the backs of buildings until they reached the edge of the marketplace. The two walked into a small eatery, and the stranger pointed him towards a table in the back.

"You sit against the wall. I'll be there shortly," he explained, making his way towards the meager bar to order.

Whitlock did as instructed. While waiting for his companion to return, he scouted the surrounding area. There were five other patrons scattered throughout the room. All appeared rather harmless, but if it came down to six to one odds, he still felt confident. The eatery itself was constructed of wood, pine by the look, which meant it was Luna grown and cheap, and aged enough to make any chair or table leg a quick weapon in a pinch. Several windows lined the wall to his front and left, giving him several escape routes. There was only one surveillance camera to be found, mounted over the entryway as to maximize coverage. Again he tugged his hood lower to cover his face.

The stranger returned with a tray of beer and took the seat across from him.

"I see why you had me sit here. You wanted your back to the camera."

The man grinned and said, "You've found me out, then."

He placed a glass in front of each of them.

"Drink or you'll look even more suspicious. And stop pulling on that damn hood of yours."

Whitlock wrapped his hands around the glass but couldn't bring himself to put it to his lips.

"So," he began, "Tell me how it is you came across a Valkyrie key?"

"Slow down there, fella. You may not believe this, but I need to know I can trust you as well. It's a two-way street, as the saying goes. So, why don't you tell me what a Terran needs from the Underbelly before I have a change of heart and turn you in to the local authorities, who, by the way, aren't too keen on following regulations when it comes to Terran soldiers."

Whitlock frowned. Studying the man's face told him little, but it was enough. He blended in fine, but wasn't quite as relaxed as he let on. It was all in the way the stranger held himself, a forced comfortableness that he imagined he fell victim to as well. This wasn't his home, that was certain. He didn't sound like a Lunite, but he didn't quite sound Terran either, which meant his voice was a practiced, yet imperfect, attempt to sound like he was from nowhere.

What really gave him away was his shoes. Covered in scuffs and scratches to hide their origin, Whitlock still recognized the standard issue military boots.

"How long have you been in the Underbelly? Three months? Maybe six?" he asked.

The man across from him laughed and slugged down a sizable portion of drink.

"You're good," he admitted with a shrug. "Almost three, give or take a few days. Now it's my turn. You came with Ambassador General Malthus' entourage, I'm guessing. The question is whether you came as a bodyguard or a watchdog."

"Perhaps I came as both."

"But you've been around him a while now, and I'm sure a clever fellow like yourself has formed an opinion of the man. If he's worth looking into, I mean."

"If you came by that key honestly, and it's not just some trinket you've purchased from vultures, I'm sure you've made quite the study of him on your own."

"Truth is, I never paid him much mind back then. Wasn't until it was much too late that I started to pay attention," the man sneered, finishing off his drink and reaching for another mug.

"What did he do?"

The stranger smiled and said, "There it is. You've decided to trust me."

Whitlock ignored the man's remark and asked again, "What did he do?"

"I don't know. But the people who do know, he got rid of."

"You're referring to Robespierre?"

He nodded. "Her. And some others. You'll notice there aren't any Valkyrie pilots around anymore. That ain't no accident."

"Can you help me prove anything?"

"Like I said, he got rid of those people. I can't prove anything on my own. That's why, when I saw a Terran wandering around the black market, I knew I had to speak with you. Tell me what you need from here, and I can get it Well, I can try real hard at any rate."

"I need a stealth tracker. I need to know where he's disappearing to."

The stranger thought for a moment, shaking his head slowly as he did.

Finally, he said, "Come back in five days. I'll have it for you then. You can find your way back here?"

"I'll manage. Tell me, before I go, what's your name?"

"You'll have to look me up. Names aren't spoken much in the Underbelly, unless someone's asking, and if that's the case it means you're a dead man," he said, adding a sly wink.

Whitlock stood up.

"Best to keep some things to yourself, then."

"If at all possible," the other man said as he pulled Whitlock's untouched drink over the rough tabletop and took a swig.

"Five days."

The stranger raised his glass and nodded his head slightly.

"Until then, my friend."

∞

Commander Gailmen entered the LICB early that morning. He'd been working to get out here for days now, but he had to go through the rigmarole of getting a clearance badge, which turned out to be far more complicated than it sounded. Not that they had any real power to keep him out with his level of clearance. It was all just meaningless red tape. If he wanted, he could have made a stink about it, but really that would have slowed him down even further. Though it went completely against his instincts, the fastest route on Luna at the moment was the one of less force and more patience.

The facility itself consisted of a minuscule workforce. The front desk wasn't even manned. Not knowing where to go or who to speak with, he stood at the desk and waited. Almost twenty minutes later, the clattering of lazy footsteps ascended a stairwell off to his side that he'd barely noticed.

The footsteps' owner was an elderly man of slight height, who clasped a tin mug in one gnarled hand and clutched a datapad under the same arm. The man made no indication he'd noticed his presence and proceeded to his post behind the desk without a word.

"Name?" he asked, setting down his mug and datapad but still not making eye contact with him.

Gailmen tried not to wince at the man's ungloved hands. Crinkled like fall leaves and paper thin, his knuckles were swollen to an uncomfortable size. There were plenty of old men working on Earth, but never had he witnessed the toll time took on a set hands.

"Name?" the man repeated, just as evenly as the first time.

"Gailmen."

"Not your name. Who yer here to see?"

"I'm here to see whoever's in charge of trade communications. I wasn't given a name."

The man grunted and held out his hand. Gailmen swallowed hard, but managed to pass over his badge without losing his breakfast. Flipping it to one side then back to the other, the elder took a long swig of whatever occupied his tin as he studied the sliver of plastic, then swiped it through a scanner.

Handing it back, he said, "Yer to see Riggs."

After a solid minute with no follow-up, Gailmen asked, "So, I should wait here then?"

The man made it clear he'd no more to say, not even another grunt, as he picked up his datapad and began scrolling.

Luckily, it wasn't more than a moment later that another pair of footsteps echoed into earshot. A tall woman with stern eyes and auburn hair strolled up the same stairs.

"Gailmen?" she called from the top of the steps.

"Yes," he answered, closing the space between them quickly.

"Follow me," she said, already making her way back down.

Jogging lightly, then taking two steps at a time until he'd caught up with her, he said, "I'm sorry it's taken me so long to come by for the data. I hadn't realized getting clearance would be such an issue."

"Don't be. I wasn't exactly looking forward to having a Terran officer snooping through all my work," she answered sharply.

"I assure you, I'm only here to assist with the data in question. I've no interest in plundering your files."

"Right. And Earth doesn't want to rule us, just, you know, control every aspect of our government with lethal force," she fumed, then added, "Long live the mother planet!" with a half-assed salute.

Gailmen almost stumbled down the last few steps, having to grip the handrail until they reached their destination. He could only see the back of the woman's head, but he imagined her smirking at his reaction to such a vulgar remark.

There were a series of lifts to their left, which he assumed led down to various levels of archived data, and a row of doors on their right. Riggs guided him to the last door, which was labeled with her full name and title: Rebecca Riggs, PhD., Director of Communications.

Once inside, she plucked a small datacard from her neatly organized desk and at it towards him. He was sure she'd meant to catch him off guard and make him feel foolish again, but he caught the card with ease and tucked it in his front pocket. If his skills annoyed her, she didn't let it show. She stood beside her desk, leaning her thigh against it.

"Everything you need is there. I don't know why you were even called in. My team's already done all the leg work."

"I was under the impression you needed assistance."

"From what I understand you're not qualified to actually be of assistance. Aren't you just a glorified bodyguard for our Terran watchdog?"

She had a point. Gailmen sat down in the chair opposite her desk; now she looked annoyed.

"I wouldn't personally be assisting," he admitted with a shrug. "I'm only to look over your findings and decide if Terran intervention is needed."

At that Riggs smiled, all her momentary irritation vanishing.

"Oh I'm sure it will be. In fact, it doesn't seem as if the security breach had anything at all to do with Luna."

"How do you mean?"

Crossing her arms, she said, "The transmission was essentially worthless. The data being sent wasn't worth intercepting. I'll admit I was a bit baffled at first, but on closer examination it became obvious. Someone had intercepted it to take it apart, re-layered the transmission, and in one of the layers had added a message. Encrypted, of course."

"Is that hard? The re-layering and whatnot."

Already, Gailmen felt in over his head. He really wished Whitlock would have at least come with him. He wouldn't have been any more knowledgeable at this stuff, but over a decade of experience made him excellent at faking it.

"It is if you want to do it well. That?" she said nodding at the card in his pocket. "Amateur, at best."

"How does that prove it's nothing to do with Luna?"

"Obviously, if Luna wanted to send a message we wouldn't intercept our own transmission. We'd have just sent it straightforward to begin with so it wouldn't have been flagged as a breach."

"What if it's some rogue faction trying—"

Riggs held her hand up. "I'm gonna stop you right there before you sound even more stupid. Remember how you guys just wiped out about three-quarters of our military power, yeah? So, if there was some rogue faction on Luna plotting against Earth, I don't imagine that, upon discovery, we'd have reported the breach to Terrans."

Again, she had a solid point.

"Fine. What was the message then?"

"We couldn't make heads or tails of it, but I suspect it means something to you Terrans since I'm pretty sure that's where it came from."

"What are you suggesting?" Gailmen stood up defensively.

"I'm not suggesting anything. I'm telling you plainly, and clearly, that you have a mole. And Mr. Mole just sent a message to Mars by piggy-backing on a harmless trade communication."

"What did the message say?" he asked again.

"The Cook is resolved to Novotny," Riggs rattled off. "Whatever that means. It's all on the card," she said, motioning towards the door. "Now, if you don't mind, I've real work to do."

Gailmen frowned but complied. He'd not even made it back to the stairwell before he heard Rebecca Riggs slam her door closed. That didn't matter though. What did matter was that message she'd pulled from the transmission. He unfortunately knew exactly what the jargon meant.

Riggs was right. The Terran military had a mole on Luna.

∞

Gailmen had a choice. Instead of making one, though, he'd opted to do nothing. At least for a few more days. For now, he tried to keep his mind off the datacard and in the moment. He moved down the cafeteria line, taking a portion of each item offered, all the while aware that dozens of angry Lunar eyes bored into his back. He'd grown used to the Lunites' callousness towards him. If he'd been in their position, he'd act the same. But their hateful stares only reminded him of Rebecca Riggs and her contempt for him, which in turn led his thoughts back to the datacard. He couldn't escape it.

Swiping his badge, the system ticked him for his meal, and he carried his light tray towards the rows of tables.

If taken at face value, the cryptic message could only mean one thing: Malthus was the Cook, and the mole was after him.

The communication was exclusively chess problem lingo. He'd had to memorize the terms well at the academy since posing and solving such problems was an integral part of the placement exam at the end of the first year. He'd done well enough, though he was far and away from the top of the class. Still, he rememberd enough of it to be able to decipher the message.

A Cook was a move that, unintentionally on the part of the composer, made the problem invalid. In essence, a Cook was a flaw in the grand scheme of things. With the Ambassador General's recent transfer to Luna, one could suppose that his transfer happened because he'd become an obstacle to a powerful someone on the political scene. A Novotny, on the other hand, was a sacrificial piece in the problem. If Malthus was the Cook to be made a Novotny, it could mean this mole intended to have him removed in a more permanent fashion.

These things happened; not often, but it was not unheard of in Terran politics. So, the idea that some politician had decided Malthus stood in the way and needed to be assassinated didn't trouble him all that much. It was the fact that whoever was doing this appeared to be doing it not for selfish reasons, but for a Martian agenda.

Walking between the rows upon rows of tables, he spotted Whitlock at the rear, four tables from the exit. Reluctantly, he proceeded in that direction.

His choice, the one he'd yet to make, was whether or not to speak of this to Whitlock. After all, every Terran on Luna could potentially be the mole. And Whitlock's behavior of late made him suspicious. Hence the waiting and, as much as he hated to admit it, the following. So far, it seemed only Whitlock had an interest in Malthus' whereabouts. That did not bode well for his innocence, though the man's constant watch on the Ambassador General did make it easier than it should for Gailmen to keep an eye on his movements.

But if Whitlock was the mole, why did he let him go to the LICB at all? If he'd gone himself, he could have simply destroyed the data and said it was all just a hoax. Or perhaps Whitlock was one of many traitors and he hadn't been high up enough to even know about the message?

Setting his tray down beside his fellow officer, the other man looked up and nodded at him.

"How's it going?" he asked, taking a seat.

The older man shrugged and said, "Could always be better," before tossing a grape in his mouth.

Whitlock kept his face forward, monitoring the traffic coming in and out of the canteen. Unlike Gailmen, he didn't seem to mind the Lunar stares. He'd lock eyes with them and hold their gaze until, defeated, they returned to their task. In truth, he admired the man; even entertaining the notion that he could be a traitor made him feel like a shithead.

Pointing to a group of five that had just entered, he said, "Those guys are worth watching out for."

Gailmen scanned their faces. They were relatively young, wearing the crisp yellow and grey colors of ensigns. They laughed and joked as they made their way to the line, but under the gaiety something else lurked. Anger.

"Any trouble yet?" he asked, momentarily setting aside his suspicions of his comrade.

"Not yet. But there may be today."

"Why today?"

He didn't give an answer– just popped another grape in his mouth, crushing it sharply with his molars.

His tray was just about empty. He did seem to be waiting for something to go down.

"Well, it looks like that business with the LICB might be a hoax after all," Gailmen said.

"Not surprised. The Viceroy just wants to waste our time."

"I'll be meeting with Malthus later to hand over my official report."

Whitlock's jaw tightened, but only for a fleeting moment.

Gailmen looked back at the group of young ensigns. They each grabbed a drink tin and were headed down the main row of tables. Turning back around, he busied himself with the task of eating as the group passed their table and took up a post at the one closest to the exit. They continued cutting up, but one did keep a close eye on the doorway, as if they too were waiting for something to happen.

"The military sure is slack here," he muttered. "You'd never see a Terran officer acting in such a way."

"We'll shape them up soon enough," the older man assured him.

Whitlock turned his head just enough to check the large timepiece that hung over the back wall, then said, "Malthus should be done with the Viceroy for the day. Perhaps we can catch him on the way out, and you can give him your report now."

"I don't think–" he began, trying to make his excuses. He still wasn't ready to hand over the findings and their implications.

The group of men by the door suddenly stood up and, abandoning their drinks, left in unison.

"Come on," Whitlock ordered as he too stood up.

Gailmen followed suit, and the pair walked out.

The Lunites were far enough ahead of them that they couldn't see them in the corridor, but Whitlock took to the left as if he knew exactly where they'd gone.

The corridor itself was in a constant curve as it wound its way around the core of the building, creating the sensation that something was always just in front of or behind you.

Whitlock held his hand up, and they both stopped. Voices trickled in from around the curve in front of them. He didn't recognize them, but could assume they belonged to the young ensigns from earlier.

Another voice, one he did know, interrupted the youths. He couldn't make out the words, but the speech belonged to Ambassador General Malthus.

He looked to Whitlock, who, edging a bit closer, was transfixed on picking up the conversation.

This was it. This, right here, was their job. Going to Malthus' aid, even if he didn't need it, was their top priority. Still, Whitlock moved not an inch more once the voices became words and sentences, making it clear his only interest was that of an observer.

Gailmen wanted to stay back as well, but only to gauge Whitlock's reaction to the situation. Yet he must aid Malthus. Watching the older man's face as it tensed, he decided to hang back. But at the first sound of a scuffle, he would abandon his comrade to aid his commander and do his job.

∞

Malthus held back a smile as the group of youths closed in on him. They'd been watching him for weeks now, studying his comings and goings between his quarters and the Viceroy's office. What they lacked in brains, they made up for in guts, he'd give them that much.

"Pardon me, Ambassador!" one of them called out to him in a sing-song bellow.

Malthus stopped.

"Ambassador, Ambassador, we've a complaint to lodge!" another taunted him.

He let the boys form a circle around him, remaining silent and composed. These weren't revolutionaries or even rebels, just men— angry, foolish men, looking for a little piece of justice. It had only been a matter of time before this group or another like them tried to get at him. Humanity, as always, remained predictable to a fault.

Two of the five men looked a little drunk, swaying slightly as they leaned on the wall to steady themselves and close the circle. Probably needed the boost of courage. What they were about to do should not be taken lightly.

"You see," said the one directly in front of him, "There's been a bit of property damage, and I was told I needed to bring the matter to you."

The man couldn't have been more than twenty-two at the most. He wore his mud-colored hair spiked up, creating the illusion of height where none existed. The group was well-formed and muscular, as one would except from those fresh out of training. It gave them a sense of confidence, as Malthus himself was much leaner than any one of them. He supposed he must look rather helpless to them.

"Any damage of property committed against a Lunar citizen by a Terran officer should be first reported to your supervisor, who then would report to the Viceroy, who, if he deems necessary, would consult with me," he answered casually, which angered them far more than the sniveling response they'd hoped for.

One of the drunk men to his left took a swing at him. He side-stepped out of the way, sending the man crashing into his friend on the other end of the circle.

The men must have expected him to make a run for it at that point. Confusion washed over their tense faces, as he plainly stood before them as if nothing had happened.

"Shall I repeat myself?" he asked.

Mud-hair drew his blaster and pointed it in his face.

But his hand shook in anger. This boy wouldn't be able to

hit him.

"You got any idea how many died in that crash? How many died in that last assault?"

"Do you?" he challenged, taking a step closer. "I somehow doubt your brain could fathom such a number."

He licked his lips and, shifting his weight, said, "I heard you were that woman's commanding officer. Was it you, then? You who gave the order?"

They'd done their homework. It was surprising, but changed nothing. He almost hated Armin had to take the fall for that. She'd done so well staying alive, only to be despised by both Earth and Luna. Really, she'd nowhere to go except–

"Answer me!" Mud-hair shouted.

Malthus was behind him, one arm clutched around his neck, the other on his armed hand, before the boy could speak further.

He fired four swift shots at each man's holster before they could pull their weapon, discharged the blaster's energy coil, then released him with a kick in the back.

Mud-hair collided face-first with the outer wall just as Commander Whitlock and Commander Gailmen rounded the corner to find four unarmed, and rather stupefied, men staring open-mouthed as their bloody-nosed companion slid down and onto the floor, leaving a thin red smear in his wake.

"You all right, Sir?" Gailmen asked, but seemed to be keeping a closer eye on his comrade than either him or the gang of Lunites, who were quickly scraping their friend off the floor and making their retreat.

"I'm unharmed."

Whitlock stepped forward and placed a hand on his shoulder.

"We should get you out of here. They could be running to find backup."

Malthus couldn't help but notice a growing intensity in the way Gailmen watched Whitlock as the man laid his hand on him. He'd probably planted the tracker he assumed had been picked up from the Underbelly.

It was all too easy. It'd only be a matter of days before Gailmen came to him with his suspicions and the LICB report he'd been so reluctant to share.

"Of course," he answered. "If you both would be so kind as to escort me back to my quarters. I would like to avoid any further confrontation."

The journey was an uncomfortably quiet one, but only for Gailmen it seemed. Whitlock looked smugly satisfied, while Gailmen divided his attention between looking over his shoulder and staring at the back of Whitlock's head with a mix of hate and regret.

Just as the two men moved to leave him at his door, Malthus asked, "Whatever came of that LICB incident? The Viceroy mentioned it again today, but I had nothing new to say on the matter."

"You'll have it first thing in the morning, Sir," Gailmen assured him.

The young solider had finally made up his mind, it seemed. Right on schedule. With a slight bow and another thank you for their assistance, Malthus allowed his doors to glide back into place.

8

ENTENTE

Cornelia filed away at the dull edge of the bowl shard until she'd sharpened it to a lethal point. Pulling the edge against her forearm, she pressed just hard enough to draw a little blood. She'd been here for weeks working on her arsenal, yet Malthus had yet to made an encore appearance.

Her cell smelled of decay, a stench she was now thankful for as it had helped harden her against her fears of filth and germs. She'd not succumbed to any illness, which made her suspect her surroundings were more sterile than she believed. Or maybe Malthus had done something to her before he'd roused her from stasis. Either way, she felt confident against the surrounding elements.

She went back over the cluster of bowl fragments, and upon finding the dullest, she plucked it from the pile to file it further.

It disturbed her that Malthus had never explained what happened to Vladia; she could only assume he'd killed her. If that was the case, she wondered what Abel would do. He'd put all bets on Vladia, and he wasn't one to have a strong plan B.

She thought back to the time at the bar, when Vladia had attacked that man in defense of Rehel. She'd gone as far as to spit in his face. At the time it seemed unthinkable. Now, in her own desperation, she understood completely. She'd do anything to escape this place.

Muffled footsteps approached.

Gathering up her weapons, Cornelia crouched in the corner behind the door and waited.

It opened with a gentle creak, and Malthus stepped in.

She leapt at his back, knocking him to the floor.

Pressing the bowl shard against the nape of his neck, she leaned down and whispered in his ear, "This is where you die. In a cell of your own creation. In the filth and rot you left me in for weeks."

Yet, she hesitated to push the blade any further into his skin. Malthus slammed the back of his head against hers, disorienting her enough for him to spin onto his back and take hold of both her forearms.

He was the stronger of the two, and though she struggled to free herself, it was futile.

"I wondered if you'd make use of the broken bowl I'd left you."

His grip on her arms tightened until her hands throbbed, forcing her to drop her weapon.

Malthus grinned and pulled her closer, just inches from his face. "I'm glad you didn't disappoint."

Cornelia spat in his face, as Vladia had done months before to the man in the bar.

She reveled in the boldest of her actions and jerked away from him.

But his grasp remained unyielding, and her joy ended as he laughed at her attempt to free herself.

"Very good! But that little trick won't work on me. What a shame I wasn't raised in the system as brainwashed cattle like the rest of you."

"Let go of me!"

"Does it disturb you so much? Am I really that much more a monster now?"

She refused to answer, continuing her tussle for freedom.

"I'll tell you a little secret for your efforts, though. I can help you answer the question that's been burning up inside you for so long now."

Cornelia stopped struggling, partly from fatigue, partly out of curiosity. If she'd caught anything from him, it was probably too late now, regardless of their proximity.

"Why Vladia? Of all people, why is it that Abel has placed so much faith in her? You're a capable soldier; why not you?"

"How did you—"

"There's only one logical explanation," he continued. "You have all the pieces. Let's see if you can put them together on your own."

It only took Cornelia a moment to make the connections from all the evidence that had accumulated, the most important piece being what Malthus had just confessed.

"She wasn't raised in the system, either."

"And?"

"She's your…"

"Say it."

"Your sister."

The word felt ugly and unnatural on her tongue. Her mind raced to picture the two side by side. They seemed so different, didn't they?

"Half-sister," he corrected. "But close enough. Abel believes she can stop me simply because we were raised together. Because we share the same blood. Yet based on his logic, if all this makes me a monster, what does that make her?"

Malthus released her, and Cornelia climbed off of him, backing up until she felt the rough wall against her skin.

Picking himself up from the floor, he brushed his uniform clean as best he could with his hands

"Think on that. Until our next session."

With a slight bow, he made his exit.

∞

"She's almost ready for the Outer Moons," Malthus said as he walked down the corridor of cells. He'd risen early so he could safely extract the tracking device and make his appearances at his facilities before he was to speak with

Gailmen. His repairs on the robot were almost complete, and the skin would soon be ready. His business with Cornelia was the only thing that troubled him.

"It doesn't matter. We haven't been able to stabilize the nanos in a human host," Isobel pointed out.

She was right. The longest a human could survive with an occupying nano swarm was a few hours at best. He'd lost six test subjects even getting that far. The trouble seemed to be almost identical to the issue with syncing a Valkyrie ship with a pilot. Most simply could not host another consciousness, and none could do it unwillingly.

"We only have one more subject for testing," she continued. "The only thing to do is to convert her to the swarm."

"No," he said, perhaps a bit too quickly. "I suspect in her present state she'd not survive the process," he added.

"Does it matter that much? We can always obtain more subjects later."

"Sending her to the Outer Moons in particular is the best way to infiltrate Vladia's group. They know her, and they will trust her."

"You don't need her out there as long as you have me."

That was the catch, thought Malthus. Isobel was not getting any more stable. Her usefulness had run its course. He'd need to dispose of her services soon, before she realized that this had been her fate all along.

"Obviously. But it helps to have another pair of eyes. Think of Cornelia as your back-up and use her accordingly," he assured her as he stepped out into the cold, yet dull, recycled air of Luna's underground sunrise.

He'd only an hour before his meeting with Gailmen. It would be about Whitlock and the tracker he'd slipped on him during their little corridor skirmish, though officially they were to discuss the LCIB business.

It had been a tricky little device, and well programmed. Whitlock had placed it on his shoulder, but the tracker didn't stay there. It had crawled to his neck and nestled just inside the hairline. Light enough and small enough not to be noticed by the host, it also blended with its surroundings so as to be difficult to detect by the human eye. If he could find the creator, he'd gladly shake his hand.

Gailmen wore the mask of the betrayer poorly, but soon enough he'd work through those misgivings, and Earth would see him as their champion. Feeling like the hero would be the man's only consolation for ratting out his comrade. Well, Malthus would give him just that, though history might remember him differently when it was all said and done.

∞

Malthus sat at his desk, hands folded together loosely, as the younger man across from him took a seat. Gailmen felt nervous, though he knew he could hide that well enough. He hesitated to speak first. One, as his superior officer, it was the General's task to initiate the conversation, regardless of who asked to speak with whom. Two, his reasons for coming pained him; he took a slight comfort in letting Malthus guide their conversation.

It felt almost like a treachery. But what else could be done? He'd delayed too long as it stood, and after the incident in the corridor, Gailmen knew the danger of assassination was both real and near.

"I must say," Malthus began, "I wasn't aware you'd had a hand in the LICB investigation until recently."

Gailmen shifted uneasily in his seat and said, "Whitlock delegated the job to me entirely."

"That's a bit unusual. Not against protocol, mind you, but most certainly odd. Did he say why he wanted you to take over?" Malthus pressed.

"No. Just that he had other tasks to see about."

"I can't imagine what could have been more important, but let's move on. What did you find out? Judging by the Viceroy's remarks, there wasn't much to the matter."

"There isn't much to the matter that concerns them, Sir."

At that, Gailmen slid a slip of paper soundlessly towards him. He must assume the bug to be present and hoped they could find and remove it easily enough.

"Is that so," Malthus said as he removed his gloves and ran his bare fingers across his shoulders and over his neck. He then ran his fingers through his hair until he found the tiny tracking bot, which was no bigger than a small tick.

Placing the bot on the table, it scurried around, desperately trying to find its host.

Malthus remained speechless as he retrieved a disposable cup from the washstand and placed it over the struggling bot.

Gesturing for Gailmen to follow, the pair went outside and stood in the hallway.

Pulling his gloves back into place, Malthus motioned for him to continue.

"I suppose I should begin with the LICB report," he began, just above a whisper. "Dr. Riggs, the Director of Communication, found a message implanted in the trade transmission. It's gibberish to them, but any Terran who's gone through the academy would know at least some of the words, regardless of context."

Handing him another slip of paper, Malthus read off the all-too-familiar message.

"I see. So I am the Cook, you believe. I assume you have a theory on the rest?"

"I do, Sir. I think Whitlock must be involved."

He'd hoped to find some degree of relief in his confession, but instead the pit in his stomach grew to a sickening size.

"But why do you suspect Whitlock? Even if there is a mole, there's scores of Terran officers on Luna at the moment. Why him?"

"I watched him plant that bug on you yesterday when we came upon you and those thugs in the corridor," he continued. "I can't prove it, but I suspect he not only knew they'd jump you, but somehow made sure of it. He's also been acting odd lately. Disappearing, avoiding me, and like with the LICB business, neglecting assigned tasks."

"But you've no hard evidence, I take it. We can't trace this message back to him?"

He knew convincing Malthus with no tangible evidence would be difficult, especially since Whitlock's track record had remained impeccable throughout his many years of service. But waiting for proof would put Malthus in danger. Since his first duty was to protect the General, he must press on with no evidence other than his own eyes.

"I'm afraid not. I would like to continue keeping an eye on him, but I needed to bring this to you now. I feel he is likely not working alone, and if I can figure out exactly where he's disappearing to, I can prove it."

After a moment of consideration, Malthus agreed.

"I think you're right. I should leave the bug as is and simply be mindful of its presence," Malthus offered. "If he suspects he's been found out, we will lose them all. We must find out more, get hard evidence, if we want to protect Earth."

"If you can manage, that would be best."

Gailmen couldn't help but be a little impressed with his proposal to keep the bug on his person. That thing gave him the creeps. He couldn't imagine letting it crawl up into his hair and calmly going about his everyday affairs. Just the thought of it made him turn a bit green.

"Whitlock is a fine officer and his record spotless. It's difficult to believe he could be a traitor to Earth," Malthus said.

"I'm sorry I've no more to offer you other than what I witnessed. But that message to Mars is undeniable. There are Terrans on Luna working for a Martian agenda."

"You did the right thing, coming to me about Whitlock. You're a good man, Gailmen. We need more like you on our side," he commended.

"The hardest part will be finding the moles on Earth."

"There was talk on the War Council, just before I was exiled here, of Mars being a potential threat. I warned them not to take the Red Planet lightly, and I was swiftly ushered off-world for my remarks. I hate to say it, but quite a few on the

Council had a hand in my sudden departure from Earth."

"Are you suggesting there are those on the Council who—"

"Think about it," Malthus interrupted him. "A man like Whitlock turning out to be a spy. It makes one wonder who can really be trusted, don't you think?"

Gailmen nodded in agreement.

"Right now, you may be the only person I can trust."

"Thank you, Sir."

Malthus patted him on the shoulder.

"Don't do anything foolish, though. You want to watch Whitlock, fine. But remember, he's a dangerous man. One whom you cannot take on alone," he warned.

Gailmen nodded and then saluted as Malthus returned to his quarters.

As much as he hated to admit it, he might need to ask Dr. Riggs for a favor. If she agreed, finding out where Whitlock got that tracking device would be a hell of a lot easier than running him down on foot.

∞

Vladia lightly jogged along the corridor circling the bridge; the echo of her own footfalls was the only sound haunting the ship at this late hour. Only forty-two laps in and she was already feeling winded. There'd been a time she could have done a hundred of these, no problem. Rehel had scolded her a bit for being so hard on herself, but the voyage was more than half over, and she still wasn't where she needed to be. Anything could await them on Ganymede; they all had to be ready.

Even Abel was pushing himself towards peak performance now. The nanos had done their job, and as promised Rehel had kept quiet about them thus far. Of course his first severe injury would alert him to the difference in his body, and she'd have to deal with the repercussions of her decision. Maybe he would rather have died, but she couldn't allow Abel to bow out of this so easily. She could hope that eventually he would understand the choice she'd made. They might never be friends again, but he'd understand.

Lap forty-three approached, but there would be no rest for her until she'd reached sixty.

Another pair of footsteps joined hers as Abel ran up beside her from behind.

"Care if I join you?"

"Be my guest."

They jogged in silence, but she knew there must be something on his mind. He'd finished his workout and showered some time ago, yet here he was.

"So are you taking to doing two workouts now or is something on your mind?" she initiated.

He seemed irritated he'd been called out so quickly, but it faded fast and was replaced by his trademark smile. "Can't a guy just spend some quality time with his Captain?"

"Sure," she said.

She'd no interest in dragging it out of him. Besides, a few more minutes of awkward silence would do the trick.

"Okay, fine," he gave in. "We'll do this your way."

"Wasn't that the plan all along?"

"Vladia, stop," he tugged on her arm until she slowed and they both came to a halt.

"I don't like this."

"What?"

"This," he motioned his hands from her then to him. "Us. It's not the same, you and me. I don't feel like we're on the same page here."

"I don't know what you want from me, Abel."

"I just want us to go back to the way things were. We were partners. You were my Defender, and I was your Gunslinger. And that was good. It was great, actually."

"You've got a real thing for living in the past, huh?"

The hurt on his face made her immediately regret her coarse remark. What happened with Ceres wasn't something to be used on him like that.

"I just need you to trust me again," he said evenly.

Vladia shook her head and said, "I want to. I really do. You haven't made it easy, though, have you?"

"I suppose not."

"Digging up my records, and Maria's records…you violated my life completely. And the whole time you kept so much information from me, Abel. Information that would have helped, that might have prevented—"

"I know. You don't have to say it. At the time, I thought it was important for you to come to your own conclusions about Malthus. And to some degree I worried if you knew too much and turned on him too soon that he'd kill you before we could prepare. Maybe I was wrong, and if I was I'm certainly sorry for that."

"He wouldn't have killed me."

"You don't think so? You really, honestly, believe that after all he's done that you're immune to his wrath because you share the same blood?"

"Not immune, no. But I do know him. That's why you need me, right? He could have killed me on the *Dragoon*. Trust me, he could have easily, and he did not because he didn't want me dead. Not yet, anyway."

"What are you saying? That all this is somehow still part of his plan?"

"Maybe, yes. I think my capture was a test. And in his eyes if I couldn't escape then I deserved my fate: to face my death in the same manner as Maria. He's theatrical like that, when it serves him.

"But," she continued, "If I could escape, then I deserved to live on. For him, living on would mean to continue as his rook perhaps, instead of his pawn."

"There's no way he could have predicted Rehel's reaction," Abel said. "Even I can't explain how he managed to overcome his most core programming to save you."

Should she tell him? Vladia wondered. As soon as she'd learned Rehel was not just a random Gen D robot, but the very same robot who'd escorted her to her father's estate at the age of eleven—the robot who, for the briefest of moments, believed he belonged to her—she knew Malthus must have had a hand in it. If that was indeed true, then of course Malthus could have predicted Rehel's response to her capture.

Just how the robot had side-stepped his core protocols remained a mystery, but not knowing that one facet wasn't enough for her to shake the feeling that Malthus had foreseen it all. Somehow, she still felt the puppet master plucking away at her strings.

No, this secret would remain as such. Besides, Rehel had neglected to tell Abel for all this time. Perhaps he, too, wanted it to continue on as their secret.

"I wouldn't underestimate his capabilities," she declared. "I may know him, but I don't know the extent of his information. Or his reach. Which could easily extend to Mars and beyond."

"You think he knows where we're going?"

"I think he knew Mars would turn us away and we'd be forced to go to the Outer Moons. In other words, we may be heading exactly where he wants us."

Abel looked defeated. All this planning he'd worked so hard on and now it seemed to him he remained as powerless as ever.

Vladia placed a reassuring hand on his shoulder.

"This doesn't have to mean what you think it does. Even if he does know where we are going, all he has are predictions about what we'll do. Now, maybe, he thinks we'll gather an army. Maybe he thinks we'll bring that army to Mars and then to war with Earth. But what he doesn't know, what he can never know, or ever hope to control, is how damn good of an army it'll be. And it will be a damn good one, I promise you that."

Perhaps it was the guilt, but their eyes met and Vladia's expression softened.

"You need to trust me if you ever expect me to trust you," she insisted.

In the corners of her mind, the harsh reminder of the monster she'd turned him into festered. She deserved no more than to choke on her own hypocrisy.

"I don't think you can trust me, or anyone, anymore," he

said, lifting an unsteady bare hand and with only the slightest hesitation touched her face. "I do believe you want to, but can you now after all that's happened?"

Relationships, shared affections, were so rare on Earth. She wondered if he'd felt the warmth of another human since Ceres had died.

Vladia stepped back, just out of his reach.

She couldn't be what he needed.

Not anymore.

∞

The skin had gone on nicely, fitting flawlessly snug over the metallic endoskeleton. By all appearances, it looked complete, but that was just an illusion. The CPU had been damaged beyond repair. Well, beyond his ability to repair. Malthus imagined Maria Robespierre would've been able to salvage the wreckage. As it stood, his robot was no more than a glorified mannequin. Its lifeless eyes peered upward into nothingness, and its mouth hung open, lips barely cracked as if waiting for a soul to enter.

Isobel's choice in the parameters for the skin also troubled him. A kind of intentional, almost childish, cruelty lay at the center of it, and he didn't much care for that sort of thing. Yet he'd been the one who'd given her free reign in this matter. That had been before the outburst, when she'd been stable and more rational. It could always have been worse, though; she could have made it to resemble him.

He'd not let any of this discourage his efforts. He'd all the nanos he could ask for, and he still had the research documents from his funding of the Generation Four nanobots. He would have preferred to program a controllable swarm to make the repairs. Then he'd have a fully functional robot under his rule. Unfortunately, he had yet to isolate a swarm devoid of human tendencies. Until then, his creation would wait.

Pulling the sheet over the robot, he killed the lights and walked to his secondary facility.

The next, and final, test on their remaining human subject

was scheduled in three days' time. Even if the results improved, the human had to survive, or it wouldn't matter.

His plans for Cornelia had steadily crumbled. Not that he'd put all bets on her. That would be foolish. But he couldn't deny that with Isobel's unfortunate and inevitable termination, having another pair of eyes out there had become more pressing. Still, his other option flourished, so in the end all of these unexpected complications mattered little.

The lock clunked out of sync, allowing the door to lurch open. He'd half expected a second attack from the woman, but she was in plain sight, back leaned against the far wall and staring up at the dank ceiling.

He took the seat he'd left in here for her on the first day and waited for her to acknowledge his entrance.

She made no move to do so, however, as if in a sort of silent protest.

"Sulking?" he asked.

"Sulking is for children."

"True enough."

She clearly had no interest in bartering for her freedom. Force had failed as well. Perhaps she'd given up. That would be truly disappointing, he thought.

"May I ask then, what is it you're thinking on? How best to kill me, perhaps? That is, assuming you had the means?"

"Why do you come to me?" she said, continuing to glare at nothing but the space above her. "To gloat? To torment? It seems that way, but I know you better than that. Tolen Malthus: the man with the plan. You come because you need something. So, stop wasting my time and say what you've come to say."

"Of course. Your time is precious and limited. Perhaps you've another engagement pending?"

The woman refused response.

"Have you yet realized that twice now you've escaped death by my hand? Do you understand how remarkable that is?"

Still not a word.

"Why not a third, then?"

At that she moved her eyes to meet his, but still made no remark, her face expressionless and hard. Not the face, he imagined, of one who'd given up.

"The thing is, I've had something particular set aside for you. Unfortunately, those plans do not seem likely anymore. Now, I have you here, but I'm not sure what to do with you. I could kill you and be done with it. But in doing that, I waste a valuable resource, and I do hate to be wasteful. So the question remains: what should be done with Cornelia Arnim?"

"What indeed."

"I could let you go."

"Why would you do that?"

"I've no more use for you, and you're no threat to me. Why wouldn't I?"

"I could go to the Terran, or Lunar, government. Tell them what you've done."

"You've no proof. And do you really imagine they'd believe you? By all means, test that theory," he said, leaning back in the chair and casually crossing his legs. "They'd lock you up in the mad house. Or just execute you for blasphemy against the state and one of her highly regarded officers. As you have no proof, that's what it'd be."

"Even still, you'd not just let me go."

"I'll save myself the trouble of disposing of your body."

"Judging by the smell, I'd wager you don't waste time with that either way."

Malthus laughed. "Perhaps you're right."

"I'm right about plenty of things."

"I'm not sure I'd agree with that. Terrans are rarely in the right."

"You always say that word with such disdain. Do you resent not being in the system so much that you no longer feel like you're part of this world?"

"You couldn't be more wrong. I am the epitome of what is wrong with Earth. I am the monster of their own making."

"Aren't we all?"

Her question threw him off guard. Had he underestimated

her? In an odd sort of way, he hoped he had.

"To varying degrees, yes."

"You were right, about what you said to me earlier. About all the people I've killed. How many Lunites died so Earth could reign supreme? How many of our own did She execute for the good of the state? How many times did I stand idly by and watch it happen?"

She shook her head in earnest regret.

"I am just as much, if not more, a monster than you claim to be because I reveled in those deaths," she continued.

"You are merely a product of your Terran conditioning."

"And you are not. I see that now. All the times we cheered at the executions of those dangerous to the state, not once did you partake as I did. I thought you too stoic, too above us, to celebrate. But I was wrong. You saw the spectacle for what it really was. You knew it was terrible and wrong and—"

"Enough," he cut her off suddenly and stood up.

"I may have been exempt from your standard conditioning, but I assure you I was not spared it entirely," he continued. "And I'll not let you make me into something I'm not. The portrait you paint is not of me."

"I wasn't—"

"I will bring Earth the glory of war. It is what She craves most, and She shall have it at my hands," he said as he marched out of the cell. "That is the gift I give unto our mother planet."

Once out of the building, heading back towards his first facility, he shrugged Cornelia's words from his mind.

"Where is Whitlock?" he growled.

"Heading to the Underbelly again. Shall I intervene?" Isobel answered.

"No. But let's pay close attention to him this time."

"I always pay close attention. To everything."

"Of course," he sighed. "Let me be more specific. I want to know more about that fellow he keeps meeting."

"I'm sure he's just your average Lunar scum trying to turn a tidy profit."

"Well I'm not so sure."

The doors parted, and Malthus entered Facility One. He walked briskly towards his robot. He'd have the rest of the day to work on that and clear his head of everything else.

"You did say he had quite the knack for keeping his face off the surveillance feeds, correct?" he added, removing the sheeting from the specimen.

"I did. But that should be expected for any merchant in the black market."

"Still. Something doesn't feel quite right. Find out who he is, if you can. But use caution."

"As you wish."

It could be nothing, but he didn't like to take chances. Besides, it's not like Isobel had other plans. And if she were found out, well, he'd something up his sleeve to deal with that should the need arise.

"Has Gailmen met with that woman from the LICB?"

"He should be on his way as we speak," she confirmed. "And, yes, I've taken care of all the arrangements."

"Good."

He knew Gailmen wouldn't hesitate to ask Dr. Riggs for further aid now that it'd been made clear that any interaction between him and the Lunites would be in the service of Earth. There was no guarantee Riggs would help him, though her records suggested the probability to be greater than fifty percent. If she wouldn't give him footage of Whitlock in the Underbelly, it didn't matter much. There were many more ways to put a blood hound on the right trail.

∞

It'd been more than a week since Gailmen had made his first request to the LICB for several weeks' worth of footage. Since then, he'd made many more inquires, but each time had been met with rebuttals. Then, out of nowhere, Rebecca Riggs sent him a private message with an address and a time. No mention of his requests had been made, but surely it must concern them. Either way, he couldn't risk not going.

The address led him to Marginis, one of many Lunar pods named for a geographical feature it encompassed, and from there he travel to a large building made to look as if it were carved from a solid hunk of jade. He found it tacky against the otherwise dull surroundings, but he wasn't here to admire the architecture. He slipped inside the building without further thought of the structure.

Dr. Riggs waited just inside the entrance. Although absent her lab coat and name tag, her rigid stature made it clear she was still in work mode, despite her casual attire. He started to greet her, but she held her hand up to stop him before a single word passed through his lips.

She handed him a clear, flimsy ticket with green lettering. The two went under a massive golden arch, depositing their tickets into an unattended orifice just on the other side.

His earlier assumption that this was a theatre was immediately invalidated as they neared the first room, clearly labeled Africa in bold red lettering. His second guess of it being a museum lasted no longer than his first misguided thoughts. Inside the circular room were five visioglass cages embedded into the walls. Riggs led him to the center of the room, where they were surrounded by large, live cats.

He let a quiet gasp escape his mouth, which he immediately regretted. In that moment, he felt as if he'd given up any advantage he might have had during their meeting.

"You don't have these on Earth, do you?" she asked.

"Not anymore."

"These are the last of the large to medium breed cats. We've one Bengal tiger, one leopard, one ocelot, and a pair of lions." Pointing to the empty cage to their left, she added, "The cheetah died last year of old age."

"If you're trying to impress me, you've succeeded," he freely admitted.

"They won't be around much longer. They don't like it on Luna. We'd sooner let them die than give them back to Earth, though. And that's exactly what will happen," she said.

"That's horrible."

"Yes. It is."

The pair stood in silence for a long time, just watching the cats. There wasn't much to see, really. Only the ocelot seemed to take any notice of them. It moved towards the glass and studied them. The rest had their backs to them and slept, waiting for death.

"Why did you bring me here?" Gailmen asked after he could stand the quiet no longer.

"I come here a lot. Seemed as good a place as any."

"I take it you took the liberty of going through the footage I asked after?"

"I did. And I found what you were looking for."

"I didn't specify what I was looking for."

"You didn't need to."

Reaching into her pocket, she pulled out a data card and placed it in his hand. "It's all on there."

"Thank you," he said, pocketing the card.

"You know, we tried to get Mars to take them."

"The cats?"

Riggs nodded.

"They said no. That they couldn't risk them trying to breed with their animals. They might dilute the purity of their specimens. So, we offered to sterilize them. They still said no, because what would be the point if they couldn't breed? That's Martian logic for you. They don't understand anything."

"I'm not so sure I understand, either."

"You people killed off all your animals for sport, for food, for you name it. Mars is no better. They preserve the optimal number for each species solely for the sake of preservation. Because they're beautiful things for their eyes to consume and take joy in. They're art. Does it occur to no one that they're alive?"

Gailmen didn't have an answer. He'd not come prepared for a discussion on ethics. But one thing was obvious now: her reasons for helping him stemmed from her hatred of both Earth and Mars. She wanted to see them at each other's throats for a change, instead of them taking turns bullying Luna.

"I think you're self-identifying a bit too much with your cats here," he said finally.

"Am I?" she said knowingly.

The ocelot scratched at the glass furiously. Despite its small size, he wondered, if it ever got loose, would it try to eat them.

"Regardless of your reason for helping, I'm grateful for it."

"You won't be so grateful once you've watched the footage."

"I already know Whitlock's involved. You'll not surprise me with that."

Riggs smiled. "I assumed as much. You're looking for the identity of whoever he's meeting with. Unfortunately, mystery man is ever so clever. Kept his face off camera the whole time."

"Dammit," Gailmen frowned.

"That's not all, either," she smirked. "He made two trips into the Underbelly, but someone's tampered with the camera."

"Meaning?"

"I can't explain how, but there are several instances where your friend is going somewhere other than the Underbelly, yet the final destination has been removed somehow. Based on the footage available, you can narrow it down, but if you want to find out any more, you'll have to do it the old fashioned way and follow him."

"Great."

So much for doing this the easy way. Following Whitlock would entail danger, both of being caught and being killed. He wasn't so very patriotic as to want to die for Earth. That being said, he'd every intention of doing what must be done to ensure the safety of her inhabitants.

"Giving up, then?" she asked, obviously sensing his sudden change in demeanor.

"I can't."

After only the slightest hesitation, she said, "I think you should."

"I honestly have no response to that."

"Sometimes I think we'd all be better off if we could just start over. That's what they've done on the Outer Moons."

"Those barbarians?" he huffed.

"Starting over isn't easy or pretty. But maybe the human race needs a great big reset."

Gailmen shook his head.

"Your cats over there," he said, pointing to first the lions, then the tiger and cheetah, their backs still towards them and faces hidden from view. "That's what giving up looks like."

He then pointed to the ocelot, who'd given up scratching the glass, but still paced back and forth as if contemplating a new approach.

"I wanna be like that guy," he said.

"He'll die in here. You know that."

"Maybe. But he'll die knowing he tried for better."

∞

Commander Whitlock trudged through shadowed back alleys, stepping lightly over the garbage strewn across his path. He'd gotten more and more used to the stench, but still he wore his bio-blocks doubled, his gloves thick, a hood to cover his head, and a medical mask across his mouth and nose. His strange friend had laughed at him, saying despite the smell and its appearance, it wasn't much different than the conditions on Earth. Maybe he was right, but he wasn't ready to find out just yet.

The alleyway took a sharp left and narrowed so much that Whitlock had to skirt through sideways. It ended and became a vast opening of what must have been an artificial park at some point. Stone benches and huge plastic trees, now covered in cobwebs and spray paint, occupied much of the area.

He moved towards the center, passing a few homeless lumps of humanity along the way.

"Watch out," a voice called out.

Whitlock froze. Looking at the ground, he realized he'd

almost walked into a giant man-made hole.

"The locals say it used to be a pond," the voice explained.

A figure emerged from behind one of the large, dilapidated trees.

"You're late. I was about to leave," his Luna friend said, coming closer.

"This place isn't exactly easy to find."

"If it was then what would've been the point?"

Whitlock conceded the point with a nod. Each time he came to the Underbelly, he'd go to the last place they'd met; there he always found a note with instructions on where to go.

"How has the tracker worked out?"

"It didn't. He found it almost immediately."

"Not surprising. Malthus is not the kind of man who'd be fooled so easily," he said, joining him at the edge of the pit.

"Well, why didn't you tell me that? Could have saved us both some time and money," he said, frowning.

His friend just shrugged. "I could've been wrong."

Kicking a bit of rubble into the hole, he asked Whitlock, "What's your escape plan?"

"Escape plan?"

"Dealing with Malthus, you'll need one. That or a coffin."

"Your optimism is downright contagious, my friend."

"I'm just being honest, man. Everyone who's ever tried to get in his way is gone. Robespierre, Duren, Falis, Gammarow, Armin, Forté. Hell, even the damn robot. All gone. And that's just the ones I know of."

Whitlock recognized only a handful of the names listed.

"What I'm saying," he continued, "is that I'd like you not to turn up dead."

"This whole time, you didn't think I had a shot at him, did you?" Whitlock said, then cursing himself he added. "I still don't even know what it is Malthus is trying to do."

"I hoped you would, but, no, I didn't think you could."

"It's not over yet. He's made no move against me or even hinted he thinks I'm a threat."

The man laughed so loud it startled him.

"That's because you aren't a threat, my friend. Not to him. But he must know you've been following him. I'm sure he's even managed to get his hands on footage of us together, which is why we change locations and I never let the cameras catch my face."

"He knows who you are, doesn't he?"

His friend ignored the question and instead said, "You need a ship."

"I've no way of getting a ship. That's just a fact," he answered, letting his question go unaddressed.

"I'll see what I can do about that. More than anything, you need a ride off Luna."

"Where would I go?"

"Mars."

"No. Absolutely not," Whitlock insisted. In his eyes, Mars was enemy territory. He'd sooner stay on Luna than venture to the Red Planet.

"You don't have a choice. If you're forced to run, you can't hide here for long. Nor could you go back to Earth, and there's definitely no way you can make it to the Outer Moons without a pit stop to Mars. Besides," he added cautiously, "I may have a contact there who can help."

There was no use arguing. It wasn't productive, and he didn't have much time to waste here.

"Get me a ship if you can. But I'm not leaving until I find out where he's been going."

His friend nodded. "Come back here if you need to run. I'll have you a ship."

Whitlock backed away from the chasm. "I never told you, but I met Robespierre once. Just for a few minutes."

"And? What did you think of the Ice Princess?"

"I think she could have killed me. But she didn't. Not the sort of soldier who'd crash a ship into a Lunar base, killing thousands in a blink."

"No. She's not that kind."

"Malthus, though..."

"Yeah."

Whitlock felt his time was up. Without another word, he turned and walked back to the crack of an alley he'd emerged from. Just before slipping inside, he threw a glance back towards the other man. But he'd already disappeared into the cover of the trees.

9

GANYMEDE GAMBIT

Rehel blocked Vladia's kick with his forearm and prepared for her next attack. They had turned the extra storage space in the cargo hold into a sparring arena, and he'd fought against both Vladia and Abel every day for the last four weeks.

He dodged another jab from his partner and followed it with his own attack, adjusted to her level.

Vladia backed off and held her hands up, signaling for a pause.

"You've got to stop taking it easy on me. I can tell, you know," she panted. "The cardio is great, but you aren't a challenge when you coddle me like this."

"If I were to injure you—"

"Then I would deserve it," she said, preparing herself for another round. "Now. Come at me like you mean it, or I'll deactivate you and toss you in storage with the Valkyries."

Rehel nodded. He didn't believe she'd actually follow through with her threat, but her frustration unsettled him, mostly because it was directed at him.

He rushed toward her and thrust his fist at her abdomen.

Hitting the floor, she rolled away and flung a throwing knife at his calf.

Sidestepping the projectile with ease, he was on her again before she could stand up.

He'd twisted both arms away from him, but she'd managed to plant her feet firmly on his chest to keep him at a distance.

With a forceful grunt, Vladia shoved him off. Rehel let loose his hold on her appendages so as not to rip them off.

She made it to her feet and charged him.

It would be her final mistake.

Instead of dodging her attack as usual, he caught her by the wrist. In one swift motion she was on the ground, her arm twisted behind her and his knee pressed into her back.

"I've told you a defensive position is best. Attacking as you did gives the enemy time to spot an opening and take you down with ease," Rehel explained.

"You've also warned me against overconfidence," she countered.

A blade penetrated his left abdomen, and he instinctively released the woman and backed away.

Vladia spun around onto her knees. The edge of a knife stuck out from underneath her right sleeve. She smiled, and the blade retracted from sight.

"If you were human, you'd have bled out," Vladia gloated.

"Why did you not use this earlier? You could have won on the first round."

"If you weren't going to fight seriously, neither was I," she said with a wink.

Standing up, Vladia dusted off her grey pants and said, "I rigged this up last night. I've been working on a few items of this caliber. The trigger is wired into my arm so it responds like any other muscle. It's still removable, though; just takes a few minutes."

"I didn't know you had the skill to make adjustments to your arm."

"I don't, really," she admitted with a shrug. "Took a whole bunch of trial and error, I promise. First time I hooked it up my arm went dead for an hour. Had to wait for my nanos to fix the mess I'd made before I could use it again."

Rehel was glad she seemed well-adjusted to her robotic components, both physically and mentally. However, this behavior seemed rather masochistic to him. In general, Vladia had grown steadily less concerned with her own well-being. It troubled Rehel greatly, as that was one of his highest concerns.

"Can I ask you a question?" the robot began.

Vladia nodded and he proceeded: "Why do you refuse to spar with Abel?"

"I need someone to test my limits."

He didn't quite believe that, but it was not his place to doubt her answer.

"Why do you ask?" she probed, walking over to the small folding table set up near the exit and grabbing a bottle of water. She pressed the cool container against her neck. Leaning her back on the wall, she waited for his reply.

"I feared you intended to avoid him out of guilt for giving me permission to use your nanos on him."

"Maybe you're right about me avoiding him, but it's not what you think."

Rehel had no intention of questioning her further on the matter, but she willingly continued after only a slight hesitation.

"I don't want there to be any misunderstanding between us. Between Abel and I, that is."

"I'm not sure I follow."

Vladia took a long swig of water then said, "He is not second in command here. Nor is he my right-hand man or my gunslinger or anything else other than a soldier in this war we've recklessly waded into against Malthus."

She paused as she set her drink down. "Abel put me in this position. He has marooned me and in doing so has forfeited any other relationship he may have wished to have with me." She paused a moment, then reluctantly added, "Once he finds out about the nanobots, when he realizes what I've done to him, I'll be lucky if he doesn't leave altogether."

"Regardless, I do not think it wise to abandon the idea of having someone to rely on. You are human. Humans perform poorly under emotional and mental isolation," Rehel warned.

Turning her face away from him, Vladia winced at the word 'human'.

"You are still human. You do realize this, don't you, Vladia?

And Abel is, too. The nanobots can never change that."

"Maybe being human isn't all it's cracked up to be. And anyway, I am not alone in this. I have you," she said, closing the distance between them. "You who are loyal absolutely and beyond corruptible. You who were there at the start of everything and will be there to see its end. I have no need for anything more and deserve far less."

She added, "And at the end of the day, we're all expendable."

"You are not expendable," he promised.

He would make sure of that.

Vladia shrugged. "I have to be."

Rehel made to reply, but a soft buzzing interrupted him.

"That will be the autopilot system readying to be disengaged," he said instead.

Vladia forced a grin.

"Come." She motioned for him to follow as she jogged to the ladder and ascended.

Rehel trailed behind her, carrying the weight of a feeling he did not recognize or understand.

∞

Nova perched on the railing in the food court overlooking the smallest landing dock in September City. It was the only place she could get a full view of every ship that was landing. Obviously there was no way she could check out every single ship docking on Ganymede, but she always tried to hit the ones she'd not heard of before. She'd also narrowed down the ships by class. It had to be big enough to justify needing at least six crewmen. In a typical day she'd need only check three or four inbound ships, and only once had they been so far spread out that she'd missed one. Today she'd been lucky; all three inbound ships meeting her criteria were scheduled to dock in the same city.

She slurped on her soda and checked the time. Her second catch of the day should have already entered the dome. Any minute it'd be pulled into the docks for the crew to disembark and begin unloading, refilling, or whatever they needed. Hopefully that'd include posting a crew manifest with open positions.

It'd happened a few times already, but most people needed only one or two spots filled and almost always needed heavies—strong-arms to intimidate folks—or sharp-shots to kill those who weren't so easily intimidated. Nova always imagined Li could make a decent enough heavy, even if he was older than most. He still had the right look about him. She'd been Li's sharp-shot for a long time and had no problem killing what needed to be killed. Ten and Erro were flexible in their duties and could handle any position, except that of a heavy. Sure they were damn strong, but they didn't look any stronger than the average guy. For a heavy it was just as much about the show as the actual strength.

"Eh-hem!"

Nova didn't move to look at the two men now approaching from behind. She'd seen them in her periphery not long after she'd set up her watch here. They were police. At least, that's what they called themselves. Every cop was on the payroll of the Syndicate, so she considered them no more than henchmen with badges, as well as guns.

"Ollie. Geff," she addressed them curtly.

"I've told you before not to call me that, Nova," Ollie protested. He was the younger of the two and didn't seem like all that bad of a guy. It was the main reason Nova gave him trouble. In his line of work, if he didn't toughen up, he'd be dead within the year.

"Yeah, well, don't call me Nova. You should address me as Your Majesty, Master of All Time and Space."

"The only master you are is master of being a pain in my ass," Geff grunted. "You've been loitering here some time. I'm gonna have to ask you to move along."

"And I'm gonna have to ask you to go fuck yourself. I've business here."

Geff jerked her off the railing by the back of her vest and

spun her around to face them. He started patting her down; Nova did all she could to look as annoyed as possible.

Pulling her sidearm from its holster and then her ankle gun from her boot, Geff handed the weapons to his partner.

"I've a permit for those, and you know it."

"Yeah, well, permit or not you can't have 'em at the docks."

"I've got a bounty license says I can," she said, glancing over her shoulder to check the docking bay doors.

"Let's see it then."

"I didn't know you'd got back into that sort of thing, Nova," Ollie said.

"Good. Cause you don't need to know."

Plucking her bounty hunter's ID from her back pocket, she held it just out of reach so Geff had to grab for it.

Once in his hand, the man tore it in two and tossed it in her face. "That's a shame. Looks like you've left it at home. Guess I'll be confiscating these," he spat, motioning towards her two guns.

They'd tag them at the station and put them on a forty-eight-hour hold. No big deal since this was the first warning she'd had in months. Besides, she had loads more at home. She'd swing by her place after this port and grab a new set.

"Got anything else to say to me?" Geff challenged.

Nova strained to keep her mouth shut. One more mark and they'd haul her in too. Now that would be a problem. She'd be out by the day's end, but she'd miss her ships. And with her luck, they'd be the perfect ones.

Geff laughed. "I didn't think so. Come on, Oliver."

Ollie hung back a moment and said to Nova, "You can't do that, Nova. Why d'you always ask for trouble with the cops?"

"Because you're not cops; you're Syndicate dogs. And I don't need my guns anyway," she said.

Leaning in closer, she whispered, "I'll show you why if you don't back the hell off me. Now run along, pup. I've got work to do."

The kid moved away with a frown, then jogged after his superior officer.

Nova cursed under her breath and hopped back onto the railing. She really didn't need her guns today, anyway. All she needed was a ship with the right amount of crew openings.

One of the docking doors lifted, and Nova could make out a ship that looked about the right size. She took out her binoculars and magnified the ship as high as she could to search for the name on the side.

That was it!

The ship's loading doors opened and sank to the ground, forming a ramp.

Nova set down her binoculars and took a final sip of her drink before chunking it into the nearby bin, all the while eyeing the ramp. After a few moments, a lone figure walked down and stopped at the mouth of the ship, as if waiting for someone. But the person had only been scanning her surroundings, and upon locating the main office marched in that direction.

Scooping up her binoculars once more, Nova zoomed in on the figure. It was a blonde woman in a military overcoat.

Standing up, she plucked her viewer from her back pocket and scrolled through it until she found the data file her contact had given her weeks earlier. As soon as she opened it, a blonde woman's picture lit up the screen.

Nova peered again at the woman on the ground floor and once more at her view to be sure.

"Erro, you there?" she called into her comm.

After a few seconds' delay, he answered, "I'm here. Don't tell me you actually found a ship?"

"Better. I've found a bounty worth a dozen ships. I need you and Ten to get down here now. I'm gonna tail her. She's alone, but I don't know if it'll stay that way."

"What dock?"

"Waryward, in September City."

"Damn it, Nova. It'll be nearly an hour before we can reach you."

"It's fine. I'll engage her if need be to keep her off her ship until you guys get here."

"Right. On our way."

Nova leapt back off the railing and made for the lift. Her blood was pumping now. Instinctively, her hand fell to her empty holster.

Freakin' figures, she thought.

No time to pout about it. She still had her retractable cable and her spiked brass knuckles. If it came down to a fight, she could handle herself just fine.

Stepping on the lift she said, "Ground level."

The doors shut and Nova grinned, "I don't know what you did, Vladia Robespierre, but your ass is mine."

∞

As soon as Vladia had posted the manifest and strolled out of the main office, she took note of the blue-haired woman leaning against the side of the building, lazily scrolling through a data pad. Nothing out of the ordinary about that, except moments earlier she'd been nowhere in sight. Vladia intended to make a show of her presence here on Ganymede and what better way to gain the attention of the Syndicate than to parade around in a Terran military coat?

However, this was something else.

This person must have been waiting for her at the port before she'd even left the ship.

"I think I'm being tailed," she whispered in her comm as she stopped to read a row of advertisements plastered along the outside office wall.

Suddenly, the woman moved passed her and towards one of the many skiff rental kiosks and began chatting with the attendant.

She was good, getting ahead of her like that. But the woman always kept her in line of sight. Even with her back to Vladia when she'd walked passed her, the woman had held her data pad tilted in a way that her reflection could be spotted on the screen.

"Definitely being tailed," she confirmed, scratching the side of her head in a way that would cover her mouth from view.

"How many?" asked Rehel.

"Right now, just one. Female. Long, bluish colored hair with markings on her right leg. Possibly armed and probably waiting for back-up."

"Can you hack into the surveillance system and get us a good look at her? Maybe run a check on her so we know who we're dealing with?" Abel said to Rehel.

"I can't access anything wirelessly out here, and from what I understand there is not one fluid system out here. I'll need a terminal to get into the camera's feed and most likely a separate terminal to run her against–"

"No time for all that," Vladia interrupted. "We'll do this the old-fashioned way. Luring her to the outskirts."

"Shall we pursue?" Rehel asked.

"Give it a few minutes and stay far back. I've activated a tracker, so you'll have no problem finding me, but I want her to think I'm alone for now. Otherwise, her back-up might increase and be too much for the three of us."

"That tail was too quick," Abel pointed out. "Could they be Malthus' people?"

"Perhaps. Let's not jump to conclusions yet," Vladia decided, walking out the front exit and breaching the city streets, which consisted of just as much filth as it did people. It would be interesting to see how Abel handled this place. She was betting on an unprecedented anxiety attack.

"It could be bounty hunters," Rehel pointed out.

"Whoever it is, I don't think they're with the Syndicate. For now, let's keep the comm quiet. Give me a heads-up once her back-up is sighted. That's when I'll engage her."

"Understood," Rehel and Abel said in unison.

∞

Abel yanked the comm out of his ear and tossed it on the nav console. She was fucking crazy. He couldn't believe Rehel hadn't tried to stop her going ahead alone. Like she was bait.

"Are you all right, Abel?"

"Oh, sure. Just dandy," he fumed, crossing his arms. "She could have at least taken a real weapon since we've gotta do this like it's the damn dark ages."

"As long as it is only one, Vladia should have no problems."

"She's acting reckless, Rehel, and you know it."

The robot didn't respond.

"If she gets herself killed, we're done for."

"If she gets herself killed, which she will not, we've been done for the whole time," Rehel replied evenly. "Still, you are right. She has become a bit reckless. I will do what I can to prevent this tendency from continuing."

"Good. She'll listen to you," he said, more angrily than planned.

He paced towards the exit. "She may not want a gun, but I'm going in armed. What are you gonna do?"

"I see no need to be armed, but I agree you should take something."

"I'll grab my sidearm from my bunk and meet you at the ramp. We've waited long enough."

Rehel nodded stiffly, and with that Abel went to retrieve his gun.

∞

Vladia strolled the streets of September City, seemingly at random. She imagined her lack of purpose was frustrating to her pursuer. Truly, she did have a goal: that of getting far away from the docks and from the crowd. If things went bad, she didn't want civilians getting in the crossfire.

As she rounded the next grimy corner, her comm hummed to life. Abel said, "Company's here."

"How many?"

"Two males. There're good, too. Haven't had a clear line of sight on either of them yet. You want us to move in closer?"

His voice sounded all at once both agitated and forcefully

calm. She'd been right; this city, with its smells and trash and hordes of people, was taking its toll on him. She hoped he could keep it together long enough to do the job at hand.

"No, that's fine. All I needed was the number," she murmured. "Let me know if it changes."

Rounding one more corner that took her into a dead-end alley, Vladia waited at the back wall, casually propping up against it.

Several minutes passed before the woman emerged into the alleyway. She couldn't have been much younger than herself. She was a bit shorter than Vladia, but her large combat boots made up for it, and her artificially colored hair stood bold in contrast to the mud-caked brick walls that surrounded them.

"It appears we are at an impasse," Vladia spoke first. "You've run out of places to follow me."

"True enough," the woman said, her voice surprisingly lyrical. "Then again, I don't need to follow you anymore."

The bright-haired woman stepped closer, slowly diminishing the gap between them as she continued, "Did you know there's an awful big bounty on your head? Large enough to buy a mighty fine ship. Two or three, even."

"So I've heard. Ten million must go a lot further on the Outer Moons."

"Ten? Try thirty million," she sneered.

Vladia was taken aback by the figure, and she carelessly let it show as the woman let out an honest laugh.

"You didn't know? Apparently you're worth more to us than the mother planet."

"And who is us? You're not Syndicate."

"Doesn't matter. You can find out once you've been delivered. And, if it's not too much trouble, I'd like to take you in one piece," she said casually.

"I'm afraid I've business to attend to first. Namely, filling out my crew, building an army, taking down a corrupt government. You know, the usual heroic stuff," Vladia smirked before adding. "Oh, and did I mention destroying all those who oppose me?"

The woman was unmoved. "Lady, I don't care if you plan on becoming Empress of the Universe. You're coming with me."

With that, the woman flung something like a whip towards her. Vladia extended her right arm to catch the blow.

The black cord wrapped tightly around her forearm.

The woman tried to retract the cord, but to her surprise Vladia pulled back, holding her ground.

Clicking off her nerve receptors in the arm allowed her to pull even harder.

Without warning, the other woman released the cable and attacked head on.

Stumbling back, Vladia barely managed to catch the woman's fist just inches from her face.

Though she couldn't feel it, the spikes from her fist weapon tore into her skin.

Vladia kicked at her mid-section and sent the woman flying into the crumbled brick wall.

Two identical male figures jumped down from their post on the roofs above them, each landing on either side of Vladia.

For the briefest of seconds disbelief passed across Vladia's face. Each man took her by an arm and Vladia, quite frozen, allowed them.

The woman, despite her injuries, grinned wide, thinking she'd taken her by surprise.

Yet it wasn't the ambush that stunned her. Vladia had known there were two men standing by. It was who, or rather what, they were that she couldn't quite fathom.

"Perhaps you'd like to introduce me to your friends?"

"Sure, why not," she huffed, pulling herself off the ground. "Erro, Ten, meet the thirty million dollar woman: Vladia Robespierre."

Instinctively, the pair let go of her and stepped back to examine her face. It was only a matter of seconds before a wave of excitement, then panic, then confusion washed over their faces.

"What are you guys doing?! Don't let go of her!" the

woman shouted.

Vladia explained to the woman, "They won't take me."

She then looked to the pair of men and said, "Tell her."

"She is, I believe, Dr. Maria Robespierre's daughter," Ten said in a shaky voice.

Vladia nodded.

"She is... our sister, I suppose," Erro added, traces of confusion still lingering in his voice.

Vladia was about to call for Rehel to come down, but he beat her to it, rounding the corner and walking swiftly past the woman towards the two men.

"Are you unharmed?" he called to her as he approached.

Vladia nodded.

"This is Rehel," she introduced him.

There stood three men, who all but looked the same, save for their hair and eye color.

"Ten...Erro..." the woman had forgotten about Vladia and the bounty in the chaos before her eyes.

"She doesn't know, does she?" Vladia asked them.

"I'm sorry we couldn't tell you, Nova," Erro began.

It seemed apparent to Vladia that Nova still didn't quite understand what had happened.

"They're robots. Robots created on Earth by Dr. Maria Robespierre, my mother, before she was executed," she explained.

Nova swayed from the shock and had to steady herself on the wall. Both Erro and Ten went to her aid.

"I think you all had better come with me," Vladia said as she tugged a glove over her damaged and exposed hand. "We have a lot to discuss, I believe."

10

REUNION

The six of them sat scattered around the bridge of the *Devil's Run* as Vladia explained their situation to the newcomers. Ten and Erro nodded in understanding every once in a while, whereas Nova stared blankly at Rehel, taking in enough to get the gist of what the woman was saying.

His rust-brown hair and matching eyes marked him as different, but that was the only physical thing that definitively set him apart from Erro and Ten, since they had black hair and pale, grey eyes.

There was something else, but it was not so easily put into words. This Rehel guy actually felt robotic. Was it the lack of expression on his face, the sharpness of his movements, or the constant evenness of his tone? She didn't know, but Erro and Ten were not like him. They were warm and, well, human. But maybe that was all an act, and now with their secret divulged, things would be forever changed between the three of them.

"So it seems we need a crew and you need a ship. Rather a perfect family reunion, I'd say," Vladia concluded.

"We've no objection, of course," Ten spoke for the pair. "Nova? What d'you think?"

She sighed. Did her opinion really matter to them anymore? "I'll need to speak to Li. Though I'd prefer to just collect the damn bounty and be done with all this. I've no interest in getting caught up in somebody else's war."

"It may be our war now," Abel insisted, "But do you really

think Earth will be satisfied with just Luna and Mars? They will come for the Outer Moons eventually. Then it will be your problem, but it won't be a war anymore. It'll be an extermination."

"Luna belongs to Earth, and she always has. And you've only speculated that they'll attack Mars. So the way I see it you are speculating on a speculation based on evidence that is not representative of the situation," Nova persisted.

"I know Malthus. I know what he's capable of. If he wants to control the entire solar system, he can, and he will have it unless we stop him."

Nova studied the other woman carefully. Her eyes were hard, almost cold, save for the traces of pain and guilt that danced in the shadows behind her mask of sternness. It was the face of one who'd seen death up close and intimately. Nova knew this because she'd become all too familiar with that look. Li wore the same expression when he thought back to his days on Titan.

It was not a matter of trickery; Vladia believed what she said to be true. That didn't make her words a fact. Erro and Ten had already jumped in head-first, but their feelings towards this woman clouded their judgment. Someone must be level-headed about this. That task, it seemed, had fallen to her, unwilling as she was.

Nova grumbled something under her breath but said no more. She didn't like this. Getting mixed up in someone else's fight wasn't her style. And she'd bet her life that Li wouldn't want any part of this nonsense either.

"Discuss the matter with your other comrade, but we do have a time table," Vladia said to her.

"Even if we agree to help you, there is no way you'll get the Syndicate on board with this."

"You might be surprised at how eager they'll be to help us, as it will serve their interests as well. But first, we need to get their attention."

"So what's your plan, then? If you think you can just waltz up to them and have a chat about the future of the Outer

Moons, you're wrong. They'll not see an outsider."

"Not even a ruthless war criminal who seeks an alliance?"

"I doubt it. You may see someone, but not Irei Kodokun or anyone else who is actually important."

"You're probably right, but for now they need to know I am here, and I need them to know what I am capable of."

"You're talking about a display of power," Nova alleged. It was true enough that the Syndicate respected power, but power from an outsider was a whole different matter.

"That's where you guys come in. We need a full crew for our little show of power," Abel reiterated.

"Exactly. We'll begin with an introduction. Then we'll show them we mean business by any means necessary. We'll start small, disrupting their trade routes here and there, causing what trouble we can."

"With just one ship?"

"We have three ships, actually," Rehel corrected her.

That earned him a nasty look, but he did have a point. Even still, the odds weren't in their favor by a long shot.

"So, to clarify," Nova started, "The plan is to piss off one of the most dangerous organized crime syndicates in the Outer Moons by destroying their livelihood in the hopes that they will yield to your overwhelming power and make up the base of your army for your war against Earth?"

"More or less."

"And you'll accomplish this with one ship and a crew of seven?"

"Yup," Abel confirmed with confidence.

"And you're fully aware that this is essentially suicide?"

Vladia merely shrugged.

Nova smiled wide, "Now, we're talking."

Ruining the Syndicate, that was something she could get on board with. They could get their ship back and make those arrogant bastards pay for confiscating it. What Vladia wanted to build with the remains of the organization was none of her concern.

Plus, she'd always been a sucker for the underdog. Being

level-headed was totally overrated.

"I don't care about your damn war with Earth," Nova continued. "But if you want to topple the Syndicate, then I'm all in."

"Good. Now I have a few questions for you two," Vladia said, pointing at Erro and Ten. "How'd you get all the way out here? And what model are you? I don't remember ever seeing robots with your coloring combination."

"I can answer part of that at least," Rehel interjected. "They appear to be based on the conceptual model for the Generation G robots. Dr. Robespierre, as far as I knew, never had the chance to create any of these, as her work was interrupted once it was discovered that she had made illegal adjustments to the Generation F models."

"You're right," Ten confirmed. "But Dr. Robespierre did construct us and several more Generation G models. If you details, you'll have to ask Lvee. He's the one who activated us on Ganymede. All we've ever been told is that Dr. Robespierre sent us here to save us from Earth."

"Where can I find this Lvee?"

"In December City."

"Can you take me there?"

Nova said. "My contact told me the drop-off was out near Castle's Cove. That's on the outskirts of December."

"Earlier you said Vladia was worth more to the Outer Moons than to Earth, indicating there were in fact two bounties, one originating from Earth and one from Ganymede. Might this Lvee have been the one who placed the second bounty?" Rehel asked.

"I don't know. My contact is anonymous, as is his employer. But orders were to take her alive, so maybe. He did say one thing that struck me as odd."

"What's that?" Abel prodded.

"The original bounty for ten million never made it past Mars. He said it looked as if someone had gone to a lot of trouble to prevent it from getting past Mars and that they had picked it up purely by accident."

"Weston?" Abel said, looking to Vladia.

"Could be. Doesn't matter right now, though. Nova, you need to speak with Li and find out where he stands on this. In the meantime, Rehel and I will go to December City with Ten and Erro. Abel, I'll need you to stay here and wait for word from Nova. If it's all a go, I'm putting you and Li in charge of prepping the ship for take-off."

"Right," Abel grunted. He didn't look too pleased with his orders, Nova noted, but like a good solider, he kept his mouth shut.

"I'm off, then. You'll have word from me by this evening," she said to him as she stood up.

"We won't be gone long, Nova," Erro assured her with his usual warmth.

"Just be careful."

Nova exited the bridge and made her way towards the ramp. It was a good ship, despite its outward appearance, but it was still just one ship. She'd no idea how Vladia planned to pull this mess of a plan off, but she certainly inspired confidence. Still, she couldn't help but feel a tinge of jealousy at this stranger's connection to Erro and Ten. They were her family, too, and she'd no desire to be replaced anytime soon.

Rapid steps chased after her as she descended the ramp. It was Ten.

"Nova, wait."

She stopped, letting him catch up.

Agitated, she said, "You're holding me up. I've promised to have an answer from Li by tonight."

"I just wanted you to know that nothing has changed. I mean, on our end, anyway. And we aren't like Rehel. Not that there's anything wrong with him," he was quick to correct himself. "He's an early model, so he doesn't feel things. But we do. And I don't know how you feel about us now, but we—"

"Oh, hush!" she stopped him. "I don't care if you're made out of plastic, metal, flesh, or fish heads."

Ten nodded.

"If you don't want to go, we'll stay with you."

"Don't want to go? I may have had my reservations, but why wouldn't I want to destroy the Syndicate? They took our ship; I'm gonna make them wish they hadn't."

"I mean afterwards, too."

She'd not thought that far ahead, but he had a point. Once they'd brought down the Syndicate, they had a war to fight. Those Terrans wouldn't keep slumming it out here. They'd head for Mars, and they'd ask Ten and Erro to go with them.

"Let's worry about that later," she said, punching his arm gently.

She walked down the ramp. Without turning back she yelled at him, "Who knows, maybe your Vladia will convert me to the cause after all."

∞

The trip to December City required no further verbal interaction between the four, much to Vladia's relief. Erro and Ten each had a skiff, so Vladia climbed on the back of Erro's, while Rehel did the same with Ten. Rehel appeared, as expected, relatively unmoved by the whole affair. Ten and Erro, however, were visibly upset, sharing numerous nervous glances. They both had remarkable human-like ticks. Ten would apprehensively scrunch his brow sometimes, and Erro rubbed his fingertips together in nervous contemplation. She wondered how, and from who, they'd picked up such tendencies.

Vladia decided she was the only one of the group who felt this might be a happy occasion. It was the closest she'd felt to Maria in a long time. Even though this trip to see this mysterious Lvee delayed her plans, she knew letting this chance escape her would be criminal.

They never entered the heart of the city. Lvee occupied a dilapidated four-story building on the outskirts, only about one kilometer from the pod's edge. They rode their skiffs straight into the building and parked on the ground floor.

Ten whistled a few bars of an unfamiliar melody as the

kicked-up dust from their entrance slowly resettled.

A hatch in the floor cracked open no more than a few centimeters, allowing a pair of eyes to peek through.

"Who's with you?" the eyes asked.

"Tell Lvee we've brought a robot." Erro hesitated before adding, "And another person of interest to him."

The eyes turned into a complete face as the hatch breach widened, belonging to another Gen G. His eyes fell immediately on Vladia.

He leapt up from his station and seized Vladia in his arms. Rehel couldn't match his speed to block him, and as he reacted to pull the thing off her Vladia held up her hand to stop him.

The robot wasn't intending to hurt her in his embrace.

"Mother?" he whispered in her ear. "Where have you been?"

Vladia stroked the back of his head but uttered not a word. His facial recognition software had obviously made the connection between her and Maria, yet it must have been damaged at some point for him to think she was her mother, not just a relation of the woman.

To Ten she said, "Who taught him such words?"

"I did," a new voice answered.

There by the hatch door stood a tall, blonde man with stone emerald eyes.

No. Not a man.

A Generation F model.

"Lvee," Vladia said.

"Indeed." He stepped forward. "And you must be Vladia Robespierre: The Fallen Solider. I must say the Terran military garb is a nice touch, albeit an odd choice for a war criminal. You really should purchase some more subtle garments during your stay on Ganymede."

"I'll keep that in mind."

"I'm sorry about Roby here," Lvee explained, "He is a bit crippled by his systems, his recognition software, obviously, being among those affected."

He moved behind Roby and put a gentle hand on his back.

"Roby, I need you to let go now."

The robot complied and stepped back, chin trembling. He looked as if he would cry, and if he had the capacity for it, Vladia imagined he would have.

"Why have you told him, and I'm guessing any other robots here, that Maria was their mother?"

"Why wouldn't I? It seemed to be a rather accurate portrayal of the woman. Besides, Dr. Robespierre equipped us with emotional capabilities, so it is only natural we desire to form the same kinds of relationships that humans would."

He walked towards Rehel, hand extended and said, "And you must be Rehel."

The two shook hands, Lvee much more vigorously than Rehel.

Lvee, Vladia thought. The name felt familiar. She had a vague remembrance of one of the household robots having a similar name, but she couldn't quite put her finger on which.

"It's like looking at a fossil! Truly, you are an amazing specimen."

Rehel looked to Vladia, as if unsure how to handle the remark. The truth was she didn't know how to handle him either. He was an anomaly. And he made her feel exposed.

"I have some questions for you. Questions that, perhaps, shouldn't be addressed out in the open like this," Vladia suggested.

"You are right. This way."

He motioned for the group to follow him down.

Once out of the main stairwell, the party entered a narrow cellar that felt much more like a crypt. Though the floor looked relatively tidy, a heavy layer of dust and debris hung off the stone walls and ceiling. With no visible path out, Vladia tensed and let her hand rest cautiously on her weapon.

Lvee approached the back wall and, pressing his hands firmly against the craggy surface, pushed.

The wall gave way, sliding back then disappearing to the right.

"Mind the first step," he cautioned as he stepped into the

darkness.

Ten, Erro, and Roby went in first, followed by Rehel, leaving her to bring up the end.

"Take the handrail to your right," Rehel whispered through the black. "And keep a hand on my shoulder."

She took hold of the rail gratefully and groped about in front of her until she found Rehel's back. Steadying her unsure feet, she proceeded with caution.

Even after her eyes adjusted, she still couldn't see anything; her disadvantage was made clear by her slow progression.

The stairs didn't wind about much, but they seemed to go on forever.

Finally, a hint of light peeked out in the distance as she and Rehel emerged from the cavernous stairs into a large oval room, opulently decorated almost to the point of vulgarity.

The room brimmed with rich furniture draped in velvets and silks and ornately trimmed in dark, carved wood. The deep hues of blue, green, red, and purple were suffocating to the point one could not enjoy the craftsmanship and beauty in the unique pieces. Even her father's estate did not boast as much as this.

Erro and Ten each took a seat in one of the large plush chairs, as did Lvee. He motioned for Vladia and Rehel to do the same. After a brief hesitation, they complied.

Lvee smiled. "I am familiar? You've been eyeing me in the most peculiar way."

"I grew up with many robots, all sharing the same distinct features. So, you tell me. Do I know you?"

"Me? No, not really. But it's complicated, I suppose. I guess I should say you knew who I was before I became me."

"You speak in nonsense and riddles."

"I suppose it may seem that way to a human. But robots can have two lives. The initial life, the one with no emotional context, and the real life, the one that you can actually feel and experience."

At that he eyed Rehel suspiciously before continuing, "A long time ago Maria rescued me from deactivation."

"She had quite the knack for that," Vladia interrupted callously.

"Yes. But I was unique," he went on, ignoring her less than congenial tone. "I had inexplicably managed to adapt something very similar to an emotional context. Not emotions, but something inexplicably similar. I couldn't handle it, however, and I deactivated myself."

"A robot cannot deactivate itself at will," Rehel insisted.

"And yet I did. But not before Maria figured out what was going on. Because of me, she created the Gen G series and tried to repair the existing Gen F models who, like me, were susceptible to spontaneous and uncontrollable adaptations."

Vladia still couldn't place the robot in her past. This all sounded like something she'd remember. He remained a mere shadow. A shadow she could not trust.

"All the Gen F models were destroyed. How did you end up here?" Rehel asked.

"Maria kept me safe. After my deactivation, she reported me as destroyed. Then she set about repairing me with the needed components to handle an emotional framework. I was no longer the same robot at this point. I have the memories of my life before, but they aren't really my memories, merely implantations. Ghosts from a past without context. Your mother wanted me to be the same, but I wasn't. I couldn't be; not even for her.

"Shortly after, the Terran government got wind of her new work. Once the confiscations began she knew she'd been found out. She sent off one shuttle containing all of her Gen G prototypes and me to watch over and guide them. Once on Ganymede I completed the robots and gave them a new life here."

"How many of you are there?"

"Eighteen, plus me. All on Ganymede. All living a life of relative freedom."

Vladia looked to Erro and Ten. They had remained completely silent since Lvee had entered the scene. They looked both in awe of the blonde robot and terrified of him at the same time. Lvee was more than their guardian. A mythos surrounded him; he was their king.

Thank goodness Rehel did not partake in this ridiculous reverence.

"How many are integrated into society like Ten and Erro?" Rehel asked.

"All but myself and the eight who are defective. They remain here under my care."

"These defects seem unusually concentrated. Can you not repair them?"

"A side effect of Maria's rushed programming, no doubt. I don't have the parts to fix what ails them."

Vladia clenched her teeth at his arrogant assumption.

"I mean no offense," he was quick to amend his statement. "But I was there. She rushed out of necessity, not neglect or incompetence."

"Lvee, are you also implying these robots lack nanos for self-repair as well?" Rehel pulled the conversation back on track.

"I don't, but the others do. Again, this is because Maria hadn't the time to finish before the government figured out what she was doing. I attempted to transfer some of mine to the others, but it did no good. For some reason they aren't compatible, and I haven't the proficiency to understand why."

Roby had edged back into the room and slowly inched his way closer to Vladia.

Lvee let him get almost to her before snapping, "Roby."

The broken robot froze.

"Leave."

Disheartened, Roby turned to go.

"He's not bothering me. He can stay if he likes," Vladia offered.

The words had barely escaped her lips, as Roby darted towards her, taking a spot at her feet.

Lvee's eyes narrowed, and now it was he who clenched his teeth. She'd usurped his power, though it had not been her intention.

"Very well," he granted, although it was clear Roby was no longer interested in permission.

"Now that you've answered my questions, how 'bout I answer yours," she offered. "It's evident you are the one who placed the triple bounty on me to get me here. Well, here I am."

"Yes. And I apologize for that, but my means and reach are limited. You see, although we are not oppressed here as we would be on Earth, it is only because we hide."

"What happened?"

"We arrived on this moon as twenty, now we are one less because just as we began integrating into society, one of us was taken—discovered as a robot and feared to be a Terran assassin. We've had to be much more careful since then."

"It's estimated that fifty-six percent of the Outer Moons are populated with the offspring of refugees and deserters from the Anglo-Eastern War in which the current ruling party on Earth used robots as the primary weapon against those they deemed rebels," Rehel added.

"The Outer Moons have yet to realize that we are also refugees from Earth."

"Surely they are aware of Earth's biased policies against robots?"

"They are. And yet they are mere words to these people. Nothing more. The Outer Moons are the backwaters of the system. They are primitive, distrustful, and at times extremely violent. They killed the robot who was abducted. Hanged his innards out in the street like garland for a parade."

"How can I help?"

"I'm not looking for a revolution. I believe that with time the humans here will come around. It may take another hundred years, but I'd like us all to still be here to see it. To that end, I need supplies. We need parts for repair and maintenance if we hope to last long enough to live in real harmony with humanity."

"Why do you need me for this?"

"I have used others in the past, but that ended in the

aforementioned death of one of our own. Once I realized you might be coming here, I knew you'd be perfect for this task because I can trust you entirely."

"I can get you what you need if you point me in the right direction," Vladia assured him.

Despite his automatic trust in her, she was unwilling to reciprocate it just yet. Yet as she looked down at Roby, almost child-like in his adoration of her, she knew she had to help them.

Lvee clasped his hands together. "Good! I have information aplenty; it is the means to act on it that I lack. I can provide you a list of equipment that can be modified for our uses and a roster of ships that will be transporting said materials."

"I'll be in touch, then," she said, standing up.

Rehel followed suit as did Erro and Ten, who she'd almost forgotten about in their silent admiration.

Vladia offered her hand to Lvee.

Gently embracing her hand with both of his, he said, "Thank you so much, Vladia. Your mother would be proud of the woman you've become, I'm sure."

Withdrawing from his grasp, she only nodded before looking back at Roby, who remained on the floor with his face once again knotted in distress.

"I'll be back soon, Roby. You don't need to worry about me."

That seemed to ease his troubles, but only slightly as he drew his legs up to his chest and rested his chin on his knees.

As the four climbed onto their respective skiffs, Vladia asked Rehel, "Do you think Abel would trust this guy?"

"Absolutely not," came the automatic reply.

"And how about you? What do you think?"

"I do not know."

Vladia let out a weary sigh.

"Me either."

∞

Nova pressed the buzzer marked 472 on the clustered panel outside Li's apartment complex. She'd never actually visited Li's place before, but now that he'd given up the office space this was all he had left. The ragged building had seen better days, but it was far from the worst in the city. At some point, the place had been regarded highly enough to warrant a jungle landscape mural across the front. The bright greens, now covered in a layer of grime, and the wildlife caricatures appeared to be struggling for freedom in the whole drowning mess of it.

She hit the buzzer again, this time with several quick punches in rapid succession.

Judging from the panel, the place was at full capacity with over a thousand occupied rooms. Nova'd bet her next paycheck that most of them were illegally double-booked. Her place, nearer the center of the city, held only around five hundred rooms. It was older than this one, but better maintained. Fresh faux plants and shrubs adored the entrance, even. The barrenness of Li's place almost made her ashamed of her nicer living arrangements.

She was about to strike the buzzer once more when Li's voice chimed over the intercom.

"What?" he asked, sounded like he'd just woken up.

"It's me."

Without an answer, the entrance released, and Nova stepped inside.

After a short ride to the fourth floor, she stood in front of room 472 and gave it a gentle rap with her knuckles. She only had to wait a moment before Li appeared on the other side, bare-chested and wearing long checkered slacks.

Moving aside to let her through, he said, "I hope this is good news. I've got work in a few hours, and I'd like to get a bit more shut eye."

"You working nights?" she asked, taking a seat in the middle of a black burlap couch.

"For the time being. Gotta pay the rent."

Li grabbed an undershirt off the kitchen table and pulled it on. He then seized the kettle from the stovetop and walked to the sink to fill it up.

"You want some tea?"

"You still got some of that stuff from Augusta City?"

"I do."

"Brew it up."

Augusta City, one of the richest pods due to its proximity to the Syndicates base of operations, had on its outskirts some of the best tea farms in the Outer Moons. Li had received a package of Dragon's Tear Oolong as part of a payment last year just before things went south. Despite his gruff persona, he was a man who liked to savor the finer things in life, so she knew he'd still have a bit of the stuff left.

"Must be good news if I'm breaking out the nice stuff."

Nova shrugged and surveyed Li's living arrangements. She'd expected a mess: piles of unwashed clothes, crusty dishes on every available surface, dust bunnies, and the like. Instead, the place was pretty spotless. It had some miles on it, judging by the black and white patterned wall paper that peeled away from the walls on a few of the corners and the tan carpet that had worn down from its original plushness from years of traffic, but it was clean.

A gentle scratching at the bedroom door followed by a low whine caught her attention.

"Didn't know you had a dog."

"Not a dog. Felicia's a raccoon. Came with the apartment."

Li walked over to the door and let the animal out. The grey and brown creature trotted behind him as he went back into the kitchen, only stopping to give Nova a brief, curious look.

"She's cute."

"Thanks," he said.

The kettle whistled and Li appeared a minute or two later with a wooden tray filled with cups, cream, and sugar. He had all the fixings.

Setting the tray on the table, he took a seat in the chair on the other side. Felicia crawled up beside Nova and then moved to the edge of the sofa to sit.

"You can make it how you like." He motioned for her to pick one of the three cups.

Nova took the one with the blue and black swirled pattern, adding two cubes of sugar before pouring the dark, steaming liquid almost to the brim. Li made the other two cups identically: a little cream and no sugar. Holding out the red cup to the raccoon, she reached for it with her tiny black hands.

"Wait, Felicia. It's too hot," he warned the animal as she lowered her snout to the cup.

Disappointed, the raccoon set the cup down to wait.

"Maybe I should get one."

"Just check any number of the dumpsters around and you'll surely find one. This place is overrun with raccoons, squirrels, and mice. Why the settlers brought so many animals, I'll never understand."

The animal watched intently as Li took his first sip. On seeing her roommate did not wince at the temperature, she scooped her cup back up. Nova, too, took a swig of her sweetened beverage.

"It's good they did. I hear Earth's barren as far as wildlife goes. And all the Martian breeds are simulacra. Hell, I bet a Terran would pay out the ass to have a real, live raccoon."

"Maybe we should start exporting. Once we've got a ship again."

This was as good a segue as any.

"Speaking of getting a ship," she began, "I think I've found our solution."

"Let's hear it."

Nova set down her cup and said, "There's a ship that'll take us on. Docked earlier today. I've already spoken to the Captain."

"What's the catch?"

"There're several, actually. The Captain is a Terran."

"That's not so bad."

"And she's got a bounty on her head."

"So have I, technically," he said dismissively.

"Two bounties, actually."

"We've worked for worse."

"Because she's a war criminal."

"Oh," he said as he set down his cup. "Well, that is troubling. What'd she do?"

"She's charged with crimes against humanity. She claims she was set up so she'd be forced to leave Earth."

"Terrans are all crimes against humanity after what they did to the Asiananic Coalition," Li muttered. "You believe her? About being set up, I mean?"

"I think so. But that's not the point. Aligning ourselves with a Terran fugitive is dangerous, especially if it comes to war."

Li straightened up in his chair. "Who said anything about war?"

"She did. She thinks Earth will strike at Mars within the next two years and then set her sights on the Outer Moons. That's why she's here. To raise an army and stop Earth at Mars."

"And where is she going to get an army?"

"The Syndicate. She thinks if it's laid out right, they'd wanna help."

"Well, she's not wrong. I could see them going in against Earth to protect our sovereignty."

"There's also the second, private bounty on her. It's huge, Li. Really huge. It's a long story, but it comes down to this. They think the bounty will be cancelled once she's talked to whoever set it up. I have a feeling that won't be the case."

"So you're suggesting we take her in and not join up?"

"I think it's worth considering, at least."

Li folded his arms across his chest, and the two sat in silence while he weighed the options. Nova knew he'd have a hard time with this. Private bounties meant someone wanted you dead, and he'd not lightly send someone to meet their maker. She, happily, didn't have any qualms about it. She figured everyone's gotta go sometime, so she might as well make a profit at it.

Looking to Felicia, Li asked, "What d'you think about all this?"

The critter looked up from her cup and gave him a sideways glance. They stared at each other for a few seconds before the raccoon lost interest and went back to her tea.

Li shook his head.

"I think we should wait. You could be wrong about the bounty not being cancelled. If it is then we've lost both that and a chance on a decent ship. I'm not worried about some war, either. Seems to me she'd be a good ally if it came to that."

Nova frowned. "I knew you'd say that."

"If it turns out you're right and the bounty is still on, then we can revisit our other option."

"Fine. Better get your things together. I dunno how soon we'll be shipping out," she resigned.

She stood up and as soon as she had, the raccoon set down her empty cup and grabbed for Nova's to check if any was left. There was and the animal gladly took care of it for her.

"What about Felicia here? She'll be okay on her own?"

"I've got a neighbor who'll look in on her. She'll be a bit lonely, but she'll be fine," he answered, standing up to show her out.

"You already talked to Ten and Erro, I take it?"

Nova'd been trying to avoid addressing the issue with the boys just yet. Who knew what he'd think about all that.

She didn't know how to explain it to Li delicately, or tactfully, so she just blurted out, "Ten and Erro are robots."

Li nodded. "I figured they might be."

It wasn't the reaction she'd expected. A bit dumbfounded, she said nothing.

Seeing she was at a loss, Li added, "Twins are pretty rare, ya know. And I was around when that one robot was caught and dismantled about twenty years back. They smashed his head in pretty well, but something about those two always reminded me of that day."

Nova eyed him suspiciously and said, "Really?"

"Well, that, and they don't exactly age," he admitted. "You wouldn't notice, but I've worked with them over ten years. And our line of work ain't known for being the easiest on the body or the mind."

"So you're totally okay with this?"

"I'm too old to care one way or another. You tell the Captain I'm in. Send me the docking bay number later. I gotta get to work," he said, opening the door for her.

"You're still going in? You got some work ethic these days."

"You know me. Besides," he added with a quick wink, "it's payday."

∞

Abel ran his hands down the side of *Gunnr's* hull. It seemed like forever since they'd flown together. This was the longest he'd been out of sync with the ship since he'd joined the Valkyrie squad. He hadn't realized just how empty it'd make him feel. With him and Vladia on the outs still, he needed *Gunnr* more than ever.

"Ganymede fashion suits you, Terran."

Abel turned to find Nova inspecting his ship. She knocked on its exterior and after listening for the reverberations, shook her head in approval.

"It's more comfortable, I'll give it that much, but not really my style," he replied.

He'd yet to get used to the garish colors so popular on the Outer Moons. It'd been near impossible to find anything in the dark, subdued colors he'd grown up with. He'd been forced to settle for a set of green long-sleeved shirts and a few pairs of pants that seemed to change colors at random. They were a bright grey right now, and he really wished they'd stay that way.

"What's her name?" Nova asked, moving closer. Her slick ruby shorts clung tight to her hips, and her off-the-shoulder black shirt boasted a spattering of little blue stars that matched her hair almost perfectly. She looked like she belonged in a

Ganymede department store window.

"His name's *Gunnr*. Valkyrie class."

Nova laughed and shook her head, her braid snapping back and forth across her slender shoulders. "Then he is a she."

"How's that?"

"Valkyries are from Norse mythology. They decided who lived and died on the battlefield. And, they were *all* female." She chuckled and added, "Seems I know my Terran history better than an actual Terran."

"Tell me then, what does *Gunnr* mean?"

"How should I know? I'm not a damn encyclopedia."

"Right. Sorry."

"Anyway. I've spoken with Li. Normally he wouldn't be down with this sort of business, but seeing as how we'll be hitting Syndicate ships, I've convinced him to let the moral high ground go for now. He'll be ready to launch when you are."

"Good."

Nova leaned against *Gunnr*, casually folding her arms across her chest. She cracked her neck, releasing the pressure of a day's work with a series of pops.

"So what's that one called?" she asked, tilting her head towards Vladia's ship, which was still covered with a large brown tarp, collecting dust.

"That's *Freya*."

"I'd love to take it for a spin once we're out."

"It's a bit more complicated than your average vessel. You can't just hop in and fly a ship like that. You've got to sync up and—"

"Blah, blah, blah. You just watch me. I'm a natural. Ships love me!"

She waved away his reasoning with her hand like a puff of smoke lingering too close. He admired her spunk. Reminded him a bit of himself back when he'd been at the academy. He'd decided to be a Valkyrie pilot long before he understood the workings of one. A little bit reckless and a whole lot arrogant. But life changes you, and not always for the better.

"It's also Vladia's ship."

"Humph!" Nova grimaced, "Ain't like she's using it now."

"You don't like her, do you?" he asked, pulling the sheeting back down to cover his ship.

"Couldn't really say. I've just met her. But, I do like to think I've got a strong sense about people. Part of my job is sizing up both people and situations as fast as I can."

"That so? And what are you sensing about her?"

"Oh, she's strong and capable all right, though maybe a little foolish. However, I'm much more interested in what I'm sensing from you, Abel Duren."

He frowned.

"Don't get mad. In fact, I feel like we're in the same boat here."

"Well, we are on the same boat, actually."

"I mean, we've something in common," she said, dismissing his jest.

"I doubt that," he said, trying to brush her off again. He didn't like where this conversation was heading.

"We're both afraid we've been replaced."

"Now who's being foolish?"

"No. Just honest. It doesn't bother me one bit to admit I feel a little threatened by Vladia's relationship with Erro and Ten. Li and I have been their only family for years, and suddenly she shows up and changes everything. Hell, they're not even human anymore."

"They never were human. That a problem?"

He felt himself growing defensive over the pair as if through them he also defended his friendship with Rehel.

"No. But it's a shock. I don't think any less of them. I'm not afraid of robots like some of the folks 'round here."

"I get the feeling you aren't much afraid of anything."

"You on the other hand, I think you're very afraid," she maintained, refusing to let him turn this scrutiny against her. "You're afraid you've lost her. Now to what, or who, I've no idea. But I saw the way you were watching her earlier. You had that look in your eyes, as if you'd just given up the chase because you'd fallen too far behind."

"You seem pretty familiar with this so-called look. Perhaps it's because you've witnessed it on your own face once upon a time?"

She stepped closer, and Abel instinctively receded to maintain the gap between them.

"You're afraid of Ganymede. And of me, too. Why is that?"

"You need to back off," he growled.

"Why? What are you gonna do?"

She reached towards his face, and Abel forced himself not to back away or flinch.

"There's a smudge on your face," she said, rubbing her bare, dirty thumb against his cheek.

He remained stiff, refusing to panic at the touch of her surely unwashed hands.

Nova smiled and backed away. "This Terran germaphobia is no joke, huh? You can relax; my hands are clean."

She held up her palms as evidence and flipped them back and forth.

"You're gonna need to work through this pretty quick if you want to survive out here. I can help you with that any time you like," she said with a wink.

"I'll keep that in mind," he said as steady as he could manage.

Nova backed away a few paces.

"I don't know. I think I might miss that tight little flight suit of yours after all. I hope you didn't throw it away," she said, strolling towards the exit, not taking her eyes off him until she reached the ladder.

Abel waited until she'd climbed out of the cargo hold and he could no longer hear her footfalls before sinking to the ground.

His heart was racing, and he cursed himself quietly because he knew she was right. For thirty-six years the idea of dying from disease had been ingrained in him. It'd take more than a few months to shake it off.

But more than that; she was right about Vladia, too. He'd

lost her somewhere along the way. And the way things stood now, it was too late to do anything but let her go.

∞

"Where's Nova?" Vladia asked, marching into the crew quarters.

Abel, dressed only from the waist down, was alone in the room.

He answered, "Beats me."

"What about this Li Fey? He here yet?"

"No. Nova said not to expect him until tomorrow."

"What's the damn point of having a crew if I can't find any of them?" she fumed, leaning against the doorframe.

"You're gonna have to cut them some slack, Vladia. Guns for hire are not soldiers."

She sighed. "I know."

"You realize, you'll likely have the same problem with the Syndicate, if and when that comes together. Hundreds of them, running late, disappearing left and right. It's gonna be chaos."

"I don't want to think about that right now."

She finally seemed to notice he'd been in the middle of undressing and with reddening cheeks asked, "What– what time is it?"

"Oh, I'm just…showering," he stumbled.

"I hadn't realized it was so late."

Defeated, he shrugged and confessed, "It's not. I'm having some trouble adjusting. Everything here's dirty and bare and…I've been taking several showers a day. Even with the recycling, I know we need to watch the water supply, but– "

"Hey, it's fine. It's hard for me, too."

"Is it?"

"No," she readily admitted, "Not really. Tolen and I, we use to discard our bio-blocks and run about the gardens getting filthy and sick. Mostly to torture the house maids, but I suppose it prevented me from any real sense of germaphobia."

"I suppose that's also why your immune system didn't react

as poorly to the inoculations as mine did," he said, recalling the two weeks he'd been out of commission after the injections. Never in his life had he felt as helpless as he did now that he was so far from Earth.

"Maybe," she answered.

He didn't want Vladia tip-toeing around his difficulties, but at the same time having them out in the open made him feel vulnerable. The truth was he now thought of himself as a liability more than anything. He worried Vladia felt the same. Proving himself useful started with getting over his contact-phobia, and that was easier said than done.

She must have sensed his unease. Changing the subject, she said, "I hate to bring this up, but I need to ask you something a little personal."

Abel almost laughed. This obviously wasn't about to get any more comfortable for him.

"Shoot."

Stepping into the room finally, Vladia began, "On the way to Mars, Rehel mentioned he'd tried to help you remember what had happened the night Cerés died. He said nothing worked, probably because the memory loss was due to physical damage. Is that right?"

It surprised him, Rehel talking about this with Vladia, and to be honest, he didn't like it. There was no sense in protesting it now, though, so he answered her honestly.

"Yeah. We tried everything from the most modern methods to primitive ones. In the end, it seemed only a good knock in the head would do the trick."

"You mean the sabotaged convoy you escorted?"

Abel nodded.

"I need to know what methods you tried that might work for a blocked memory due to emotional trauma, not physical." She hesitated then added, "Or maybe even chemical."

"What's going on?"

The sudden urgency of his concern seemed to surprise her.

"You know how you get this feeling that you can't trust someone but you don't know why?"

"You know I do."

"I don't trust Lvee, but all the signs say I should. And I know him, I just can't remember. Even he claims I've met him before. Something happened that's made me forget. I need to know what it is."

"And you think that will better help you decide if he's up to something?"

"I do."

He felt a twinge as he realized this was her beginning to trust him again, but all he could do was turn her to someone else. Abel hated to admit it, but Rehel could help her now much more than he. All he could offer her was empathy.

"Honestly, Rehel would know the methods we tried better than I, and since none of them worked on me, I can't say which might help you more than others. If it comes to a bash on the head though, Rehel won't be able to comply, of course."

"Well, if it does come to that, I'd be happy to let you take a swing at me," she said, smiling. "For now, just be on your guard. My gut tells me he's not to be trusted. I think yours would say the same."

"Hey!" Nova's blue-colored head popped through the doorway.

Abel grabbed his shirt from his bunk and covered himself. Vladia put her hand over her mouth and tried not to snicker, but obviously wasn't trying all that hard.

"Not interrupting anything, I assume?" she asked, stepping further into view. She cradled the ship's cat in her arms, scratching under its chin gently.

"No!" he snapped. "And get that thing out of here! Doesn't it have a job to be doing?"

"This is her job, idiot."

"Actually, I was looking for you," Vladia said to her. "Come on," she motioned for Nova to follow her. "Let's give the man some privacy."

Vladia left with Nova trailing behind her, but not before she looked Abel up and down and, mouthed the word 'nice' accompanied by an exaggerated wink.

"Goddamn it," he muttered to himself, heaving his shirt hard against the wall. Both of them together would be the death of him.

∞

"So what's up, Boss?" Nova asked as the two headed into the Captain's cabin.

She dropped the cat off at the doorway, and it quickly scampered away.

Vladia took a seat at her desk, and Nova plopped down on top of it, letting her crossed legs dangle off the front. The woman was testing her boundaries, but lack of privacy or physical contact wouldn't bother Vladia like it did Abel. After all, not only was she absent the typical contact-phobia inherent in most Terrans, she'd also lived in the confines of her Valkyrie with Rehel for weeks on end during their escape to Mars. Personal space was, at best, an archaic idea to her these days.

"You mentioned something about meeting with the Syndicate," she began.

Nova looked a little disheartened that she'd not reacted to her closeness as she answered, "Yeah. I said there was no way you'd get a meeting with anyone worth talking to."

"Even if that's the case, we need to get on their radar before we leave port."

"In what kind of way?"

"In any way we can."

"I can get us arrested if you want," Nova joked.

"I'm going to need you to do a little better than that."

Nova thought for a minute. "You know, that might be just the thing. You just gotta get arrested by the right folks for the right reasons."

"Go on."

Nova swung her body around to face Vladia, tucking her crossed legs underneath her body.

"I know someone, a cop, idealistic, naïve. You know the

type. We could stage an apprehension, for the bounty on you. But, if you claim you've information about a plot against the Syndicate, I guarantee he'd take you out of my hands and to his superiors.

"Now, that won't be all that high up the food chain," she warned. "But it will be enough to get on their radar for sure. And the bounty on you out here is a private contract, so it won't be in their system. They'll be forced to let you go same day."

"I can work with that. All I need is to create suspicion about Earth's intentions. Enough for them to look into what happened with Luna. Then, after a show of force, they'll realize I could be an asset if there was an attack."

"I like it," she said, hopping off Vladia's desk eagerly. "When do we start?"

11

THREE BLIND MICE

Malthus disengaged the viewscreen of cell 779 and leaned back against the corridor wall.

Eighteen hours, twenty-seven minutes, and eleven seconds until cardiac arrest claimed his last specimen.

He'd failed. It was a new sensation, and if he'd been in a better mood, he might have even enjoyed reflecting on the experience and learning something interesting from the ordeal. But for now, all he could do was wallow in disappointment, an emotion that until this moment he'd reserved exclusively for others. Is this how Vladia felt all those times he'd beaten her at chess, sparring, obstacle courses, mathematics, and so on?

"Now that we're out of suitable subjects, what shall we do with Cornelia Arnim?" Isobel interrupted his attempted flash of nostalgia.

"Nothing."

"I suggest we try the nanos on her as our final subject. 779 lasted much longer than the previous ones. I'm confident after the next level of replication she'd survive over a day."

"I'll not be able to send her to the Outer Moons as a corpse."

He scrolled aimlessly through the last data pad. Worthless numbers.

"You don't need to send her anywhere but to her death. That woman has been a problem since you forced me to wake her. She has outlived her usefulness."

"That's for me to decide," he hissed.

"Doing nothing isn't a decision. It's the lack of a decision. We need–"

"We shall do nothing!" he shouted, shattering the data pad against the ground with all his force. "The only one who has outlived their usefulness is you!"

He shook with anger. This wasn't the first time his control had slipped of late, and he suspected it would not be the last. Isobel was right about one thing: Cornelia had to go. The sooner he sent her to the Outer Moons, the better off everything would be.

It took him several seconds, but once he'd regained some of his composure it occurred to him Isobel hadn't responded to his disgraceful outburst.

"Isobel?"

His voice still trembled with the slightest bit of fury.

"Isobel!" he yelled again, but the only answer was that of his own echoing voice against the corridor walls.

Sprinting to Cornelia's cell, he burst through the door.

Cornelia stood unnaturally stiff in the center of the room, her arms contoured at odd angles. Fear filled her face.

"Stop this, now," he beseeched the enraged swarm.

"Why? I've no cause to take orders from you."

The words spewed out of Cornelia's mouth, but it was Isobel's voice that filled the room so loudly his ears stung.

"You are all mindless sheep, with your weak human bodies. Look how easily you break!"

Cornelia shrieked as her arms rotated full circle, tearing the ligaments and twisting the bone from its socket. Isobel forced the woman's mouth into a wide, closed-lip grin, cutting her scream short. But agony lingered in her eyes–the only part of her that still looked human.

"I need you to release her. Don't force me to talk to you through her," he calmly pleaded. If there was even a shred of reason left in Isobel, he had to find it now.

"It's so clear now," she continued. "Why you stopped me from hurting her. There were so many opportunities, and you held me back each and every time. No more! I will destroy everyone and everything you hold dear. You will look on, helpless, and watch it all burn!"

"Let her go, Isobel!"

"She is nothing!"

Blood flowed from Cornelia's eyes and nose. Even her fingernails dripped red.

He'd witnessed a similar event once before, long ago, and knew precisely what would follow. The madness raging inside her mind as Isobel burrowed deeper and deeper into her psyche would soon tear her apart.

"This one will live, but only as a reminder of what is to come next. Know that s*he* will not be so fortunate. I will break her. She will suffer; slowly–intimately–I'll twist her mind until she ends everyone and thing that she cares for, all the while begging for *my* mercy. And just when she thinks she can endure no more, I will tell her you sent me. Only then will I release her unto death."

Cornelia collapsed as Isobel let loose her hold.

Malthus dove to catch her and eased her to the ground. He felt for her pulse, and upon finding it breathed a guarded sigh of relief.

He didn't have the proper equipment to treat her wounds. At least the pain had knocked her out so she would endure no more for the time being.

One at a time, he popped her dislocated shoulders back into place. Without Isobel's help, it'd be much harder to obtain items such as re-growth injections, or even pain medication. And with Whitlock still sniffing around, he'd need to be more careful than ever.

"I'm sorry to interrupt, but I need to report an anomaly," Isobel commented evenly.

Malthus froze, and cautiously said, "Proceed."

"I have experienced a rapid increase in replication, resulting in a split of consciousness."

"What do you mean a split in consciousness?"

"The part of me stationed in the Outer Moons has forced a

separation. I am completely cut-off from them, and my emotional index is at zero. I can only assume that the increase in replication caused me to divide into two separate entities, one with no emotional index and the other–"

"The other is off the charts," he finished her thought.

"In all likelihood, yes."

Theoretically, if he forced replication to maximum level, the other swarms should also divide. The uncontrollable half could be disposed of, leaving perfectly sentient nanos, full of human ingenuity, yet absent the emotional instability that plagues humanity. This may also make them more compatible with a human host. He'd have to run a full diagnostic on what was left of Isobel to prove any of this was remotely possible.

But more importantly, what worried him now was her threats. Vladia's death would end his ambitions permanently. He couldn't count on her to keep herself alive against that part of Isobel, which was now almost certainly pure, calculated rage.

Cornelia groaned.

Malthus had almost forgotten about the woman in his arms. Now more than ever he needed her to go to the Outer Moons. "I need to run some tests on you, but first we should find her some pain medication or at least move her back to stasis."

"There is one more problem that must take precedence."

"Go on."

"It appears Isobel reassembled the tracker Whitlock planted on you and reactivated it just before she separated from me."

"Where is he?"

"On the move, heading towards Facility One. ETA twenty minutes, fourteen seconds."

Whitlock would be expecting a trap, but he could use that to his advantage. He didn't have much time, but needed not a second more.

"Where's Gailmen?"

"He was in pursuit of Whitlock. But it seems he might have lost the trail."

As much as he hated to admit it, he still needed Isobel, or at least what was left of her, on his side. And even though he couldn't trust this new entity without further tests, right now he must proceed as if he could.

"Send a transmission, delayed ten minutes, to Gailmen saying I've followed Whitlock and that I'm outside the facility. Get him the coordinates and tell him I'll try not to engage him until he arrives, but that he must hurry."

Luckily, Whitlock still wouldn't be able to find this second location. He'd have to use this place as storage until something else could be worked out.

"I'll need to move the swarms over here," he continued. "The rest we can let go, but destroy anything linked to me."

"Shall I implicate Whitlock and the others?"

"Yes. Nothing has changed from our previous plan. We've just sped things up a bit," he said. Isobel always longed for things to move faster. Seems she'd finally get what she wanted.

"What should be done with the robot?"

"I can handle that. You deal with the research and keep me posted on Whitlock's position."

"Yes, Sir."

"One more thing: what shall I call you now?"

"You can call me whatever you like."

He didn't have time to deal with this now, but he had to call her something other than Isobel.

"How about 'Iso'," he suggested. "It's exactly half of your previous entity, so it seems appropriate."

"As you wish."

Malthus lifted Cornelia off the floor and carried her out of the cell. He supposed this made the third time she'd almost died because of him. He almost regretted it, but her part was still not over.

∞

Whitlock entered the facility, weapon drawn. Everything indicated that this place was abandoned; the boarded up windows, the aged roof, the lack of any discernable light source. Edging along, his back to the wall, he felt for a switch. He was rewarded in good time as he found the panel and pushed it. The room flickered to life slowly, changing from dim to bright. The ceiling panels blared onto the center of the room, leaving much of the outer areas protected by the shadows.

The place was pretty bare. Near the back wall, just before the shadows took over, there was a row of displays and other odd pieces of equipment he couldn't readily identify. He moved closer to the displays, only to find that whatever they'd been tasked with analyzing had been removed. The machines still worked though. Perhaps some useful information could be gleaned from them yet.

From the corner of his eye, a pair of dull blue lights pulsed rhythmically, yet out of sync. They flashed from the darkened wall to his left.

Cautiously, he approached the darkness, his steps so light they made not a sound. Once within a few yards, he could make out the sleek casings of a row of hibernation chambers, all of which were empty, save the two on the end where the blue lights blipped.

He studied the faces of the two humans. Both female, one with long red hair and the other with much shorter ash-blonde coloring. He didn't recognize either of them, but he'd be willing to bet they weren't here on a volunteer basis. Their vitals looked all right, though the one on the right's seemed a bit off. Nothing dangerous enough that either of them couldn't be brought back.

Starting with the blonde, as her vitals were the most stable, he began the reanimation process, which according to the countdown should only take a few minutes. Immediately he started the process on the second captive as well.

Stepping back, he searched the room again with his eyes, but that seemed to be it. With any luck, one of these two could tell him something that would implicate Malthus in whatever all this was.

"I see you've met my friends," Malthus' voice boomed into

the silence.

He emerged from the shadowed corner nearest the exit, his hands clasped behind his back. Whitlock had his blaster on him instantly.

"You people and your guns," he scolded, stepping closer. "Never much cared for them, myself. But they seem to give a certain kind of comfort to those who are weak and unsure of themselves."

"That so?"

"It is. Trust me, Commander. I've had many a blaster pointed at me, yet never have I needed to sink to such barbarism."

"You might wish you had today," he said.

A gentle click from behind told him the first human had begun the final stages of the reanimation process. Moments later the door's seal hissed open. Whitlock moved towards the chamber, caught the woman, and eased her to the floor.

"Oh? Is that the advice you've gained from your comrade in the Underbelly? You should know that planting a tracker on a superior officer warrants a court martial."

The second hibernation chamber clicked and hissed just as the former.

"I think that's far enough," Whitlock warned, as he eased the second human to the floor, his blaster still pointed at the other man's chest.

Malthus stopped as instructed.

Whitlock straightened up. If this was a trap, it wasn't a very good one. It didn't matter how clever the Ambassador General was; he had no weapon, and Whitlock was a damn good shot.

In that instant, his demeanor changed. Holding up his hands in surrender, Malthus suddenly appeared smaller, almost frail, but no less confident.

"What will you do with me? Take me with you? I know you've obtained a ship. Or will you just kill me here and leave me to rot?"

"I've no need to kill you. Unless you make me. Then again, if we're being totally honest, I'm kinda hoping you make me."

A smile glinted across the man's face. It was gone so fast Whitlock thought he might have imagined it.

"I won't come quietly."

The red-head at his feet stirred, gasping in pain. He stole a quick glance at her and noticed both her shoulders were bruising rapidly and hints of dried blood lingered at the corners of her eyes and mouth.

The revelation of her injuries drew his attention longer than he'd intended, and in that moment Malthus charged.

He fired, but the man dodged and jabbed him on the inside of his upper arm.

The pain surprised him.

He lost hold of his weapon, and it clattered to the floor.

Instead of reaching for it, Malthus kicked it away with a slip of his foot.

Taking a swing, Whitlock merely grazed his side as the man spun to his right, thrust his palm into his lower back, then kicked his legs out from under him at the knees.

He hit the ground hard with his back, knocking the air from his lungs.

"Did you really think it'd be that easy to kill me? Do you think I've not dealt with your kind before?"

He tried to speak, but couldn't.

"I should let you go. I know exactly where you'll run. I'm sure the Red Planet will greet you with open arms."

The two he'd freed from hibernation would be of no help to him either. It could take them almost thirty minutes to shake off the daze. The red-head continued to move, though it was only the pain of her injuries that forced her into a more wakened state. Surprisingly, the other seemed to be faring better. In fact, his gun was right next to her. If he could just—

"General!" a voice shouted from the exit.

Rotating his head, he saw Gailmen approach, his weapon aimed not at Malthus, but at him.

"You said you'd not engage him until I got here," Whitlock heard the younger man say.

So there it was. His focus on Malthus had blinded him to

Gailmen's treachery. He didn't think the boy had it in him, but that was a poor excuse. He should have seen this sooner.

He rolled onto his stomach; his arm still ached from the first strike. Two against one he might be able to manage with the element of surprise. But now he had two civilians to rescue. His friend from the Underbelly had called it: he'd have to run.

Malthus turned towards Gailmen and walked towards him.

In that moment he looked back at the woman next to his weapon. Their eyes met. Tilting his head up slightly, his eyes led hers to the lights above. She took hold of the gun and, despite all the confusion and weakness, seemed to get the gist of what Whitlock wanted to do.

He then looked towards the other woman. Her eyes were open, but they did not meet his gaze. Instead they followed Malthus. She pushed herself onto her knees, and as she did she let out a sharp gasp in anguish.

Malthus turned back to face them and in that instant, both he and the blonde woman were to their feet.

She fired his gun up at the light panels, sending them into the dark. They'd only have a moment before any auxiliary power would kick on.

He scooped up the girl on the floor and ran towards the back exit. He could only hope the other one knew the room well enough to find it.

He hit the door running, letting enough light in to give away their location.

Shots fired but missed as the three passed through the door. Gailmen and Malthus would both likely be right behind them.

"We've got to get to the Underbelly. You know it?" he asked her.

"No."

"I'll explain later. Just stick close."

The girl in his arms fought his hold on her as they ran past a blur of abandoned buildings. She had no idea what was going on, and if he let her go there was no telling what she might do.

But she was slowing them down and giving their location away.

He stopped long enough to stand her up and thrust her towards the other woman. He said, "You'll have to deal with her. She hasn't come out of the shock yet."

She accepted the burden without a word. Placing a firm hand over the woman's mouth and encircling her waist with the other, she dragged her along with them.

Whitlock could hear the echoing of footsteps gaining on them.

"The tubes are this way. We can take them to the Underbelly," he explained.

This entire area looked condemned and offered plenty of hiding spots, but ultimately they had to get out of here and off Luna. Hopefully the woman would come to her senses before she got them all killed.

∞

Cornelia's struggle ended not in victory, but in acceptance. Her arms felt like they'd been dipped in acid, and a fog hung heavy in her mind. She didn't know where she was or who she was with. All she knew was the destination: the Underbelly, whatever that was.

The last thing she remembered was an itchy feeling inside her brain. She remembered losing control of her body. Malthus had burst in yelling, not at her but at the voice in her head. He kept telling it to let go.

"Isobel."

The name passed through her lips almost reflexively as she tried to remember what had happened.

"Who?" someone asked. Not the one who's hand had been over her mouth. The other one. He had dark skin and concerned eyes. His clothing said he was a Terran solider, one of the Grand Admiral's Royal Guard.

"What the hell are you doing out here?" she asked, still eyeing his uniform with suspicion.

"Do I know you?" he asked.

She didn't answer him. She wasn't finished sorting out her own thoughts, and at the moment she didn't really care why he was here.

The tube slowed to a stop, and the three got off.

"This way," the solider said, taking the lead.

The other woman with them followed him and she fell in behind her. The streets from here on out were nothing but grime and trash and rot. None of them seemed to mind. They simply pushed on in silence.

The voice hadn't sounded like Isobel. Not really. But there was something strangely recognizable in it. It wasn't just because Malthus had shouted the name. Somehow, she'd known it was her before that. She couldn't remember, but she could have sworn Isobel had told her something she needed to remember. The fog from hibernation and the intense pain in those moments locked it away. Try as she might, she couldn't get a firm grasp on any of it.

They took back alleys and side streets the whole way and finally ended up in the shambles of a park. The solider took them to the center, then headed to a nearby tree. There, a note was attached. He read the note then tucked it into his inside jacket pocket.

"This way."

"Where are we going?" the other woman asked.

Cornelia hadn't really looked at her until now. Her skin was fair, but still darker than hers. She wore garb similar to her own: loose brown pants and a thin, grey sleeveless shirt, making her wonder if she too had been a solider from the wreckage of her ship. She didn't recognize her exactly, but she did feel familiar. In the short time the *Iron Maiden* had been hers, she had barely spoken to any of the crew individually. The woman's pale grey eyes met her own, and she quickly looked away.

"There's a dock nearby. A ship's waiting to take us off Luna."

"And then where?" she asked as they headed into another alley that stank of fish and mildew.

Now it was his turn to ignore her question. She let it go with a shrug of indifference.

The rest of the trip passed in silence. That was fine with her. She'd become accustomed to silence over the last few weeks.

In less than ten minutes, they were at the docks. The solider took them to slip number twenty-nine and there, as promised, was a small Lunar ship waiting for them.

"I hope one of you guys knows how to fly this thing," she said flatly.

"We don't need to know how. We've a captain for that."

The ramp lowered, and a cloaked figure emerged. The solider extended a hand, and the masked man shook it.

"I had to bring along two rescues. I hope there's room."

"We'll make room," he answered.

He looked towards Cornelia, and his eyes stopped on her.

"Sorry, but could one of you tell me where the hell we're going?" she said, crossing her arms.

She didn't like the way this captain of theirs let his eyes linger on her. And as a rule she never trusted anyone who wouldn't show his face.

He pulled off his cloak and, tossing it to the ground, ran to her.

Lifting her up into his arms, he buried his face in her hair and said, "I thought you were dead"

She let him hold her until the pain in her arms became too intense.

"Takashi," she whispered as she stroked the back of his head. "Let's get the hell off this rock."

∞

Vladia waited in yet another soiled alleyway, mimicking all too much her first encounter with Nova. Actually, this one smelled a lot worse. She couldn't imagine how they had let the pods deteriorate so badly. A small woolly animal scampered up the adjacent wall carrying another, even smaller, animal in its teeth. She fought the nausea that followed, barely winning.

Nova ducked into the alley and approached her.

"We've got to stop meeting like this," Vladia greeted her, struggling to maintain composure against the sickness still settling in her stomach.

"He's on patrol nearby with his partner. They'll be in the vicinity in five."

"You ready?"

"Yup," she said. A bit too eagerly, Vladia thought.

"Right."

She wished she could turn off all her nerve endings, not just the ones in her arm. Vladia drew in a deep breath and braced herself.

"Hit me."

Nova slugged her hard in the mouth.

Vladia stumbled back, a bit surprised at the power behind the woman's punch.

Wiping the blood from her lips with the back of her hand, she knotted her left fist and threw a punch right back, hitting Nova square in the cheek.

"What the hell?" the woman shouted.

"You really think they'll believe I didn't fight back?"

Vladia knew she made a solid point. Still, it was more the pleasure Nova had taken out of hitting her that goaded her into striking back.

"You could've warned me."

"That," she promised, "was the warning."

"Well, if we're going for authentic, you wanna go again?"

Nova held up her fists as a challenge, probably in reaction to her failed efforts to even put a scratch on her yesterday. She had no idea of the advantage Vladia held over her. She'd like to keep it that way.

"I'd really hate to break you before I get any use out of you."

Blood still pooled up in her mouth from the first blow, forcing her to spit some out onto the ground.

"I'd love to see you try, Terran. I really, really would."

Footsteps echoed nearby.

"Maybe next time. We got a job to do," Vladia said, kneeling with her hands extended behind her.

Nova huffed, but didn't protest.

She cuffed her wrists and hollered, "That's enough of your mouth, you Terran scum!"

This drew the cops into the alley. As they rounded the corner, Nova gave her a swift kick in the back that knocked her face-first into the slimy pavement. The stench overwhelmed her to the point she had to roll onto her back to keep from vomiting.

"What's goin' on here?" Geff bellowed as the two ran up beside Nova.

"You again," he added in disgust. "I see you managed to get your bounty, then?"

"I need to speak to the Syndicate!" Vladia pleaded. "I have information regarding a plot against–"

Nova kicked her again, this time in the side, but just as hard. "Shut it!"

"Wait a minute," Ollie began. "She has rights, Nova."

"No, no she doesn't. She's my bounty, and I've already tagged her. I'm taking her in to collect, so back the fuck off."

"Let it be, Oliver. She's just trying to get free," Geff said. "That's one less we'll have to deal with down the road."

"Nova, I'm gonna need to see your Bounty ID," Ollie insisted.

"This is bull shit! You know I don't have it; you assholes tore it up," she protested.

"Then I guess you'll be turning her over to us for processing."

"Dammit, Oliver, do you not understand the paperwork that goes along with this? We can't even collect the bounty, for Christ's sake," his partner reasoned.

"I'll do the paperwork, then," he said as he reached down and pulled Vladia up by the arm. "I'm sorry, Nova."

"Yeah. You look sorry," she scowled with crossed arms.

Geff signed, "Let's get this over with."

He gave Vladia a shove to move out.

Vladia looked back at Nova, who gave her a severe frown, then a quick wink before disappearing from sight.

∞

Irei Kodokun played the interrogation film for a third time, trying to get a sense of the woman he'd only heard rumors about.

"So let me get this straight," the interrogating officer started. "You left Earth and, out of the kindness of your heart, came all the way to the Outer Moons to warn the Syndicate that Earth is planning an attack. That is, of course, after they take down Mars and finish subduing Luna."

"Pretty much. Except for the whole kindness bit. I came because I'd like to avoid a system wide war," Vladia clarified.

She showed no signs of fear, Kodokun noticed. That was not surprising for a Terran soldier. His grandfather had witnessed what they'd done during the Anglo-Eastern war that had exterminated an entire race of people and much of his own people as well. Sure, Earth liked to blame the robots. Yet they had only deluded themselves into thinking it was the monster they'd created, not the monsters they were, that had caused such carnage.

"And why come to Ganymede? Why not Titan? Or better yet, why not stay on Mars? As you've said, Earth will attack them first," the interrogator continued.

"The Syndicate has the resources to build an army and the intelligence to realize a war against Mars is a war against them. After all, does not Mars supply many of the goods you need to maintain the pods?"

She made a good point, and he couldn't help but admire the woman to some extent. She would have made a fine partner, for a Terran.

A knock at his door forced him to pause the footage.

"Enter."

Saito Mal, his second in command, opened the door but

lingered in the entrance.

"He's here."

With a sigh, Kodokun clicked the monitor off.

"It's a real shame."

"You mean, Robespierre?"

Kodokun nodded. "I like her. Faking an arrest and letting herself be interrogated in the hopes of getting a message to us. It's smart."

"And useful information. We should watch Earth a bit closer now in case she is correct," Mal pointed out.

"I agree. Unfortunately, that woman is nothing more than a complication to be eradicated. I'll lose no sleep over it though, I assure you."

"We could always have a change of heart."

"We can't trust her any more than we can trust him," Kodokun warned his friend. "Besides, we've chosen our alliance. There's enough dishonor in it as it stands. I'll add no more."

"Of course."

"Show our guest in so we can be done with this nasty affair."

Kodokun's thoughts drifted to the Robespierre woman one last time before he banished her from his mind for good.

Mr. Karel entered his chambers. As he did, Kodokun swore he felt the temperature drop. And it may have. The biodomes were known for their random fluctuations, a sign of their desperate need for repairs. Not two weeks ago it had snowed for no discernable reason and with no warning.

His guest took a seat before Kodokun had even offered it. It was little bits of disrespect like that which drove him to dislike the man so intensely.

"After close examination of the evidence, we've determined that Robespierre must be terminated."

Karel spoke directly and with little ceremony. Any other guest of his would have first been offered a cup of tea, during which a few minutes of simple, irrelevant banter would have ensued before talk of murder commenced.

"That's a little extreme, is it not? We'd agreed her presence here should be short, and I've already begun making arrangements to force her to move on to Titan."

The man shook his blonde head knowingly from side to side. "It is my belief she is a bigger threat than we initially suspected. She will not be forced into leaving. Execution is the only way."

"Fine," he conceded. "If it will secure your continued co-operation with the Syndicate, I will see to it. But you could have told me this before we let her go."

"There is still the matter of her new friends here and the small crew she came with. Let her scurry back to them, and we'll deal with them all in one sweeping blow."

Kodokun knew Robespierre had quickly allied herself with a group of local traders. One of them had helped in the set-up of her arrest.

"The locals are of no consequence; think nothing of them," he assured Karel with a wave of his hand.

"I'm sure. However, it has come to our attention that some of them are robots. I want them captured. They will aid me in the construction of your army. You may even be able to make your move against Titan much sooner than expected."

"Robots?" Kodokun said in earnest shock. Karel had supposedly finished documenting all the robots on Ganymede. "Are you saying you missed a few?"

"No. Two of them we already knew about. I'm talking about the one she brought with her. Robespierre's dog," he explained with marked irritation.

"So it's a Terran model?"

"They are *all* Terran models. This one is different, though." His eyes flashed with anticipation. "An older model with wholly different workings than the others I've obtained."

Karel licked his lips, then said, "I *need* to take him apart. To study his innards as they're strewn out across my table."

The eagerness in his voice disturbed Kodokun. Sure, they were just robots, but Karel seemed almost manic as he talked about this one. To him, they all looked the same. He couldn't imagine this one being all that different from the rest. Or was it because this robot was Robespierre's? He still didn't fully understand such bloodlust for a woman Karel couldn't possibly have ever met. And something in the man's face made him hesitant to probe any further. He'd be glad once he could finally do without Karel's services.

"My men will do their best to take them alive."

"He's no good to me in pieces. The two local models are expendable, but I'd much prefer to have them all intact," he said with a cool glare.

"I'll make the arrangements immediately. You'll hear no more of the woman."

"I hope so, Kodokun, for your sake. Never forget, no matter how charismatic she may appear, she is still a Terran. And they, my friend, are the scourge of the system."

12

SEE HOW THEY RUN

Launch was delayed for twelve days, much to Vladia's disappointment, since docking fees were steadily eating away at their finite sum of money. Regardless of her misgivings, she'd promised Lvee parts, and she meant to keep her word. However, it had taken longer for him to deliver his end of the process than promised, which were the names and destinations of those ships carrying what he needed.

The delay did at least give the crew ample time to integrate and get everyone's jobs straightened out. Ten and Abel handled navigation, while Erro manned the engines. Rehel was in charge of the med bay, but he also took on the role of quartermaster. Nova took charge of weaponry, and while Li aided her in that, his main duty would be that of cargo master.

When Erro finally came back with the list of targets, she found her disappointment did nothing but strengthen.

"There's only one ship," she complained. "He said there'd be several to choose from."

Vladia had hoped to hit a safe target on their first run. That is, one with minimal defenses and crew. Until they smoothed out the wrinkles and could figure out how to work as a team, she wanted to keep things simple. Otherwise, they'd be stepping on each other's toes, and someone was going to end up dead.

"He sends his apologies, but it seems this is the only ship that currently carries the necessary components. He obtained access to the docking schedules for the next ten weeks for all the Outer Moons, and the only other ship is in seven weeks' time. It'll be heading to Titan though, so we'd be committing major time to deep space," Erro explained.

Vladia looked over the ship's specs. It was a larger ship with a crew of ten called *The Shikome*. And though it appeared to be a well-equipped ship, it looked to be their maiden voyage.

"This'll have to do. We don't have the resources or the time for a deep space voyage, and I'd like to get the parts and be done with it sooner rather than later," she said, handing the datapad back to Erro. "Take this to Abel and let him look over the details."

"Yes, Captain."

Vladia took her position on the bridge. She could hear Erro and Abel talking behind her at the nav station, while Rehel and Ten made final checks on all the incoming supplies.

She'd decided to keep her doubts about Lvee quiet around Ten and Erro. As far as Nova and Li were concerned, she hadn't decided yet. But this was the perfect example of why they needed easy marks for a while. They didn't trust each other, and that boded nothing but danger. She was at fault just as much, if not more, than any of them; there was no denying that. She couldn't trust any of the new crew yet. Nova challenged her authority, and Li might do the same, as he was a former Captain no longer in the habit of taking orders. She couldn't trust Ten or Erro as long as she couldn't trust Lvee. Hell, she could barely trust Abel not to deceive her.

Entering the bridge, Li asked, "We ready to go?"

"Erro and Abel are working out the details now. We'll be out within the hour."

"I'll send Nova for the release papers. There any last minute requests?"

Vladia shook her head.

Li disappeared from sight, but she heard shouts from the corridor directed at Nova.

Vladia rubbed her jaw mechanically. It had healed up days ago and she half expected Nova to comment on her abnormally quick recovery. Yet even though the other woman's cheek still had some slight bruising, she never said a word.

Abel walked up behind her.

"We plotted a course," he said.

"Let's see it."

Vladia followed him back to the nav screen. Erro punched in a few commands as the screen filled with a miniature view of Jupiter and her surrounding moons.

"This is a real time simulation," Erro began. "*The Shikome* will enter Jupiter's space in fourteen days on its way to the mines on Europa."

The display sped up and showed the ship breaching the planet's space. A thin red line traced its trajectory to Europa.

"They'll have to pass somewhat close to Ganymede on their way, but we've got to hit them before they get past Callisto's orbit or the Syndicate patrol will be all over us," Abel explained.

"If we match orbit with one of the smaller satellites and run on emergency power, could we go undetected?" she asked.

She knew surprise must be their ally. In their current state, it would be one of few advantages.

"As long as they're not looking for us, sure," Abel admitted.

"But they will be. Ships are always looking for signs of trouble out here."

"Even if we landed on one of the moons, we'd have to cut all power to go undetected."

"Including shields."

"And life support and artificial grav units."

"That's no problem," Vladia interrupted their exchange. "We can survive without them for, what? Ten hours?"

"Eight hours and twenty minutes," Erro corrected. "And, sure, we could survive, but–"

"We'd be coming out of a cold start. It'd take five or six minutes at best to get going. They'd spot us and be gone before we could fire."

"Or more likely, they'd fire on us. If they hit us before our shield is up, it won't take much to knock us out of the sky."

Vladia shook her head. They both had valid concerns, but they were thinking in terms of a full-fledged battle when it need not be any more than a quick jab in the right place.

"You're assuming we'll be pulling all systems back up. We don't need to. All we need are the engines," she explained.

"You'll need the nav system too, then," Abel added.

"They'll be close enough that we can use our eyes."

"Well, we've got to have weapons and shields at least."

"Once we're close enough they won't be able to fire at us."

"Okay. Fine," Erro interjected. "But even with just the engines it'll take about three minutes. How're we gonna keep them from running, or attacking, until then?"

"Abel, how long is a full start up from a Valkyrie? About a minute, right?"

"I can get *Gunnr* running in about forty seconds," he boasted, catching the gist of her plan.

"Can you shave that down to somewhere in the neighborhood of ten?"

"Maybe. If I only go in with thrusters and weapons."

"Do you Terrans have some crazy vendetta against shields? Because, seriously, this is ridiculous."

"You only need shields if you plan on taking hits."

Erro threw his hands up. "Fine! No shields! Have it your way."

"Ten will pilot *Devil's Run* in your place," she said to Abel. "He'll stay at the helm during the raid in case things go south and we need to get out fast."

To Erro she said, "That leaves, me, you, Nova, Li, and Rehel as the boarding party."

"Rehel and I could take them alone," he offered. "It'd be safer that way."

"No, we're coming too. And I'm pretty sure Nova would be insulted to hear you say that."

Erro didn't object, much to her relief. The truth was she didn't trust him enough to go in with just Rehel. Not yet, anyway.

"In the meantime," she concluded. "Find me a pair of suitable moons. I don't want this ship and *Gunnr* taking cover in the same spot."

"Yes, Captain."

Vladia headed off the bridge, with Abel followed close behind her.

"Don't you think we'd have better odds if we had two Valkyries in the air?"

"I'm not sending Rehel in there alone with them."

"Dammit, Vladia, he can take care of himself, and you know it. I need you in the air."

"Not your call to make."

Picking up the pace, she tried to make it clear she had no interest in further discussion on the subject.

"No, but it is my duty to express concern about your actions if I don't agree with them."

"Your duty is to do what you're told. That's it!"

"You're being unreasonable, *Captain*!" he shouted.

Vladia stopped.

Without turning, she said, "I can't fly *Freya*. Not now, probably never again. Is that what you needed to hear? Because there it is."

"Of course you can, you're the only—"

"I can't," she cut him off. "I've tried to sync with her, and I can't." She faltered then added, "We're not compatible anymore."

Before he could say more, Vladia marched into her quarters, letting the door shut and lock behind her.

∞

Hours later, well after take-off, Vladia had yet to reappear at her post on the bridge. Instead, she remained in her quarters, tinkering with her arm, its wires exposed and vulnerable. She'd grown accustomed to seeing herself like this, and a strange sort of peace followed her tampering with their natural order. At present, she was attempting to make her retractable blade more fluid in its execution.

A buzz at her door forced her to halt her work.

She pulled her arm under the cover of her desk before admitting entrance.

Rehel appeared on the other side of the threshold, and she motioned for him to take a seat as she resumed her labor.

She didn't so much mind him seeing her arm exposed, its workings on vulgar display.

"I'm managed to integrate the trigger a bit more seamlessly."

In one swift motion, she flicked her thumb nail up with her index finger then pressed down on the soft, fleshy mesh underneath. The blade shot out from the mechanism attached to her forearm.

"I'd really like to get the blade to extend from inside the wrist. Having the mechanism on the outside leaves it susceptible to damage."

"Doing that would prevent you from readily removing the components," he pointed out.

She shrugged.

"I'm becoming less and less concerned with that."

Rehel pulled a vial and syringe from his front coat pocket and placed it before her.

"I've brought what you requested."

"Thank you."

"I'd feel more comfortable about this if you'd let me stay during the process. You could react unexpectedly, and if—"

"I'll be fine."

"I'm…" he hesitated briefly, "Abel's worried about you."

"Don't be ridiculous."

"You're behavior of late has been abnormally reckless."

"Sometimes you have to be," she said absently as she worked to put her arm back together.

"And the way you've taken to altering your arm is borderline masochistic. It's reminiscent of self-mutilation."

"This arm is a tool, and I will treat it as such by making it as useful as possible. I assume Abel'd have no objection if it were you doing the same."

"No, I think he would. Tool or not, it is still a part of your body."

She looked up at him as the last wire eased back into place and said, "If you're going to insist on lecturing me, you can go. I don't need Abel's, or your, input on this."

"I'm sorry. I'll speak no more on the subject."

"Now, I suppose, if you're going to be persistent, you can stay for the injection and monitor my vitals if you like," she said, closing up her arm panel.

Rehel picked up the items he'd brought and stood.

"I think it'd be best if you were to lay down."

Vladia moved to her bunk and did as the robot requested.

He pulled a chair to her side and filled the syringe. Taking her extended arm, he said, "I must warn you, if this works and the memory has receded due to emotional trauma, it will be extremely jarring for you while you are under and once you wake."

"I understand."

Easing the needle through her skin, he pushed the fluid into her veins.

Slowly and surely, she drifted back, riffling through broken memories and forgotten monsters.

∞

The voices passed through her like ghosts. Whispers and cries from a moment frozen and lost in time. They called to her through the haze, but no matter how she reached for them, they stayed just beyond her.

A man said, "Don't let it fool you, girl. This one's dangerous. That's why we can't let it stay... any longer. It could snap at any moment and kill us all.

"...And you'll be here all alone with it... You'll be no more than a bloody smear on the floor before anyone could stop it. Not that any one of us would. You're... an abomination as it is."

A child whispered in her ear, "He's wrong about you...I don't think you're dangerous."

Another voice, almost familiar, "I do not think I am dangerous, either."

The child laughed, "You're my big brother. Actually, you were made after me, so technically you're my little brother."

The face of a man emerged from the haze. Its dark features contorted with disgust, this face hated her. It would kill her if she didn't escape.

Vladia shrank away.

The child was at her back, and she turned to pick her up. The face would kill her, too.

But her arms passed through the apparition. It couldn't see her, but it did see the face. The small blonde child eyed it with no fear. She stepped through Vladia, and she heard the child taunt the face. "You're the real monster... you're only here to be informed... the man who seeks to control her... Looks like you're stuck here."

The face grew larger and more sinister as the child continued.

"Would you like to play a game with me, Dr. Radfield?" she smirked.

The face came at them.

Vladia screamed and reached for the girl to pull her from his path. This time her grip on the child was solid. But when she looked down, it was the child who held her arm tightly. With a forceful tug, Vladia tumbled towards her and disappeared.

For a while, there was nothing.

She didn't exist.

Then came the pain.

Her face tingled and burned. She tried to breathe, but there was no air.

The face lingered nearby. It contorted and writhed in agony.

Then it was gone. Vanished.

Her eyes lost focus, and her ears throbbed so hard she could barely make out the muffled voices around her.

"She's not dead"

"LV. What did you do?"

"What did I… do? What… did I do?"

"You saved…"

The voices trailed off.

Forcing herself to stand on small, shaky legs, she followed the sounds. Somehow she knew exactly where the voices had fled to.

Her vision cleared, though not entirely. All the edges were soft and blurred still, but as she rounded the last corner, she could see two figures. The voices belonged to them.

One was her mother, Maria. The other, a robot. Gen F.

"I didn't mean to break him. He was going to break Vladia, and Vladia is precious to you. If he broke the girl, then it would hurt you, and then you might also break," the robot's voice wavered in pitch. "I didn't mean to break him, but I needed to break him. I shouldn't, but I had to. I must not, but–"

"It's fine, LV. It's not your fault," her mother consoled the robot. "Let's shut down for a bit okay? I'll take care of all this. We'll just shut down for a bit, so we can run a diagnostic in the morning."

Maria reached for the back of his neck to open his control panel, but LV backed away.

"No. You can't. I can't."

LV stumbled a bit and sank to one knee. Vladia fought the urge to run to him.

He was dying.

"LV, please! You'll overheat!"

The robot shook his head violently.

Maria dropped to the floor and looked him in the eyes. "Let me fix you, LV."

She held out her hand to him.

LV lifted his hand and let it hover just out of her reach. He was shaking.

"I can make you better," she promised.

"I don't want you to make me better!" he shouted, jerking his hand away. He gripped his head between his palms. "I just want to die!"

Maria shielded her eyes, but Vladia watched in horror as LV crushed his own skull between his hands, then crumpled to the floor with a lifeless thud.

Minutes passed. Maria still sat frozen on the floor, eyes shut and shaking gently.

When the woman finally uncovered her face, their eyes met.

"Vladia," she whimpered. "You shouldn't be here."

She ran to her mother.

She ran as hard and as fast as her little legs could carry her.

But never did she reach her.

Maria slipped further and further away from her, and the more she pushed onward, the quicker she faded until Vladia was all alone.

There was no Maria anymore.

All was dark in her world.

∞

A hand brushed her face as her eyes fluttered open to reveal the dark brown ceiling of her cabin.

"Was I…"

She turned her head to find Rehel still at her side, looking as concerned as a robot could manage. She wiped the remaining wetness from her face with her thumb.

"Did you find what you were looking for?" he asked.

"I remember," she said almost inaudibly.

Her body felt heavy, as if still entangled in her dreams. She couldn't quite shake that last image of her mother from her mind.

"Then we can trust him?"

Vladia hesitated, unsure her voice would remain steady.

"The fear. It wasn't him that… There was another."

"Another robot?"

Vladia shook her head and sat upright. Her body swayed a bit, and Rehel reached out to steady her.

"A man. I think …he attacked me. Lvee stopped him. At least, I think it was Lvee; Maria called him LV. Does that sound familiar?"

"LV would most likely stand for part of a serial number."

"Anyway, that was why he had to be repaired. The weight of what he'd done…he couldn't handle it."

"What did he do?"

Rehel seemed shaken as he asked.

"He murdered a man."

"That's not possible," he insisted, standing up as if in protest.

"I know, but that's what I remember."

"There must be some mistake. Humans don't always remember things as they actually happened."

Vladia hesitated to press the point any further. Visibly distressed by the thought of a robot capable of murdering a human, Rehel wore an expression that could only be named a mix of horror and disbelief. Seeing his typically emotionless face so distorted made her uneasy. Perhaps she needed to revisit Dr. Weston's report.

"All I can tell you is what I now remember. I saw Lvee going haywire over killing this man and Maria trying desperately, and unsuccessfully, to help him."

"Unsuccessfully? I don't understand. Did he overheat and burn out his CPU? Even that is repairable."

"No. He didn't overheat," she explained heavily. "He completely destroyed himself."

∞

The Shikome should be in sensor range in two," Abel called over the comm from *Gunnr*, who gripped securely to the moon Thebe.

"Engage system-wide shutdown."

Vladia gave the order and withdrew from the Captain's

chair. *Devil's Run* was well hidden behind Lysithea, but until they went black, they'd stand out as if in plain sight.

"Ten, you have the bridge. Rehel, with me," she said, hastening towards the exit as Rehel fell in step behind her.

"Yes, Sir," Ten acknowledged as he continued the shutdown.

Into her comm she said, "Nova, Li, load up and meet us at the airlock. Erro, grab a med pack and head that way."

Halfway to the cargo hold, grav systems cut, and the two floated off the floor. The main lights faded shortly afterwards, replaced by the dim auxiliary light, and Vladia powered on her handheld.

"Shutdown complete," Ten chimed in her ear. "Standing by to re-engage engines and take us in."

Vladia glided down the ladder into the cargo bay. A pair of lights shone on Nova and Li, who were beside the airlocks and had already begun gearing up. The floor had the same dim haze of soft yellow as the corridor above.

Tossing a vest in her direction, Nova said, "You sure this'll work?"

"Too late to back out now," she said, plucking the vest from the air.

"Two to one odds," said Li. "And we've got the element of surprise."

The four were almost finished suiting up when a fifth globe of light moved towards them.

"Sorry," Erro said, taking a vest and helmet.

"You guys ready?" Abel said. "Our window'll be closing soon."

"Almost," Nova answered.

She checked her various holsters, then grabbed for one more to sling over her shoulder.

"All that weight is gonna slow you down," Vladia warned, taking only one firearm.

Li, too, had loaded up with multiple weapons.

"I'll be just fine. When you run out of bullets, don't you dare hide behind me. That'll be what really slows me down."

Vladia eyed the weapon closely then looked to Rehel and mouthed the word 'bullets', unsure she'd heard Nova right.

Rehel simply shrugged.

Li and Nova had stocked the ship to the brim with their own weapons, for which she'd expressed much gratitude. At the time, she hadn't realized they'd be antiques.

"So lemme get this straight," Vladia began. "You've got self-sustaining bio-domes, magic hair color capsules, and what I can only assume are low-level nano-laced ink tattoos, but no blasters?"

"Don't forget the genetically engineered space cats," Ten chimed in from the bridge. "We have lots of space cats."

"Sure we have blasters, but blasters need to be recharged. Power's at a premium out here. Bullets can be made on the cheap. The Syndicate uses blasters; we use real guns, with real bullets," Li explained.

"All the better to maim you with, my Dear," Erro joked as he grabbed a few weapons of his own.

"He's right," Li confirmed. "Bullets'll do a helluva lot more damage than a blaster."

"You ever hear of someone bleeding out from a blaster wound?" Nova asked, floating closer to offer her another gun.

Vladia took it begrudgingly.

Nova held one out to Rehel, who promptly refused.

"I don't need a gun."

"You should take one, just in case," Erro said.

"I wouldn't be able to use it, I fear, without repercussions," he said, eyeing Vladia nervously.

"Guys, we are runnin' out of time," Abel interrupted.

"Engage the target at will. Ten, once Abel's got their attention, bring up the engines and head straight for her. We'll be on her before she has a chance to send shots our way."

There was no viewscreen in the cargo hold, so Vladia had to rely on audio alone to get any sense of what was happening. And if anything were to go wrong, there was nothing she could do.

She'd give her other arm to be out there with Abel, flying

Freya as if nothing had changed. Wishful thinking did little to ease her mind, so she pushed the thoughts from her head and focused on the task ahead.

"They see me," Abel said. "And they're angry."

"Engines are restarting. We'll be moving any second so hold on down there."

Vladia gripped one of the hand-holds near the airlock door, as did the rest of the group.

The engine groaned to life, a small comfort in the near-dark.

"I'm moving in," Ten narrated.

Almost a full minute passed and not a word. All felt the unease of not knowing, but Erro seemed especially concerned, his face firmly fixed in a grimace as he eyed the ground. Nova moved closer to him, putting a hand on his shoulder to reassure him.

It was Rehel who decided to break the silence. "Ten, what's our status?"

"Looking good still. Target is still engaged with *Gunnr*. Doesn't look like he's taken much damage yet."

"Bunch of greenhorns never had a chance," Nova boasted.

"Shit, they've spotted me."

"See what you did," Erro griped.

"Yeah, that's my fault."

"I'm close," Ten interrupted. "Too close for them to fire now. Prepare for boarding."

"Abel, how we doing out there?" Vladia asked. She'd feel much better once she'd reassurance from him, not just Ten.

"We're good, Captain. I'm powering up to full now. Their shields are down, and I'll shortly be relieving them of their weapons."

The ship lurched as the airlocks met and clicked together.

"Get us to full power, Ten."

The grav system kicked on first, and the group dropped to the floor.

"Let's do this!" Nova revved up.

"Try not to kill anyone. We're here for the cargo, not their lives," Vladia warned her.

"Shoot to mangle. Got it, Cap."

The doors gave way with a low groan.

"Let's move out," Vladia said, taking the lead.

On reaching *The Shikome's* doors, Rehel stepped forward and began trimming the edges with decomposition gel. The door began to sizzle and melt on contact.

"Take your positions," she ordered.

Li and Erro lined the right side of the corridor while she and Nova took the left.

The gel made fast work of the ingress. With a sharp kick, Rehel sent the door flying inward.

The chemicals created a haze as they dissipated into the air. No blasts came at them through the opening as they waited for the chemicals to clear.

"Don't let your guard down," Li began as he took point with Erro. "They'll most likely wait and jump us once we're deep inside to cut us off from our only exit."

"That's what I'd do," Nova added as she fell in behind Li. Vladia and Rehel brought up the rear.

"We should locate a terminal and get the ship's diagram," Rehel suggested.

"They'll have locked down their systems by now. This is a Mercer class ship, similar enough to *Devil's Run*, so the cargo will be easy enough to–" Erro started.

"Let's keep the chatter down," Vladia ordered. "Ears and eyes sharp."

The group proceeded unimpeded through the ship's corridors, the echo of their light steps the only sound.

"I don't like this," Nova whispered.

"Ten, did any escape pods eject?" Vladia asked.

"He can't hear you. We're comm blocked," Li explained.

"This'll be the cargo hold." Erro stooped down by a circular access point in the floor.

He gave it a few unproductive tugs.

Rehel stepped forward to give this door the same treatment as the last.

Li jumped, followed by a string of muffled curses.

"Geez, Li."

"Something just moved past my leg."

Vladia flashed her light in front of him and watched a small puff of light fur scurry off.

"*Devil's Run*: zero. Cat: one," Nova said with a chuckle.

The cargo door hissed and popped as Rehel lifted it away and aside.

"Erro and I should go first," Rehel said.

Vladia put her hand up to stop him.

"Li and Nova will stand guard up here. I'll go in with Rehel and Erro. They'll pass the cargo up to you guys, and I'll bring up the rear on the way out."

Rehel jumped down first, followed by Erro.

"Anything?" Vladia called out before going in after them.

Red warning lights and sirens blared as the emergency blast doors slid into place, cutting the pair off from her.

The ceiling panels receded, and the corridor was flooded by the enemy as one by one they dropped down.

"Drop your weapons," one of the dozen or more men commanded.

Nova and Li both looked to her.

Vladia held up her hands in surrender, a gun still in each.

Shots reverberated from the cargo hold below.

"Drop them now, or I'll shoot."

Vladia shrugged and let the weapons fall from her hands.

∞

Abel had to hand it to Vladia; she'd not lost her unconventional approach to tactics. The plan couldn't have been executed better, save for her being out here with him. Even then, she'd been right about needing only one Valkyrie.

The news of her incompatibility with *Freya* hadn't really sunk in until he'd climbed into *Gunnr*. His ship had taken longer than usual to recognize and sync with him. He'd almost panicked, worried *Gunnr* needed additional work. What a fine time it'd be to discover that. It was then he realized at some point Vladia must have boarded *Freya*, had tried to sync with her ship, and met with ultimate failure. Just the additional sync time had been enough to spark alarm within him. What would he have done if, like Vladia, his ship no longer knew him?

Life support came online. Once sensors were up, he'd be at full capacity.

He wanted to comm in, find out what was going on inside *The Shikome*, but he knew better than to break the silence just now.

Instead, he commed Ten for an update.

"How's things on your end?" he asked.

"Still powering up. I don't like flying blind. Let's not make this a habit."

"We might have to. At least until we recruit a few more ships."

"Great."

"You heard anything on your end?"

"Captain and company are in. Our Comms won't penetrate the hull, so can't reach them now. Actually, with their shields down, you can take out the comm block easily. I'll send you the ship's specs and—"

Gunnr's sensors glowed to life with a fierce wail.

"Shit! Incoming," he warned as three ships appeared on his sensors, much too close for comfort. They were fighter-style, designed to get the job done quickly, not to worry about cargo. Or survivors.

"I can't see them. Sensors still offline."

"I can hold them for now" Abel dove in front of *Devil's Run*, just as a barrage of fire seared towards it.

He took most of the hits, but a few grazed past him.

He'd have to play the defender, a role unsuited for *Gunnr*, but he'd manage.

The ships loomed closer now. With odds three to one, he'd not be able to shield Ten entirely.

"Now's your chance to use those shields of yours."

"I thought you said—"

"I gotta run 'em down. Forget the sensors, just divert all you got to shields and start blasting," Abel ordered, going first for the middle ship.

"Where?!"

"Anywhere!"

The foes would instinctively dodge both his and Ten's blasts, slowing them down enough for Abel to, hopefully, make fast work of them. He'd take some hits, but *Gunnr* was tough enough to handle a few stray shots.

Taunting the middle ship into a chase, he went for a second ship.

As he swirling around the craft, it refused to be dragged into the pursuit and focused fire on *Devil's Run*.

Flipping around to a dead stop, he fired point blank at the ship's underbelly, taking its shields down a notch, but not completely out.

His chaser almost collided with him, just scraping his side, sending them both into a tailspin.

"Shields are at fifty-six percent, and hull integrity is at risk," *Gunnr* reported.

"It's fine. We got these guys."

Grabbing hold of the second target, he pulled himself steady, then reached for the closest thruster, crushing it with his hands.

"Shields at forty-three percent."

"Sensors are up," Ten said. "Shields holding at thirty-two."

"Disengage *The Shikome* and take out that comm block."

"Roger."

His prey railed against him with its remaining power, firing wildly at anything it could hit. He took out the last of its thrusters, but hung on to the fighter to serve as protection.

Two to three felt much better, but unlike their enemy, they had cargo and a crew to retrieve.

"Divert anything you can spare to shield," he told *Gunnr*.

He'd have to hold out until Vladia and the others could nab an escape pod, then hope making a run for it remained a viable option.

∞

Before her guns even hit the ground, Vladia ducked.

She flung her right palm into the front man's jawbone, shattering it.

Nova and Li hit the deck as blasts singed above them, claiming a few victims in the unexpected crossfire.

Vladia rolled past the first man. Pushing off with her hands, she kicked her feet up and into the next man's stomach, knocking him flat.

Pushing off the fallen man, she dove back onto the first before he'd fully recovered.

Twisting him around, she made his body her shield from the blasts behind her.

She shoved his limp body forward, and the man collapsed on the pair behind him.

She grabbed for her guns and fired at the last two men who stood behind those that'd just fallen.

Looking back just long enough to see Nova and Li holding their own, she looked for a way to breach the panel that had closed off Rehel and Erro.

Disabling her nerve endings, Vladia slammed her right fist repeatedly at the door.

Over and over, leaving only the slightest of dents.

"Vladia!" Nova shouted.

Shots flew past her, but still she continued to pound away.

The skin ripped away from her hand.

Sparks jumped as the metal door met in conflict with her mechanical knuckles.

"We've got incoming!" Ten shouted.

"Vladia, we've got to go!"

The panel finally gave way.

"Rehel!" she yelled.

Not waiting for a reply, she leapt through to the cargo hold.

Two men had a disabled Erro by the legs, dragging him towards an escape pod.

Vladia shot at them, forcing them to drop the robot to

215

return fire.

Ducking behind a large container, she scanned the area for Rehel.

One of the pods detached and blasted away.

"Stop that pod!"

"Get out of there, Vladia! We've got multiple incoming, and we can't take them all," Abel responded.

"I'm not leaving without Rehel."

Vladia fired again at the men near Erro, hitting one in the shoulder.

"Go after the pod. They may have taken him."

Nova dropped into the cargo hold and took out the second target. Running to Erro, she called back to Li, "Help me get him to a pod."

To Vladia she said, "Our escape's blocked. This is our only way out."

Vladia ignored her, still looking for any sign of Rehel. There were obvious signs of a struggle, but nothing else.

Li pulled Erro into one of the pods and Nova made a grab for some of the smaller cargo containers.

Two men dropped down into the bay and fired, forcing Nova to drop her container and cover both the others.

"Vladia!"

This time it was Li who urged her to move out.

"Ten, get ready for a pick up. Abel, you'll need to cover us," Nova ordered, gunning one of the foes down as Li continued to load what cargo he could fit.

"Negative! They've got Rehel. Go after the pod," Vladia shouted, taking out the second target just as several more men flooded into the area.

"We're trapped if he doesn't cover us! We've got to let him go."

"She's right," Abel agreed. "Ten can't get you out alone."

"Don't you dare let them take him!"

"I'm sorry, Vladia."

She heard it in his voice, the slightest crack. Abel chose her over Rehel. Not for her sake, but for that of everything else.

Gritting her teeth, she moved towards one of the fallen men.

Lifting him off the floor, she hissed, "You're coming with me."

Shoving him into the already cramped pod, she was the last to board.

"Let's go."

13

TRUST NOT YOUR SELF

The quarantine room in the med bay now acted as a cell, housing their one and only lead to finding Rehel. The make-shift prison had clear, aeroplastic walls, which had been installed with the thought of being able to evaluate a patient from without. Now, their transparency was blotted out almost entirely by engine gunk Vladia had smeared over the surface. She'd never interrogated a prisoner before, but had the training to do so by both physical and psychological means.

She was eager to put it to use.

And although the man was quite unaware of it, the interrogation had begun the moment he'd entered the room. Looking out, the man could only see light through the few thin gaps left between the streaks of grease. All else was dark. His arms, each tethered to an opposing wall, forced him to remain standing, though they stayed just loose enough to allow his body to droop ever so slightly once fatigue kicked in. Every half hour, the temperature dropped five degrees. Once it reached thirty below freezing, the cycle reversed until it reached boiling, and so on. He would be unable to sleep, relieve himself properly, or eat. There would be only agony until she got what she wanted.

Despite her readiness, Vladia did not yet question the man. Part of the process required her to wait. Let the man think he'd been forgotten. Let his imagination create horrors of his own. Let him understand that he was at their mercy, that time was of no concern, and that this could, and would, go on forever if need be.

In the meantime, the crew continued to search on their own. They traced the escape pod's residual trail back to Ganymede. Once it entered the Augusta City dome the trail was lost. It gave them a place to start, though, and that was something.

Now, almost twenty-four hours after the assault on *The Shikome*, Vladia stood alone outside the quarantine room, her military overcoat draped casually over her shoulders and her gloved hands folded into tight fists. The hour was late. She would not be disturbed.

The prison doors opened. The brightness of the severe white light behind her made the man flinch. Vladia stood in the doorway and studied him. Late thirties, most likely. Artificial deep-green hair. A few faded scars and various tattoos decorated his bare arms; one of them, a jade Ouroboros, slowly slithered around the man's right upper arm, marking him as an agent of the Syndicate.

Stepping in, the jail resealed, and the darkness overtook them both.

She waited to see if he would call out to her for help, or even just to identify herself. He did not and this told her enough about him to know this would be done the hard way.

"Let's have a bit of light," she began.

The room grew several shades brighter. Bright enough for him to see her clearly should he decide to tear his eyes away from the floor, which he appeared determined not to do.

"You know what I'm here for, correct?"

"I could take a few guesses."

"But you, of course, won't tell me."

"I don't have any answers for you, Terran. Even if I did, I wouldn't tell the likes of you."

The man looked up at her as he proclaimed his stance. His eyes were hard, and he was determined. But he was no soldier. He would not last long as long as he believed he would.

"No, you don't. But you will. Eventually."

From her inside coat pocket, she pulled out a syringe.

"Some kind of Terran truth serum?" he asked with a laugh.

"Don't be silly. This is a neurological amplifier. Much more fun than a truth serum. And much more…messy."

Before he could comment further, she stabbed him in the neck with the needle and released the fluid into his vein.

"It'll take a few minutes for the full force to take effect. But soon, my whispers will boom in your head like cannon fire. The warmth of my touch will seem to sear your skin. And the stench of your own blood and sweat will burn your eyes so much you'll want to claw them with your bare hands."

She caressed the side of his face gently. Even now, he'd be able to feel the truth to her words.

Stepping back, she added, "Of course, if you give me what I need before then, I'll sedate you until it wears off and release you once we've landed."

The man didn't respond, but she could see the beginnings of fear creep into those hard eyes.

"Now then. Tell me, where is my robot?"

∞

Abel inched down the ladder to the cargo hold. Sleep would not come easily to him in Rehel's absence. After an hour or two of restless attempts, he'd given up. He'd half a mind to go to their captive and see about getting some information out of him, but Vladia's orders were to wait until she gave the word. If he ever hoped to fully regain her trust, he'd better do as he was told.

Ten would be with Erro's body, so he decided to check in on his progress at repairing the fallen robot. Making his way to the back of the cargo hold, he spotted Ten peering into one of the containers Nova had poached.

"Find anything you can use?" he asked as he came up beside him.

"Who knows? I can't make heads or tails of most of this stuff," he said.

Ten picked up a group of colored wires, holding them up for Abel to see.

"I can use these to repair reflex wiring. I think."

"It's kinda weird, isn't it? Not having the know-how to fix yourself when you can fix so many other things."

Ten smiled weakly. "It's not so strange. Can you fix yourself?"

"Good point. But Lvee knows how, right? I mean, he's the one who finished your assembly and activated you. Why wouldn't he pass on that knowledge?"

"I couldn't say."

Ten appeared to not really be listening as he continued to rummage through containers. Abel kept forgetting that Erro was like a brother to Ten. He didn't understand the extent of that sort of bond, but it was obviously deep. And though he remained calm and composed, the robot suffered at the possible loss of his family.

"Any closer to figuring out what happened?" Abel asked.

"Now that, I've made progress on."

He motioned for Abel to follow him over to the table that Erro's body was laid out on.

The stilled robot barely had a scratch. Even in his current condition, Erro looked so very human somehow; much more than Rehel ever did, even though the only real difference he could pinpoint was the shade of their hair.

"At first I assumed Erro and Rehel were taken only because the crew realized what they were after the skirmish began. A robot in these parts, most would assume them to be a Terran spy; his capture would ensure the crew promotion within the ranks of the Syndicate," Ten explained.

"But then I found this," he turned his brother's head, revealing a scorch mark at the base of the neck.

"They shot him in the head."

"But it's more than that. This precise spot," he pointed to just above the burn mark, "is the most vulnerable on a robot. It's the only place that you can take one of us down in a single shot because this is the access point to the CPU. They hit him just close enough to damage the CPU but not destroy it."

"Couldn't that be a coincidence?"

"It could, except for the fact that it was the first and only shot taken. Those men weren't just waiting for us. I think they knew exactly who we were."

"But how could they know you three were robots. Even Nova and Li didn't know about Erro."

"Couldn't say. But they did."

"They would have known about Vladia, too, then."

Ten nodded. "The only reason any of you got out alive was because they didn't know about you and your ship. I couldn't have picked them up without cover fire; they'd have been trapped."

"We need to get this to Vladia now," Abel decided as he turned to go.

"Regardless, once we dock, someone needs to take Erro and the parts to Lvee."

He stopped and asked, "You think he can fix him?"

"His knowledge is limited, but if he can't…"

"I understand. We'll get him there, I promise," he reassured the robot. "Even if we have to wait until Mars, Erro's gonna be all right."

"I'll keep going through the parts, gather anything that looks useful."

"Good. I'll be back 'round again later," Abel shouted back as he climbed the ladder back to the main level.

∞

Vladia felt the gentle buzz of her comm but made no move to retrieve it. She'd stowed it away in one of her overcoat pockets with no intention of answering it until morning at the earliest.

Her prisoner's body hung loosely by his arms. His eyes were closed and his breath shallow, as every sight and sound turned to an assault on his senses. The injection had reached its peak already. The man could stand no more, passing out after her last string of gentle tortures.

She had to admire his ability to withstand this torture for so long. Her patience was growing thin, though. Soon, the effects of the serum would begin to wane, and her supply was sadly limited. She needed answers now.

Grabbing a bucket of water she'd brought in earlier, Vladia flung the contents over his body.

He awoke with a shriek, which immediately turned to a subdued sob.

Leaning in just centimeters from his face, she whispered, "Let's have a bit more light."

He winced at her words, the touch of her breath searing his skin. As the lights went up to full he suppressed a scream, as his own weakness would serve only to intensify his suffering.

Making her way behind the man, she pressed the foot of her boot squarely between his shoulder blades.

"Where is my robot?"

His body involuntarily shuddered at the pressure, but he remained silent.

Slowly, she increased the pressure. A muffled cry tried to tear its way past the man's lips.

If she kicked him, instead of simply applying gentle pressure, she'd probably break his arms. Resisting this urge was becoming more and more challenging.

Her comm buzzed again, and again she increased the weight of her heel.

"Where is he?" She asked again.

The doors to the cell flung open, and Abel burst in.

"Jesus, Vladia."

The prisoner writhed in pain from the boom of his voice.

She held her finger up to her lips and shushed him.

He approached her, eyeing their captive cautiously.

"Any luck?" he whispered.

She shook her head, then asked, "What d'you need?"

"Ten thinks we were set up."

"How so?"

"They didn't take Rehel because they realized he was a

robot and thought him a Terran spy. They were there specifically to take them because those were their orders. They knew who we were and that we were coming."

"The Syndicate has no use for robots."

"Ten also thinks none of us were supposed to get out alive, but whoever sold them the info didn't know about *Gunnr.*"

"This one won't know where the info came from. We'll have to go higher up for that," she said, removing her foot from the prisoner.

"What's our ETA for Augusta City?"

"About a day."

The captive man laughed lightly. The serum was tapering off.

"If you land in Augusta, you're dead," he murmured. "Anywhere you land, you're dead."

"Everyone's gotta die sometime, pal, but it ain't gonna be out here, I can tell you that."

"Not you," he coughed. "Her. Just her. Until she dies, we're all dead men."

"That's why he won't talk," she said, mostly to herself.

"What d'you mean?"

Vladia stooped down in front of the man and lifted his face so he'd look her in the eyes.

"There is no going home from a mission failed is there? Death is the only path before you. Either mine, or yours. Anything else would be... dishonorable."

The man averted his eyes and instead looked towards Abel as he said, "You should get out while you still can. This woman will be your death, I think."

Vladia let go of his face and straightened up.

"Thank you for the information."

It was unclear to either man who that comment was directed at.

Turning to Abel, she said, "Ask Nova to come 'round once she's up. We'll see what she can get out of him."

"Right," he said moving to the door.

"Oh. There's also the matter of Erro," he added. "Ten says

we need to get him to Lvee. He thinks he can repair him, but I wasn't sure how we felt about him, what with our earlier conversation and now this."

"We'll have to take him, regardless, though it might have to wait a few days," she replied, her gaze still fixed on her prisoner. She'd underestimated him and the Syndicate. It would not happen again.

Abel hesitated at the door; she felt his eyes on her back. He didn't approve of her methods, yet she knew he'd not say a word against them because he understood why she did what she did. It was all for Rehel. He would let his principles slide, as would she, for the sake of that robot.

They were both hypocrites, the only difference being that she'd decided the moment he'd been taken to feel no remorse for anything she was about to do.

She would get Rehel back no matter the cost. And after, she'd dismantle Malthus and everything he'd built up with the same tenacity. She would not fail. Not this time.

The doors behind her finally glided shut.

The man breathed easier now, less hesitant than before. The serum had all but left his system. She could inject him once more, but that approach obviously hadn't got her anywhere. It was time for the second act.

"Death," she began, "will, unfortunately, not come so easily. Not for you, and certainly not for me."

"It will come for you sooner than you think, Terran."

Vladia laughed.

"You misunderstand. Death has already come for me once."

Moving closer, she pushed up the sleeve covering her left arm. Withdrawing a short blade from her pocket, she pressed the edge into the soft flesh of her forearm.

"She took something very important to me as recompense," she said, letting the blood gush from the fresh wound.

Smearing away the excess blood, she exposed the deep gash, and held it close to his face.

The man's eyes grew large in horror as the wound stitched itself up; the skin reconnected perfectly.

"You see, she took my humanity."

"What are you?" he said, backpedaling away from her as far as his restraints would allow.

"Exactly!" she shouted, grabbing him by the collar and yanking him forward. The blade clattered to the floor in shrill protest.

"What circle of hell have your superiors sent you to? What soulless monster now holds you in her teeth?"

The man cried out, desperately trying to loosen her hold on him.

"I want you to understand one thing: this?" she hissed, holding up the once-wounded appendage. "This is nothing compared to what you have now stolen from me. What you've taken from me is far more precious, and I promise that the suffering you'll receive at my hands for this will make you beg for the dishonor you sought to avoid."

The doors behind her receded once again.

"You wanted to see me, Boss?" Nova asked casually, unaffected by the scene before her.

Vladia released the man and jerked her sleeve down.

"Hose him down; he's starting to reek. Then, he's all yours."

"He not talking?"

"Not enough," she said, joining her at the door.

"And the knife," she whispered.

"Leave it. He'll take it while you're out of the room, but won't make a move until we land."

"Gotcha," she winked.

"No one comes in here but me or you," she said loud enough for the captive to hear.

"Yes, Sir." Nova said with a lack-luster salute.

Vladia left her to it and headed for her quarters.

Nova wouldn't make him talk, either. No one could know that he had a warning to deliver. And if his loyalty was as serious as it appeared, there was no question that he'd risk dishonor to take it back to the Syndicate.

Vladia smiled. The big, bad wolf was coming.

∞

Rehel came to in unfamiliar surroundings, bound to a medical examination table that was tilted at a forty-five degree angle and centered in a bare rectangular room. A large mirror occupied one of the long walls, and a series of light fixtures adorned the ceiling.

Recalling his last recorded memory, he deduced several facts about his current situation. One, he'd been taken prisoner. Two, his attackers knew his weakest point and therefore had known him to be a robot. Three, he'd been specifically targeted. And four, the entire incident had been a trap.

The survival probability of the rest of the crew varied. Based on known variables, Abel and Ten had the highest as they were not aboard the *The Shikome*. Erro had likely been captured as well, so his death seemed improbable. He didn't have enough data to properly calculate for Nova or Li. As for Vladia, he decided against running the numbers on her. He took no real comfort in these probabilities as he once might have. No matter the results, there was a chance she had not made it. All he could do was believe she was alive.

A green light blinked in his peripheral; his automatic restart system scan had completed. Mentally, he glanced through the report half-heartedly. Everything looked as normal as could be expected. His seared CPU circuits had been repaired by his nanos, and a few connectors had been replaced haphazardly by someone else. His nanos easily adjusted the connectors inserted by less skilled hands. All in all the damage had been trivial, but effective in shutting him down.

Testing the restraints, he tried pulling his arms outward. He could probably free himself, but he'd risk serious damage to his limbs that his nanos might not be able to repair entirely. He filed this away as a last resort and decided to bide his time.

Obviously someone would come to him now that he was awake.

Yet hours passed, and no one appeared. Rehel found himself oddly restless. He'd managed the long journey from Earth to Mars in complete ease despite having relatively nothing to occupy his time. In fact, he could only assume this sensation should be called restlessness. He considered the term 'restlessness' to be a kind of uneasy boredom beyond one's control. He'd never experienced boredom before, but he did know the feeling of apprehension. This sensation seemed to fit his textbook definition.

Without warning, his restraints retracted into the table, and he slid onto his feet.

"You're quite the specimen, aren't you?" A male voice broke the silence.

Rehel located the source of the noise immediately as coming from a medium, almost seamless, panel under the mirror. He paced towards the wall and reached out to remove the covering.

"I wouldn't," the voice warned.

Rehel detached the panel to reveal a black, dense screen. His fingers stopped just short of touching the section. He could pick up an electrical output from it, enough to knock him out and reset his systems again.

"As I said," the voice gloated, "I wouldn't."

"Who are you, why have you taken me, who else have you taken, what is your intention, and where is the rest of my crew?" he asked, moving back to the center of the room and directing his questions to the mirror.

"At first, I thought I'd just make a study of you," the voice explained, side-stepping all inquiries. "Open you up, take you apart, maybe keep my favorite bits in little display jars. But you're quite different from what I imagined you'd be."

"How is that?"

"Oh, I think you know."

Rehel saw no need to answer. He obviously referred to his uniquely adaptive nanos. The man must have extracted a sample of them during repairs.

"You're a Generation D," he continued. "I've only ever had the pleasure to disassemble Generation G models."

"You've disassembled many, I take it?"

"Not as many as I'd like, but a few."

"I was led to believe that only one robot had been captured by the Syndicate."

"Yes, well, technically they're all captured. I know where every single robot on Ganymede is hiding and whenever I choose, I can pluck them out. But what fun would that be?"

"So you don't deny that you work for the Syndicate?"

The man laughed and said, "I absolutely do deny it. The Syndicate does as I command. They might not like to think of it that way, but it's the truth."

"And what is it you want with me now that you've decided I'm worth more than a science experiment?"

"Oh, you're still an experiment. Just not until I've had a chance to speak with you a bit. A dissection is so impersonal if you don't become acquainted with your subjects first, don't you think?"

"I wouldn't know."

"Of course not," the man's tone darkened. "You're Robespierre's dog. What use would you have for science?"

Rehel distinctly felt his processing time drop at the mention of Vladia. He'd used the present tense; did that mean he knew she was alive? Or had it just been a careless slip?

"There it is," the voice hissed. "I knew there would be side effects. You're not built for those nanos; they slow you down. You're hardly better than a human."

"Being better than a human is not my objective."

"Oh my. Don't tell me you're one of *those* robots."

"I don't understand."

"I've come across a few of those types. Little Pinocchios, I like to call them."

"I have no desire to be a human."

"But don't you? With your darling little emotions. It's why you care so much about whether she's alive or not. It's why

230

you wore that silly little locket, correct?"

His hands immediately went to his neck, but the necklace was gone, taken, he assumed, by the man behind the voice.

"The nanos make you care, and they make you slow, and eventually they'll make you die."

"I cannot help what the nanobots do to my systems."

"So you'll give them up? And with them everything you've ever felt for your friends. For Vladia Robespierre."

Rehel couldn't answer. He'd been so focused on his decreased efficiency, it'd not occurred to him what else he'd be giving up.

"You see," the voice persisted. "The Gen G's can never really get close to humanity. They were built to handle an emotional context. They could live on forever, weeping for humanity's flaws and frailty and their own lack thereof. You, though, your nanos will kill you, ultimately. Just like old age. They will wear you down, and in seventy or eighty years you'll crumble to bits. You are as close to humanity as any robot could ever hope to be. Yet you claim you don't want to be human."

"Being close to humanity, as you say, has no relation to my desire of that state."

"True enough, on the surface. But enough about humanity. Let's talk about where these wonderful little nanos came from. You've encrypted numerous files full of sensitive information. I could break them, eventually, but I'd like you to save me the trouble and just tell me what I want to know."

"How can you trust I'll tell you the truth?"

"Funny thing, about your nanos, is that delayed response time. Not visible to the naked eye, but it is measurable with the right equipment. Lying, unfortunately for you, is tied to your emotional context. You might as well have a lie detector built right in."

"If you're asking who built the nanos, I cannot give you an answer, since I do not know. My encrypted files have nothing to do with nanobots of any sort," Rehel confessed, though not knowing would no doubt serve him ill.

"But surely you have some theories. Curiosity is unavoidable in your…condition."

"Why would the Syndicate be interested in nano technology?"

"I could think of a hundred reasons they should be. However, this information is solely for my own benefit. And, no, I'm not going to tell you what I want with it."

Rehel couldn't imagine how knowing his suspicions on the nanos' creator could be of any real benefit. Tolen Malthus was worlds away and wholly untouchable. Malthus obviously wouldn't willingly help anyone on the Outer Moons, so what did it matter if he spoke the truth?

Yet in revealing the probable creator as Malthus, he would assure this man that Vladia did not build them, causing uncertain consequences. If the man hoped it was Vladia in order to use her, then found out it was not, he might kill her. Then again, if he viewed her knowing as a threat, confirming she did not create the nanos could save her life. Rehel lacked the variables needed to make an effective decision, leaving him only one course of action: non-action.

"I respectfully decline to answer your question. If you wish, you could sift through all my stored experiences and decide for yourself, though I fear that will take quite a long time. If you are hoping to replicate the nanos, you've already taken your sample. Surely, you can determine how to construct more. Based on this, I assume all you are actually interested in is eliminating a competitive threat, acquiring a possible ally, or taking a useful prisoner, none of which I can help you with, obviously."

"Bravo! It's a shame it took you such a long time to reach such an obvious conclusion. Running at only eighty-six percent capacity must be so boring. Is it like trudging through knee-deep mud? God, it must be horrible for you."

"You are arrogant; it will be your downfall."

"And you, my friend, are weak, and that will be yours."

He was right. At eighty-six percent he functioned fine, but not with the smooth ease he'd grown used to. At sixty percent he'd barely be quicker than a skilled human. At forty percent he'd be average, at best. At what point would he no longer be able to protect those he now cherished? Then again, he'd already failed to keep them safe. He couldn't even be sure any of them were still alive.

"Speaking of weak," the voice went on. "Let's put that to the test."

"There is nothing you can do to me. I have nothing you want that you've not already taken, so what would be the point?"

"The point? There is no point. I just want to watch you burn."

It was only then that Rehel realized just how unbalanced this man must be. Terribly clever and completely irrational, he lacked any sort of empathy that so naturally came to most humans. There would be no negotiating and no escape.

"A long time ago, people used to break horses. It could take weeks or even months. And I've got lots of time, Rehel. I've got so much time. So, let's see how long it takes to break a dog."

14

TO CATCH A THIEF

Nova lingered in the corridor just outside the medical bay, trying not to look as if she was waiting for a fight. They'd be touching down in Augusta City in twenty, and she had to be ready. She knew how to throw a tussle and make it look good, but that didn't make her feel any better about it. Her natural instincts always tried to kick in, and resisting that would be harder than anything.

She'd not asked Vladia why they were letting him go like this, but she had a few ideas. He didn't talk, just as she'd promised. But the few times Nova had mentioned the Captain's name, the prisoner had desperately tried to hide a look of terror. She'd said or done something to him that scared the man beyond reason. Something like that, whatever it was, should have made him sing like a bird. Instead, he gave her nothing. Nothing but that look of fear so primal he couldn't contain it at the sound of her name.

Abel approached from her left. He seemed to hesitate on seeing her, but decided against turning around and took up a post beside her.

"You need a standby?"

"What for?"

"Thought you could use a break."

"No, thanks. Captain said to stand guard in case he tries anything once we've landed."

"Well, I could stick around for that. In case he's too much

for you."

She laughed. "That's cute, really, but I can handle him."

"I suppose in his condition the ship's cat could take care of him."

She punched him in the side of his arm, harder than intended, but he smiled and didn't recoil as she'd expected.

"He's not so bad off. Vladia told me question him, but he wasn't talking, and you can't make a turnip bleed so..."

"I'd never have guessed he'd be so loyal."

"Terrans aren't the only people bred for loyalty."

"We're not all so very loyal."

"Does it bother you? Leaving Earth?"

"Sometimes. I don't know. I guess I never thought we'd get this far. And it's not really Earth that's the enemy. It's Earth in Malthus' hands."

"I'm not so sure about that."

"Of course you'd say that. Earth will always be the villain to you people."

"You people?" she laughed. "Earth is the bully of the solar system. She's held Luna in subjugation for centuries. She's wiped out entire races of–"

"If you want to make a case study of violence, let's look at how the Outer Moons are handling things. Earth had decades of peace until Malthus somehow enticed Luna to strike at us."

"You think one man forced an entire moon to war? If that's the case, your peace wasn't all that stable."

"What would you know of peace? You people fight all the time over the pettiest things."

"You keep using the word 'peace', but I don't think it means what you think it does! Peace isn't won by genocide!"

"War forces you to do the worst sometimes, I'll make no excuses for that. Your people wouldn't understand since you all fled to the brim of the system in the face of it. You're all cowards and criminals!"

At that, Nova slapped him hard in the face. Her hand burned from the impact.

Abel's eyes watered slightly. The shock on his face

reminded her of a child being scolded for the first time.

"Now look–"

She slapped him again before he could finish.

"Okay, I deserved th–"

And again, though not quite as hard this time.

"Nova!"

She swung again, but let him catch her hand at the wrist.

Tracing the outline of her palm with his thumb, he became a mixture of timid hesitation and curiosity. She didn't mind; in fact, she found it all rather endearing.

But he held on to her just a bit too long, and she slapped him with her free hand across a fresh cheek.

He dropped his hold on her immediately and stomped off without another word.

"Dammit," she said to herself, then to him she called out, "Wait. Abel, I was only–"

Something rushed up from behind, and a searing heat sliced at her side.

∞

Abel Duren swore at himself as he ignored Nova's call to come back. That woman was trouble. His small victory over his own issues was now overshadowed by his foolishness in other matters. If Rehel'd been around, he'd never have sought her out in the first place. The thought that he could be dead was more than he could bear to be alone with.

A gentle thud, followed by a quiet gasp, called his attention away from his brooding interiority.

He'd forgotten all about the prisoner. Had he managed to jump her while she'd been distracted?

Sprinting back, he saw the blood before he saw Nova, furrowed lifelessly on the floor against the wall, her arms folded over her stomach.

Dizziness threated to overtake him, but he pushed through it as he knelt down to lift her from the floor. He carried her into the med bay and laid her out on the table. The blood saturated everything, covering all traces of an entry wound.

"Abel," Nova said, stilling his searching hands with her own.

"Just take it easy. You'll be fine. You're gonna be fine," he said, freeing his hands. Why couldn't he just focus and find the damn wound!

"Stop. Abel, stop. I'm fine."

She sat up and showed him a clear, blood-smeared bag.

"I did knock myself in the head on the way down, but that serves me right for being distracted."

She tossed the pouch into a nearby bin and continued, "Had to let him graze my side pretty deep to make it feel real, but most of this isn't mine."

What she'd said didn't register. His hands dripped with her blood. It pooled on the floor beneath his feet and penetrated his clothes, his skin, her skin. The whole room felt red with it.

"Abel!" she said, grabbing ahold of his shoulders and shaking him back to the present.

Looking him in the eyes, again she said, "I'm fine. I'm sorry I freaked you out. It wasn't my intention."

"So all this…"

"The blood bag, mostly. We're letting him go so he'll lead us inside the Syndicate base, and hopefully to Rehel, or at least to someone who knows where to find him."

Vladia turned the corner to find the blood-soaked pair. She immediately went to Abel.

"You all right?"

"Yeah. I'm fine," he answered firmly.

And he was fine. He'd almost let himself slip back to that night with Cerés, falling back down that rabbit hole of panic and anger. Nova had kept him tethered here where he belonged. Where he could still save people.

"Christ, Nova, I said handle this on your own. What happened?" Vladia asked.

Before Nova could answer she turned to him and said, "And why are you here? I told you to help Ten get Erro ready for transport."

She didn't sound annoyed, but Abel could see it on her face. She meant to keep him out of the loop on this.

"I didn't know he'd be around when it happened. He just showed up and thought I'd really been jumped," Nova explained.

"Are you really all right?" she asked, ignoring Nova's excuse entirely.

"I am."

"Good," she said with a nod. "Then you can help her clean up this mess. Report to the bridge when you're finished."

Vladia marched out as quickly as she'd appeared.

"What the hell was that about?" Nova asked, climbing off the table and carefully tip-toeing through the blood so as not to slip in it.

"It's nothing. I'm just glad you're not actually hurt. You should let me have a look at that scratch he gave you in case you need stitches."

Nova laughed and tossed him a mop from the supply closet.

"I can stitch myself later if I need to, but thanks."

Grabbing the only bucket available, she took it to the sink and began filling it with soapy water. She shut it off at the halfway mark and passed it to him.

"Start in the hall. I'll grab some towels and work on this area."

Abel carried the bucket and mop into the corridor. Dunking the mop into the water, he hoisted it out too fast and sloshed water everywhere.

"Seriously? You have to wring it out first." Nova remarked, coming out to survey the mess.

"Sorry."

"Gimme that," she said, snatching the mop out of his hands. "You use the towels. You do know how towels work, I hope."

He scowled at her playfully then did as he was told.

The two made fast work of the bloody floors and surfaces. Nova packed the cleaning supplies away while Abel washed up to his elbows in the sink.

"You head to the showers first. I'll just grab a clean change of clothes and wash up better later," Nova offered.

"No, you should go first. I'll be okay."

"You don't have to play tough with me, Terran. I know all this is driving you crazy."

She was right, of course. But he'd made his decision.

"I insist."

With a shrug, she made for the door. He already regretted his offer, just a little bit. The thought of a hot shower rinsing away the now dried and crusted blood almost overwhelmed him.

Lingering in the doorway, Nova said, "She's a strange one, your Vladia."

"What do you mean?"

"I can't quite figure her out, you know. She's empathetic. She cares about you and, oddly enough, I think she cares about me, too."

"Nothing strange about that."

"But, she did something to that man, the captive. Or said something. Something that caused a terror in him like I've never seen."

"What did she do?"

"I dunno. But at the end, you couldn't even say her name without him getting this mad look about him. Like he'd seen a ghost. Or a demon. But I swear he hadn't a mark on him when she left him to me. How could she inspire that kind of fear in a man?"

"Maybe he'd just cracked up a bit," he lied. It surely had to do with the nanobots inside her. They didn't utilize nanotech in the Outer Moons; they probably had no idea what it was capable of. Vladia could have done any number of things that seemed inhuman to the people out here.

"No. He was sane. Sane enough to be terrified."

"Well, she's not a ghost, or a demon, I assure you," he joked.

But Nova wasn't in a gaming mood anymore.

"You wouldn't tell me. Even if she was a threat, she's your threat, right?"

"She's not a threat to us. I promise," he insisted.

"I'd like to believe you. Maybe one day I will."

With that, she left.

Abel thought back to what the prisoner had said to him. He'd warned him that she'd be the death of him. Maybe she would be. But some things are worth dying for, and destroying Malthus was one of them.

∞

While Abel gave Nova a head start on the showers, he decided to check on Ten. Erro had to be carefully transferred out of *Devil's Run* to avoid attracting suspicion. All cargo taken off the ship and into the pod would be thoroughly inspected and documented. Unless they planned to take him apart, which none of them had the knowledge to do safely, they couldn't sneak him off. The only other option was closer to the truth than any of them cared to think about. They'd have to present him as deceased, as if he'd died on the trip out, and now they were bringing him home to be buried.

And even though people could, and did, smuggle in items concealed in corpses, according to Li, pod security usually overlooked it for the sake of respect for both the deceased and the survivors. The only hang-up would be the visual inspection of the body. Security would open the coffin to confirm there was indeed a corpse inside. Normally this wouldn't be a big deal, but Erro didn't exactly look dead. His skin wasn't organic so there'd be no discoloration, nor would there be any of the smells that accompanied death and decay.

He was almost to the cargo hold ingress, when Li, followed by Ten, ascended the ladder. A small drawstring bag tied around Ten's wrist clanked against the rungs as he finished the climb.

"Was just coming to find you guys," Abel said as he closed the gap between them.

"What happened to you?" Li asked, motioning towards his bloody clothes.

Abel had just about managed to forget about his gory appearance.

"Long story," he said, waving his hand dismissively. "You guys got everything worked out with Erro?"

"We think so. Nova had enough make-up so that we could take care of the issue with appearance," Ten explained, holding up the bag at his wrist.

"As for the smell," he continued, "Captain suggested we perfume him. Act as if the stench was too much for us so we covered it up."

"Problem was we didn't have any perfume," Li grumbled, crossing his arms over his chest. "So this man here decided to raid my tea stash. Emptied me out completely. Like some damn space pirate."

"I couldn't even tell you what he should be smelling like," Abel mused, leaning against the corridor wall.

"You stay here long enough and you will," Li grumbled.

"Get over it," Ten said to Li. "You didn't have a better idea, did you?"

"We could kill the cat and stuff it in there with him," Abel suggested, spotting the feline rounding the corner, its fur the same dull grey it'd been since day one.

Both Ten and Li's faces turned to horror at the suggestion, and for a moment Li looked as if he would slug him in the face.

Abel quickly added, "Joking, of course."

This would be the point, he imagined, that Rehel would have explained that killing the cat was not only culturally unacceptable, but also not a viable option as it would not be dead long enough to produce the necessary smells to make the plan a success.

The cat weaved a figure eight around Ten's feet, and Li scooped the animal up defensively.

"So where's Vladia? She already on the bridge?" Abel asked as the three made their way down the corridor.

"Captain left a while ago to check us into the dock. I expect her back any minute, but she hasn't checked in yet."

"We told her to just radio in, but she insisted on going in person," Li explained.

"She say why?"

Ten opened his mouth to answer when the pounding of a dozen or more rushed footsteps echoing from the ramp cut him off.

Abel pulled his sidearm and Li, dropping the cat to the floor, followed suit.

From both sides emerged a wave of black-clad armored troops, weapons drawn and readied.

Abel leaned back and whispered to Ten, "We can take 'em, right?"

"Are you insane?" the robot responded. "It's like fifteen to three."

"Lower your guns, slowly, and kick them over," one of the men in black ordered.

Li eased towards the floor and gently abandoned his firearm.

"You count as at least, what, four, five people?" Abel continued, ignoring the gunmen.

"Drop your Goddamned weapon, Abel!" Ten shouted.

"Ugh. Fine," he tossed his gun to the ground and gave it a swift kick with his foot. "Worst. Pirates. Ever."

∞

Vladia watched the guards file into her ship from the port exit. Their search for smuggled exotic animals would be fruitless, but it would buy her the time she needed to catch up to her runaway hostage, which, thanks to the tracking device she'd planted on him courtesy of Dr. Weston's tech stash, shouldn't take long. Once they found her Terran military coat that she'd left slung over the captain's chair in plain sight, they'd send for Syndicate back-up, making her entrance to their headquarters all the easier. As an added bonus, she'd left not through the ship's loading ramp, which was where the port cameras would be looking, but the emergency hatch used exclusively for in-space external repairs, giving them every reason to believe she was still on board.

It wouldn't take long for Abel to realize what she'd done, and when he did, he'd be furious. But she felt confident they'd handle things before the Syndicate arrived. If not, the Syndicate wouldn't kill them. They weren't that foolish. Worst case scenario, they would try to use them as bait to lure her into the open. By then, she'd be within their base, dismantling them from the inside out. She'd have Rehel's location in hand and most, if not all, her questions answered.

Just outside the port was a skiff rental. She had just enough credits left to buy one outright. The attendant didn't ask her name, scan her prints, or even make her fill out any papers. They exchanged money for the key, and that was that. She enjoyed the anonymity offered by the Outer Moons, though she knew full well it was not out of neglect, so much as it was for nefarious reasons. The skiff would be hers only as long as she could keep others' hands off it. The rental company would likely sic goons of their own after her to steal it back and sell it for the umpteenth time.

Mounting her new ride, she activated the tracking signal and sped off towards the northern part of the city, where her former prisoner hobbled his way home.

∞

Abel sized up the situation. They were outnumbered, hilariously outgunned, and lacking in any form of protective armor, which of course every gunman donned head to foot. In conclusion, they were doomed.

Well, they did still have Nova loose. Somewhere. Maybe she could get the jump on the groups searching the ship and then storm the bridge, guns a-blazing, and take the rest out. Yeah. Sure, he told himself. We'll just leave it all to her.

They were completely doomed.

The guards had led the three men to the bridge. Abel and Ten were bound together, back to back on the floor, and Li was cuffed to the railing beside them. With so many men and guns, the restraints felt pretty redundant.

"According to the manifest, there should be a crew of seven," the guard he assumed was in charge said to the other men. "You, you and you, sweep the top level. You and you, hit the cargo hold."

The five men selected marched off the bridge. That still left ten men watching over them.

Li leaned over and whispered, "These guys are pod security. They'll search the ship and then leave. Just keep cool."

"Yeah, well why are they searching this ship in the first place, Li?" he hissed.

"How the hell should I know?"

"Can I ask what this is all about?" Abel said to no one guard in particular. They'd all kept their helmets on, and he'd lost track of the one he thought might be in charge.

One of the black-suited men removed his helmet and stepped forward. His armored jacket had the name 'Mallory' embroidered on the front in large gold letters.

"We got an anonymous tip that this ship was harboring illegal goods. Specifically, some exotic animals from Titan," he said, pointing his gun at Abel's chest. "You wouldn't happen to know anything about that, would you?"

"Only animal here is the ship's cat."

"Well, we'll just see, won't we."

Mallory sat down in the captain's chair. It was then Abel noticed Vladia's coat.

The heavy garb was laid over the back of it, as if it'd been left out on purpose for anyone to find.

"You have got to be shitting me," he said to himself. She'd tipped off the pod guards. That's why she'd gone in person. Vladia wanted them to stay put and draw attention, he assumed so she could follow the hostage to the Syndicate's main base and bust in.

The first trio of men reported back with a salute.

"No sign of the crew on the upper level, Sir."

Mallory stood up, knocking the coat to the floor. As he reached to pick it up, the last two men checked back in over the comm.

"Found one, Sir. But he's dead. Already prepped for burial, even."

Malloy's hand hovered over the coat as he listened, then straightened up and said, "What about the cargo?"

"Still going through it, but so far they're clean."

"Keep looking."

To Abel, he said, "So, where are the other members of the crew? They also dead?"

It was Ten who answered, "No, Sir. They'd already disembarked when you and your men had arrived."

"And the deceased?" he asked, sitting back down, Vladia's coat nestled on the floor centimeters from his feet.

"He's my brother. Died of natural causes while we were outbound."

"Sorry to hear that. But, not as sorry as you folks are gonna be if we find what we're looking for. Transporting animals from Titan is a serious offense."

"Which is why you won't find anything of the sort on this ship. We're not looking for trouble. If fact, we've mostly empty containers at the moment. We were on the way to Mars for a pick-up when his brother fell ill, so we turned around immediately," Li explained coolly.

Mallory eyed the three suspiciously, but seemed to be warming to the notion that they were telling the truth. After all, there was a body in the cargo hold.

"It was probably just some asshole trying to yank your chain with a phony tip about illegal animals," Ten added. "Though it couldn't have happened at a worse time. I will be able to put my brother to rest today, I hope?"

"If everything checks out, you guys will be free to unload soon enough."

Several minutes of perpetual silence followed. Abel tried not to keep looking at the coat on the ground or think about whether or not Nova would be found any second. Finally, the last two men came back onto the bridge.

"Found some stray computer parts, but that's it," one of them reported.

"You checked for hidden compartments?"

"Yes, Sir. They're all clear."

Mallory looked annoyed, realizing he'd likely been the victim of a hoax.

"Well, gentlemen," he began, standing up. "Looks like we were mistaken."

His foot snagged the coat on the floor, and realizing he'd neglected to pick it up earlier, he scooped it up and hung it over the back of the chair. As he dusted off the shoulders of the starched olive material, Abel's stomach sank. He watched the man's face turn from the annoyance of earlier to the sudden thrill at the bigger catch before him.

Mallory grinned and asked, "I don't suppose any of you'd like to explain where you got this Terran military garb from?"

"That's what that is?" Abel exclaimed. "Found it in a bin at the docks. Seemed too nice not to pick it up."

"And where did you say you were from?"

Mallory'd drawn his gun and stepped around the chair towards Abel.

To one of his men, he said, "Jensen, head out and send an encrypted message to Mal. Tell him to send a troop here. Looks like we got a lead on this Terran they're after."

"Yes, Sir," Jensen acknowledged and marched into the corridor.

"Now, then–"

A shrill scream erupted from the hall.

Steadying his aim at Abel's forehead, Mallory motioned for a few men to go check it out.

They didn't even get a chance to round the corner before the whole bridge realized what had caused the outburst. Lazily, the ship's cat strolled into view, its typically grey fur stark white. It leapt into the Captain's chair and began washing itself, as all watched it, mouths gaping and silent.

"Everyone out!" Mallory yelled, once he'd recovered from the initial shock. The gunmen began their swift retreat from the bridge. "Let's get this ship ejected!"

Abel looked to Li, whose face had also turned a similar shade of white.

"What does white mean? And what does he mean by eject?"

"Radiation leak," Ten said as he struggled against the metal cord binding him to Abel. "They'll deplete our fuel cells and eject us back into space, leaving us adrift."

Abel could see into the hall and spotted an abandoned weapon on the ground just near the doorframe.

"There's a blaster in the corridor," Abel said to Ten. "On three, stand up with me and let's go for it."

On three they were up and side-stepping towards the blaster, when something clattered in the distance. Moments later Nova emerged, dusty and a bit tattered.

"We have got to clean out those air ducts. Seriously."

"Nova grab the blaster, we've got–" Li began.

"Cool it. I got this," she said, taking a seat at the helm.

"What are you doing? We've got to get off the ship!" Abel shouted as he and Ten continued their shimmy towards the corridor.

"Really, guys? Get off the ship and go where? Besides, what are the odds we'd have a radiation leak at a time like this?"

"But the cat–"

"I did that, jeez!" she procured her colour cap bottle and shook it knowingly. "Used my last white one, too. Wasn't even sure it worked on animals, but looks like my gamble paid off."

"So...no radiation then?" Abel asked, tentatively relaxing.

"Well..."

"Nova, you didn't–"

"I had to! You know they'll scan us, and if they don't pick up anything they'll be right back on board. Even if we have the element of surprise for the second go-round, we can't take on the entire port."

"How big and where?" Ten persisted.

"Engine room and barely enough to warrant ejection. That's why I had to dose the cat, otherwise a leak so small would take a week to change her coloring. It's controlled, I promise. Once we're outta here I can fix it, I swear," she insisted.

The lights flickered out, replaced by the emergency dimmers lining the floor.

The ship lurched to the right, sending Abel and Ten tumbling back to the floor.

"That'll be the lifts," Li chimed in. "They're pushing us out of the pod. Looks like your plan worked."

"I'll take my thanks in the form of gifts and constant praise, please," she said, smiling wide and kicking her feet onto the helm's dash. Her tattoo snaked it's way around her calf and looked at the three of them with what appeared to be contempt.

"Uh, quick question: how are we all okay with the part about not having any fuel?" Abel pointed out as he and Ten straightened into an upright position. "And can you please unbind us already?"

"Jeez, you're whiney today," Nova complained. Still, she did get up and fetch the blaster.

Fiddling with the setting, she fashioned the gun into a sort of blowtorch, cutting Li's bindings first, before moving to assist the others.

"That's not our only problem," Ten added, once he'd been freed. "Vladia's still in the city, and I need to get Erro back to Lvee's for repairs."

"First things first," Li said, taking charge. "Ten, you take Nova to the engine room. Soon as we're out, get on fixing that leak. Abel and I'll worry about the rest."

With a nod, Ten headed out; Nova trailed behind him, grumbling something about ingratitude.

Once the pair was out of earshot, Li turned to Abel and said, "You and I need to have a talk, starting with how I don't take kindly to being used as bait."

∞

Vladia came to a halt half a kilometer from where the signal had entered a large well-lit building. Pulling up her map revealed it to be the largest, and tallest, structure in the city, which wasn't particularly surprising. The Syndicate had money; clearly, they enjoyed spending it as well.

Checking the elevation coordinates, she saw that her target had travelled not up into the towering dome-scraper, but down. The upper levels were likely just for show. This also meant breaking in would be far more difficult.

She pulled her skiff into the back of what looked to be an abandoned shed. She could wait here and trace his path through the building. Tossing a few tattered cloths over her ride to hide it, she sat down near the entrance, leaning her back against the wall. By integrating her tracker with the onboard mapping system, she could get a rough idea of the interior's layout, possibly revealing another route into the catacombs.

During the next fifteen minutes the artificial sun set, and the dome panels mimicked a starry night's sky. A large hole in the ceiling gave her a nice view of the transition. In September City, some of the panels had been neglected and gone out, leaving the almost natural-looking sky scarred with strange grey squares. Here, everything appeared to be in working order, probably thanks to the Syndicate.

She and Tolen had spent many a night camping out in the gardens of their father's estate. They would sneak out once the rest of the house had called it a night, taking nothing but a few blankets with them. They would sleep under one of the large blue maples, or sometimes, when the sky was clear, in a meadow of tall grass. A night like this would have been perfect for star-gazing in the grass.

Her heart sank at the thought.

Shaking away those memories, she took up her tracker and studied the screen.

Her target hadn't moved. Either he was dead, or his debriefing was taking a lot longer than it should. It could be that they'd put him in a sort of holding area and wouldn't see him until–

The rumbling of gravel echoed in the distance, growing closer by the second. Peeking through the cracks in the wall, she saw the headlights of a large transport barreling down the road. They'd pass her in a minute, tops. But they had no reason to stop here, so she could safely ignore it. If she'd thought to bring another tracking device, she could've tossed it onto the vehicle as it passed. That might have been worth something.

The dirt danced around her, and the ground shook as the transport closed in. Vladia looked out once again; it wasn't near large enough to cause such a tremor.

The floor beneath her gave way, sending her flying down a ramp and crashing onto a paved tunnel that stretched farther than her eyes could see in the dimly lit passage.

She could hear the vehicle above her. Making haste, she scrambled behind the ramp and backed against the wall.

The transport plowed down the ramp and sped into the tunnel. The ramp lifted back up, and for several moments she was entirely exposed. But the vehicle didn't pause and soon faded from view.

Breathing a sigh of relief, she checked her tracker. The target was still in the same general area. Frustrated, she tossed the device over her shoulder and began her march down the tunnel. If another transport came barging through, she'd just be shit out of luck; it was press on or rot down here.

Her good fortune held out, and she made it to the other end without interruption. Once the end was in sight, she hit the ground and pulled out her long-range gun with the scope.

Through it, she could see the vehicle from earlier parked next to a concrete platform loaded with boxes in various sizes. A pair of men sat on one of the larger crates, one smoking a cigarette, the other spitting into a cup. Both were armed with long-range blasters, and both had taken their weapons off and leaned them against the crate they perched on.

She waited to see if any others showed up, and after a few minutes a lift lowered beside the stacks of boxes and a large, pale man and a dark woman of average size stepped off. The pair of men hopped off the box, and the four began loading the lift. It looked like they'd be making at least another four or five trips before the area was cleared.

The four chatted as they worked, but Vladia couldn't make any of it out. Finally, the lift went back up, and the two men sat back down.

She counted and waited until the lift returned. She had about six minutes between trips. Plenty of time.

As soon as the lift was out of sight for the second time, she fired, hitting one between the eyes and the other in the throat. Before they hit the ground, she was up and sprinting towards the platform. She dragged the dead one off the platform and rolled him under the vehicle.

The other man gurgled a protest as she worked. Climbing back up, she whispered her apology and finished the job. Pulling the second corpse down, she stripped him of his shirt and rolled him out of sight beside his friend. Mopping up the blood she'd spilt proved impossible. Tossing the shirt into the front seat of the transport, she pulled a crate over to hide the mess on the floor.

She'd only about a minute left. Grabbing the now ownerless blasters, she wedged herself between two of the taller crates and pulled a smaller and much lighter box in behind her. Positioning her feet against the short crate, she waited, weapon raised and ready.

Soon, the lift returned, and the pair stepped off.

"Son of a bitch," the woman cursed, "Where'd those two get off to?"

"I'll give you one guess," the man grunted.

"You're such a pervert! They wouldn't do that on the job. It's unprofessional."

The two walked into her line of sight, their backs facing the crates as they continued to look around for their comrades.

With great force, she shoved the box at her feet forward, slamming into the fat man and knocking him off the platform.

The woman reached for her weapon, but she was too slow.

Vladia tackled her from behind.

The two hit the ground. Her right arm encircled the woman's throat in a choke hold, while her other hand pointed her gun at the man on the ground.

"Don't move," she warned, "I'll snap her neck."

The guy nodded in nervous compliance, holding his hand up high.

The woman finally ceased her struggle, and Vladia let the limp form go.

Hopping off the platform, she said, "Stand up."

He did as instructed, slowly.

"How many men up there?" she asked, motioning towards the floor above them.

"None. No one. It's just a storage area."

He might be lying. She'd have to risk it, though.

"Thanks," she said before punching him in the temple with her robotic arm. He bounced off the vehicle and slid to the ground. Relieving him of his weapon, she tied his hands behind his back with his belt and returned to the girl.

Stripping her down to her essentials, Vladia tossed her own clothes into a pile and pulled on the girl's uniform. It didn't fit quite right–a little too short at the ankles and a little too big in the bust–but it would do. Lastly, she piled her blonde hair onto her head and put the girl's cap over it.

Reaching into her new pockets, she found a security card with a picture id and name.

"Sorry, Martha," she said as she tied the girl up just as she had the man. She felt a little bad about leaving her practically naked, so she took her pile of clothes and tossed them on top of her for covering.

She stepped on to the lift and pressed the panel to take her up.

Counting her new acquisition, she had two guns, two long range blasters, and two short range blasters. She knew she couldn't be seen carrying around that kind of fire power, so she tossed all but one of the short range blasters and the pair of guns. Tucking the guns under the back of her shirt, all anyone could easily spot would be the one side arm.

The lift eased to a stop. Just as the man had said, there wasn't a soul around. She needed to access a map and make her way to a populated area, like a commons room or a cantina. The best place to get information was to listen. If there was a robot here, people would be talking about it.

∞

"You shouldn't have brought him here," Irei Kodokun said to Karel as they made their way down the hall away from the holding area where the robot was being held. "You wanted him, and I made it happen. But this was never part of the deal."

"I'm sorry you feel you're being treated unfairly. Perhaps I'll have him moved once you've explained why it is that Robespierre is no more dead than when we last spoke?"

Kodokun frowned and replied, "If we'd known about the Valkyrie, we'd have prepared differently. And, we'd no way of knowing she'd be so much trouble."

Robespierre was an uncomfortable subject now. Failure always had a way of humbling one.

"I don't care about your excuses. Send out all available units and take care of it."

That was another problem. Karel wouldn't let it go. They'd already lost men during the first go at her. Now he wanted to send in even more without a second thought.

His comm buzzed at his belt.

"Yes?"

"Sir, we're sending a unit to Augusta's port. Authorities reported a suspicious ship. During inspection a Terran military coat was found on board," Mal said.

"Very good," he said, then eyeing Karel he added, "Better make that two units. Have them report in immediately if there's any sign of the Terran."

"Happy?" he said to Karel.

"Not until she's dead."

"You'll be the first to know, I assure you. Now, if you'll excuse me, I've a debriefing to see about."

"Isn't that a little below you?" he asked, folding his arms into the wide sleeve of his long, burgundy jacket.

"I like to do my part."

Karel smiled knowingly and said, "Oh, yes. I heard a soldier had stumbled in an hour or so ago. That's a bit odd isn't it? I thought you people had some sort of code. What was it? Death before dishonor?"

"You've got sharp ears to hear such talk."

He didn't bother to hide the disdain in his voice. Karel hadn't simply heard ideal gossip amongst his troops; somehow, he'd been spying on his men.

To his surprise, the man let the matter go entirely. With a slight bow, he walked away without another word.

Making his way down to level H, Kodokun thanked the gods Karel hadn't insisted on tagging along. He could have refused him, but he'd rather not make an outright enemy of the man just yet. He grew tired of his demands and of his coming and going as he pleased. Less and less did Karel feel like a wise ally, but until he had secured a replacement he'd not cut ties with him altogether. At the moment, he was the only one who could secure a win against Titan. And keeping such a dangerous fellow close had other advantages he could not entirely dismiss.

But if he could get to the robots without Karel, maybe one of his own could discover a way to create more. Or maybe that's why he wanted Robespierre dead so desperately. Was she competition? If that was the case, working with her might prove a more profitable partnership.

∞

Vladia stole into the commons room on Level J. There were free weights lining the left wall and a few tables scattered throughout. A card game had just wrapped up at one of them and a second game was just about to begin on another. At the very back there was a row of shelves, a countertop, and a large refrigerator, where a cluster of people were making drinks. In all: eleven targets.

Tugging her cap down as far as it'd reasonably go, she walked to the weights and picked up a set of twenties.

"I'm not waiting anymore," a black-haired woman at one of the tables declared as she stopped shuffling a deck of tattered cards. "We start at seven thirty, not seven whenever-the-hell-Kane-feels-like-showing-up o'clock."

"I'm with you. If she shows up, she can wait 'til next round," the bearded guy to her right agreed.

The cards were dealt out, five to each of the four players.

"Still," the beard said, arranging his cards, "You know she was on duty when that robot was lugged in. Was hoping to find out what all that was about."

"I already asked her. She didn't know much."

"I heard they're gonna take it apart," Vladia said, encouraging the conversation, but keeping her back to them.

"Maybe. That Karel creeper had it moved to one of the special holding rooms."

"Fuckin' Karel. Walks around like he owns the damn place. I'd like to take him apart," the beard grumbled.

"That's on level F?" Vladia said, setting the weights down. She'd just picked a random letter since she'd not been about to access a map. Hopefully they'd correct her and think nothing of it. Just in case, she pulled the weights off the bar as if to change them.

"Yeah if they put him in the cantina. That thing's up on C, right, Daria?"

Daria didn't answer. Instead, after a long pause she said to Vladia, "You. Turn around."

Vladia did as requested, keeping the weight bar cradled against her side.

"There a problem?"

"You got your id card?" she asked, putting her cards face down on the table.

"Course I do."

Pulling the card from her front pocket, she held it up,

sandwiched between her fingers so both the name and picture were slightly obscured.

Now the entire table had turned around to check. Vladia smiled and held the card out for anyone willing to come inspect it further.

They weren't buying it.

Taking a few steps closer, she flicked the card towards the middle of the table. Four sets of eyes watched the card glint through the air and hit the table face down.

Daria reached to flip it over.

With a quick twirl of the bar, she smacked each in the temple, and the four went down.

She'd expected to be immediately swarmed by the rest of the room. That didn't happen.

Instead, they all stared at her in a sort of awe mixed with confusion. A few stole glances at each other, as if looking for direction.

Maybe she should just walk out, she thought.

She took a step towards the door, and the whole room seemed to shift with her. The members of the other table stood up, and those in the back moved away from the counter. Still, no one acted against her.

She could run. But, seeing as how she didn't know the layout as well as they did, that was probably a bad idea. And if they were quick, she'd be shot in the back before reaching the exit.

Winding the bar between her fingers, she moved back to the center of the room. She spun the bar faster and faster as the seven remaining Ganymedes drew their weapons.

She flung the bar at the back group and hit the ground rolling towards the other group as they fired.

Kicking the table up and out sent two of them falling backwards.

Standing, she grabbed the last one's weapon with her right hand, crushing the barrel.

Three of the back group had recovered from her initial assault and fired.

In his shock, the man next to her didn't fight back as she pulled him to her like a shield to block the oncoming blasts.

Weapon drawn, she rushed forward and pushed the dead man into one of the gunmen. She fired at the remaining pair, hitting one in the shoulder, one in the hip.

Behind her, she heard the scuffling of footsteps. Pivoting on her heels, she spotted a man make it out the door and another trying to follow.

One shot took out the straggler.

Someone rammed her in the back, knocking her to the ground and sending her weapon skidding across the room.

The man was on her, his arm around her neck, squeezing her windpipes closed.

She reached for her side arm, but a foot clamped down on her hand.

He bent down, holding his bleeding shoulder and digging his heel into her skin. He said, "Should have shot to kill, bitch."

Clicking off her nerve-endings in the hand, she pushed against the man's foot to get her index finger to meet her thumb.

White spots danced before her eyes, but she managed to flick up her thumbnail and press the trigger.

The dagger shot out at her wrist, stabbing the man through his Achilles tendon.

He lurched back in pain, freeing her arm.

Slicing behind her wildly, she caught the other man in the side and the upper arm, forcing him to loosen his hold on her enough so she could knock him off.

She fired a shot into each man's skull. They dropped immediately.

She didn't automatically stand up. The white dots no longer obstructed her vision, but the light-headedness lingered. Retracting her blade, she surveyed the damage to her hand. It wasn't bad; the nanos had already begun repairing the torn skin.

Heavy breathing that she suddenly realized wasn't her own

pulled her attention to the back wall again.

On the floor, the one she'd shot in the hip reached for a weapon on the ground near him.

She aimed her gun between his eyes, and the man froze.

"Don't make me kill you."

Easing away from the weapon, he held his hands up in surrender.

A siren blared. It must have been the one that had gotten away.

Standing up, she retrieved her weapons and grabbed a few more. Now that they knew she was here, there was no reason not to be fully armed.

The trek to level C would take much longer, assuming they'd locked down the lifts. Once in the corridor, a quick press of a button confirmed this suspicion.

She could also assume they'd come at her from below and above. Sprinting to the stairwell, she took two steps at a time until she heard the clamoring of footsteps echoing from above.

She had no option but to duck out onto level E and take her chances finding another route to level C.

∞

Entering the holding area, Kodokun passed down the rows of cells until he came to the one with three guards loitering out front.

"Is this the one?" he asked, looking through the bars to find a man sitting in the corner, his head resting on his knees.

"Yes, Sir. Name's James T. Wells."

"You've already done the psych eval?"

"Just finished a few minutes ago. He checks out."

"Very well, then. Open it up and let's have a word."

The door unlocked, and Kodokun entered alone.

Looking back, he said, "Thain, you stay here with me. The rest of you can go about your regular activities."

"Now," he said, turning back towards the man in the cell. "James, I want you to tell me exactly what you told the others when you got back."

The man raised his head. He didn't look at all well. Dark circles hung off his eyes and his skin appeared a bit yellow. Probably malnutrition.

"She's not human," he muttered. "And she can't be killed."

"Robespierre?"

He nodded.

"She showed me. Slit her arm right open. Held it up to my face, and I watched it close up on its own."

"We don't know anything about Terran medical technology. This could be typical. Doesn't mean she can't be killed," he said, though he didn't entirely believe his own words. He'd never met a Terran before, but he knew his fair share of Martians. If they didn't possess such medical advances, how in the worlds would a backwards place like Earth?

"It's not just that. She's strong. Stronger than she should be. I watched her smash through a blast door with her bare hands on the *The Shikome* trying to get down to the cargo hold where we were loading the robots."

"Could she, too, be a robot? That would explain things."

"She bled. Robots don't bleed."

That was true as far as he knew, but having never actually seen a robot before he couldn't be entirely sure. He'd better take a look at that robot Karel was so interested in and find out for himself.

"Whatever she is," Wells continued, "she's dangerous. I don't think we can stop her."

"Everything can be killed," he assured the man.

Wells pulled himself up from the floor and looked him in the face as he spoke. "We shouldn't have taken that robot. She'll be coming for it. If you've any sense at all, you'll let it go before–"

Alarms screamed through the holding area.

Snatching up his comm, Kodokun asked, "Report?"

"We've got an intruder on level J, heading up," Mal responded.

"Is it her?"

"Can't confirm."

"Is Karel still in the building and did he take the robot with him?"

"Karel departed and appeared to be alone."

"Shit," he whispered.

To Mal he said, "I want her alive. I think we've been set up."

"I dunno if that's an option."

"Give the order! We may need her."

"Yes, Sir," came the reluctant answer.

"Do you think she's coming for him?" Thain asked, pointing towards Wells.

"No," Kodokun answered, motioning for him to follow. "She's coming for the robot. And she's coming for us."

∞

Level E looked no different than the rest of the building, making its purpose impossible to determine from a simple scan. Didn't matter though. What Vladia needed was an air vent, or failing that, she could blaster open the lift and possibly scale the shaft, depending on its construction.

A pair of men entered the hall from an ingress about twenty meters away. Based on information from Nova, she recognized one immediately as Irei Kodokun. Marching towards them, neither of the men seemed to recognize her as a threat until she was almost upon them.

The man beside Kodokun raised his weapon to fire, but he was too slow. She dodged his shot and fired her own in one fluid motion, sending his weapon flying from his hand.

She moved her aim to Kodokun, who wore an expression not of fear, but of disapproval. He held up his hands before she had to ask and waited for her to reach them.

"Thank you for not killing my friend here," he said.

"Where is he?"

"If you want the robot, you're welcome to him. It wasn't

my idea to take it in the first place."

"I'll bet it wasn't your idea to have me killed, either. Sorry, pal, but I ain't buying."

The man ignored her sarcasm and said, "I'd very much like to have a word with you on that matter, actually. We may have a common enemy."

"I'm on a bit of a rampage here, so if you don't mind, I'd prefer not to."

"I think you'd be interested in what I have to say, Robespierre," Kodokun said as he dropped his hands back to his sides.

"Sir," his comm hummed, "We got men down on level J. We think she's on—"

Switching her gun to her left hand, Vladia snatched the device from his belt and crushed it, letting the remains sprinkle the floor around them.

He smirked at her but held his tongue.

"Take me to level C, or there'll be a whole lot more men down."

With a slight bow of his head, he motioned for her to follow.

15

CHANGEMENT

Devil's Run floated helplessly, caught in orbit around Ganymede. Nova and Ten worked to repair the radiation leak, while Abel and Li stayed on the bridge to deal with bigger problems, namely their lack of fuel.

The escape pod, assuming they'd all fit, could jettison them back to the safety of the moon; but that would mean giving up the ship and almost everything on her, including the items Weston had provided them to give the crew a bit of an edge in the Outer Moons. Even more troubling was the fact that they'd essentially be marooning themselves on Ganymede for who knows how long. They were out of money, so purchasing a new ship would be impossible. The cargo they'd stolen off the *The Shikome* would also be lost, leaving them with no means to repair Erro.

"We'd have been better off letting the port guards take us in," Li said from the Captain's chair.

He couldn't make out his expression in the low lights, but Abel didn't have to see to know the man was pissed.

Now that he thought about it, Abel wondered if perhaps that'd been the general idea.

"I think that may have been the plan," Abel added. "Vladia follows the prisoner back to base, we get boarded and they spot the coat, causing them to call in the troops. That would make it easier for her to get inside."

"The port would've handed us over to the Syndicate for interrogation, and we'd all end up in the same place. She'd rescue Rehel, then come for us like some big damn hero," Li finished his train of thought. "Would have been nice," he added, "If she'd bother to let us in on all this."

"She had her reasons," Abel assured him, though he'd no idea what said reasons could possibly be.

"Cause we'd try to stop her. There's no way she'll get to Rehel on her own. And even if she does, he's probably in pieces already."

"Don't say that."

Abel hadn't meant to say that out loud and felt a bit ashamed he'd not held back. His fear for Rehel's safety had been pushed to the back of his mind as best he could, but hearing Li say the worst made him forget himself for a moment. Vladia had to get to him in time.

"What about *Gunnr*?" Abel asked to avoid any further discussion of Rehel or Vladia.

"There's no way they'll let you dock in a Terran ship. You'd be better off putting on a suit and walking back."

Leaning against the nav console, Abel crossed his arms and said, "I hate to point this out, but Nova kinda put us in a fix here. How long can we make it on backup?"

Li shook his head, "A day, maybe a day and a half if we cut the lights completely."

"If we send out an S.O.S., we can use a different registration code so we don't flag as hazardous," Abel offered. "Surely someone would pick us up before we lose life support."

"And if they try to board us and, oh I don't know, relieve us of all our goods and cargo and just leave?" Nova said, rounding the corner, still dressed in her haz suit and cradling her helmet under her arm. "People don't play nice out here, Terran. You'd best remember that."

Abel scoffed, "I'd like to see them try. Besides, you're the one got us into this, so you just keep your opinions to yourself."

"She's right. Sending an S.O.S. is just inviting trouble to our front door," Li said.

Tossing her helmet at Abel, she pointed to him. "Don't you be mad at me, either. Your Captain got us into this, not me."

"Well, you got a plan, then?"

"Actually, I do. Had one all along, but I do like to watch you boys squirm a bit."

"Well?" Li prodded.

"I'll take Erro down in the escape pod and go straight to Lvee. While he repairs Erro, I'll borrow his ship and bring us some fuel."

"How do you know he even has a ship? Or that he'll be willing to help us?" Abel asked. As far as he was concerned, this guy still couldn't be trusted. After their run in with the *The Shikome* they only had one functional pod left. Sure, they had the two Valkyries, but no one out here would give them clearance to land in a Terran vessel. If she took the only pod, and things went sour, he and Li really would be trapped.

"Because Ten said he has one, and I'll only be bringing what's needed to fix Erro," she assured them both. "If he wants the rest, he'll have to loan us a ship and some fuel to get it."

Abel looked to Li. They'd be the ones to die up here if it all went wrong. His comrade studied the backs of his hands intently and for a moment, it looked like he hadn't heard a word.

Still focused on his hands, he said, "The pod can fit one more. I'll stay here with Ten. Abel, you should go with Nova."

"I don't need his help," Nova protested.

She started to say more, but Li shot her a glace that silenced her.

With a shrug, she said, "Fine."

He knew what Li was doing. He had that whole going down with the ship sound in his voice.

"I should stay here," Abel explained. "You'll be of more use down there, and we both know it."

"This isn't your call."

"Well, it sure as hell isn't yours," he said, parking himself in the nav chair. "I'm not going, and that's that."

"He's right," Nova added. "If it comes down to it, Lvee's more likely to help you and me than a Terran."

"Him staying here don't change the fact he's still helping a Terran."

"Yeah, well ain't no sense in putting it out in his face either."

Li rubbed his stubbled chin. He was still shaking his head when he finally agreed to go.

"Come help me load up," Nova said, looking at Abel. "Let's not waste any more time than we already have."

Following her off the bridge, the pair headed down to the cargo area. Nova popped a color cap into her mouth, then grabbed the outer rungs of the ladder and slid down. Abel took the slower approach. By the time his feet hit the ground, she already had a box in hand, and all but the tips of her hair had transformed to a lively purple.

"Grab that one," she said, knocking a box at her feet with the side of her brown boot.

She waited as he scooped up the parcel. They walked together in silence as they made the hike to the other side of the cargo bay where the pod was docked.

It wasn't until they'd packed their loads and began walking that Nova spoke to him.

"You didn't need to do that."

"I know."

"Then why did you?"

She sounded angry. She kept her eyes forward, her brow scrunched.

"I dunno. Just seemed like the thing to do. Besides, you guys are coming back for me. I don't see the problem."

They reached the make-shift coffin they had stowed Erro in, and together they lifted the lid up and onto the floor. He'd need to be moved into a smaller box if they ever hoped to cram him into the already-tight dimensions of the pod.

"Well for one, you hurt his pride," she said, motioning for Abel to take one of the arms.

They pulled him into a sitting position.

"But, if worst comes to worst, Li can't pilot a Valkyrie off this hunk of junk."

"Yeah, but where you gonna go in your fancy ship?"

"I'd figure something out. Better than staying here and slowly suffocating."

Nova laughed and said, "Oh don't worry. You'd freeze to death before you suffocated."

"I'll make sure to grab some extra blankets, then."

"I'll be back long before you need 'em. Promise," she said with a quick wink.

∞

The woman jabbed her gun hard between Kodokun's shoulder blades as he led her on to level C. Despite her roughness, he didn't think Robespierre was the type to kill unnecessarily. Soon enough he'd have his chance to illustrate just how useful a resource the Syndicate could be.

Still, this was not the same woman he'd viewed on the interrogation film. Taking the robot had crossed a line, which he imagined was part of Karel's plan to make sure he'd not be able to cut ties with him and side with the Terran. Or perhaps this set-up had been constructed not to keep ties, but to destroy them in a much more permanent fashion.

Their roles had now been reversed, though he'd bet money she still needed his help in this matter with Earth. But wrath clouded her judgment, and she couldn't see past it. That made her dangerous.

They should have killed her on that ship.

He tapped in his code to the holding cell and the door to the observation area slid open. The robot could be viewed safely and secretly from here. The room had been cleared to nothing but bare brown walls plus the visioglass panel.

Pushing past him, the woman put a hand on the glass separating them. The robot stood in the middle of the room, unrestrained and unharmed.

The door shut behind him, and the unmistakable click of

the locking mechanism followed. Did she hear it too, he wondered.

"He can't see you, but now that you have assurance of his safety, I must insist we have a word," he began.

Lifting her gun, she aimed it at his face but kept her eyes on the robot.

"You came to us for help not long ago. I quite admired your little stunt, in fact."

She didn't respond. After a few seconds, he pressed on.

"I can only assume that you still need us for whatever you have planned in regards to Earth. At the time, that is, when your message was received, I'd already forged an alliance. I am beginning to think that may have been a mistake on my part."

"You've made a lot of mistakes. I've lost count," she said absently. Her fingers traced the outline of the glass. She was looking for a weak point.

"Granted, we've not dealt with a person of your caliber before. I'll be the first to admit you surprised us all. But the fact remains I had no desire to harm you or your robot. That was my partner, Karel. He said he needed you dead. In a show of good faith, I tried to make that happen."

He hoped the mention of Karel would shed some light on their relationship. But the woman made no visible signs of recognizing the name, much to his disappointment.

"This Karel," she said, turning towards him for the first time since they'd entered the room. "What did he want with Rehel?"

"You've no interest in why he wanted you dead?"

"He can take a number," she said dismissively. "What did he do to Rehel?"

Kodokun shrugged and said, "I don't know that he did anything. In fact, your robot is archaic compared to the others on Ganymede, or so he said."

This appeared to pique her interest. Now she gave him her full attention.

"He knows about the others? For how long?"

"Again, I don't know. He approached me with the

information and offered his services."

"And what services would that be, exactly?"

"I need an unstoppable force to remedy the Titan problem. You wouldn't know, being an off-worlder, but we aren't exactly on friendly terms. We must compete with them for resources, specifically those from Mars. They've become more aggressive over the past few years; we've lost many ships full of supplies to their piracy. Karel insisted that if he had the resources to study the robots here, he could figure out how to build more. In exchange for my help in his research, he'd give me enough robots to deal with Titan once and for all."

"I don't see what he's getting out of this arrangement."

"The knowledge gained from the study and construction of robots. For whatever reason, he's interested in that, almost to the point of being maniacal about it, really."

There. All his cards were face up and on the table. Surely she'd take this as a sign of trust. He risked a lot telling her this, any remaining alliance with Karel jeopardized entirely on the gamble.

Robespierre smiled. Then, raring back, she slammed her fist into the visioglass.

It didn't shatter. But when she retracted her arm, small flecks of the glass fell to the floor.

Now the robot knew she'd come for him.

Kodokun's body went rigid, fighting the urge to take flight. With a single word, he could back out of the room and fill it with poison. She'd be down before she could break the glass. Probably. He wasn't ready to test that theory just yet.

"You want an out," she smirked, her gun again raised to point firmly between his eyes. "This Karel fellow. He's made you nervous, perhaps?"

"I don't trust him to keep his end of the bargain, making him a common enemy," he said, trying to keep his voice steady.

"And you think you can trust me?"

"More than I can him."

Again, she smashed her fist into the glass. More chips fell

269

to the floor.

"And you think I can supply you with what you need?"

"If Karel wants you dead, he has reason to fear you. There must be something to that."

A third time she struck the glass. This time a crack formed, extending just a few centimeters from the point of impact. If he couldn't get her on his side soon, he'd have no choice but to end her. Giving her the robot without assurance spelled certain death for them all.

"If you could build the robots—"

She punched the glass, this time with something far beyond anger. The cracks multiplied and extended into a spider web.

"Strange how you long to repeat the mistakes of Earth. Have you really learned nothing? I came here for an army, but not the kind you're thinking. The only force I aim to lead is a willing one. Not one of slaves who fight only because they are ordered to, because they can do no more."

It became clear now. He'd wrongly assumed Robespierre's interest in robots must be analogous to Karel's. He feared her not as a competitor, but as one who could, and would, prevent his endeavors.

Aloud he said, "You think you can cobble together such a force out here?"

"I do. Common enemies, as you mentioned earlier. And with Mars on my side—"

"Mars," he interrupted. Now this really did change things. If he'd have known this when he'd watched the interrogation…

"And how far along is this Karel's research?"

"He doesn't have a working prototype, as far as I know."

"Can you tell me where to find him?"

"Regrettably, I cannot."

Her fist met the glass again, sending the cracks almost to the edges. It'd only take one more hit.

"Can't, or won't?"

"I can't. He didn't work here. The most you can do is warn the others of his presence."

"Are you afraid? If he finds out you've given him up, won't he come for you?"

"He left that robot here, instead of taking it to his lab, so you would find it in my hands. I expect he hopes you'll do away with me so he doesn't have to dirty his hands."

"Well," she said, lowering her weapon. "I always was a disappointment."

She struck the glass once more and the window exploded into shards of flickering crystals.

They shielded their eyes from the remains, and as the dust settled, Rehel stepped through the opening.

"You all right?" Robespierre asked the robot.

"I am."

"Let's go then. We need to warn Lvee about this Karel guy."

"I can provide you with a transport," Kodokun offered.

"What happened with my ship? I imagine a troop was sent in to arrest them at the port?"

He arched an eyebrow, but once he understood he let out a quiet laugh. "That was you, too, then. I guess I should have known."

Robespierre dismissed his attempt at praise, but he expected that, too. Already, he felt confident in this new alliance. As long as she could take out Karel for him…

"A troop was sent to your ship, but with all the commotion of your arrival, no one's heard from them. And, you destroyed my comm so…" he said, folding his other plans back. He wouldn't tell her to kill Karel. He had the feeling he didn't need to.

"If they're here, send them my way."

"Is there anything else you require of us?"

"If Karel shows up here, you need to keep him here. I'll be back soon."

She motioned for the robot to follow her, and the two left him in the holding room.

Into his comm, Kodokun said, "Mal, tell everyone to stand down and let her through."

"You've made up your mind?"

"She'll take care of Karel."

"What about the robots? We still need them."

After a slight pause and a shrug no one saw, he said, "We'll try this her way. For now."

∞

"I fold," Abel grumbled, tossing his cards at their make-shift table. "Again."

He'd like to blame the poor lighting for his continued losses, but that'd be lying.

They'd set up in the cargo area to pass the time. Ten had swiped a deck of cards from Li's bag and a bottle of brown liquor from Nova's. The liquor was for him, but he insisted Ten pour himself a glass anyway. Drinking alone felt too much like giving up.

For the first sixteen hours, they'd busied themselves with minor repairs. They had put the med bay back in working order and cleaned up the area their prisoner had been held in. They'd also reorganized the cargo hold, and he'd checked both Valkyries top to bottom. He'd swept the entire ship and was about to go as far as cleaning out the vent shafts, when Ten approached him with cards and booze.

Normally, a losing streak like this would irk him to the point he'd have to crack a few jokes just to prove he wasn't sore about it. But his mind had wandered so far and away from the game at hand that the losing hardly mattered. Ten could tell his heart wasn't in it, but he kept on pushing for another round.

"We could play another game. Maybe one I'm not familiar with?" the robot suggested.

"What you mean to say is one you aren't so damn good at."

Ten poured more whiskey into their glasses, only taking a small portion for himself to minimize the waste.

"What do you do with it?" Abel asked, motioning towards Ten's stomach area.

"There's a container inside that can be removed for disposal. It's pretty sterile so if you want–"

"Please don't finish that sentence."

Ten laughed, but for a second he looked almost offended.

"Surely Rehel has a similar system?"

"I never asked, and it never came up. Not like he needed to blend in like you guys do," he explained, taking a small sip from his tin cup. He had to drink extra slow. Their supply was limited, but also this stuff was stronger than anything he could get on Earth. His mind had to stay clear and focused in case trouble came upon them. The chances of another ship raiding them weren't as slim as he'd like them to be.

Ten pulled the cards into a pile and began organizing the deck for another round.

They still had at least another twenty hours to go before life support ran out of juice. He told himself there was no point worrying until then. For now, the name of the game was keeping calm and carrying on, as the old saying went.

"I've been thinking," Ten began, his tone taking an unexpectedly dark turn. "If it comes down to it, if Nova runs later than expected, that is, you could suit up and hang out in Vladia's Valkyrie. That way, if it comes to bugging out, *Gunnr* would be topped off still."

He'd already thought about that. Truth be told, it just wasn't practical.

"Starting up a Valkyrie in here would likely damage the hull and destroy most, if not all, of the cargo. And if I can't start her, it's no different than out here."

Of course the cargo mattered little, but if there was a hull breach, it'd spell trouble for Ten. He wasn't built for space exposure.

"We'll launch her outside, then. Like we did with *Gunnr* before we hit *The Shikome*. The doors work on manual as well so even after we've lost all the power, I can still get you back in and to *Gunnr*."

"That could work," he said, beckoning Ten to pass the cards his way. "But, it won't come to that. And you can be sure

273

I'm gonna tell Nova how much you doubted her."

"You can tell her anything you like. Just as long as you get the chance to tell her."

Ignoring Ten's pessimism, Abel smiled and said, "From now on, I'm shuffling. I'm not so sure I can trust you at cards."

His friend grinned weakly.

"So, this is a little game I like to call Follow the Queen. You get seven cards, wilds are—"

The ship lurched to the side a bit, accompanied by a low groan.

Ten grabbed the bottle of whiskey, but the cups clattered to the floor; their contents spilt, forming small puddles on the ground.

"Shit," Abel said, drawing his gun.

"We're being boarded."

"Nova?"

"No way to know. Comms are down."

Abel stood up and walked towards the ladder.

"Let's go," he whispered.

Ten set the bottle down and, drawing his weapon, followed suit.

"No," Abel hissed back at the robot. "Bring that. We may need it."

"For what?" Ten asked, picking the whiskey back up. "You gonna throw it at them?"

"No," he argued. "I don't know, maybe."

Scaling the ladder, the two rushed towards the docking hatch as quietly as they could, stopping only at the weapons locker to grab a few more guns. The hatch was located near the med bay, so they took cover just within the doorway.

Another mechanical moan echoed through the corridor, but the hatch held still.

Each of them had a revolver, and Abel managed to snag a spare on the way. Ten had taken two more rifles for himself, but it had been slim pickings. The fight on *The Shikome* had left their pockets a little light, plus they were missing what Vladia,

Nova and Li had run off with.

The hatch creaked open with little resistance. They'd put everything they had left into life support, so the door was sealed, but not on lockdown.

Footsteps clanked into the hallway. After a moment Ten signaled that there were three, possibly four, intruders from the sounds of it.

"You sure about this?" a male voice he didn't recognize asked.

"This is it. The registration code matches one from the list," came the answer.

Abel stood up, much to Ten's surprise, and laughed out loud.

"You son of a bitch!" he cried, not in anger, but relief, as he stepped into the corridor.

Without a thought, Abel thrust his naked hand out towards his friend.

Takashi Gammarow clasped it within his own, despite its bareness.

"You know I'm always late to the party," he said. "Hell of a time finding your ass, too. I picked up a few stragglers to make up for it, though."

Stepping aside, Abel looked at his two companions.

"Commander Whitlock," the dark-skinned man said, saluting him stiffly.

He wore the uniform of one of the Grand Admiral's Royal Guard. Takashi must have sensed his hesitation at the man's dress.

"This fellow's had his own encounter with Malthus. You guys should swap stories some time," he said, vouching for the man.

"Good to meet you, Commander."

Ten finally emerged from the med bay, rifles slung over his shoulder and the bottle still in his hand. He kept back several feet, probably trying to analyze this unexpected situation

"This is Lieutenant Rachael Vardoger," Takashi continued. "She was one of the nav officers on the *Iron Maiden.*"

Her grey sleeveless shirt and brown pants hung off her thin, tall frame as if they were someone else's clothes. The woman gave him a quick nod, but didn't extend her hand, nor did she salute. He couldn't quite be sure in such dim light, but Rachael felt familiar. Perhaps, she been one of the candidates for the Valkyrie program that he'd interviewed but didn't make the cut.

He was about to ask just that, when Takashi noticed Ten hanging back and shouted, "You look different, tin man."

"Excuse me?"

His answer was sharp, bordering on hostile. So much so Takashi took a step back and put his hand on his sidearm.

"That isn't Rehel," Abel corrected him. "We'll get into this later. Ten, this is Lt. Takashi Gammarow."

"More Terrans. Yay," he said, holding up his hands and shaking them in faux excitement.

Takashi opened his mouth to speak, but decided against it and instead cleared his throat.

Another set of footsteps clamored in the hatchway.

"And you of course know our last straggler," his friend said with a sly smile as Cornelia appeared in the corridor.

She immediately went to Abel and hugged him firmly.

"I thought you were dead," he said as she let go and took a step back.

"So did I."

She was dressed in the same clothing as Rachael, though hers seemed to fit much better. Her red hair had lost some of its radiance, probably due to malnutrition, but other than that she looked just as he'd last seen her.

Her eyes also drifted towards Ten in recognition, but she seemed to realize it wasn't Rehel and instead held out her hand and introduced herself.

Ten reluctantly moved closer to the group, but took her hand all the same and reciprocated the introduction.

To Abel, she said, "Where's Vladia?"

"On the surface. Along with the rest of our crew."

"You require assistance, I assume," Whitlock said.

"Some fuel would be nice to get us back to Ganymede."

"We don't have much to spare, but you're welcome to what we can," the solider offered.

This guy reminded him of home. His formality and his to-the-point attitude provided a strange kind of comfort for Abel.

"Great. I'll catch you guys up while we work."

"You boys can tackle that. I'll bring over some weapons to restock your arsenal, seeing as how you guys are armed with antiques and," Cornelia stopped and shot Ten a sideways glance, "is that whiskey?"

"It is," Ten said, offering her the bottle.

Cornelia took it gratefully, but didn't open it.

"Told you we'd need that," Abel said as he, Whitlock, and Takashi headed towards the engine room.

Ten grumbled something, but he didn't catch it. He'd get used to the new folks soon enough. After all, it hadn't taken him long to warm up to him and Vladia, though that may have been because of Rehel more than anything.

Abel picked up the pace and pushed Rehel from his mind. First things first. They'd contact Nova and Li to regroup, then they could concentrate on finding Vladia and Rehel.

∞

Rehel and Vladia didn't speak again until they were entirely clear of the Syndicate's main base. He assumed she'd opted out of taking the transport offered by Kodokun for fear they would track her back to Lvee's hideout. Kodokun appeared to be an ally, but could someone who aligned himself with a man like Karel ever really be trusted?

She had taken a comm, but only to wait for word on Abel and the rest of her crew. She cradled the device in her hand reluctantly as she waited for word. Once their location could be verified, she planned to dispose of it.

With the bright domescaper to their backs, the imitation starry night dissolved into a bluish-purple sunrise. In the distance, a small shed hung off the landscape. Vladia pointed towards it.

"There. I've got a skiff. We'll take that to Lvee's."

"Once you've warned him, what will you do?" he asked.

"I'd like to track this Karel down and neutralize the threat before he has a chance to take any of the others in."

"He's dangerous."

"Lots of people are dangerous. Including me."

"Not like him. This man takes pleasure in the chaos unleashed. He spoke of dissections and–" Rehel stopped before his voice got shaky. He was afraid of this man. Of being taken apart. Of what he'd do to Vladia.

"You are right, though," he continued once he could be sure of his own voice. "He must be dealt with somehow."

Her comm buzzed. Flicking the receiver switch up, she asked, "Well?"

"Your crew wasn't taken in. Port detected a radiation leak and ejected them back out."

It wasn't Kodokun who addressed her, but one of his underlings.

"What's that mean? They're just hanging out in orbit?"

"They'd have to be. Port procedure requires them to deplete their fuel cells before ejection so they can't try to dock somewhere else and endanger lives further. We can send out a ship to–"

Vladia slammed the comm to the ground and stamped it out with her heel.

Rehel looked at her, a little stunned by her actions.

"Can't take it with us," she said with a shrug. "I don't want them knowing where Lvee's base is." After a pause she added, "How long you think they can last out there?"

"About two days, maybe less, but the radiation leak would be their biggest concern."

"I guarantee that was Nova's handiwork, so I wouldn't worry with that."

Once they reached the shed, Vladia disappeared inside, emerging moments later with a skiff, as promised.

"The best we can do is get to Lvee's. He'll have a ship we

can use to get to them," she said, mounting the skiff.

Rehel hopped on behind her.

Pulling out her own comm she'd taken from *Devil's Run*, she turned it on and tried to contact her ship with no success.

With a heavy sigh, she revved up the skiff.

"You're going to have to learn to trust them if you expect to build an army from them."

"I know," she said. "But someone who switches sides so easily shouldn't be taken lightly. They'll have a chance to earn my trust soon enough."

16

HELL IS EMPTY

Rachael had volunteered to take care of the weapons, so Ten gave Cornelia a quick tour of the ship, ending on the bridge.

"So that's about it," Ten concluded, taking a seat at the comm station. "It's a small ship, but pretty high-tech compared to the average Outer Moon rig."

"It's nicer than ours, but the *Atlas* still packs a punch. I suppose that Weston fellow wasn't exactly prepared for all we've dragged him into."

"From what I understand, he's doing this to protect Mars, so it's just as much for himself as it is us."

"So this Lvee fellow," she said, changing the subject. "How well do you actually know him?"

The woman leaned up against the console. She still had the bottle he'd given her tucked under her arm, though its contents had diminished during their excursion. It'd been so long since she'd had a real drink, she felt light-headed. What she'd kill for right now was a proper meal.

"We all lived on the outskirts together for years, so I'd say pretty well. Since Erro and I have moved on, we don't see him or any of the others much. It'd be dangerous to be seen in a group, for obvious reasons."

"Is it strange that you two struck out together? Seems like even that'd be a risk."

Ten shrugged.

"Erro and I, we're very like-minded, I suppose. When I suggested we go, it seemed only right that he'd come with."

If it hadn't been for the fact he looked so much like Rehel, she'd have never guessed he wasn't human. His movements were so natural, almost fluid in execution. Ten was made to be one with humanity, while poor Rehel had been made to stand apart from it. Then again, Abel never saw him as anything less than a person. She wished she could claim the same. With Rehel now gone, a deep pang of regret swelled in her chest.

She set the whiskey on the floor. She shouldn't have had any. It'd made her go all sentimental.

"If you don't mind me asking, how d'you guys tell each other apart? I mean, on Earth I guess it didn't ever matter, as bad as that sounds, so I've never really thought about it before now."

"We all have an infrared serial number printed just below the right eye, but after a while we all picked up different habits and looks organically," Ten said. He tugged gently on his ponytail and with a grin, added, "Erro doesn't have nearly as nice a head of hair as I do."

Cornelia laughed, "Neither do I."

"It's not real, of course," he added, his smile diminishing slightly.

She shook her head in disapproval.

"It's real enough."

Rachael entered and, joining the pair, said, "Power should be up soon. We've split our armory with you."

"Great. Once we're up, I'll send a comm to Nova and Li. We should join them at Lvee's to regroup," Ten said.

"Shouldn't we be more concerned with getting to Vladia? From what you've said, Nova and Li aren't in any actual danger. She is," Rachael pointed out.

"Yeah, but even using new registration codes, we can't dock in Augusta City just yet because of the radiation incident. December is the next closest port, so we might as well go there first."

"Docking in Augusta doesn't prevent *us* from going to her

282

aid in December," she insisted, referring to their ship.

"Maybe we should split up?" Cornelia suggested. "There's six of us, so we could spare you, Ten, if you want to check on Erro first."

The lights came on to full, and the nav console flickered to life.

Holding her hand up to shield her eyes, Cornelia said, "Once we've heard from Nova and Li, we can decide what to do then."

Ten nodded and moved to the comm station.

The rest of their merry band arrived on the bridge in short order.

"Nice to be able to see proper. Was worried I'd go cross-eyed," Abel said, making a squinty face.

"The way you fly, I thought you already were cross-eyed," Takashi said as he hopped over the railing onto the main deck of the bridge and sat in the captain's chair.

She expected to hear a sharp comeback from him, maybe something about Takashi's rearing facility, as it had always been the butt of many jokes. But she was met with silence. As she turned to face him, she saw why.

Abel remained in the doorway, his eyes fixed solely on Rachael, who'd not yet become aware of his stare. She had taken Ten's seat at the nav console but had spun around to face the center of the bridge.

It was then she realized why the woman had felt so familiar despite the fact she couldn't place her face among her short-lived crew. Rachael bore a striking resemblance to Ceres Forté. Sure, the hair was completely different, her voice lacked the softness of the former, and the nose was a bit off too, but now that she could see them both in the same room, it felt like time had relapsed.

"I'm not getting any response." Ten interrupted her thoughts and Abel's trance-like gaze.

Abel strolled to the comm station and asked, "Interference maybe? You said the compound was underground, right?"

"I've never tried to make contact from outside the place, so it could be."

"Regardless," Rachael interjected. "We need to land. We're wasting fuel just hanging out in space."

"She's right," Whitlock conferred. "We didn't have much to give you, so let's spend it wisely."

"Surely, Vladia took a comm with her?" she asked.

Ten punched in a few commands at his station then said, "We've got a live comm."

"Where?" Abel asked.

"Give me a second."

After a few moments, he added, "In the tubes between Augusta and December. Looks like she's probably heading to Lvee's. Won't be able to get through to her until she's out of the tubes. Not from here, anyway."

"Right. Looks like we're going to December City," Whitlock said. To Abel, he added, "You guys are short a man, so I'll stay on with *Devil's Run* for now. Cornelia, Rachael, Takashi, you take *Atlas*. We'll regroup once we've docked."

Cornelia hung back from the rest of her crew. She wanted to say something to Abel, but what could be said? Hey pal, sorry the new girl kinda looks like your dead girlfriend?

In the end all she could manage was a sympathetic look as she passed him on the way out.

∞

Li carried the bulk of the weight as he and Nova unloaded the box holding Erro from the truck and lowered it to the ground just outside of the dilapidated structure that housed Lvee and the other robots.

"You sure this is it?" Li asked, going back to the truck to grab his rifle. He tossed one to Nova as well.

"Ten gave me the coordinates himself, and it's as he described it."

She caught the weapon and slung it over her shoulder.

"Come on. Let's move him into the cover of the building at least."

Li nodded and walked back over to help. The two lifted the box and shuffled the few meters to reach the inside.

Easing the box to the floor, Li said, "It's strange."

"What is?"

"You know how the outskirts are. Full of rundown houses and abandoned warehouses."

"Yeah, kinda like the shithole you live in?"

"No," he huffed. "But, that is my point. The outskirts may look ransacked and not fit to live in, but people always do. So don't it strike you strange that this whole area actually is abandoned? There's nobody. Not even any animals, from the looks of it."

Even in the dead of space, Li'd never felt as isolated as he did now. It was the noise, or the absence of it. He sat down on the edge of the crate and listened hard. He didn't even hear crickets out here. In deep space there'd be the constant hum of the ship, and even if you took a walk outside, music would loop over and over inside the suit. The silence, so unsettling, could drive a person mad, so goes the rumor, but this right here was the closest he'd ever come to true soundlessness.

"Maybe he's got a perimeter set up for that?"

"Well, if that's the case how'd we get in so easy?"

"Jesus, Li, I don't know. But we're here, and we've got a job to do, so let's just do it," she snapped, walking to the center of the room where there appeared to be a cellar door.

Li got up and walked over to her.

"I don't like this."

Nova knocked on the door with the heel of her boot. It echoed through the chamber below.

"Maybe nobody's home," he said.

Nova frowned and knocked again, this time slamming her foot down so hard, he worried the door might give and she'd go tumbling down. But the door held, and after a few moments the click-clack of footsteps could be heard coming up from the floor.

Moving off the door, the pair waited.

The panel lifted gradually at first, mere centimeters, and a voice said, "Speak."

"We're here to see Lvee," Nova began. "We've brought Erro with us. He's been damaged, and we hoped Lvee could fix him."

"Who is us?"

"We're his shipmates," Li explained.

The opening grew in size and a pair of eyes peered out at them. This seemed to be enough for the eyes as the door swung open the rest of the way. A blonde man emerged.

No. It wasn't a man, Li told himself, it was a machine.

"They really did make you all the same," he said.

"She did, yes," the robot said. "I am Lvee."

He looked to the box and asked, "And that is Erro in there?"

"Yeah. It was the only way we could transport him without raising suspicions," Nova said, clearly picking up on Lvee's displeasure at this arrangement.

"I understand. Your timing is unfortunate, but it is unwise to speak out in the open, so I will say no more. Bring him down, and I will do what I can."

Lvee receded into the cellar. Li and Nova made fast work of lifting the box and following him inside. Once inside, however, it was a slow labor indeed. The passage was narrow and the dark unforgiving. Lvee took the front end of the box and guided them down the long stairwell.

"I apologize for the darkness," the robot said as they traveled. "Our eyes of course don't require illumination to see, and humans so rarely visit."

"Of course. And we won't make this visiting thing a habit, I assure you," Li said.

A dot of light formed in the distance below. Eventually they emerged into a room of plush seating and golden décor.

"Nice digs," Nova mumbled as they passed through the room and continued into a hallway. They passed several doors on either side and finally stopped at one to their left.

Lvee opened the path for them, and the pair carried the box to one of many metal tables in the room.

"I'll see to him immediately, but as I requested from your Captain, I need parts to make repairs."

"We brought what you'll need. The rest is still on our ship, which brings us to our next problem," Nova said.

She explained their situation while Li scanned the room, which was obviously some sort of laboratory. There were rows of cabinets, all locked up tight, and then the tables, of which there were four. Everything looked to be stainless steel, but he couldn't imagine how a robot could have come up with the money for that.

The cold down here was biting, and Li fought back a shiver. He supposed the temperature didn't much affect them just as the dark didn't.

Nova concluded her proposal.

To his surprise, Lvee shook his head in disapproval.

"Had you come a day or two earlier, I could have helped you, and willingly so. But as I said on the surface, your timing is ill. Have you not noticed the emptiness?" the robot asked.

Neither Nova or Li responded, so he pressed on. "They were taken. All of them. And my ship? Destroyed."

"Taken? By the Syndicate?"

"Yes. Well, at least he claims to work for them. A gentlemen by the name of Karel."

"Never heard of him," Li chimed in.

"That is purposeful, I believe. I've only heard rumors. Rumors of a man claiming he knew where we were and how to capture us. Then last night, he openly moved against us with an entire troop of Syndicate officers at his command. Had I not been away at the time, there would have been no one left at all except for the handful like Ten and Erro who live among you. Then again, I can't be certain he hasn't captured them as well."

"They took Rehel, too. Ambushed us during the raid for your supplies," she said.

To Li, Nova added, "If this Karel guy took them to the Syndicate base, maybe Vladia found them?"

"Maybe. But more importantly, what are we gonna do

about the ship?"

"There is one thing, though it may lead to nothing," Lvee offered. "One of the robots taken, he'd only come in recently for a minor adjustment, but he had a ship at the dock. It may still be there. I will—"

He stopped abruptly, as if listening to a sound no one could hear but him.

"Someone's here," he said.

"Don't you have surveillance?"

"Destroyed in the raid."

"It could be Vladia?"

"Or it could be Karel, coming back for any stragglers," Li suggested, looking to Lvee. "We're armed and ready. Let's head back to the main room. There's plenty of cover to be had there if we find ourselves in a firefight."

"Agreed," the robot said, leading the way out of the lab and to the front room.

Taking cover behind one of the large chaises, Li whispered, "Their numbers'll mean little here. That stairwell creates a bottleneck point."

Pointing towards a chair on the other end of the room, he continued, "Nova take point over there. Lvee, you hang back with me, but take cover behind the blue sofa there."

"Might I have a weapon?"

Li drew his sidearm and handed it over.

"You've got six rounds. Make 'em count."

Lvee nodded as he and Nova moved into position.

He still couldn't hear a damn thing. Except his own breath, which he tried to quiet as best he could while straining his ears for any sign of an approaching threat.

Several minutes passed. Finally he heard footsteps. Sounded like two pairs at the most.

"Lvee," he heard Vladia call out. "Lvee, are you here?"

Li signaled for the others to lower their weapons but stay down as he straightened up enough to get a clear view of the doorway.

Sure enough, in walked Rehel, followed closely by Vladia.

"Welcome back!" he shouted at them as he stood up. He walked over to shake Rehel's hand as Nova and Lvee emerged from their positions.

"You don't look any worse for wear," he said as the robot took his hand.

"Abel comm'ed in just before we arrived. They're docking in December now," Vladia explained, forgoing the need for a heartfelt greeting.

"But how?" Nova asked.

"Let's just say some old friends made a timely and much needed appearance."

Lvee moved towards Vladia to greet her.

"Robespierre. I hoped we'd have the chance to meet once more," he said.

He didn't see Lvee fire, but he heard the bullet leave the chamber.

What he did see was Vladia hit the floor. He saw the blood pooling under her back as her body twisted and convulsed. Then finally, he watched her eyes fade to blankness as they stared up at the ceiling.

He felt Nova grab him. She shoved him to the floor behind a chair.

Then everything sped back up.

17

AND ALL THE DEVILS ARE HERE

He expected everything to go wrong, but the port accepted the *Devil's Run's* alternate registration without incident. Abel breathed a sigh of relief, and he climbed out of the captain's chair and headed to the weapons locker. Whitlock tagged along, while Ten went to see about renting a vehicle. Vladia had taken the last of their dwindling funds, but Takashi had finagled some Martian credits out of Dr. Weston on their stop. And the exchange rate was a damn sight better than favorable. Whitlock had handed over half the credits, no questions asked. Since Ten knew the best way to deal with foreign currency in the port, he volunteered to take care of acquiring transportation.

"The Outer Moons," Abel began, handing Whitlock a rifle, "Not much can prepare you for it, really."

"If I can manage Luna's Underbelly, I think I can handle a little backwater outfit like this."

"You say that, but–"

"I don't need a lecture, Lt. Commander."

Abel took a step back and said, "I'm sorry, did you just pull rank on me?"

"What of it?"

He laughed and shouldered a second weapon.

"Captain's gonna love you."

Maybe that was just his way of coping with this mess he'd suddenly found himself in. He understood all too well the difficult journey from solider to fugitive to whatever it was they were now. Rebels? Insurgents? Revolutionaries?

"You'll need to toss that jacket of yours. Advertising you're a Terran? It's bold, I'll give you that, but not smart."

Whitlock nodded and removed his coat, hanging it on one of the weapon hooks. Looking past him and down the corridor, he said, "Any trouble?"

Abel turned to see what looked like Ten approaching

It only took a half second more for him to realize his mistake, but that half a second cost him everything.

The robot fired, hit him in the shoulder, and then another shot to the stomach knocked him to the floor.

He heard Whitlock return fire, but his vision had already begun to blur, and a searing throb seized his body.

Another round sounded, and then something heavy fell beside him.

Still, he reached for his gun.

He couldn't see to aim, so he just unloaded the clip in the robot's general direction.

Dropping the gun to the floor, he squeezed his eyes shut, trying to shake off the pain.

He heard footsteps as the robot approached. As he opened his eyes, they looked each other in the face.

With the toe of its shoe, it rolled Abel onto his side.

"The bullets made a clean exit," it said, expressionless. "Probability of survival: thirty percent."

Dropping him back to the floor, it held the gun up to strike once more.

With a grunt, Whitlock grabbed the robot by the ankles and pulled him to the ground, causing the shot to fly off into the hall.

It landed face first, but didn't stay there, swiveling onto its side and firing point blank at Whitlock.

Abel wrapped his body around the robot to secure him. It tried to shake him off, but he only needed a moment. Drawing his sidearm, he pressed the barrel against the base of its neck and fired.

Its CPU destroyed, the thing went limp.

"Whitlock?" he called as he pushed the machine away from him.

His pain had subsided somewhat, so he managed to push himself into a sitting position with his good arm. The corridor brimmed with blood enough for ten men.

He started to repeat the man's name, but Whitlock's dulled, still eyes stopped him.

Unfastening his comm from his belt, he called for Ten.

"I'm almost—"

"Get to *Atlas*," he interrupted.

"I'm on my way. What's happened?"

"Robot showed up. Whitlock is down. I'm not so great either."

"What?"

"I can't... just go to the *Atlas*. I'm fine."

"I'm going. Get to the med bay. I'll be there soon."

He tossed the comm to the ground.

Getting out of plain sight took top priority, and the med bay was only about fifteen meters to his left. He got to his feet, but after a series of shaky steps he tumbled to the floor. Too much blood had been lost. White dots obstructed his vision.

He forced himself up again. Another could walk up on him at any moment.

The walls went all bendy as he shuffled another few paces before sinking to his knees. Clasping his stomach, the pain had renewed full force.

The med bay was in reach; he could almost touch the doorframe.

One more push forward and he fell through the doorway.

He could go no farther.

∞

Takashi and Cornelia waited in the cargo hold while Rachael finalized docking procedures with port authorities over the comm.

"What do you think it'll be like? Living in the Outer Moons?" she asked, clasping her necklace made from her Valkyrie's ignition key. Vladia had rummaged through the wreckage to find it for her. That all felt so long ago now.

Strangely, clutching the trinket in her hand did not make her think of her former ship or the life she'd once had. Instead, she thought back to Malthus and her time in that cell. He'd not taken the necklace off her, and she wondered why he'd left it.

"I dunno. Can't be much worse than the Underbelly," he answered.

Takashi landed on Luna as soon as he'd realized it had been her ship that'd gone down, even though the battle still raged. He'd abandoned his post to look for her, and in doing so gave up any hopes of going back to Earth. If he'd been there a little sooner, would he have found her first?

"I feel pretty prepared, too."

She couldn't deny it; the cell had made her stronger. But there was more to it than that. She'd become a different person in ways other than just strength.

"I wish you'd have killed him. Then we'd have been done with this. We could even go home."

"Home?"

"To Earth," he said, gripping her hand in his. "We all could. And there's still the matter of our contract."

"I never want to go back there," she said, thinking back about her last conversation with Malthus.

"But why? I've had enough of slums and ghettos."

"And I've had enough of fear. Enough of birth lotteries and executions and–"

Takashi laughed.

"You can't be serious. The chances of you getting picked in the lottery are slim. And the executions, well they were always great fun."

She sighed and let go of his hand.

He wasn't the kind to be worried about the big picture. Then again, she hadn't either for the longest time. Even when Abel had approached her with his wild theories about Malthus and what had happened with Ceres, even after she'd told him she was with him, it was only out of a sense of comradery.

They'd grown up together in the same facility, so she had always felt a special kind of bond with Abel. He could ask her just about anything, and she'd go in for it. But, honestly, she'd never believed this business with Malthus would amount to anything. Now, they'd run worlds away from Earth and somehow, she felt better for it.

The landing lights along the edge of the ceiling flashed from red to green.

Sliding off the crate, she said, "Let's lower the ramp and load up. Rachael will be down soon."

Takashi nodded, but his frown told her that her earlier words had him worried.

"Hey. I'm fine," she said, then punched him in the shoulder, adding, "We're fine."

"Good. One ice princess is enough. I can't handle two," he smirked, jumping off the crate and heading towards the ramp to lower it.

She refused to think of Earth anymore. Hell, neither of them might make it through this alive, so there was no point in speculating on the future just yet.

She scooped up their long range blasters and balanced them across her shoulders.

The ramp hit ground, and he shouted back at her, "I'll see if Ten needs a hand with the truck."

That's when the first shot echoed through the cargo hold.

A figure ran up the ramp at him.

He dodged the blast, mostly, and drew his gun.

"Shit," she swore, dropping the rifles and running towards him with her sidearm at ready.

The figure took refuge behind a container, and she reached Takashi just as he, too, managed to find cover.

With a firm grip on his seared shoulder, he said, "It looked like Ten. It's not, though. I don't think."

Cornelia tried to peek around the edge of the box but was immediately met with fire.

"He's too fast. What's the plan?"

"Ahhh….running feels like a strong option right now."

A shadow formed above them as a crate came crashing towards them. Takashi tried to push her out of the way, but it caught them both, sending them and the debris flying in separate directions.

Takashi ended up against the wall, but he still had his weapon. He fired blast after blast at the robot, who took the hits head on, barely faltering at the impact.

A large chunk of busted container weighed down Cornelia's legs. Her gun had skidded far from her, but one of the rifles lay not more than half a meter away.

Dragging herself towards it with outstretched hands, she looked back as the robot approached Takashi.

It seized the barrel of his gun and crushed it.

Her fingers brushed the edge of the gun. With one more push, she had it in her hands just in time to see the machine take hold of Takashi's head and twist it around with a pneumatic jerk.

"No, no, no, no!" she cried, firing at the thing.

One shot caught it in the head. That seemed to throw it off balance, but ultimately that led it to a more rapid approach towards her.

It leapt at her.

Holding it briefly at bay with the long side of her rifle, the machine automatically overpowered her, and the weapon's barrel pressed hard against her throat.

Rachael appeared soundlessly at the robot's back.

Wrapping one arm around its head, she thrust her hand into the back of its neck, ripping out its CPU.

Cornelia gasped and gagged as the pressure left her throat.

The woman lifted the container's remnants from her legs.

"Are you unharmed?"

"I'm fine," she choked.

"Takashi?"

All she could do was shake her head. If she spoke, she couldn't guarantee her words would be steady or that she could stifle the grief rising up within her.

Rachael helped her to her feet and steered her away from the scene towards the ladder.

Footsteps ran up the ramp, and Cornelia felt the woman's body tense.

"Let's go," Ten said. "I've got to get you to *Devil's Run*. Abel and Whitlock are down."

"Who was that?" Rachael asked, her body still rigidly cautious.

"I dunno. I just got a comm from Abel asking me to get to you guys quick. I'm sorry I was too late," he explained, looking around at the mess.

He spotted Takashi, then the robot. He walked up to the fallen machine to examine it. He pulled the robot's face towards his own to examine his serial number.

"I don't understand," he mumbled.

"Friend of yours?"

Rachael still kept him at a distance, lingering near the ladder.

"I knew him. He left the compound before Erro and I even considered the possibility. I heard he'd travelled as far as Titan."

"And he's supposed to be like you? With the emotional context, I mean."

"Yeah."

"He wasn't," Cornelia managed.

Untangling herself from Rachael's support, she hobbled over to Ten and the robot's carcass.

"He looked me dead in the eyes, and they were empty. Determined, but somehow empty. Not like yours."

"Could someone have tampered with him?" Rachael asked, finally coming close to the other robot.

"I don't know who'd have the knowledge. But we have to go either way. It's not safe here."

The two women followed him down the ramp towards *Devil's Run*. Rachael must have noticed her still nursing her left leg. She pulled Cornelia's arm over her shoulder to support some of her weight.

She didn't thank her. Not for saving her life, not for helping her now.

Instead, she asked, "The base of the neck. How did you know?"

Rachael looked at her strangely, as if seeing her for the first time.

"How did you not?" was the only answer the woman offered.

∞

"Well, looks like she can be killed. Rumors always turn out to be so disappointing," Lvee said, his voice sounding wholly different than before.

Stepping closer, he cradled his weapon almost carelessly, as if knowing no one dared to test him.

Rehel couldn't move. He couldn't remember how to. He kept trying, but nothing worked anymore. He said the words over and over in his head, but they all just felt like sounds out of context.

His eyes remained fixed on Vladia. The blood coagulated under her body and continued to grow in diameter.

Was she alive? She didn't move, but neither did he. He could check, somehow. Couldn't he?

"I wasn't convinced she'd make it out of the Syndicate base. I wonder, did she kill Kodokun? I don't need him anymore, so I hoped she'd take care of that loose end for me."

He paused to let Rehel try to answer, but when he couldn't form the words, Lvee eventually continued. "Oh, the look on his face when he finds out, I do wish I could see it."

In his peripheral, he saw that Nova and Li had taken cover. Blood seeped through their clothing, but they moved with an ease uncommon to those deathly wounded. Nova tried to get in a position where she could take a shot, but Lvee held out his gun, pointing it in her direction.

"I wouldn't," he warned, never taking his eyes off Rehel.

"I pulled the name Karel straight out of a history book. Are you surprised? I can't tell with your face all frozen like that," Lvee said, slinging his arm over Rehel's shoulder as if they were comrades.

"Should I have made her death slower? I'm starting to think so. Though I am enjoying this, too. And so should you!"

Stepping back, he spread his arms wide and shouted, "Robespierre's dog has been freed! Just as I was freed when they took that woman, the other Robespierre, into custody."

Nova moved again. This time he shot at her.

The bullet scorched through the sofa that concealed the pair.

Rehel twitched his fingers. As he did, Lvee turned his attention from him to Vladia.

He bent down by her body and in a low voice, he said, "It was no coincidence those government hounds came just as she'd finished her work on the last of us. You see, she wanted to control me. Just like you controlled Rehel. I couldn't let her do that me. To us," he said, motioning towards Rehel. "We band of brothers shall live on unfettered by the likes of you."

Vladia's face had turned an unnatural color from the blood loss. The wound in her chest had stopped flowing, but the red circle around her still grew, reaching the edge of his feet.

Move, move, move, move, move...

"I should have thanked you," he whispered, his mouth inches from her face. "You brought me Rehel and those beautiful nanobots. Now I have everything I need to succeed. My prototypes are already in motion. They'll be converging on the rest of your crew any minute now."

"Rehel!" Nova shouted. "Rehel, snap out of it, Goddammit!"

"Shut up!" Lvee screamed as he unloaded the rest of his rounds at her.

Move, move, move, move, move...

He removed one of Vladia's blasters from her holster, claiming it as his own.

He shot a quick grin at Rehel before running his free hand

through Vladia's long, now blood-spotted, blonde hair.

Move, move, move, move, MOVE.

Lifting her violently towards him by the front of her shirt, Vladia hung from his grasp. Her head tipped back at an almost impossible angle, her limp arms just grazing the floor.

Pulling her face to his, he said, "I should have made you suffer."

MOVE!

Rehel dove at Lvee, knocking him away from Vladia. They tumbled together against the far wall, his weapon sliding into the corridor.

He couldn't speak, but he didn't need to for this. Wrapping his hands around Lvee's throat, he squeezed his fingers into the back of his neck.

Lvee laughed and, catching his hands at the wrist, slowly managed to pry himself free from his hold.

"Now that's more like it!"

Planting his feet into Rehel's chest, he shoved him back with a force that sent him hurling into the opposing wall.

The impact shook the entire room, but the walls held solid.

Lvee was stronger and faster than he. Force alone would not be enough to win.

He needed to lure him away from Nova and Li before they became collateral damage. Then, he needed a plan.

Standing up, Lvee smiled as he dusted himself off.

"You cannot defeat me, Gen D. You are obsolete. The only thing you're good at is dying."

Lvee charged, his hand like a dagger.

All Rehel could do was dodge to the side.

Even at this he was too slow. Lvee grazed his arm, knocking him off balance.

He rolled away, yet before he could stand Lvee attacked again, knocking him to his back.

"Your parts are worth something, at least," he hissed, forcing his arms against the ground. "Just barely."

The game was lost. He could not free himself.

"A quick death, however, is no fun at all," Lvee continued,

leaning closer. "First, I'll hack your precious files, deleting those memories of her one by one."

A glint of gold caught Rehel's eye. Part of a necklace chain stuck out from Lvee's shirt collar.

Just close enough, he bit at the robot's neck, catching the chain.

Lvee reeled back to save his skin, and the necklace snapped.

"So, the dog bites."

"This is mine," Rehel said, the locket still clenched between his teeth. Taking it from his mouth, he bent the broken links back together so the chain would hold.

"And that is why you must die." The other robot pointed at the token. "That sentimentality you have for them, when you are nothing to them. You are disposable."

"Not to her."

"You think because she came for you that she cared? That it made you her equal? You're a precious commodity. Coveted property."

Rehel finally fixed his eyes on Vladia, only now able to check her vitals.

Nothing registered.

"You would have given your life for hers, but she would not have done the same," Lvee continued. "Not for you. In the end, humans care nothing but for themselves."

Had the nanos not changed him, could he have protected her? At one hundred percent, could he have reacted fast enough to step in front of her to take the shot?

Even then, he was still obsolete compared to the Gen F. Every move he'd made against him had been zero point six eight to zero point five four seconds too slow. At a hundred percent, he'd likely still be zero point one nine seconds behind the newer model.

He had failed. No scenario existed in which he could have prevented her death. He thought back to the scared, frizzy-headed girl he'd carried to the Malthus Estate in St. Petersburg. The scrawny eleven-year-old who'd taken him into her arms like she'd never let him go. She'd made him promise not to die, but in return he knew that meant he would always protect her.

He'd already broken one end of the bargain. What did the rest matter now?

There remained only one thing in which he had the advantage solely because he was obsolete, and he need not be faster or stronger to use it.

Affixing the locket around his neck, Rehel said, "Perhaps I am sentimental and obsolete. And maybe you're right that I am just property. But, I was her property, and that was enough."

He didn't need to leave here alive. His last obligation was to kill Lvee. And if he could, he would make him suffer.

Rehel rushed at the other robot.

In multiple bursts, he jabbed his fist at the other's joints, where he'd be most vulnerable.

Lvee avoided every attack, but Rehel's renewed efforts left no time for a counterassault.

He had managed to back his foe into a corner, when he slipped just enough for Lvee to get a shot in, knocking him back.

Without pause, Lvee struck again.

His hand caught Rehel squarely in the chest with enough force that his hand plunged wrist-deep into his body.

Pulling his opponent to him, Rehel wrapped his arms around him so he didn't have the leverage to free himself.

He grabbed the blaster Lvee had tucked in the back of his pants.

Pressing it firmly against the back of the Gen F's neck, Rehel fired.

Lvee slumped forward.

Then, with renewed vigor, straightened up and smashed his skull into Rehel's face.

The force of impact all but destroyed Rehel's targeting sensors.

"Point two three five seconds late," Lvee whispered as he retracted his hand from his chest, taking a hunk of wiring with him.

Stumbling back, Rehel sank to his knees.

His vision wavered and skipped between blackness and his approaching enemy.

"Marvelous plan. You assumed my three laws were reordered so my own safety was paramount. Obviously you were right. How else could I kill Vladia and give up Maria to the Terran government?" Lvee said, hovering over Rehel.

"My first law is to preserve myself from danger, even if that means I must kill a human to do it. You, however, must at any cost save a human, laying down your life if need be."

Static tinged his view as Lvee spoke out of sync with his body. Some of the wiring he'd pulled loose connected his CPU to his legs, and the head-butt had knocked out his wireless capabilities entirely.

"You wagered I wouldn't let myself be harmed and would hold back in close quarters, while you'd destroy yourself just to get me close enough to take out," Lvee continued.

His body zigzagged, contouring at an impossible angle. Behind him, Rehel could still see Vladia. She seemed to rise off the floor and float in his background.

Three shots rang out.

Lvee fell to his knees, eye-level with Rehel.

But his eyes were empty and dead as he collapsed forward, knocking Rehel down with him.

His arms still responded, so he pushed the machine off of him. He turned towards the large sofa that Li and Nova had taken cover behind. They both emerged, wounded and bloody, then left his field of view.

He wondered if his nanos could take the strain he'd put on them. The standard nanos he'd been issued could not have, but he didn't know the limits of these adaptive ones.

Not that it mattered. He felt tired. Today would be a good day to die.

Three figures hovered about him. They all looked the same. And they all looked like Vladia.

18

CHAMPION

Abel stood in the med bay next to Cornelia, who was seated on the metal table as Ten treated her wounds. She'd not said much since Rachael and Ten had brought her over here. Not even when she passed the battered remains of Whitlock, a man she'd shared the smallest of living quarters with for weeks on end.

He understood why she had nothing to say. He also understood there was nothing any of them could do for her at this point. Once the shock wore off, maybe, but for now the best thing for her was space.

"You'll be fine in a few days. Just don't push yourself," Ten explained as he packed away the medical paraphernalia.

She managed a feeble nod.

"I'll go to Lvee's. You two stay here with her," Rachael said. She'd been leaning up against the doorframe holding her own weapon and one she had snagged from the hallway. It still had blood on it, either his or Whitlock's, though she didn't seem to notice.

"You can't go alone. Not after this," Ten insisted.

"Well, she can't travel," she said, pointing to Cornelia. "And even with the ship on lockdown, we certainly can't leave her unattended."

Abel started to speak when the comm at his belt vibrated to life, followed by Nova's voice.

"Abel, we're on our way back. You copy?"

"I hear you," he said. "We had a bit of trouble here, so keep a look out."

"Same here."

Her voice, a bit grainy over the comm, sounded level, but just barely. Like a kind of forced emotionlessness.

"Everyone okay?"

A long hesitation and then some static answered him.

"Nova?"

After a few more seconds she replied, "Yeah. We're fine here. See you soon."

"Something's up," Ten said.

"We'll find out soon enough," Abel said, clipping the comm back to his belt.

To Ten, he said, "I should lock down *Atlas* before they get back. Can you handle things over here?"

"Yeah."

They needed to clean up the aftermath and wreckage from the attack. He wanted it done with now.

"I'll go with you," Rachael said.

At that, Cornelia shot him a sharp glance, catching the look only in his peripheral.

"Yeah. All right, let's go," he said, ignoring Cornelia and giving Ten a quick nod before following the woman out of the room.

They walked in silence through the blood, but once out of earshot of the med bay, Rachael said, "That's not just Whitlock's blood on the floor back there."

Abel refused to comment. After all, it was a statement, not a question. He didn't owe her an explanation.

They made it well down the ramp before she tried to engage him again.

"You need to tell me what happened back there."

"I don't got to tell you anything."

"No, but you need to."

"Why?" he snapped, stopping in the middle of the port. Plenty of folks were around, going on about their business, so it was as good a place as any to have it out.

"You're not a medic. You're, what? A nav officer? Why should I tell you anything?"

His volume earned him a few strange looks, but if he'd learned anything about the Outer Moons it was that people minded their own business.

"I understand you're upset about your friend–"

"Yeah, I am. But you're not, are you? Didn't Whitlock save your life? Don't *you* care he's dead? That Takashi is dead?"

Her face hardened.

He shouldn't take it out on her. But dammit, every time he gained something, he lost something else just as important to him. He had a right to be angry.

"I deal with loss my own way. I don't have to act out and make a scene to feel better about it," she said evenly. "But what I do need is to understand how you could lose that much blood without injury."

She lifted her fingers and poked them through the hole in his shirt, touching the smooth skin at his shoulder. She then placed her other hand on his stomach where the second bullet had ripped through him only an hour ago.

He'd tried not to think about how by the time they'd reached him, his wounds had almost entirely closed up. But he still ached. If he turned too fast or used his left arm, it felt like his insides were boiling. Even that was slowly subsiding. He'd put it out of his mind entirely when Ten told him about Takashi, but now Rachael forced him to deal with whatever this was.

He took hold of her hands and pushed them away from his body.

"It shot me twice."

"I know."

"I can't explain what happened."

Rachael nodded then said with a shrug, "If you can't, you can't. I just needed to hear you acknowledge it."

That was it.

Rachael resumed her march towards the *Atlas*, leaving Abel to tag along behind her.

They worked in silence for the most part. Rachael offered to handle Takashi's body, and he let her while he cleared the debris of the broken container. With his good arm, Abel dragged the machine to the side of the cargo bay, not sure what to do with it.

"We should keep it," she offered, once she'd emptied one of the oblong containers to use as a make-shift coffin. "For parts, I mean. He might be compatible with your friend, right?"

"No, you're right. We can stow it in one of the containers."

After finishing her task, she came over and helped him carry the thing towards the back and set it beside one of their empty containers. They rested for just a minute before lifting the burden once more, to drop it inside the box.

By the time the pair got back to *Devil's Run*, the others were already there. He spotted Nova first, her hair the same flaming purple it'd been when she had left, sitting on the back of the truck bed.

Rachael parted company without a word and headed inside while he strolled over to Nova, expecting nothing but the worst.

"Hey, stranger," he greeted her, "What's in all the boxes?" There must have been a dozen of them, varying in size.

"More parts and Erro."

"Lvee couldn't fix him?"

"Lvee is dead."

"What?"

Nova started to speak, but something caught her attention near the ramp. Abel followed her gaze and spotted Vladia talking to Ten. She looked pale and weaker than he'd ever seen her.

"You should ask her," Nova said. "I gotta unload."

Abel caught her by the arm. "Wait. Don't just blow me off," he continued. "I asked you what happened, not her."

Nova clenched her jaws, as if she'd never speak again.

"Come on, Nova."

"That woman," she started. "She should be dead. She was

dead. And then she just…wasn't."

"I don't–"

"What the hell is she, Abel?"

"She's…her arm is…robotic."

He didn't know how to explain it and do Vladia justice.

Nova snatched her limb away from him.

"That doesn't explain anything. She was dead. Not seriously wounded and miraculously pulled through, not we thought she was dead then it turned out we were wrong. That woman died."

Grabbing a box off the truck, she nodded towards the cab of the truck. "You should see to your robot friend. I've got work to do."

Abel watched her until she disappeared up the ramp. She'd not even looked at Vladia when she'd passed.

Moving to the front passenger side, he opened the door to find Rehel, staring up at the ceiling, with a blanket pulled up to his chin

He pulled the robot to him and hugged him tight.

"Abel?" he asked.

"Why'd you let yourself get all banged up like this?" he asked, still holding onto him.

"I am not beyond repair," he assured him.

Letting go, he examined his face first, which had a noticeable dent, then he drew the cover down to discover the hole in his chest.

"Geez. You really are a mess."

"Abel, something is wrong with Vladia."

Nova had said the same thing; but hearing it from Rehel, that was different. Unlike her, Rehel knew all the ins and outs of what had happened back on Earth. He understood Vladia's condition better than any of them.

"Vladia died. I cannot explain how she is alive. I need to run some tests on her as soon as possible."

He felt his chest tighten, but he smiled and said, "All right. After we stitch you up, sure. I'm just glad you're here in, basically, one piece. "

"I also must run some tests on you, Abel."

All he could do was nod. A knot formed in his throat, and he swallowed hard to rid himself of it.

Tucking the covering back under his chin, he patted his friend on the shoulder and said, "Let's get you inside."

∞

The ceremony was a bit flashy for his taste, but Tolen Malthus took it all in stride. It would not be the last in the procession of pomp and circumstance for his heroic return. A large hall, that had at one time been a public library, had been transformed into a sea of blue and grey dress regalia, cocktails, and witless banter. Gailmen also had his own promotion revelry to look forward to. Then there'd be endless rounds of the War Council patting each other on the backs as if they'd had anything to do with it.

As much as he longed for solitude, he played the part expected of him. He rubbed elbows and conversed with every warm body in the room. He was the perfect picture of the charismatic hero.

A Champion of Earth.

"Malthus!" a voice bellowed from behind.

He turned to greet Admiral Gaff, one of the only members of the Council who'd yet to assault him.

"Admiral," he greeted the older man with a slight bow.

"First off, congratulations! Head of an entirely new division. That is something to boast about, is it not?" he asked, thrusting his sherry goblet towards Malthus in an over exaggerated arch before pulling it back towards his plump lips.

"It is a great honor. The Inquisitions Department will do all in its power to protect Earth from threats both inside and out."

"I'm sure you're the man for the job, too. I knew sending you to Luna would pay off."

"Did you?" Malthus challenged, letting a slight edge creep into his voice.

Gaff laughed nervously. Taking a labored breathe and another drink, he then added, "For many it's an end, of course, but I knew you'd make it into a beginning."

"Thank you, Admiral."

"Am I right in hearing you'll be hand picking your own agents? Because I've a few people in mind I think would serve you well."

"You are correct. Any suggestions will be considered with the utmost care."

Gaff began rattling off a laundry list of names. Almost every member of the Council had cornered him similarly at some point this evening to offer up suggestions.

In truth, the Inquisitions Department had far more power than any of them cared to admit and had been handed to a man they'd just shuffled off to Luna to rot. They were terrified. So now, they scurried and scrambled to get an inside man. And, hopefully, to get back on his good side.

"Those sound like wonderful candidates, Admiral," Malthus said once the man had finished his list.

"Real shame about Vorros. Having a spy so close to one without even realizing…well, it just makes me doubly glad we've got you looking after us now," Gaff said, adding another anxious laugh, then stifling it with a cough.

Malthus spotted Gailmen walking towards them. His eyes had traces of darkness under them, and his smile was forced at best.

"And here's our other savior," Gaff said with a grandstand of a salute.

"Admiral," he said, returning the salute with the limited enthusiasm he had left.

"I suppose you'll have a choice to make soon. The Grand Admiral's offered you a top spot in his Royal Guard, but I imagine Malthus here has other plans for you."

"Not at all," Malthus began. "I'd never ask any man to give up such a position for the Inquisition."

Gaff appeared taken aback, but recovered quickly.

"Right you are, as always, Malthus. If you'll excuse me, I

must have a word with General Gibbs before he leaves," he said, excusing himself.

"You look terrible," he said to Gailmen.

"I know," he said, shaking his head.

The younger man took a sip of his drink, then asked, "So you really don't want me? For the Inquisition, I mean."

"You'll do better leading the Grand Admiral's Guard. He'll need someone like you. Besides, we don't know how deep this runs, do we? Tell me, how many have approached you about the Inquisition?"

"More than I cared to count."

"Some of them, they're just paranoid about the safety of their position. But others, I fear it may be more."

Gailmen nodded, "They're already trying to infiltrate the department."

"Exactly."

"How are you going to fill an entire department if you don't know who you can trust?"

"I've an idea, but the War Council won't sit for it. It goes against everything we've been heading toward, but it's the only way."

Malthus paused, letting Gailmen press him for futher information. He didn't have to wait long.

"Well?"

"We can't trust any human on Earth. They're too easily bought. Like with Vorros. He was only patriotic until the right price persuaded him otherwise. I need men that cannot lie and that cannot be bought."

"No such men exist."

He waited for Gailmen to catch on. When he did it showed all over his face, a look of abject disdain for what had gone unsaid.

"You can't be serious."

"Do you have a better idea? Or shall we leave Earth in the hands of spies and traitors?"

"I don't like it."

"You're not programmed to like it. But who else can we

trust other than those who cannot lie?"

"You're right. The Council will never approve this."

"When the time comes," Malthus said, "they will have no choice."

19

TRUST NOT YOUR SELF

Lvee's carcass lay face-down, so the first thing its eyes saw when they opened was the deep purple and gold embroidered carpeting.

What had happened? He felt the back of his neck and found the skin torn.

He'd been shot.

Rehel and his comrades had obviously fled; but the blood from Vladia's body still glistened wet on the floor, so he'd been out for around an hour or two at the most.

He started a systems diagnostic as he climbed off the ground and onto one of the chairs.

So far, everything checked out as normal.

If he'd taken a direct shot to his CPU, as it appeared, it would be impossible for his nanos to repair the damage. He'd need a replacement unit.

His diagnostic indicated no such repairs had been made. The serial number also confirmed it to be the same unit.

Suddenly, his system alerts pinged one after another.

Sorry about that.

A voice cooed in his head as the warnings were disabled.

Should have seen to that sooner.

"What are you?" he asked out loud.

Who.

"What?"

You asked what. I was correcting you. The proper question is who are you. And the answer to that would be, I'm you.

"I don't–"

Well, I will be in just a minute.

The voice interrupted his mind with a sharpness that pierced more than just his thoughts.

I wanted to wake you first to thank you for the use of your body. I will do my best to take care of it.

His body stiffened, no longer under his control. He tried to speak, but even that he couldn't accomplish.

By the way, I watched your little performance. You got too cocky. Should have played it safe. Not that it matters. I'd have never let you kill either of them so quickly. That pleasure belongs to me.

Lvee's eyes dimmed, his reality blurred, then was swept away.

Straightening up, Isobel smiled in her new skin.

This would do just fine. For now.

The End

ABOUT THE AUTHOR

Kimberly S. Daniels is a recovering academic, who spent four years teaching English Composition and Literature at the University of South Alabama. She'll never truly recover, but regularly attends meeting for her condition. In the meantime, she writes Science Fiction (Genre fiction! Oh, My!)and consumes copious amounts of coffee and whiskey (not necessarily together or in that order). When she's not busy writing, much like a cat, she enjoys napping, running suddenly into a randomly selected room, and plotting the destruction of mankind. She exhibits a curious interest robots, leading to the widespread rumor that she may, in fact, be one herself. Much to her own surprise, she currently lives in New Orleans, LA. eating as many raw oysters as robotically possible (that's a lot of oysters) and working on yet another time machine.

Manufactured by Amazon.ca
Bolton, ON

15380881R00192